EYES OF A STRANGER

OTHER BOOKS AND AUDIO BOOKS
BY CAROL WARBURTON:

Edge of Night

Before the Dawn

EYES OF A STRANGER

A Novel

CAROL WARBURTON

Covenant

Covenant Communications, Inc.

Cover illustration by David McClellan.

Cover design copyrighted 2005 by Covenant Communications, Inc.

Published by Covenant Communications, Inc.
American Fork, Utah

This is a work of fiction. The characters, names, incidents, places, and dialogue are products of the
author's imagination, and are not to be construed as real.

Printed in Canada
First Printing: July 2005

11 10 09 08 07 06 05   10 9 8 7 6 5 4 3 2 1

ISBN 1-59156-864-1

Dedicated to my parents,
Leslie Buchanan and Evalina Whipple Payne,
children of the Mexican Mormon colonies.

ACKNOWLEDGMENTS

My appreciation goes to members of the Hatch family of Colonia Juarez, Mexico, for their help in researching this novel. Also to Dorothy Keddington, Ka Hancock, and Charlene Raddon for their encouragement and suggestions during the months of writing. A special thanks to Angela Eschler, my editor at Covenant Communications, for her helpful suggestions and encouragement. Each of you has helped to make this a better story.

PROLOGUE

Soft afternoon sunlight filtered through the pines and oak, painting dappled shadows onto the forest floor and highlighting the slender figure of the young woman who waited in the trees. She stood erect, her large brown eyes anxious as she absently tucked a wisp of wavy black hair into the heavy braid that hung to her waist. Where was Ricardo? Why hadn't he come?

Worried, she stepped from the shelter of the trees to peer along the path that skirted the meadow. Although Teresa Maria Acosta owned no mirror, she knew she was beautiful. At sixteen her beauty was sung throughout the villages, and offers of marriage had come from as far away as San Miguel. But Teresa had no interest in her numerous suitors. Her heart and dreams were centered on Ricardo Rafael de Vega, only son of Don de Vega, one of the wealthiest land owners in the state of Chihuahua, Mexico. Numerous prayers to the Blessed Virgin had granted Teresa her dearest wish, for Ricardo returned her love and daily slipped away to meet her in their sanctuary among the trees.

"Ricardo." Teresa momentarily forgot her concern as she placed a hand on her stomach to feel the subtle distention of her waist. "And little Ricardo," she added, although Ricardo wasn't yet aware that she bore his child. *I will tell him today,* she promised herself.

Teresa smiled as she pictured his face when she told him the news, imagining how his eyes would light with pleasure as he pulled her close and murmured, *"Nuestro niño . . . nuestro hijo."* It would be a son, a fine, sturdy boy who would one day inherit the vast El Rancho Valle Grande that sprawled across the Sierra Madre, encompassing hundreds of acres of rich grazing land and tracts of oak and pine. Valle Grande was only the beginning of the holdings. Ricardo had told her of two smaller ranches and a large home in Mexico City.

It wasn't easy for Teresa to picture her son growing up amid the luxury of the de Vega household. The task became more difficult when she tried to imagine herself, one of the de Vega servants, sitting down to dinner with the haughty Señora de Vega. Teresa shivered at the memory of the señora's anger when she'd failed to polish the silver urn to suit the woman's taste. She wouldn't let herself think of what his *madre* would say when Ricardo told her they had secretly married.

A sudden gust of wind caught the edge of Teresa's shawl and whipped it against her face. Engrossed in her daydream, she hadn't noticed the angry ranks of clouds invading the sky. Teresa glanced up as the first of the clouds moved across the sun, obliterating its face and plunging the forest into twilight. A hush fell over the meadow, and for a moment the wind stilled. Teresa glanced nervously at the mountains framing the valley. They were obscured by dark clouds that swirled in ominous silence, portentous of a violent mountain storm.

"Hurry, Ricardo," Teresa whispered.

As if he'd heard her, Ricardo emerged from the forest, the quick stride of his black-clad legs showing his eagerness to be with her. Teresa smiled while her eyes drank in the autocratic tilt of Ricardo's head, the fine aquiline features and black hair—all gifts from his forebearer Don Federico de Vega, who had sailed from Spain more than one hundred and fifty years before. The patch of white hair growing near the crown of Ricardo's head came from his mother. Whether the haughty señora liked it or not, the distinctive marking might have been passed to her grandson, the tiny *niño* who would one day inherit Valle Grande.

When Ricardo raised a hand in greeting, Teresa ran to meet him. A moment later she was gathered into his arms, her face pressed against his braid-trimmed vest while his hands caressed her neck and shoulders.

"Querida." The affectionate term of endearment was a whisper in her ear. "I thought I'd never get away . . . and now the storm." Ricardo glanced at the threatening sky and guided her back through the trees to an abandoned shepherd hut.

"What kept you?"

"Padre." A frown furrowed Ricardo's dusky forehead, then he smiled, making Teresa's heart constrict with tenderness. "But we will not talk of him or Mexico City or Isabel . . . only us." Ricardo pulled her to him while his lips moved over her cheeks and eyelids.

Teresa savored his closeness and the pressure of his hands. After a moment, she pulled away. "You spoke of Mexico City. Does that mean you'll be leaving?"

Ricardo's nod was barely perceptible.

"When?"

"Mañana."

Tomorrow. Teresa flinched as a jagged streak of lightning flashed across the sky. Her eyes searched Ricardo's face while she waited for the thunder to subside. "Has Don de Vega found out about our marriage? Is he sending you away?"

"No."

"Then why?" Teresa's voice broke. "And who is Isabel?"

"I don't wish to speak of her."

Teresa stiffened. Was Ricardo tiring of her?

Ricardo placed his hands on her shoulders. "Please, don't be upset. Don't spoil the little time we have left."

"Then tell me why you must go."

Ricardo sighed and looked away. "I must go to marry Isabel."

"No . . ." The word slipped out before Teresa could stop it. "But you are married to me."

"I know, Querida." Ricardo took her hands. "Try to understand. This marriage to Isabel isn't of my choice. It was arranged many years ago, though it wasn't to take place for several years. Now . . ." Ricardo's expression turned grim. "A letter has arrived from Don Diago, Isabel's father. Her mother is ill. They want the wedding to take place now . . . before she dies."

"What about us?"

Ricardo gathered her close. "We'll continue to meet . . . to love."

"But you'll be married to another woman . . . twice married. That isn't right."

"I know . . . but I'll be married only in name to Isabel." He paused and looked deeply into her eyes. "Listen, Querida. You must never tell anyone about our marriage. Never. Things won't go well for me if Padre or the church find out. It must remain a secret . . . our secret. Do you understand?"

Teresa nodded, though inside she felt as if she were shattering into tiny pieces, like a beautiful vase smashed on the tile floor of the parlor. What was Ricardo saying? What was he thinking?

Ricardo touched her cheek with his finger. "Remember my heart will still be yours, as it's been from the day I first saw you carrying flowers into the parlor. Since then there's been no other . . . only you." He bent his head to hers and rested his lips on her cheek. "When I inherit the ranch, I'll build a house for you in the meadow. Every day I'll come to see you." He raised one of her work-roughened hands to his lips. "You shall have servants to wait on you. No more scrubbing and cleaning, Querida, only love and happiness and niños. Our niños."

Teresa swallowed a tortured sob and laid her face against his shoulder, biting her lip to choke off sound. The low murmur of his voice went on as he planned their future and reaffirmed his love. Teresa scarcely heard him. Her thoughts had turned to their niño, her mind hearing the taunts of children running after her *hijo*—her son. Teresa shivered, not liking to think of the name they would reserve for her. "No!" Teresa pulled away. She would not have everyone thinking she was Ricardo's mistress. Never that.

"What's wrong?"

The concern on Ricardo's face stopped her tongue. She couldn't tell him. Not when their time was almost gone. She raised her hand to his face, trying to memorize the curve of high cheekbones, the feel of his firm, square jaw. After today it was all she would have of him. Just the memory. She must leave.

Lightning followed by a resounding crack of thunder drew them apart. Ricardo scowled at the lowering sky. "I must go and arrange for the journey." He bent his head for one brief kiss. "I should be back by the end of the month. Promise that you'll be here waiting." When Teresa hesitated, Ricardo lifted her chin with his finger. "Promise?"

Teresa nodded, hoping the Blessed Virgin would forgive her for the lie.

"Come. Madre will be asking for you."

They walked together until they reached the meadow where Teresa paused and turned. "You go first. We mustn't be seen together."

Ricardo nodded and pulled her to him. "Remember, I love you." As he released her, he removed a gold ring embossed with the de Vega crest from his finger. "To seal our marriage and love," he said, sliding it onto hers.

Teresa caressed the ring as she watched Ricardo stride past stalks of Indian paintbrush and columbine, his dark-clad figure growing small and indistinct. When he reached the trees, Ricardo turned and waved.

A crash of thunder rent the valley, drowning out Teresa's *"Adiós,"* and sending a gust of rain against her face to mingle with the tears running down her olive cheeks. "Adiós, Ricardo," she repeated in a whisper.

* * *

Teresa sat on a wooden bench beside the sagging doorway to her brother's one-room hut and gazed down at her twin sons. Each day her milk waned while the babies' needs increased, their pitiful, insistent cries attesting to hunger and feeding her fear that they would starve.

If Ricardo de Vega had chanced upon the isolated farm a two-day journey south of his ranch, it's doubtful he would have recognized his beloved Teresa. A difficult delivery followed by a high fever had diminished the Mexican girl's strength and devoured her beauty. Of late, even the smallest task left her weak, and today she could do no more than sit in the sun, warming her frail body and praying to the Blessed Virgin to increase her strength so her milk would flow to fill the eager mouths of her niños.

"Madre de Dios, ayúdame por favor."

Hearing her voice, one of the twins opened his black eyes and gazed at her.

"Ricardo, *mío.*" Teresa smiled down at the baby swathed in her best red shawl. Rafael, the second twin, dozed fitfully on the bench.

Like his brother, he was wrapped in a shawl, its soft yellow hue the only way Teresa could differentiate her sons.

As she studied the tiny faces, she marveled again at their perfection. Their miniature noses and creamy skin proclaimed their Spanish ancestry, but she liked to think the eyes and hair were hers. "Our little hijos," she crooned. "A perfect blending of our love. You shall live. I must see that you live."

Teresa began to plan. If she could find someone to nurse one of the twins, she would have enough milk to satisfy the other. But which one would she keep and how could she bear to let one go, even for a few weeks?

Torn between her resolve to save her sons and her need to keep them near, Teresa closed her eyes and leaned against the wall of the hut. Each day her babies grew weaker. She must act soon—today—or it would be too late.

Teresa called to her brother who was husking corn by the corner of the house.

Pedro Acosta frowned and pulled the husks away from an ear of corn, then laid it in the sun to dry. Only then did he straighten and go to his sister.

"Please . . . I need you to go to the village."

Pedro's frown deepened. "*Por que?* You know we have no money. If I leave the corn to go on some foolish errand, it won't dry and we'll starve."

"The niños are already starving." Teresa struggled to keep her voice steady. "Please, Pedro. You must take one of my children to the padre. Ask him to find someone to nurse him . . . just until I'm strong again. Then I'll have enough milk for them both. But now . . ." Teresa's eyes filled with tears.

Pedro looked away, not wanting to see his sister cry. There had already been too many tears. And now the niños . . . always crying. How was he to provide for so many hungry mouths? He clenched his fist. If he could discover the name of the man who had done this terrible thing to Teresa, he would kill him. But Teresa refused to reveal the name of her lover. Each day she grew weaker, his beautiful young sister wasting away like a lovely mountain flower stripped from the soil and left to wilt in the sun. But perhaps there was hope. If

Teresa only had one baby to feed, maybe her strength would return. It was a chance Pedro was willing to take.

"All right." He reached for the red-clad niño, the one who cried the loudest.

Teresa hesitated. *Not little Ricardo.* But when Rafael gave a pathetic whimper, she let her brother take Ricardo. He was the strongest and would weather the journey the best. Teresa's heart ached as she looked at her little hijo.

"Wait!" On impulse, she took little Ricardo from Pedro and went into the hut. When she was certain Pedro hadn't followed, she slipped the ribbon that held Ricardo de Vega's ring from around her neck and placed it over the baby's head. "To keep you safe and bring you good luck," she whispered, burying the ring in the folds of the shawl. Teresa kissed Ricardo's satin-soft brow and snuggled him close, then she turned and took him to her brother.

"Remember, it's only for a few days . . . a few weeks." With tears coursing down her cheeks, Teresa Maria Acosta watched Pedro carry the baby down the dusty path, her throat contracting into a painful lump as little Ricardo's dark head grew smaller and then disappeared.

* * *

It was late afternoon before Pedro Acosta reached the crossroad. Not liking his sister's errand, Pedro's steps slowed and stopped. What if the padre demanded money for his services?

The Mexican scowled and jiggled the squalling baby. Even if the padre agreed to take the niño, there was no guarantee the baby would live. The villagers were as poor as Pedro. How could their wives produce any surplus milk? His frown deepened. Since the deaths of his wife and child, he cared for no one but his sister. If taking Teresa's son to the padre would make her happy, he would comply. But the task was distasteful.

The baby's cries increased. As Pedro looked at the angry face, a thought entered his mind. Why not take the child to the *Mormones*? A slow smile lifted Pedro's mustache. Of course. Why hadn't he thought of it before? The Mormons with full barns and numerous wives would have ample milk for Teresa's son. Hadn't they taken him in when he was hurt and given him work after he recovered?

Pedro remembered one woman in particular—Sister Cameron they had called her, wife of the man who'd given him work. Since she was childless, she was certain to welcome Teresa's hijo and could arrange for someone to feed the niño. White skin or brown, it shouldn't matter to the baby, and Teresa wouldn't need to know.

His drooping mustache lifted higher as he recalled the hams he'd seen in the smokehouse, the chickens scratching in their pen. The Mormons were always good for a handout. Perhaps they would even pay him for the pleasure of having the baby. Pleased with the thought, Pedro turned his back on the path that led to the priest and hurried along the track to Cave Valley and the Mormones.

CHAPTER 1

Mexico—1907

Matthew Cameron maneuvered his horse through a heavy stand of aspen, his dark eyes on a cow that had wandered off to birth her calf in a stand of trees. Now that the birthing was complete, he was anxious to get the cow back to the meadow. He'd heard a mountain lion the night before and had seen its tracks by the stream that morning.

When the cow and calf rejoined the herd, Matt started his horse in a watchful circle around the cattle, the jaunty set of his Stetson hat shading his handsome features while his dungaree-clad legs hugged the saddle, his lithe muscled body and the brown mare moving as one.

Although no stranger to herding cattle, this was the first time he'd had the responsibility of his father's entire herd. He'd brought them up from the flats of Colonia Cortéz to graze in the mountains near the abandoned Mormon settlement of Cave Valley.

Matt savored the crisp evening air, preferring it and the lush growth of the mountains to the heat and desert of Colonia Cortéz; but Joseph Cameron had become discouraged by the short growing season in Cave Valley and had moved his family to a farm on the outskirts of Cortéz when Matt was six. Now, at eighteen, Matt was ready for a life of his own. If he proved himself with the cattle, perhaps his adoptive father would be willing to help him. A place of his own was what Matt wanted, a ranch in the mountains where a man could stretch and ride as far as he pleased. No matter what else happened this summer, Matt was determined to show his father that despite his brown skin, he was a son Joseph could trust.

The memory of his father's parting words ran through his mind. "Remember, I'm counting on ye, Matty. See that ye dinna let me down."

"I won't." Matt had clasped the Scotsman's big hand. "None will be lost."

It was a promise Matt intended to keep, but the sudden illness of his younger brother had complicated the matter, leaving Matthew alone with the cattle while another brother accompanied the sick boy back to Cortéz.

Remembering his promise, he urged his horse into a canter and started the cattle back to the meadow. Although twilight lingered long in the mountain valley, the memory of cougar tracks made him anxious to get the cattle into the corral.

After herding the Durhams into the pen, Matt dragged logs close to it and built a fire. With only one to stand guard, he would have to rely on the fire for help. He worked quickly, bringing his blanket and rifle from the lean-to, going to find the ax. By the time darkness came, Matt had finished eating and had chopped enough wood to last the night.

"All right, puma, I'm ready," he said, needing the sound of his voice to bolster his confidence.

The night was cool and full of stars. Matt gazed at the sky where the crescent of a new moon seemed to hang just beyond his grasp. Something, perhaps the stillness, was making the cattle restless. He heard their soft lowing, saw their nervous movement. The first hour slipped by, then another. Despite his resolve to remain alert, he grew sleepy.

A piercing cry made him jerk. Heart pounding, his eyes searched the darkness. The scream came again, making the hair on the back of his neck stand on end. The cattle bunched closer, tossing their heads and bawling while the hobbled mare snorted in alarm.

"Easy, girl." He studied the far side of the corral. That was where the cougar would try.

Cradling his rifle, Matt grabbed a burning stick from the fire. If he could start a second fire on the far side of the corral, he could patrol the entire pen and keep a better watch for the mountain lion.

A loud bellow startled him as he hurried along the side of the pen. He hesitated when he saw that the new calf had been jostled into a corner and had tumbled outside, it's loud bawling mingling with another yowl from the cougar.

Matt set down his gun and quickly arranged kindling, praying the calf would stay close to the pen. Just as he set torch to sticks, he saw a dark form with glowing eyes limp toward the calf.

He scrambled for his rifle and got off a quick shot as he rushed back to the calf. The cougar paused, glowing eyes seeming to lock with his. Then it leaped, knocking Matt to the ground before he could fire again. The cat's teeth sank into the flesh of his shoulder. Matt gasped at the searing pain and rolled with the cougar in a frenzied struggle for life, trying to pry the powerful jaw from his shoulder amid snarls and a tangle of claws ripping and tearing. He flung his leg over the muscled haunches of the cat and tried to flip him over.

A whip whistled through the melee of fur and dungarees and struck the cougar on the side of the head. Snarling, the puma released its hold on Matt and turned to face the dark outline of a man who lifted his arm and sent the whip snaking through the night to snap furred flesh from the cougar's neck.

Seeing his chance, Matt grabbed his rifle. While the whip held the cougar at bay, he took shaky aim and squeezed the trigger.

When the cat fell, Matt struggled to his feet, holding his shoulder as he peered at his rescuer. "Thank you," he rasped, unaware of the blood staining his shirt and dripping through his fingers. A loud buzzing in his ears drowned out the stranger's reply. Matt's vision blurred and he swayed unsteadily before pitching forward, his fall broken by his rescuer.

"Ave Maria," the rescuer said when he felt the wetness running down Matt's arm. His words were lost amid the bawling of the calf and Matt's whispered plea to rescue the animal. Instead, the man dragged Matt toward the fire.

"No . . . the calf . . ."

The man continued to pull Matt over the rough ground, his broken exclamations mingling with a roaring in Matt's ears.

"The calf . . ." Matt's voice became a whisper as the stranger laid him by the fire, the man's Spanish features clearly outlined by the pulsing flames. Matt blinked to clear the fog from his brain. Was it just an illusion? As black eyes met his, Matt gazed up into a face that was an exact mirror of his own. The full mouth moved, and a voice spoke in Spanish as blackness started near the top of the man's head and slid downward over the sharp nose and full lips, obliterating the features until only whirling darkness remained.

* * *

Matthew wakened to brilliant sunshine and the scolding of a squirrel perched on the roof of the lean-to. Thinking he'd overslept, he tried to roll out of his blanket. Pain knifed through his shoulder and made him gasp and stop.

"Lie still," a low voice commanded in Spanish. "You have lost a lot of blood. If you move, you will start bleeding again."

Matt turned his head to look at the man who had spoken. When he saw the dusky face, memory returned. "I . . . I thought I was dreaming."

A smile split the handsome features of the young man who squatted beside the blanket. "It's no dream, though I find it as strange as you to look into a face exactly like my own. See . . . even our hair is the same." The Mexican touched the patch of white hair growing near the crown of his head. "*Tío Pedro* didn't tell me about the hair or that you speak Spanish."

"Tío Pedro?"

"My uncle . . . our uncle," the Mexican corrected. "Too bad he didn't live to see our meeting. All these years he knew about you, but he didn't tell me I had a twin *hermano* until just before he died."

Died. Twin brother. The words tumbled through Matt's aching head, conjuring up pictures of two brown babies playing in a sunny dooryard, two laughing boys galloping horses across a meadow. Identical. Mirror image. God had intended them to be together. What had torn them apart?

Matt closed his eyes. "Our uncle is dead?" His voice faltered as his dry lips formed the next question. "And our mother?"

The Mexican's mouth drooped as he rose and ambled to the fire, his baggy white pants and shirt masking his muscular, brown frame. "She died a few months after Tío Pedro took you to the Mormones.

As Matt watched his twin, an uncomfortable thought crept into his mind. Was this how he appeared to others—unmistakably Mexican with no trace of *gringo?* Matt pushed the thought away and concentrated on what the young man was saying.

"After that, it was a matter of staying alive. Tío Pedro was a poor man . . . too poor to bring another hungry mouth to his table." He paused and turned a slab of meat with his knife. "Are you hungry?"

Matt shook his head. "Just thirsty. Could I have a drink?"

His brother nodded and dipped a cup of water from a bucket in the corner of the lean-to. As he helped Matt drink, he shook his head. "When José told me he'd seen a *vaquero* who looked just like me—even the hair— well, I came to see for myself." He paused while Matt took a few awkward sips. "God must have been watching over you. If I hadn't come . . ."

"You saved my life."

"*Sí.* But isn't that what hermanos are for?" The appraising look in his twin's eyes made Matt uneasy. "Do you know how often I've envied you . . . wished Tío Pedro had taken me to the Mormones instead of you?"

Matt shook his head.

"Often, my brother. More often that you might think." The Mexican straightened and looked toward the corral. "If I had but half of your cattle, I would be a rich man. Given one or two, I could be happy."

Tension tightened Matt's stomach. "The cattle aren't mine."

"Whose then?"

"Joseph Cameron's."

"You are his son, no?"

"Not really."

"Ah." The Mexican's dark eyes searched Matt's. Then he gently patted his arm and rose. "You are tired. So much talk isn't good." A smile crossed his face as he reached for his whip. "Rest well, hermano, and do not worry. Rafael will see that no harm comes to you or the cattle."

* * *

Long shadows stretched across the meadow when Matthew roused again. He lay for a moment, letting his eyes follow the horse-shoe-shaped course of the tree-lined stream that fed into the Piedras

Verdes River. Behind it, spanning the horizon from north to south, were the serrated peaks of the Sierra Madre robed in forests of oak and pine and crowned at the summit with slabs of granite.

For Matt they symbolized his beginning. It was here his dark-skinned mother had given him life. Invisible threads still drew him to them, their gossamer strands gently pulling him back to the rugged canyon that had witnessed his birth. Each summer he followed their call, his heart quickening as the desert floor gave way to foothills, then the highlands where Joseph Cameron sent his cattle to graze.

Instead of finding his mother, Matt had found his brother. His twin. Turning onto his good side, Matt peered out of the lean-to, looking for Rafael.

Seeing the empty cattle pen, Matt struggled to his knees, gritting his teeth as he cradled his shoulder and tried to stand. "If that Mexican's stolen the cattle . . ." The words died when he saw the Durhams grazing on the far side of the meadow and Rafael riding the brown mare near the edge of the herd. "I'll be . . ." Matt chuckled and lowered himself back onto the blanket. He was weak as a kitten and thirsty. A cup of water sat by his pillow. It seemed his Mexican brother had thought of everything.

I must stop thinking of him as a Mexican and remember to call him Rafael or hermano, Matt thought, still not recovered from the shock of discovering he had a twin brother. He was sure the Camerons had never suspected. All these years he'd had a twin, the two of them looking exactly alike, maybe even thinking alike . . . neither knowing about the other. He closed his eyes, still not quite believing it.

The bawling of a calf brought Matt's attention back to the cattle. A short time later, his brother ambled into the lean-to.

"So . . . you're awake."

"Sí."

"Are you hungry yet?"

"A little."

"*Bueno,* because I'm starved." Rafael squatted by the fire and stirred the contents of a pan. "Have you ever eaten boiled cougar?"

Matt grimaced. "No."

"Neither have I," Rafael confided. "But the broth should be good for you, and I am hungry enough to eat almost anything."

"Even cougar?"

Rafael grinned as he ladled the broth into a tin plate. "*El tigre* is not so brave now that he's lost his skin."

"What about the calf?"

"In the corral with his madre. *Por diablo,* he was a noisy one. And you?" Rafael grinned as he ambled over to Matt.

Matt's eyes took him in, both mesmerized and disturbed by the sight of the bronzed face, the grubby brown hands protruding out of dirty sleeves. *This is how I would look if I hadn't been adopted by the Camerons—Mexican, and a poor and dirty one at that.*

"All night you were talking, though it was in *Inglés* so I couldn't understand," Rafael went on. The spoon hovered above Matt's opened mouth. "How did you learn Spanish?"

"At school." Matt's stomach quivered as the warm liquid slid down his throat. It tasted better than he expected and he opened his mouth for more. "My mother . . ." He paused. How could he explain Helen Cameron's complex personality and her zeal for learning? "She learned Spanish too, so sometimes we speak it at home."

Rafael's dark brows lifted. "Why would a *gringa* learn Spanish?"

"She's a midwife and spends a lot of time helping the Mexicans."

Rafael continued to spoon the broth into Matt's mouth. "This man you call your padre, what does he do?"

"He's a farmer." He swallowed another spoonful of broth. "Raises cattle, too."

"Is he as wealthy as Tío Pedro said?"

Not liking the turn their conversation was taking, Matt motioned the spoon away. "Others are richer. Since he has three wives and fifteen children, he works hard to feed us all.

"Fifteen niños?" The dark brows lifted again. "*Madre mía,* how does he feed so many?"

Matt thought of the long hours the sturdy Scotsman spent in his fields. "It isn't easy."

"And you say he doesn't count you as his son?"

Matt looked away from Rafael's probing brown eyes. "Sometimes." The answer, like his voice, was tentative. Although Joseph Cameron had given him his name, Matt knew Joseph didn't love his dark-skinned son as wholeheartedly as Helen did. "Since he has nine sons of his own, I'm not the first in line for either his affection or his money," Matt concluded.

"I see." Rafael glanced outside. "I must see to the cattle."

Matt felt a stab of apprehension when Rafael picked up his whip. What if his attempt to discourage his brother from expecting a reward had spurred him to steal the cattle? He rolled onto his side and peered out into the graying shadows. If Rafael started for the corral, he'd have to try to reach the rifle. Instead, his brother walked toward the horse, and when he returned he was carrying Matt's saddle. Matt pretended to be asleep, but pretense became reality as he slipped into fitful slumber, always aware of Rafael's watchful presence during the mountain-cooled night.

* * *

Thereafter, Matt ceased to worry about Rafael stealing the cattle. Gradually his strength returned and by the end of the week, he was able to take a few steps around the lean-to.

"What happened to your *amigos?*" Rafael asked one evening.

"My friends?"

"José said there were two gringos with you . . . two boys with light hair."

"They're my brothers . . . my adoptive brothers," Matt amended. "George got sick, so Harry took him home. Harry should be coming back before long." Matt frowned, counting the days since the boys had left. "I want to thank you again for staying to help. I can't pay you, but maybe . . ."

Rafael put up his hand. "Since we're hermanos we will not talk of pay. It is what our madre would wish."

"Did Tío Pedro ever tell you about her?"

"Sí." Rafael paused and looked out of the lean-to. "Sometimes when he was sad, Tío would talk . . . especially just before he died."

"What did he say?"

"That she was young and very beautiful." Rafael's brown eyes seemed to grow darker. "Tío Pedro said she was the most beautiful girl in all of Chihuahua."

"Did he tell you her name?"

"Teresa. Teresa Maria Acosta."

The name seemed to mesh with the picture of the smiling Mexican woman Matt conjured up whenever he thought of his birth mother. "I wish I could remember her." His voice was unsteady. "What about our father? Did Tío Pedro tell you about him?"

Rafael's features hardened. "He had no name, or if he did, our tío did not know it. You see, we are illegitimate."

Sickness settled in Matt's stomach. This wasn't the first time he'd been called such a thing—albeit the choice of words had been much harsher. Fred Murdock had hurled it at him when Matt had beaten him in a fight. Although Fred's mother made him apologize afterward, the name had stayed like a dark stain in the back of Matt's mind.

"You don't seem surprised."

"It's rumored among the Mormones." Not liking to dwell on the subject, Matt slid a gold ring from his finger. "Did Tío Pedro ever mention this?"

Rafael stared at the ring. "Where did you get it?"

"It was on a ribbon around my neck when Tío Pedro brought me to Helen Cameron. She gave it to me last year for Christmas."

Rafael took the ring and held it close to the firelight. *"Caray!"* he whispered, running his finger over the raised crest.

"Do you recognize it?"

"No . . . though it must be valuable. A valuable ring," Rafael repeated, handing it back to Matt. "Too bad Tío Pedro isn't here to tell us about it."

Tension collided with fingers when Matt reached for the ring. He knew Rafael was lying—knew it, but didn't know why.

* * *

Why? The question circled through Matt's brain and followed him as he wrapped himself in his blanket that night, interrupting his sleep and making him start whenever Rafael got up to check on the cattle. Sometime he must have slept deeply, for when Matt awoke the next morning, both Rafael and the mare were gone.

Matt scowled his displeasure. He should've known Rafael couldn't be trusted, especially after he'd lied. But had he lied? As he reached for his boots, Matt noticed his naked ring finger. A quick survey of the lean-to showed the rifle was missing, too.

He slammed his hand against his boot. "The thievin', lying Mexican!" As he spoke, he felt a twinge of guilt. Wasn't he a Mexican too? Did that make him a liar and thief? Matt pushed the thought aside, even as he acknowledged that he'd suspected—no expected—Rafael to steal from him. It had been there from the start; his own judging and feeling of superiority. Regardless, he was positive Rafael had recognized the crest on the ring.

Matt's anger simmered throughout the morning, and every time the cattle wandered off he felt like swearing. He was so caught up in his anger and misery he didn't notice Rafael had returned until his brother loped the mare across the meadow. "Where's my rifle and what have you done with my ring?" Matt shouted.

"They are here." The ring flashed on Rafael's finger when he pointed to the rifle nested in the scabbard of the saddle.

"Thief!" Matt yelled, wondering how someone who'd shared the same womb with him could steal with such unrepentant nonchalance.

Rafael smiled and pulled on his left ear, a gesture Matt recognized with irritation as his own. "Si, but since I came back, I am no longer a thief, no?"

"Why did you come back?"

Rafael swung his leg over the saddle and sprang to the ground. "I don't know, hermano. But the farther I rode, the more I knew I must turn back. It was as if our blessed madre were whispering in my ear, telling me we must go together to find our padre."

The contrite look on Rafael's face nibbled at Matt's anger. This was his brother, the vital part of his identity for which he'd been searching. "You recognized the crest on the ring, didn't you?"

"Sí. I have seen it many times on the de Vega cattle, and it hangs over the gate to the de Vega *hacienda*."

Mattt had heard of the wealthy *hacendado*—the landowner whose holdings spread over much of northern Chihuahua.

"Don't you see what this means, hermano?" Rafael grasped Matt's good arm. "Our padre is rich, and he has only one son . . . a niño so sick he must spend his time visiting doctors in Mexico City. It is the lament of Don de Vega's life. He wants strong sons to carry on the family name."

"We have no proof. Just the ring. How do we know our mother didn't find it or . . ." Matt couldn't bring himself to say "steal."

"You are mistaken, hermano." Rafael removed his *sombrero* and touched his hair. "This is our proof. The white streak. Don de Vega has one too, though it isn't so noticeable now that his hair is turning gray."

Matt's eyes moved from his brother's hair to his face.

"Tío Pedro suspected. Once he took me to the de Vega ranch. The guards wouldn't let us in, and when Tío Pedro refused to leave . . ." Rafael lifted his shirt and turned.

Matt's insides twisted at the sight of the ugly scars crisscrossing his brother's brown back. "How did you get those?"

"From the de Vega guards. After they finished, they said they would kill us if we ever came back." Rafael lowered his shirt. "Needless to say, we did not return. Since then I have learned to use the whip. And someday, hermano . . ." Rafael fingered his quirt. "Someday I will return the favor."

"Your whip can't get you into the hacienda."

"But the ring can. Remember we are two young men, not a scrawny boy and a sick old man."

Matt's jaw tightened. "I can't go with you. The cattle . . . my father."

Rafael's voice turned scornful. "*Señor* Cameron is not your padre." He stepped closer and gave an excited laugh. "Think of it, hermano. We are about to become rich, so rich you can buy Señor Cameron a hundred steers to replace these."

For a moment Matt was carried along by his twin brother's enthusiasm. If he went with Rafael, he would become part-owner of the biggest ranch in northern Mexico. Then practicality crept in. "Even if Don de Vega's son is sickly, what makes you think he'll welcome his illegitimate sons?"

Rafael strutted like a rooster, his arms outstretched, a wide grin stretching his features. "Are we not strong? Can't we ride and rope cattle? That puny son of his can't even get on a horse." Rafael laughed and threw an affectionate arm around Matt. "Forget about the Mormones and come with me."

"I don't know." Thoughts of Helen made him hesitate. Although his Mexican mother and Don de Vega had given him life, Helen Cameron had carefully shaped and molded it, her arms offering shelter and comfort while her faith gave his strength. And what about his promise to Joseph Cameron? He couldn't just walk away. Nor could he forget about the Mormons. Wasn't he a Mormon too? Matt took a deep breath and met his brother's eyes. "I can't go with you, Rafael. My father . . . Joseph Cameron is depending on me."

"Fool!" Rafael spat the word.

"Perhaps." Matt managed a smile. "But you can go."

"How? It will take days to walk to Valle Grande. And when I get there . . ." Rafael looked at his dirty clothes. "They will throw me out like they did before."

"If you were better dressed, maybe they wouldn't throw you out."

"Where would I get new clothes?"

"I have some extra ones in the lean-to. You can take mine."

For a second Rafael's face brightened, then he shook his head. "A vaquero without a horse fares no better than a poor *peón*."

Matt eyed the mare, reluctant to let her go. "I'll need the rifle, but you can take the mare . . . but only after you've helped me get the cattle back to the corral."

"How will you take care of the cattle after I'm gone?"

"Harry should be back by tomorrow . . . maybe even today. He'll have his horse and the pack mule. We'll make out all right."

While they rounded up the cattle, Matt suffered pangs of remorse. Rafael was right. They should be going together to find their father. If it weren't for his promise . . .

A short time later his remorse changed to unease as Rafael stepped out of the lean-to dressed in Matt's clothes. A wide grin stretched the Mexican's handsome features, his pride in the borrowed shirt and dungarees evident. "Now no one can tell us apart. It is strange, no?"

"We may look alike, but you're not me."

"Sí, but I doubt even our blessed madre could tell us apart."

"Maybe that's why she put the ribbon around my neck." Matt's eyes fastened on the ring. "When you're through with it, I want it back."

Rafael's eyes narrowed. "Why, hermano?"

"You won't need the ring after you've met Don de Vega. Our mother gave it to me, and I want it back."

Tension tightened the muscles in Rafael's lean jaw. Then he shrugged. "Since I'll be with our padre, it's only fair that you should have the ring. Where should I look for you?"

"I'll be here until fall. After that, you can find me in Colonia Cortéz."

"That is far away."

"Since we're brothers, I'll expect you to find me. If not, I'll come after you."

There was a moment of silence while the brothers gauged each other. "I can see you are a man who doesn't like to be crossed. Neither do I, hermano. Maybe it's a trait we inherited from our padre, no?" Rafael flashed a quick smile. "It may take me a while, but I will come."

"*Gracias.*" Matt held Rafael's gaze. "Let me know how it goes."

"Sí." Rafael extended his hand. "Until then, hermano."

He gripped his brother's hand—a brown hand with narrow, tapered fingers, exactly like his own. *He's not me,* Matt's mind cried out as he watched Rafael mount the mare and lift his sombrero in farewell. "He's not me." The words came in a rasp and seemed to hang in the air, mocking him and chiding; for as Rafael rode away, Matt felt as if he were gazing after a reflection of himself.

CHAPTER 2

Fourteen-year-old Sabra Lindsey stuck a tentative, pink foot into the sun-dappled water of the Casas Grandes River. The cool liquid swirled around her toes, bringing welcome relief from the heat radiating off the Chihuahua desert.

"It's not very cold," she called over her shoulder.

"What if someone sees us?" Becky Wilson asked.

"They won't." Sabra grimaced when she noticed her friend had taken off only her shoes and stockings.

"I thought I'd just wade," Becky said, not quite meeting Sabra's gaze.

"Suit yourself."

Sabra waded into the river, her breath catching as the water crept past her bloomer-clad knees and up toward her middle.

"Be careful," Becky cautioned. "Remember, you can't swim."

Ignoring the warning, Sabra continued into the water. Except for during flood time, the Casas Grandes was little more than a shallow stream and certainly not anything to cause worry. Even Papa said the river was safe. But Samuel Lindsey had never intended for his daughter to swim there. This cooling respite from the heat was reserved for the male inhabitants of Colonia Cortéz, not the female, and most certainly not for a female clad only in a muslin chemise and bloomers.

Sabra paused to brush a strand of chestnut hair away from her heat-flushed cheeks. The promise of beauty lurked in the finely chiseled features and enormous green eyes, eyes that sparkled with mischief as Sabra scooped up a handful of water and threw it at her friend.

Becky's squeals rose above Sabra's laughter. Forgetting her resolve to stay dry, Becky hitched up her skirt and waded after Sabra. Splashing and laughing, they fell into the water in a tangle of muddy legs and dripping clothes.

Sabra surfaced first, coughing and sputtering as she clambered out of the muddied pool, hair streaming dankly over her face, the wet chemise clinging to her skin. Instinct alerted her to someone watching them, the knowledge streaking like lightning from a summer thundercloud to make her pause and look around.

"Becky . . ."

Something in her tone silenced Becky's sputters. In the resulting stillness they heard a rustle followed by retreating footsteps and stifled laughter.

"It's Hughie. He and Vern were trying to follow me." Worry trembled through Becky's voice. "What if he tells Mama?"

"He won't." Sabra said, although Becky's little brother was a notorious tattletale. "Maybe we'd better get dressed," she added, looking down at her drenched chemise.

Subdued, the girls wrung out their clothes on the riverbank. When Sabra reached for the shirtwaist she'd left behind a clump of willows, she couldn't find it. "Someone's taken my clothes!" Her gaze darted along the edge of the river. The towering cottonwoods and low-growing willows made ideal places for a boy to hide. "Hughie Wilson, get back here right this minute. Do you hear me?"

The soft trill of a meadowlark was the only reply.

"I mean it, Hughie. If you aren't back with my clothes by the time I count to twenty, I'll tell Sister Moffit you put a blow snake in her outhouse."

The continued silence changed Sabra's anger to concern. Having Hughie tattle was bad enough. To be forced to walk home in her bloomers and chemise was too horrible to contemplate.

"Hughie!" Becky's shrill voice pierced the somnolent afternoon air.

"Is something wrong?" a male voice called.

Before Sabra and Becky could hide in the willows, Luther Hawkins came at a run from a nearby cornfield. The shock on his face when he saw the two girls was as great as their dismay.

"We . . . we fell into the river," Sabra began. "But we're not hurt . . . just a little wet."

Vaguely aware that Becky cowered behind her, Sabra watched color suffuse Luther Hawkins's weatherworn face. "I'll . . . I'll get your mother," he stammered.

"No . . . please. We don't . . ."

But Brother Hawkins was already hurrying through the trees.

The long ride back to town seemed to take forever, the girls sitting in the backseat of Papa's buggy with the quilt Mama had brought draped around their shoulders. Sister Wall shook her head when the buggy passed, while Myrtle Hamblin turned to stare, her eyes as large as Mexican *pesos*. Becky ducked into the folds of the quilt, but Sabra lifted her chin and pretended not to notice. Why had she thought swimming in the river such a wonderful idea? Why had she called so loudly for Hughie?

Later that evening Samuel Lindsey asked a similar question, his voice filling the house. "Why? What possessed you to do such a harem-scarem thing?" Samuel hadn't trusted himself to speak when he'd first seen Sabra. Even now he wanted to shake her. Instead, he took a deep breath and repeated the question. "Why?"

"We were hot."

"You could have washed yourselves off with cool water."

"That's not the same."

The lines tightened around her father's mouth. Samuel Lindsey wasn't a big man, but there was something about him that exuded power, his gray eyes seeming to penetrate those with whom he was speaking, the planes of his handsome features taking on a flintlike sternness. "Whether it's the same or not doesn't matter. What matters is that you went swimming in your . . ." Samuel couldn't bring himself to say "drawers."

"Rob and Del go swimming in their underwear all the time."

"Rob and Del are boys."

"So . . . ?"

Afraid of what he might do, Samuel began to pace the parlor—four paces to the window with its crocheted lace curtains, six paces back to the wide double doors. "It just isn't done," he finally said. "Young ladies don't act this way. It was bad enough when the whole town saw you wearing Rob's dungarees. If you keep it up, no one's going to want to marry you."

"I don't care," Sabra retorted. "I don't need some stupid man to take care of me. I can take care of myself."

Samuel's lips twitched. "You can certainly do that. I've never met such a feisty girl. But . . ."

"I won't be prim and proper, either," she interrupted. "I don't want to be like other girls. I want to be me, Papa, not someone all frippery and silly. I'm me and . . ." Tears halted the tirade. Sabra looked down at the rag carpet, hoping Papa wouldn't notice her tears.

"I'm sorry, hon." Samuel's voice was contrite as he put a calloused hand on her narrow shoulder. Why did she always want to take a different road? Couldn't she see the danger? Samuel could, and what he saw frightened him. Sabra was like a young colt, kicking against the traces—tossing her head, always questioning and defying. His hand tightened on her shoulder. Heaven knew how much he loved his daughter. He'd loved her with an overpowering tenderness from the moment Sister Cameron laid the squalling mite in his arms. Now his love was tempered with an element of fear. Sabra was fast changing from child to woman, her nondescript brown hair deepening to a rich chestnut color, the planes of her piquant features softening into something very close to beauty. He'd seen the older boys' sidelong glances. Before long they'd want to do more than glance. "Promise me you'll think before you do things, Sabra. Promise?"

* * *

That night after Sabra went to bed, she heard the murmur of voices floating up from the kitchen. Curious to know what was keeping her parents up so late, she stole down the stairs to listen.

"I don't know what to do with her," Mama was saying. "I suppose if we look at it from Sabra's viewpoint, what she did was no worse than what half the boys in Cortéz have been doing. But still . . ."

"It certainly doesn't help her wobbly reputation," Aunt Mae said.

The presence of Papa's second wife surprised Sabra. By unspoken agreement, a plural wife didn't infringe on the privacy of the other wife's home when their shared husband was present.

"Much as I'd hate to see her go, maybe you ought to send her to live with your brother in Utah," Aunt Mae continued. "If she's someplace where people aren't already talking about her . . ."

Sabra couldn't believe what she was hearing. When she and Mama didn't see eye to eye, she could always depend on Aunt Mae to listen. Now Aunt Mae was suggesting that Sabra be sent away.

"Maybe Mae's right," Elizabeth sighed. "We've tried to make her more ladylike, but you know how she is. And after today . . ." Mama sighed again. "It will break my heart to see her go, but if it will help . . ."

Sabra's stomach tightened.

"No," Samuel stated. "Sabra may be a mite wild and independent, but she's young yet. Only fourteen. Give her another year. If she hasn't changed by then, we'll consider Salt Lake."

Her father's reprieve offered a glimmer of hope, but it couldn't dissolve the fear of being sent away. It circled above her all night, interrupting her sleep and sending her dreams galloping to her haven on the bluff.

Sabra awoke before dawn when the sky was still strewn with stars. They beckoned just outside her window, whispering of freedom and the silent sweep of the bluff where she could be alone. Her upstairs bedroom with its gingham-draped dressing table and curtains seemed suffocating. She kicked back the sheet and went to the window. A slight breeze ruffled the curtains, and the stars called with increasing urgency.

A short time later she was riding across the flats on her sorrel mare. Sabra rode astride, having donned the new divided riding skirt her father had bought for her after the escapade with Rob's dungarees. Elizabeth Lindsey disapproved of the new fashion, certain it would only encourage Sabra in her tomboyish ways, but Samuel had overruled his wife, pointing out that a divided skirt was more modest than a bunched up dress or a pair of boy's breeches.

"Thank you, Papa," Sabra called to the yellowing sky. "And thank you, God, for making such a glorious morning." She laughed and pushed back the straw hat she'd donned from force of habit, letting it and her nutmeg-colored hair tangle together in the freshening air. It was always cooler on the bluff—cool and wild with a sense of peace. If only her parents could understand her need to run free, away from the hot kitchen and rooms filled with noisy, teasing brothers.

The Mormon practice of having more than one wife had filled Samuel Lindsey's quiver until it overflowed with children—all of them boys except for Sabra. Being the only girl had its advantages, for Aunt Mae, Papa's second wife and Mama's sister, was as delighted by the arrival of a girl as Elizabeth was. Together they showered Sabra with affection and lace-trimmed pinafores, reveling in her accomplishments and taking turns sitting by her bed when she was sick.

Everything would have gone well if Sabra had shown interest in the normal female things. But she preferred to be outside with her father and brothers, sitting on her father's lap as he cut a swath of alfalfa with the horse-drawn mower, or riding pell-mell after the cows on her favorite horse, Buttons. Everything her brothers did, Sabra tried too. Even swimming.

The sky was golden with dawn and the air still cool as Sabra cantered her mare up the steep incline of the bluff overlooking Colonia Cortéz. When she reached the top, she reined in the horse and looked across the mesquite-studded valley where the Casas Grandes River wound like a long, brown serpent, its course marked by cottonwoods and willows.

Cortéz, a town founded by Mormons fleeing the United States for the practice of polygamy, lay nestled in a bend of the river. Like its sister colonies, it bore the Spanish name of the Mormons' adopted country, but its design was purely American. Had a stranger happened upon the tree-lined streets and gabled, two-story dwellings, he might have thought he'd strayed across the border into the United States.

To Sabra the well-planned town symbolized all that was right and wrong with her life. The shaded yards and flower-scented gardens surrounding sturdy, brick homes were like the warmth and laughter mingling through her structured days. Sabra tried to comply with the rules governing her conduct, knowing they were couched in love and patiently given, but there were times when the need to be free of restriction filled her with a restlessness she found difficult to contain.

"I won't go to Utah!" Sabra shouted at the breeze. "I don't care what Mama and Aunt Mae say, I won't go!" Even as she spoke, the more practical side of her wondered how she could prevent it.

Frowning, she dismounted and tethered the mare by a solitary acacia. "And I won't spend the rest of my life cooped up in a hot, stuffy kitchen. Scrubbing and cleaning . . . that's all Mama and Aunt Mae do."

Voicing her frustration helped. The expanse of the desert did the rest, seeming to absorb her into its vastness along with the rocks and cacti and creosote. She closed her eyes and lifted her face to the burgeoning sun, letting peace and silence roll over her, savoring the soft breeze as it soothed and caressed.

When Sabra opened her eyes, she gazed over the broad sweep of the Casas Grandes Valley and the farms bordering the river. The green, cultivated fields presented a sharp contrast to the desert. *Papa's right,* she thought. *I am a wild thing. If I can't be outside, I'll shrivel up and die.*

Using the peaked roof of John Simmon's gristmill as a landmark, Sabra counted across the fields until she found her father's farm. Everything looked so small from up on the bluff. The haystacks resembled overturned straw baskets, and the two horses grazing in the grain field appeared no bigger than mice. Sabra stiffened and her eyes narrowed. What were horses doing in their grain field?

Not waiting to discover the answer, she ran back to the mare. A moment later they were flying down the hillside, her problem and the need to be alone forgotten in the rush to reach the farm.

This wasn't the first time someone had staked horses overnight in her father's grain field. A circle of close-cropped foliage and fresh horse droppings had greeted her father several times, but each time Samuel left one of his boys to watch the field, the horses hadn't appeared.

"I've caught them red-handed," Sabra cried, laughing as she pictured her father's surprise when she brought the horses up to the barn.

Although her father suspected that one of their Mexican neighbors was "borrowing" the grain field, there had never been any proof. Now when the Mexicans came to claim the horses, Papa would have all the proof he needed.

"Come on, Buttons!"

The horse responded with a burst of speed as they rushed past mesquite brush and spiky Spanish bayonet. On they galloped, past the community pasture and gristmill, then down the lane leading to the farms. Sabra's long hair and battered hat, its ribbon fastened under her chin, streamed behind them. When she reached the field, Sabra slowed the mare, her mouth tightening at the sight of the damaged grain.

"Look at what they've done," she grumbled, thinking of the milk and sacks of corn her father gave his Mexican neighbors. "They should be grateful. Instead, they do this."

Sabra dismounted and jumped the ditch at the top of the field. One of the horses resisted when she tried to lead it out of the field, but the other followed her, encouraging his balky companion. Hearing a shout, she turned and saw a Mexican running toward her with a stick in his hand. Her heart jerked when she recognized Carlos Garcia, a sulky, seventeen-year-old who sometimes worked for the Mormons. Why did it have to be Carlos? Why not one of the Mexicans who was friendly?

"*Alto!*" Carlos shouted.

Sabra ignored his command to stop and urged the horses toward her mare. Before she could reach them, Carlos threw the stick. Clinging to the rope of the shying horse, Sabra scooped up a rock and hurled it at the advancing Mexican. The sound of stone striking flesh forced a startled grunt from the young man. He paused, an ugly scowl tightening his features as he rubbed his leg. Then, with a curse, he rushed toward her.

Sabra grabbed another rock. "You come one step closer and I'll throw it . . . only this time I'll aim at your head."

Carlos stopped and appraised her out of glaring, black eyes, his hand sliding inside his baggy shirt.

Sabra's mouth went dry. Did Carlos have a knife? She watched his eyes move over her in a calculating manner, saw him point to the horses.

"You can't have them until you talk to my father."

Carlos's eyes narrowed and an angry flood of Spanish poured from his lips.

Although she only understood a smattering of what he said, Carlos's vehement expression and voice left little doubt about his feelings. "*Caballos . . . mis caballos,*" Carlos concluded, lifting his hand in a menacing gesture and pointing at his horse.

"No." Sabra's heart pounded into her throat, its erratic hammering filling her ears with a steady staccato. Suddenly that staccato changed to the drumming of hooves. Someone was coming.

A subtle change in the Mexican's expression told Sabra he was aware of the rider too. Their eyes locked and the muscles in her raised arm tensed, ready to hurl the rock if Carlos moved.

"What's going on here?" a male voice yelled.

When Carlos leaped to snatch the ropes, Sabra swung the rock at his head. Before the stone connected, strong fingers grabbed her hand and forced her to drop it.

"Are you trying to get yourself hurt?"

Sabra whirled to face the rider, mistaking his olive skin and dark eyes for one of Carlos's relatives. Then she recognized Matt Cameron. "Let me go!"

Matt's fingers tightened. "Not until you tell me what's going on."

"Carlos staked his horses in our grain field. Now he's trying to get them back. Thanks to you he's succeeded." Sabra lunged for the ropes, but Carlos sidestepped, his face breaking into a grin when Matt yanked her back. "Let me go!"

"Calm down so I can hear Carlos's side of the story."

"Carlos's side!" Sabra's voice jerked with fury. "You know what he'll tell you—that he's innocent as a baby. Then he'll twist things to make it look like I was stealing his horses."

"Were you?"

"Of course not! I was taking them up to the barn. If Carlos wants them back, he'll have to talk to Papa and pay for the ruined grain." She gestured toward the field. "He can't have the horses back until he talks to Papa."

"I don't think Carlos will like that."

"Of course he won't. That's why I had the rock."

A smile tugged at the corners of Matt's mouth.

"It's not funny. If you're afraid to stop Carlos, let me." She glanced at Carlos and saw him sidling away with the horses. "He's getting away!"

Matt called in Spanish to the Mexican. Carlos paused, a wary look crossing his face as he glanced at Sabra. *"La tigra,"* Carlos began.

Cat! Sabra knew what Carlos was saying—knew it just as she knew Matt was amused. She caught the glitter of laughter in his eyes, sensed it bubbling through his chest. Seeing it, she stamped her riding boot onto his instep. Instantly, Matt's arm curled around her neck, forcing the air from her throat as he pinned her against his chest. Her vision blurred, and for a second she thought she would faint. His hold loosened a bit as he forced her face up, his angry, black eyes glaring into hers. "If you so much as move, you'll wish you hadn't." Then he thrust her aside and went to Carlos.

Shaken and trying to catch her breath, she watched Matt and Carlos in amicable conversation. The scene was so pleasant, she half expected to see them walk off together with the horses.

They're in cahoots, she thought. *Fred Murdock's right. Matt's more Mexican than he is Mormon.* Before she could decide what to do, Carlos had handed the ropes to Matt and ambled down the lane to the Garcia farm.

"Now what do you plan to do?" she demanded. His actions had put her off balance.

"Get you back home where you belong." Matt paused and scowled. "What were you doing all alone out here?"

"I rode up to the bluff. When I saw horses in our field, I came to take them home." Her pointed chin lifted and her eyes flashed. "If you hadn't interfered, I'd have done it, too."

"Like heck you would have. Did you know Carlos was carrying a knife? If I hadn't happened along, you could have been hurt."

Sabra's knees went weak. "He wouldn't have used it." Using anger as a cover for fear, she hurried on. "How come you just so conveniently happened by? I'll bet you and Carlos are in cahoots. Fred says . . ."

"I know what Fred says." The muscles in Matt's jaw tightened. "If you're fool enough to believe him, I'm sorry I didn't leave you to Carlos." Matt dropped the ropes and mounted his horse.

Sabra immediately regretted her accusation as Matt rode off. She knew Matt hadn't done anything to warrant Fred's taunts. But regret didn't make her take back the words. Matt had treated her like she didn't have any sense . . . as if she were wrong instead of Carlos.

Trying to get the Garcia horses to follow Buttons didn't improve Sabra's temper. First one would balk, then the other. She tried everything—talking, cajoling, finally yelling. She was glad Matt had ridden off. Having him laugh at her was the last thing she needed. Then, for no apparent reason, the two horses turned docile and followed Sabra as if they'd been doing it all their lives.

The horses' cooperation lifted Sabra's mood. It improved further when she pictured the look on her father's face as she rode into the yard with the horses. He'd be pleased, maybe so pleased he'd forget she'd gone swimming in her drawers. Even Rob and Del would be impressed.

Caught up in thoughts of her homecoming, her good humor had grown until it included Matt, who'd stopped to check on his father's cattle. "I'm sorry," she called. "I don't really believe what Fred says."

Matt neither answered nor looked at her.

"I've never believed Fred."

"Never mind."

"But I do mind. I know how it feels to be wrongly accused."

Matt paused. "Like stealing watermelons from Brother Patton's melon patch?"

"That wasn't me." Sabra was defiant.

"I know. It was Harry and some of his friends."

"Hmph. Harry sure took his time owning up to it."

"That's Harry's way. Quick to dance, but slow to pay the piper." Good nature returned to Matt's features. "Do you know what Carlos called you? La tigra . . . a wild cat with a wild temper."

Sabra tried to suppress a smile. "I do have a bit of a temper."

"Bit! My foot feels like a horse stepped on it."

Laughter bubbled in her throat and spilled out in a delighted giggle. "It was Carlos's fault. If he hadn't thrown a stick, I wouldn't have gotten mad and hit him with the rock."

At the mention of the rock, Matt's face grew serious. "In spite of what you think, that could have turned into a nasty situation."

"Maybe." Sabra lifted her chin, ready to do battle. Matt's steady gaze put her off. She pushed self-consciously at her tangled hair, understanding now why the older girls pinched color into their cheeks whenever Matt was around. She forced her eyes away from his dusky face and concentrated on the rutted lane winding between the fence posts. Dew-wet grasses clustered along the irrigation ditch, and a mourning dove broke off its mournful song and took flight.

"What did you tell Carlos to make him give back the horses?"

"I just mentioned that Mr. Lindsey would probably ride to Casas Grandes for the sheriff. The threat made him decide to go home and get his father. I told him if they promised to not do it again, they'd probably get their horses back."

"If he tries it again, he'll be sorry."

"I believe you. I think Carlos does too." Matt smiled as he took in the uncombed hair and freckled nose of the girl who'd challenged Carlos. Though he wouldn't go so far as to call her a wild cat, she certainly had spunk, a quality that sat at odds with her large emerald eyes and full red lips. "Your parents should have named you Nutmeg."

"Why?"

"It suits you and goes with your hair."

Sabra wrinkled her nose. If one of her brothers had tagged her with the nickname, she'd have been upset. Coming from Matt, if felt like a compliment. She glanced at him, noting his blue cambric shirt and the dark blue bandanna knotted around his neck. Most of the older boys dreamed of becoming cowboys. Having spent the summer in the mountains, Matt had achieved both the dream and the status that accompanied it. "When did you get back from the mountains?"

"Yesterday. After running loose all summer, some of the cattle weren't happy to find themselves fenced in again. I rode out to check on them."

Matt stroked the neck of the black gelding his father had given him to replace the brown mare. His worry about giving it to Rafael had been for nothing. Although Joseph had frowned when Matt told him about the Mexican who'd saved his life and helped with the cattle, in the end he'd voiced his approval. "Ye did the right thing. 'Twas a brave thing the laddie did. He deserved a reward."

Matt's tale of the mountain lion had been expansive, but his description of Rafael had been deliberately vague. Twice he'd been on the verge of telling his parents about his twin brother. Each time he'd opened his mouth, something stopped his tongue. A similar numbness had spread to his brain, leaving him uncertain and torn in what he should do and say. Part of it related to the shame he felt at knowing for certain he was illegitimate. There were other factors too, his fear that Joseph Cameron would love him less being the most prominent.

Sabra's voice jerked Matt back to his surroundings. "I'm glad you happened along this morning."

"So am I. If you don't mind, I'll hang around 'til Carlos and his father come for their horses. We don't want any misunderstanding."

Sabra nodded. The Camerons often acted as interpreters when disputes arose between the Mormons and their Mexican neighbors.

The warmth of the sun on their shoulders and a chorus of mockingbirds calling from an apple orchard lulled Sabra and Matt into a comfortable silence. Ahead, Cortéz rose like a shady oasis, its carefully tended gardens and lawns serving as evidence of the ingenuity that sent water from the Casas Grandes River coursing through ditches to give life to the arid land. Windmills turned lazily in the morning breeze, their steady rhythm pumping water from underground wells to augment the precious river water.

Most of the Mormons had built their homes in town, preferring the safety and camaraderie of close neighbors to the isolation of farms. Soon men and boys would start the daily procession out to the fields, driving milk cows to pasture, then staying to hoe or irrigate their crops. Matt felt a sense of homecoming as he and Sabra turned down Hidalgo Street. Smoke curled from chimneys, and he could hear neighbors calling to one another as they did morning chores.

When they turned into the hollyhock-bordered lane leading to the Lindsey barn, Sabra reined in her mare. "Please, don't tell Papa what happened."

Matt's dark brows lifted. "Why not?"

"He'll be angry. So will Mama. They might send me to live with my uncle in Utah if they find out about the fight . . . how I hit Carlos."

"I take it you don't want to go to Utah?"

Sabra shook her head.

"I see."

Matt's steady gaze made her feel uncomfortable. "Please. It's important."

"I can see it is." Matt continued to appraise her. Until now, he'd taken little notice of Delbert Lindsey's little sister, though he'd heard remarks from his aunts about her undisciplined behavior. As Matt took in the freckled face, with a streak of dirt on one cheek, he felt sorry for the girl.

Before he could agree to her request, Sabra started her mare down the lane, pulling the Garcia horses after her. "Forget it," she flung over her shoulder. "I should have known you wouldn't understand."

Matt urged his horse forward. "Who said I didn't understand?"

"You did . . . or at least I thought . . ." Her voice trailed off when she saw his grin. "Does that mean you won't tell?"

"My lips are sealed."

"Thanks." Matt's smile made her feel warm and strange inside. "I just hope Carlos doesn't say anything."

"He doesn't want trouble, either. Not after that knifing last spring."

"But he might say something to Papa."

"That's one of the reasons I'm sticking around. Since I'll be interpreting, I can censor what your father shouldn't hear."

"Will you?"

Matt nodded. "But I think you should stay inside the house until after the Garcias leave. Seeing you might remind Carlos of what you did and . . ."

Sabra giggled. "I wish you could've seen his face when I hit him. He thought he could just walk up and take the horses." Her exhilaration returned. "Come on, you nags. Let's show Papa and the boys what we found."

* * *

Elation stayed with Sabra for the rest of the day, heightened by Matt's wink when he followed Samuel into the kitchen after the Garcias left.

"You're safe," he whispered.

Since her mother was watching, Sabra had to rely on a smile to convey her gratitude. She ducked her head and concentrated on peeling potatoes, aware of the happy circle of warmth gathering around her heart.

Sabra wondered at the strange turn of events as she undressed and prepared for bed that night. She blew out the lamp and went to the window where a moon the color of freshly churned butter cast mellow light into her room. She was too tired to puzzle out why the idea of friendship with Matt excited her or how it had actually come about. She only knew it had happened and that she was pleased.

"Nutmeg." Sabra smiled as she whispered the name. Then she knelt and said her prayers, unaware she was still smiling when she climbed between coarse muslin sheets and fell asleep.

CHAPTER 3

Excitement slipped through the bedroom window and touched Sabra with a shivery finger just before the sun peeked over the distant hills. She rolled over and smiled. It was the sixteenth of September, Mexico's Independence Day, an event the Mormons celebrated with almost as much enthusiasm as their Mexican neighbors.

Breathing in the tantalizing odor of freshly baked biscuits, Sabra pulled on her shirtwaist and brown skirt. Biscuits were but the beginning of good things. After the parade, there'd be a picnic and games, followed by a dance.

When prayers and breakfast were over, Sabra and her brothers set out for the parade. Others were already there, seeking shady porches or grassy spots under the trees. Sabra walked with Rob and Del, her older brothers, while eight-year-old Willie ran ahead, his shirttail hanging out between his suspenders.

"Don't go too far, Willie," Sabra called. "Mama said you can't have any chocolate cake unless you stay with me."

"That should keep him close," Delbert chuckled. He nudged his younger brother Rob. "What did Mama bribe you with?"

"Chicken . . . all that lovely fried chicken." Rob gave Del a friendly shove. "How about you?"

"The same." Del rubbed his stomach. "Nobody fixes chicken like Mama, though Sis here is makin' progress." He grinned at Sabra. "That was mighty good water you boiled for us last night. Keep it up and you might learn how to cook."

Del dodged as Sabra swung her fist. "Just wanted to see if you're in good enough form this year for us to win the three-legged race again," he teased.

"You don't have to worry about me," Sabra assured him. Although her brothers liked to tease, she counted herself fortunate to have eighteen-year-old Del and sixteen-year-old Rob as her companions. "Wouldn't you rather ask Rosella Clawson?"

Del shrugged. "She might not enjoy such things . . . her being so pretty and delicate-like."

Sabra pulled a face. Anyone with two eyes could see Rosella was a complete ninny, but all of the young men were so smitten with the blond from Utah that they failed to notice. "Why don't you ask her anyway?"

"I might." Del put his arm around her shoulder. "In case she turns me down, we'd better practice first."

Just then Willie gave a shout. "Look! The bandwagon's ready to go."

Sabra glanced up the street and saw Aunt Mae and her children waving at them from a shady place under a tree. "Over here, Sabra," Aunt Mae called. "I sent Jake over early to save a good spot."

Sabra and the boys hurried across the dusty street to join their aunt and the other half of Samuel Lindsey's brood.

"Did your mother get her new skirt hemmed?" Aunt Mae asked.

Sabra nodded, aware that Aunt Mae had spent a good part of the previous day helping sew the skirt and Spanish costumes Elizabeth and Samuel were wearing in the parade. She studied Aunt Mae's pleasant, round face, wondering if she resented being left to mind the children while her shared husband and his first wife rode with the leading citizens in the Independence Day parade. Days like this made Sabra glad the Church had issued the Manifesto discontinuing polygamy. She reached for baby Joey who chortled and grabbed the ribbon dangling from her straw hat. The baby's protest when she tried to rescue the ribbon drowned out the opening bars of the Mexican anthem.

Everyone came to attention as Bishop Harris, who carried the Mexican flag, started his prancing gray stallion down the street. A gaily decorated bandwagon followed the eagle-emblazoned flag. Sabra's eyes flew to the riders behind the bandwagon. Pennants with the names of all the Mexican states fluttered over the heads of the men, while the ladies riding at their sides held the flags of the capitals.

"There's Mama and Papa!" Willie cried.

Sabra's throat swelled with pride when she spied her father. At fifty, Samuel Lindsey's face and bearing were those of a much younger man. Although his curly black hair and mustache were laced with gray, his eyes and handsome features sparkled with life and good humor as he doffed his sombrero to acknowledge the shouts of his sons.

An unsmiling Elizabeth rode on Buttons, her gathered turquoise skirt flowing over the mare's rump in a colorful cascade. Unlike her husband, Elizabeth bore the marks of time on her face, its lines attesting to nine difficult pregnancies and four small graves in the Cortéz cemetery. Even so, there was a quiet dignity in her tall figure, one enhanced by the black lace *mantilla* worn over her hair and still-pretty features.

Sabra wished her mother would smile instead of looking so solemn. Why couldn't she be like Papa? Then she remembered how Mama had sat up after everyone had gone to bed to finish her skirt and put the finishing touches of braid on Papa's black vest. Mama had been up again before dawn to fry chicken and bake a cake so her family could enjoy the picnic. No wonder she looked tired and older than Papa.

"Mama." Sabra felt the sting of tears when her mother acknowledged her wave with a tentative smile. Willie and his half brothers took up the cry, their exuberant shouts making Elizabeth blush and shake her head.

"Make sure you stay with your sister," Elizabeth mouthed.

Willie nodded and grabbed Sabra's sleeve, pointing to the carriage carrying the queen and her two attendants. "Look, Sabra."

Swaths of red, white, and green bunting draped the open carriage. A young man wearing black trousers and a short jacket trimmed with silver braid held a Mexican flag over the heads of the queen and her attendants whose red, white, and green dresses were arranged to resemble a second flag.

Sabra grimaced when she saw that Rosella Clawson was the queen. She might be pretty, but why had the parade committee chosen a girl from Utah to reign over the festivities? Just then the man holding the flag glanced in Sabra's direction, making her forget all about Rosella.

Warmth, mingled with shyness and excitement, swept over her when she recognized Matt Cameron. Sabra watched him almost furtively—Sabra who was never shy, who didn't care two pins what boys thought of her or whether they noticed her presence. She cared now, pushing at the untidy scraps of hair straggling out from under her straw hat while her eyes searched Matt's sombrero-shaded face for any sign of recognition. Had he seen her? Would he wave?

"I wonder why they chose Matt to ride with the queen?" Del asked.

"'Cause he's Mexican and today is Mexico's Independence Day." Rob grinned at his brother. "Better watch out, Del. Rosella's making sheep eyes at him."

Del's frown deepened. "Why didn't he stay in the mountains until Rosella went back to Utah?"

"'Cause he lives here," Sabra snapped. She gnawed on her lower lip and tried not to notice how Rosella kept smiling up at Matt. "Rosella doesn't. They should've chosen a girl from Cortéz to be queen."

"That may be true, but it's not something you should say out loud," Aunt Mae countered.

"Why not?"

"It's not polite." Aunt Mae leaned her head close. "But I'll tell you a secret if you promise not to tell."

"I promise."

Aunt Mae's voice lowered to a whisper. "Remember how Brother Clawson brought new band instruments from Utah at the beginning of the summer? Well, when the parade committee heard they were returning to get Rosella this week, they voted to show their appreciation by making his daughter the queen."

"Too bad Mabel Anderson's father didn't think to buy a new bandwagon," Sabra quipped, noting the first attendant's forced smile. "If he had, maybe Mabel would have been queen."

"Sabra!" Aunt Mae tried to suppress a giggle.

"I'm sorry," Sabra apologized. But she wasn't, not when Rosella kept smiling at Matt.

When the parade was over, Sabra hurried with her brothers to the grove of trees adjoining the combination church-schoolhouse. The locust and black walnuts, planted fifteen years before, provided welcome shade for picnics and ward socials.

Today the grove teemed with people. Children were everywhere, laughing and dodging among the trees while parents spread quilts and arranged food in the shade. The smell of fried chicken vied with the aroma of root beer fizzing in crockery containers recently taken from the cool cellar under the church.

After three helpings of chicken followed by a generous piece of chocolate cake, Del lay back on the quilt. "I ate too much."

"Pig." When the epitaph failed to get a rise, Sabra tickled his nose with a piece of grass. Del jerked and his blue eyes flew open. "Are you going to ask Rosella to be your partner for the race?" she prodded.

Del frowned and closed his eyes. "Naw."

"Why not?"

"She's the queen. Rosella can't very well race and hand out prizes at the same time, can she?"

"I guess you're stuck with me."

"That's all right. I doubt Rosella can run very fast anyway. But I ain't racing 'til I've had a little *siesta*."

As her brother closed his eyes, Sabra went to look for Becky. As she crossed the school yard, she became aware of whispers, then a few snickers, and finally Hughie's friend asking how she enjoyed her swim. She was on the verge of giving the obnoxious twelve-year-old a piece of her mind when she saw Matt coming toward her, the black *charro* costume exchanged for dungarees and shirt, his crisp, dark hair freshly combed. Sabra was aware of her shyness and the quickened rhythm of her heart. Matt ran with the older crowd, those old enough to be courting, so she didn't expect him to take much notice of her. She did hope he'd speak, though.

"There you are. I've been looking all over for you."

"You have?"

Matt nodded, but his eyes were on Hughie's friend. "They're about to start the races and I need a partner."

Sabra felt a little addled. "Partner . . ." she stammered. "Me?"

Matt didn't seem to notice her confusion. "Sure, I know a winner when I meet one. Let's show them what we can do."

Hughie's friends, who'd been playing marbles, stood up. "Why don't you let her show you how she goes swimming in her drawers?" the bigger one mocked.

There was a tiny moment of silence before Matt advanced on the two boys. Eddie Whipple brushed dust off his pants and tried to ease away, but Sam Murdock stood his ground, his head lifted in defiance.

"I'm going to pretend I didn't hear you say that." Matt's voice was low. "But if I ever hear talk like that from you again, I'll grab you by the ear and take you to the bishop." His hand shot out and grabbed Sam's shoulder, his tone lightening. "Speaking of showing people things, did I show you where I got clawed by a mountain lion?"

"No, but Harry told Archie about it."

"Well, if you're real good, I might show it to you sometime." His hand tightened on the boy's shoulder. "But if I ever hear you say mean things about Sabra, I'll deal with you like I did with the mountain lion." Matt paused and looked hard at Sam. "Understand?"

"Sure, Matt." This was from Eddie.

Sam nodded and swallowed.

The two boys couldn't seem to get away fast enough, Sam mumbling something about helping his father set up ropes for one of the races.

Matt turned back to Sabra, who'd watched the scene with a mingling of astonishment and admiration. "Are you ready?" Matt asked.

Sabra nodded, knowing in some unfathomable way that her life was about to change. Instead of storming and kicking, she would follow this man without protest, happy just to be in his presence as she was now, matching her step with his while excitement swirled inside, swelling and building until she thought she would burst.

They were halfway across the school yard before Sabra remembered her promise to Del. "I can't race with you. I promised Del I'd be his partner."

Matt's grin vanished. "Trust Del to have the luck. First Rosella. Now you."

Sabra stared at him, totally confused.

"Rosella asked Del to help her hand out prizes," Matt said.

That might explain Matt's chagrin, but it didn't explain how he and Del could be so dumb about Rosella. A sudden thought made her take heart. "If Del's handing out prizes, he won't be able to race."

"You're right!" Matt's grin came back. "Come on, Nutmeg."

Sabra needed no further encouragement. She followed Matt as he pushed through the crowd. Several racers were already there, waiting on the grass. Matt handed his bandanna to the man in charge of the race and extended his right leg.

Sabra flushed when she realized she must offer her left leg with its scuffed high-top shoe and dirt-streaked stocking. She glanced at Rosella, who sat in a chair under the trees. Tiny white slippers peeped from under the hem of her skirt, and her hair looked as if it had just been combed.

Sabra shoved a strand of unruly hair back under her straw hat. *I don't care,* she thought. *I can run faster than a hundred Rosella Clawsons, and Matt knows it. That's why he chose me.* Forgetting her scuffed shoes, she grinned up at Matt.

"Ready for a practice run?" he asked.

At her nod, he placed his arm around her shoulder. Sabra concentrated on synchronizing their rhythm, but the pressure of Matt's arm on her shoulder, the feel of his long leg against hers, broke the thread of her concentration. She missed a step, making them stumble and almost fall.

Matt's hold tightened as he tried to keep his balance. "Are you all right?"

"Yes." Unable to meet Matt's eyes, she felt heat rush to her face. What was wrong with her? Sabra took a deep breath and tried to put her topsy-turvy emotions back in their proper place. *Pretend he's Del or Rob. If you trip in the race and make a fool of yourself, it will ruin everything.*

The thought brought a return of recklessness. "The others haven't got a chance," she whispered with an impish grin. Protected by the "he's my brother" thoughts, she was able to meet his warm, brown eyes with only the suggestion of a tremor.

Matt's smile matched Sabra's as he squeezed her shoulder. "Put your arm around my waist and hang on, Nutmeg."

Sabra felt Matt's muscles tense as the man dropped his hand to begin the race. They sprang forward as one, their feet striking the turf, then lifting quickly to pass a less fortunate couple who'd fallen in a tangle of petticoats and smothered giggles. They kept their rhythmic pace, concentrating on the next step, not daring to look back, each aware of the steady cadence of a couple just behind them.

"It's Fred Murdock," Matt said between ragged gulps of air.

Knowing Matt's dislike for Fred, Sabra strained to stretch her legs without breaking rhythm. "We've got to win . . ." And they did, streaking across the finish line two paces ahead of Fred and his partner.

Sabra threw her arms around Matt's neck. His happy laughter sounded in her ears, and his exuberant embrace threatened to crush her ribs. "I knew you were a winner, Nutmeg!" Releasing her, Matt knelt and untied the bandanna.

Friends hurried them to receive blue ribbons, their praise making Sabra feel a part of the older crowd. Instead of being Del's little sister, she was Matt's partner and someone of consequence.

Sabra laughed and glanced at Matt, certain he was as proud as she was. Her joy seeped away when she saw his dark eyes focused on Rosella. Now she knew why Matt had asked her to be his partner. Not because he admired her spunk, or because they were friends, but to impress Rosella.

* * *

Sabra's high spirits had returned by the time she arrived at the dance that evening. Her animation increased when fiddles struck up a tune.

"Gentlemen take your partners for the quadrille," the dance manager called.

Sabra sat next to Becky on a bench along the side of the hall. Although she knew better than to expect Matt to ask for the first dance, she harbored the hope he might seek her later. Rosella or no Rosella, Sabra was determined to one day catch Matt's eye.

It was easy to pick Matt out of the crowd of men and boys who surged across the floor. He was wearing the black charro suit again, its deep tones setting off his handsome features and accentuating his dark hair and brows. Sabra wasn't surprised when Matt stopped and bowed before Rosella Clawson. She knew he would, just as she knew his doing so would start tongues wagging.

"That Cameron boy looks just like a Spanish *matador*. And Rosella. Have you ever seen a prettier girl?" an older woman said.

Sabra pulled a face and looked away, but Edith Murdock's next words jerked her attention back to the conversation.

"Matt may be handsome, but I'm glad he isn't dancing with my daughter. Do you know what Fred saw Matt doing?"

"No." The women's heads bent closer.

Sabra strained to hear the words. "When Fred was in Casas Grandes, he saw Matt come out of a *cantina*. Fred's sure he'd been drinking. The men he was with were riffraff . . . maybe even bandits."

There was shocked silence.

"Is Fred sure it was Matt? He's always been such a nice boy."

"It was Matt, all right. Fred saw that white streak in his hair. Don't breathe a word of this to Helen. If she found out, it would break her heart."

The muscles in Sabra's stomach tightened. Fred Murdock was lying. Everyone knew he didn't like Matt. Just the same, it made her sick inside—sick and angry that people would talk that way about her friend. Her eyes sought Matt, who was taking his place on the dance floor with Rosella.

Rosella still wore her crown, its gilt points shimmering like a halo above her silky curls. Until tonight Sabra had paid little heed to the girl from Utah. Now each detail of Rosella's person was noted—her dainty features and long-lashed blue eyes, and the *dress*. Even Sabra had to concede that the white ruffles and lace were lovely and gave Rosella's faintly flushed face the appearance of an angel.

Sabra glanced down at her brown skirt and white shirtwaist and wished she'd worn something more feminine. Then Rob asked Sabra to dance, making it impossible to think of anything except having a good time.

"Balance all," Uncle Ernie, the caller, directed. "Now bow to your partner and swing once around."

The dancers complied, stamping their feet and gliding over the cornmeal-slicked floor in rhythm to accordions and fiddles.

"Alamande left, swing the ladies to the center of the set," the bandy-legged Englishman continued.

Sabra was swung to the middle, grinning as she took her place with the other women who made up their set. No one in Cortéz would willingly miss one of the dances, especially the Independence Day Ball.

Since waltzing was forbidden in the colonies, polkas, schottisches, and reels interspersed the square dances. Sabra danced them all, partnered by brothers and half brothers, plus a bevy of teenage boys who felt at ease with the high-spirited girl who often joined them in a game of ball.

Everyone but Matt, Sabra thought, unprepared for the hurt when she saw him hurry to claim Rosella for another dance. She wasn't the only one upset by Matt's behavior. Rosella's father frowned each time Matt led his daughter to the floor, his heavy jowls shaking with disapproval while his eyes followed the couple through the steps of a quadrille. Brother Clawson's annoyance increased when Matt ignored his scowling presence beside Rosella at the beginning of the next dance.

When Matt reached to take Rosella's hand, Brother Clawson put an arm on his daughter's shoulder. "You've danced enough with Rosella for one evening."

"Papa . . ."

"No, Rosella. You've displayed yourself enough with this Mex . . . this young man." Brother Clawson glared at Matt and escorted Rosella to a male cousin.

Shock and astonishment stilled those close enough to hear the conversation.

"Serves him right," Del whispered, taking Sabra's arm.

Sabra pulled her arm away. "How can you say such a thing? Brother Clawson was rude!" As she spoke she noted streaks of humiliation stain Matt's olive cheeks. She watched him hesitate, then hurry out the door. Sabra started after him. "Matt . . ."

Del jerked her back. "Where do you think you're going?"

"To help Matt."

"He doesn't need your help. For Pete's sake, Sabra, stay out of it."

"He's been insulted."

Before she could say more, Papa was there, his arm going around her shoulder. "Easy, Sis. No one's been insulted. And even if he had been, there's no need to start a revolution."

"But Matt . . ."

"Matt will be fine," Papa assured in the tone he used to soothe her out of a temper. "Besides, I haven't had a chance to dance with my daughter."

"Sabra, please," Del hissed. "Everyone's watching you."

"I don't care." She knew Sister Murdock and some of the women were looking at her. "Why aren't they staring at Brother Clawson? He's the one who was rude."

The scrape of fiddles drowned out Samuel's reply. A moment later she and her father followed Uncle Ernie's calls through the steps of a reel. Sabra held her head high, aware of the stares and busy tongues. She knew what they were saying. *Sam Lindsey's too lenient with that girl. Look at her. It's time he took her in hand.*

The threat of Salt Lake City circled through the cry of the fiddles and clutched at Sabra's heart. What if her behavior made her father change his mind? She wanted to cry—for herself, for Matt, for her parents who suffered the embarrassment of a daughter who didn't conform. Too proud to cry, she bit her lower lip, wishing she could run outside and vent her hurt into the desert night. Instead, she followed the other dancers through the reel, clapping and pretending enthusiasm she didn't feel.

Pride got her through the leave-taking and the walk home, but as soon as she stepped inside the house, Sabra started up the stairs.

"Sabra!" Samuel's voice caught her in midstride.

"Yes, Papa."

"Your mother and I would like a word with you."

She sighed, knowing from Papa's tone that this was not the time to argue. Willie and Rob were sent to bed, leaving Sabra, her parents, and Del in the kitchen.

"Would you two like to tell me what set off the fracas at the dance?"

"Brother Clawson didn't want Rosella to dance with Matt 'cause he's a Mexican." Sabra's eyes flashed as she recalled the indignity.

"What has that to do with you?"

"He was rude. He had no right to say that to Matt."

Samuel frowned. "I still don't see what this has to do with you."

"Sabra's gone soft on Matt," Del said. "She thinks 'cause he asked her to be his partner for the race, he's in love with her."

"I don't either!" Sabra shouted. "You're just jealous 'cause Rosella likes Matt more than she does you."

"Liar!"

They faced each other across the table.

"Children!"

Samuel's stern voice reminded Sabra about Salt Lake City. "I'm sorry, Papa." She clutched the side of the table so she wouldn't fly at Del. "Brother Clawson was still rude."

"That may be, but it doesn't give you the right to criticize your elders." Samuel's tone softened. "He was only trying to protect his daughter."

"From what? Matt goes to church. Isn't he as good as anyone else?" Before her father could reply, she hurried on. "I'll bet if Del had danced with Rosella all evening, Brother Clawson wouldn't have said a word." Sabra's green eyes filled with scorn when Samuel failed to answer. "It's true, isn't it? Brother Clawson acted that way just 'cause Matt's a Mexican."

Samuel sighed and looked away. "It's not that simple. There are reasons you're not old enough to understand."

"Stupid reasons," she retorted, forgetting Salt Lake City and the need to be circumspect. "I'm glad the Clawsons are leaving. If they stayed here, they might infect the whole ward with their prejudice." She paused and lifted her voice in a trilling imitation of Rosella. "I can't associate with you, Sabra. You have freckles, and God doesn't allow anyone with freckles into the celestial kingdom."

"Sabra!"

Silence settled over the kitchen as Samuel leaned across the table and glared at his daughter. "Maybe you should be sent to your uncle's."

Sabra's chin trembled and her eyes filled with tears. "Being sent away won't keep me from speaking my mind, Papa. Nothing can do that. I'm sorry I upset you and Mama. Del too. Tonight wasn't much fun for him, either. It's just that Brother Clawson was cruel, and I didn't like seeing Matt hurt."

Unable to bear the steadiness of Sabra's gaze, Samuel lowered his eyes to the oilcloth-covered table. Would he ever understand this daughter and her mercurial personality—raging and spewing a burning tirade of accusations one moment, then so honestly contrite it was difficult to know whether to react with anger or forgiveness. *Dear God, help me know what to say.* While Samuel waited for an answer, Sabra hurried on, anxious to explain her outburst and make things right with her parents. "The Clawsons aren't the only ones who are prejudiced. Fred Murdock's always saying mean things. Once he called Matt a . . ." Even Sabra's devil-may-care attitude wouldn't let her say the forbidden word. "Anyway, he says mean things," she hurried on. "It's unfair. Aren't we supposed to judge a person by his actions instead of by his looks? Like Uncle Ernie? No one makes fun of his bowlegs. In fact, everyone loves him 'cause he's so kind and cheerful. It should be the same with Matt."

"I've never said anything mean about Matt," Samuel defended.

"I know . . . and I know you and Mama would never be like Brother Clawson. But there are some . . ." Her mouth tightened. "Did you know Lucy Hamblin's father told her she couldn't marry Matt 'cause he's Mexican? Have you ever heard anything so silly? Not that Matt would ever want to marry such a nitwit, but . . ." Sabra shook her head, so caught up in what she was saying she failed to see the quick glance exchanged by her parents. "The members of the ward should let Matt know they don't approve of what Brother Clawson did. It would make Matt feel better . . . his mother too." She looked at Samuel, who was usually the first to champion a good cause. "Could you bring it up in priesthood meeting, Papa?"

Samuel rubbed his mustache in a bid for time. If he refused, there'd be another scene. If he agreed? Sam glanced at Elizabeth. What could he say to help Sabra understand how he and the ward felt about Matt? He'd discussed it with his neighbors after Joe Cameron arrived in Cortéz with his adopted son. It wasn't that they hadn't taken to the little boy. Matt's quick smile, his goodness, and his willingness to help had made him a favorite. But there was the matter of his race to be considered.

Sabra's steady gaze made Samuel uncomfortable. He looked away, wondering how to explain the complex situation. Didn't the Book of Mormon teach that the Mexicans, through their Lamanite blood, were a chosen people, remnants of the House of Israel? Samuel's youngest brother had gone on a mission to the Mexicans. But to marry one? Samuel shook his head. His home, his food, anything he and his neighbors could spare was gladly shared with their Mexican neighbors. Everything except their sons and daughters. "I'm not the bishop," Samuel hedged.

"You can talk to him. Please, Papa. It's not fair for Matt."

"I'll see what I can do." Samuel didn't quite meet his daughter's eyes.

Sabra came around the table and gave him a hug. "I love you, Papa."

Guilt diminished the pleasure Samuel usually derived from his daughter's demonstrations of love. He looked imploringly at his wife.

Elizabeth was as much at a loss as Samuel. "It's past your bedtime. Past everyone's bedtime. Tomorrow will be here and none of us will be ready."

Sabra smiled at her mother's practicality. "Good night, Mama." She laid her cheek against Elizabeth's face and added, "I'm sorry if I embarrassed you tonight. I didn't mean to."

"I know you didn't."

Sabra looked at Del. "Are you still mad at me?"

"Naw."

Sabra squeezed Del's arm, then hurried up the stairs, certain that Samuel's capable hands would halt the prejudice and make things right again for Matt.

CHAPTER 4

Matt left the house shortly before daybreak, carrying his bedroll and enough provisions to take him through the days he'd be away. His departure was quiet. He didn't want to waken Helen after the upsetting night they'd just passed.

"I'd like to stay away forever," he told the black gelding. "If it weren't for Mother, I would."

As Matt finished tying his bedroll to the saddle, Joseph came through the gate separating the yards of his first and second wives. Since coming to Cortéz, the broad-shouldered Scotsman had shaved off his beard, but he clung to his mustache, brown in hue like his thinning hair.

"Yer up early this morning, lad." Joseph's piercing, gray eyes noted the bedroll. "Where are ye off ta?"

"Anyplace, as long as it isn't Cortéz."

Joseph's face grew solemn. "I heard aboot last night. 'Twas hard for ye, I'm sure, though I doot Brother Clawson meant it the way it came out. Most likely . . ."

"He meant it. He's afraid my brown skin might contaminate his daughter."

"Och, now, lad. Brother Clawson's a good man, and I'll nae ha ye speakin' ill of him."

"But it's all right for him to speak ill of me . . . is that what you're saying?"

The two men faced each other, dark eyes boring into gray eyes.

"Nae, lad, that's nae what I'm sayin'. Brother Clawson was outta place. Since he's leavin' tomorrow, I see nae need to make a scene."

He looked away from Matt's accusing eyes. "I ken ye've been hurt, Matty. I don't blame ye for bein' angry. But 'tis something ye'll have to get used to." He hunched his shoulders, hating what he felt duty-bound to say. "Ye see, 'tisn't just Brother Clawson. There're others who feel the same."

"Why?" Matt's voice vibrated with anger. "Why don't they think I'm good enough to marry their precious daughters?"

"'Tisn't that. There's nae better lad in the colonies." Joseph rubbed his chin with a calloused hand, wishing he could shield Matt from more hurt. "Yer mother and I didn't want it to come to this, Matty. We hoped . . . thought they'd eventually accept ye, but . . . " He shook his head, the gray eyes shimmering with tears. "I'm sorry, son."

His father's unexpected display of emotion took Matt by surprise. He ducked his head and pretended to adjust a strap on the saddle, not knowing whether to laugh or cry. *He loves me. Father really loves me.*

"It's not your fault," Matt mumbled. But it was. At least in part. Hadn't Joseph's treatment of him and his mother set the example for the rest of the town? Look who had nice brick homes and kitchens with piped-in running water? Not Helen, that's for sure. But Aunt Lou and Aunt Kate, the mothers of Joseph's natural children, had both. It wasn't fair, and it wasn't fair that Joseph's children had only to breathe to win his praise while Matt had to excel to gain his notice. Look how hard he'd worked all summer. Small wonder the towns-people thought he wasn't good enough. Hadn't his father's daily actions borne this out?

Love and respect warred with resentment. Matt gripped the saddle to keep the accusing words from boiling out. He mounted the gelding, anxious to put as much distance as possible between himself and the Scotsman.

Joseph placed a hand on Matt's thigh. "Don't do anything rash, Matty. Remember, yer mother loves ye and so do I."

Not trusting himself to speak, Matt nodded and urged his horse down the lane, keeping it at a brisk pace until he reached the Independence Day carriage. Still swathed with bunting and wilted flowers, its dejected appearance mirrored Matt's feelings. He averted his gaze to stem the hurt, while memories rushed past with fragmented pictures of the smiling crowd and his soaring elation as he'd ridden on the float with Rosella, certain that at last he'd won the town's acceptance.

Matt made a derisive sound in his throat. Rosella's father had taught him a bitter lesson about acceptance, one he wouldn't soon forget. "To heck with the pompous, old man!" Matt jerked the reins and pressed his heels into the gelding's sides. "To heck with anyone who doesn't think I'm good enough for their daughter!"

He took satisfaction in the harsh words, but throwing away eighteen years of responsible upbringing wasn't as easy. When Matt neared the Cameron farm, he saw one of the Durhams grazing on the ditch bank. "Dumb cow," he grumbled, slowing the gelding. "Don't you know enough to stay where you belong?"

The cow lifted limpid eyes and continued to chew her cud while Matt dismounted and opened the gate.

"I don't know why I'm even bothering with you," he went on. "I should leave you to bloat or be stolen by Mexicans." Matt gave a bitter laugh. "Mexican. That's what I am. Do you hear that, Matt Cameron? You're a Mexican. A lousy, thievin' Mexican!" He hurled a rock at the cow, making her flinch and jump the ditch. "Take that!" he hollered, picking up another rock. "And that . . . and that!" Sickness clawed his insides when he heard the stones strike the cow. Fighting tears, he rushed at the animal and drove her back into the pasture.

Matt sagged against the gate after he closed it. "I'm sorry," he told the animal, giving in to tears. It had always been like this—not quite fitting in. Matt's tanned skin and Spanish features set him apart from the Mormons as much as his education and upbringing set him apart from the Mexicans. Where did he belong?

The answers Helen had poured into little-boy ears were no longer enough. *"You belong to me and your father."* She'd held him close as she rocked him in her cane-back chair. *"When I couldn't have children, God heard my prayers and sent me you. Not in the usual way, it's true, but you're mine, Matty. You belong here with me . . . with your family."*

Now her words seemed empty, like husks of corn left to dry and shrivel below the cob. His hopes, like the protective covering around the corn, had been stripped away, leaving him defenseless and ashamed. In his mind he saw a gaunt-faced peón, the permanently stooped shoulders and shuffling feet of a villager; it filled Matt's heart with quiet despair. *Is this who I am?* Part of him railed against the cruel image while the rest of him accepted it. The poor peóns and Don de Vega were as much a part of his heritage as Helen and the Mormons. Somehow he must try to weave the varied threads together, meshing them into a pattern of symmetry and value.

Matt straightened and wiped his face with his sleeve. As he did, he saw Sabra Lindsey watching him from the back of her mare. His first impulse was to jump on his horse and gallop away, but something told him she would only follow. He frowned and glared at her. "What are you doing here?"

"I just came out for a ride."

"And found me blubbering like a baby. Bet you can't wait to get back so you can spread it all over town."

Sabra shook her head, afraid that if she said the wrong thing, Matt would bolt and run. "I won't say a word to anyone. I promise."

As they regarded each other from opposite sides of the dusty lane, Matt's defenses crumbled. Sensing it, Sabra slid from the mare. "Where are you going?"

"Away."

"Not forever, I hope."

A little smile flicked across Matt's lips. "Just for a few days. I need to sort some things out."

Sabra led her mare across the lane. "I don't blame you . . . and I don't blame you for being upset. Brother Clawson was awful."

"He was also right. I am a Mexican . . . something I've been dodging most of my life." Matt held out a calloused, brown hand. "When I was little I even tried to wash the brown away. I took a scrub brush and a bar of Mother's lye soap and scrubbed until my hands were raw. Then I cried."

"What did your mother do?"

"She coated my hands with lard and flour and assured me she and God loved brown-skinned little boys just as much as white ones. I was content for a while, but it never stopped me from wishing."

Sabra rubbed her freckled hand. "Just like I keep hoping my freckles will go away." She giggled. "Did you know I used a scrub brush on them, too? It was Papa who found me. He told me my freckles were pixie dust, a favor the fairies sprinkle on those they wish to honor." Sabra jammed her hands into the pockets of her riding skirt. "Unfortunately, the fairies got carried away." She smiled. "Mama says it's partly my fault . . . that if I'd remember to wear my hat and gloves, the freckles would go away." She grimaced and lifted her face to the sun. "I'd rather be free."

Sabra closed her eyes, her face raised to the sky while the rays of the sun bathed her in a wash of golden light that highlighted her milky skin, the deep red of her lips, and the curve of dark lashes lying across her cheekbones.

Until that moment, Matt had never thought of Sabra as anything other than a gangly girl whose spunk had gained his admiration. Now, as he took in the slender form, he felt a sudden desire to kiss her delicate cheeks. He ran a finger over the dusting of freckles on Sabra's nose. "Don't ever be ashamed of your freckles, Nutmeg."

Sabra's green eyes flew open, a trail of confused emotions playing across her features as she raised her hand toward Matt's face. Losing courage, she rested it on his hand, her fingers curling protectively around Matt's palm. "Don't you ever be ashamed of your brown skin."

They gazed at each other, shy and self-conscious, each intensely aware of the other. Sabra was the first to look away. She stuffed her hand into her pocket again. "Are you going back to the mountains?"

"Probably." Matt looked at the mighty peaks of the Sierra Madre sprawling to the west, their rocky ridges etched against the horizon in shades of purple and mauve and blue. *Home,* they whispered. But Cortéz was home, too. Matt sighed, no longer knowing where his home was. "Maybe I'll try to find my father."

"Father? But . . ." Sabra paused. "You mean your real father?"

Matt nodded, wondering how such an untidy scrap of a girl had managed to unlock the sharing of confidences. For a moment he was tempted to tell her about Rafael and Don de Vega, but the knowledge of who his parents were was still too new, something with which he hadn't yet come to terms. Until he did, he would keep the story to himself. "It's only a rumor."

"Does your mother . . . does Sister Cameron know?"

Matt shook his head. "It would hurt her. I couldn't do that. I left a note saying I was going away for a few days." He paused, his eyes holding hers in a steady gaze. "Will you do me a favor?"

"Yes."

"Will you tell Mother you saw me this morning and that I'm all right?"

Sabra nodded. "I'll tell her you're fine. Nothing more."

"Thanks, Nutmeg." Matt's boyish grin was back.

"It's the least I can do to repay you for helping me with Carlos," she answered.

Matt's grin widened. "I did get you out of a tight spot."

"Well . . . maybe."

Laughter came easily, like water slipping over smooth stones, washing away the last of the constraint between them.

Matt tugged on one of Sabra's braids. "So long, Nutmeg." He put a booted foot into the stirrup and swung himself into the saddle. "Try to stay out of trouble while I'm gone."

"I will."

Sabra's smile overflowed with caring. It pierced Matt's loneliness like sun bursting through dark clouds after a summer thunderstorm. Perhaps the situation wasn't hopeless. Surely there were others like Sabra, others who cared.

Matt clung to this thought as he urged the gelding away from the ditch bank. When he turned to wave, Sabra's slender image imprinted itself onto his senses and followed him into the mountains like the echo of a beautiful song.

CHAPTER 5

Three days later Matt halted his horse on a ledge overlooking El Rancho Valle Grande. Surrounded by jutting ridges of lava and pine, the valley stretched for miles, its north perimeter melding with misty blue haze in the distance. Matt's pulse quickened as he looked down on the red-tiled hacienda and sprawling outbuildings of the ranch. Was it here he and Rafael had been conceived? His thoughts turned nostalgic as he pictured his Mexican mother hurrying to meet him, happiness lighting her eyes when she called a welcome.

Matt pushed the picture away and started the black gelding down the steep trail. His welcome might be less than friendly. A lot depended on Don de Vega and Rafael. Matt was filled with misgiving. Why hadn't Rafael returned with the ring?

Common sense told him Rafael had probably been too busy enjoying his new status to think of the promise. But pockets of worry wouldn't let the matter rest. Rafael had given Matt his word. What had happened?

The need to know had pulled Matt to the big valley, excitement building as the miles fell away. Perhaps now he would find his roots. If he got to know his real father, maybe he could come to terms with who he was.

Holding to this thought, Matt started down the steep path marked by lichen-spangled rocks with tiny flowers pushing between the cracks. Tall pines and heavy undergrowth crowded his path, and he was forced to detour around a boulder. The narrow, rock-strewn trail wasn't the main entrance to Valle Grande, but it would get him there. He could already see patches of meadow through the thinning trees.

When Matt reached the floor of the valley, the hacienda lay before him, its whitewashed walls gleaming in the afternoon sun. He heard a dog bark in the distance and saw smoke curl from one of the chimneys.

"Valle Grande." Matt spoke the name aloud, hoping the sound of his voice would loosen the knot in the pit of his stomach. What if his father refused to see him? Not wanting to think of the possibility, Matt spurred his horse across the meadow. Cattle bearing brands similar to the crest on the de Vega ring were grazing on autumn-tinged grass. They were short-horned Herefords instead of the inferior Chihuahua cattle seen on most Mexican ranches. Don de Vega obviously knew his business. But would he welcome another son?

As if someone had heard the question, a vaquero rode out of the hacienda gate, his approach more cautious than friendly.

Matt reined in the gelding and raised his hand toward the cowboy. *"Hola!"*

The vaquero halted and gave a smothered exclamation. Firing a shot into the air, he galloped his horse back through the gate

Instinct told him to turn and flee, but his desire to see Don de Vega and Rafael overrode them. Since the valley was isolated, perhaps unexpected visitors were always welcomed in this manner. Matt didn't have to wait long to find out. In a matter of minutes, armed men rode through the gate and spurred their horses into a circle around him.

Heart pounding, Matt repeated his greeting. "Hola."

Instead of responding, the men rode closer and brandished their guns.

"I've come to see Don de Vega. If you would take me to him . . ."

A vaquero gave a derisive snort. "Insolent dog. You were told to leave."

Before Matt could respond, a rope coiled around his arms and jerked him from the saddle, pain and jagged light exploding inside his head when he hit the ground. Stunned, Matt lay still for a moment. What was happening? "Please, I must see Don de Vega." It took him a few seconds to realize he'd spoken in English. He repeated the request in Spanish.

"Don de Vega will see you, all right," the vaquero spat. "But not before you tell us what you've done with the cattle."

"Cattle?" Matt closed his eyes and tried to think. "I don't know anything about any cattle."

The vaquero urged his horse closer. "Don't try to play dumb. We know you took them."

Matt slowly got to his feet. What had Rafael done? "You don't understand. I'm not Rafael. I'm his brother . . . his twin brother."

"Liar!" A flick of the vaquero's wrist uncoiled the rope and freed Matt's arms. "*La patróna* said you were a liar. Another whipping is what you need. When I get through with you this time . . ." An ugly smile split the vaquero's broad features and he raised his arm.

A sharp command halted the vaquero. "What's going on?" The man who'd spoken stopped when Matt turned to face him. "Madre mía!"

Matt had often imagined meeting his father, but nothing had prepared him for the electric shock that shot up his spine, jarring his heart then vibrating down to his fingertips. He closed his eyes, then quickly opened them, feeling a confused emptiness as he watched a stranger walk toward him. The man was dressed in black, unrelieved except for a white ruffled shirt and dark string tie. His black attire made the steel-gray hair with its streak of white all the more dramatic.

"Padre." The stranger's cold dark eyes shattered the word before it reached Matt's lips. There was nothing of welcome. Only anger and smoldering hatred.

"What are you doing here?" Don de Vega demanded.

"I came to see Rafael. Didn't he tell you about me . . . that we are twins?"

"No." The coldness in Don de Vega's voice matched that of his eyes. "You did not tell me about a twin brother because you do not have a twin brother. I've had enough tricks and lies. If you think you can ingratiate yourself with me again, you are mistaken." The full lips tightened. "Tie him up, Benito."

"You don't want me to use the whip?"

"We will leave that for the *jefe*, though he should be whipped too for failing to find him." A harsh smile touched Don de Vega's mouth. "It wasn't very clever to return to the valley. Now you will see how the de Vegas treat those who cross them. Lock him in the guard room, Benito."

The numbing shock that had held Matt speechless suddenly fled. "I'm not Rafael. Look . . ." Matt's fingers worked at the buttons on his flannel shirt. He shrugged it off to expose his back. "I don't have any scars. Rafael has scars on his back."

"It is true," Benito whispered. "I put some there myself. Years ago . . . then again last month." The vaquero's gaze flicked from Matt to Don de Vega. "There are no scars on this man's back, *El Patrón*. Only the big one on his shoulder."

"I'm not blind," Don de Vega spat. He studied Matt in silence. "Come with me."

Matt picked up his hat and reached for the gelding's reins.

"One of my vaqueros will see to your horse," Don de Vega said.

Matt reluctantly handed the reins to Benito and followed Don de Vega, his legs still quivering from the fall. As he walked, he noted the arrogant tilt to the Spaniard's head and the tailored black suit. Matt felt nothing except an overwhelming desire to sit down and collect his scrambled thoughts.

Don de Vega had reached the graveled carriage approach that was outlined by whitewashed rocks. Although the wrought-iron gate stood open, a barefoot boy hurried to pull it wider, his brown face a study in curiosity. Neither Don de Vega nor Matt paid any heed to the boy. Matt's attention was focused on the iron crest outlined in fretwork above the gate. It was an enlargement of the design on Matt's ring, one so distinctive he wondered that no one had guessed his true parentage.

Bright geraniums spilling from clay tubs greeted Matt, their cheery color repeated in flaming bougainvillea that climbed the hacienda wall and trailed to form a canopy over a fountain. Matt recalled the hours Helen spent coaxing marigolds and phlox to grow in the desert's arid soil. Here, lush growth was everywhere, though the sight of a servant carrying water to the geraniums made him suspect that beauty did not come without effort, even in the big valley.

When they reached the hacienda, Don de Vega nodded briefly to a servant as she opened the heavy oak door. Matt glimpsed grill-covered windows and saw a stone lion guarding the entrance. Darkness closed around him when the door shut. As his eyes adjusted to the dimness, Matt became aware of color—bright *serapes* patterned in vivid shades of red and yellow, and fresh-cut flowers spilling from a pottery urn.

"This way." Don de Vega opened another door, his black-clad body silhouetted against the light pouring through a grilled window.

It was a room that smelled of leather and freshly polished wood. Matt paused in the doorway, noting the sunlight dancing across the massive desk before it lost itself in richly bound books lining the walls. When Don de Vega turned to face him, he forgot everything else.

They were of a similar build, broad shouldered with narrow waists and hips. Although twenty years separated the two men in age, Ricardo de Vega was still in his prime—a man to be reckoned with. Matt felt the full impact of this as they measured each other, his confidence and the carefully hoarded dreams about his father dissolving under the arrogant gaze.

"Rafael never told me he had a twin." Don de Vega continued the inspection, his brown eyes on a level with Matt's.

Angry that Rafael had conveniently forgotten to mention him, Matt suffered Don de Vega's close scrutiny with growing irritation. "Where's Rafael? I need to talk to him."

"First, you will tell me why you came here. If you think you can soften me up because of your madre . . ."

"Madre!" Anger boiled up in Matt's throat. "Thanks to you I have no mother. If it hadn't been for the Mormons, I wouldn't be alive, either."

Matt glared at Don de Vega, wondering how he could feel so much animosity toward a man he'd just met. Then the years of Helen's careful training surfaced. *He's my father,* Matt reminded himself. *In spite of what's happened, he's my father and I owe him respect.* Matt lowered his eyes and took a deep breath. "Look . . . I didn't come to fight. I came to . . ." He shook his head. "I'm not sure why I came. Rafael was part of it, but I wanted to meet you, too." Matt glanced at Don de Vega, noting the lines at the corners of his mouth, lines that suggested years of bitterness and frustration.

Don de Vega seemed more intrigued than angered by Matt's outburst. "You were with the Mormones? I have had dealings with those gringos. How did you come to live with them?"

"Tío Pedro took me there and asked them to keep me until my mother was better. He never came back."

"Ah." The Spaniard nodded. "That explains your accent and clothes, but not Rafael." The dark eyes probed. "How did you find out about him?"

"Last spring I took my father's . . . Joseph Cameron's cattle up to the mountains. While I was there . . ." Matt then related what had happened. Don de Vega's dark brows raised when Matt told him about the cougar, scowled when Matt related how Rafael had taken his horse and ring.

"So. He stole from you too?"

"Not really. He came back and asked me to go with him. He said we should go together. That it was what our madre would wish."

Don de Vega gave a derisive chuckle. "Rafael is talented at using sympathy. Let me guess. Did you not then give him the horse . . . perhaps even the ring?"

Feeling foolish, Matt nodded. "I only loaned him the ring. He promised to bring it back after he'd proven who he was."

"You were naïve to expect such a thing. Though, since Rafael no longer has the ring, he couldn't return it to you." The Spaniard opened the desk drawer and withdrew a small brown box. "I keep the ring in readiness for my son's—Felipe's—saint's day. It belongs to the de Vegas, not you."

Something stronger than Matt impelled him across the room to confront his father. "That ring is mine. Madre gave it to me. I want it back."

Startled silence filled the room. Don de Vega's eyes narrowed. "No one speaks to me that way. Especially not a mongrel raised by gringos."

Matt could feel his heart pounding. "I may be a mongrel, but the ring's mine." His voice cracked with emotion. "It's all I have of my mother."

Don de Vega leaned across the desk, the harsh lines of his face relaxing. "So, you care about her?"

Matt nodded and held his father's gaze. "I may not remember her, but she gave me life. She is my mother."

The arrogance drained from Don de Vega's face. He sank into a leather chair and picked up the ring. "Teresa . . ." His voice was a sigh, a quiet mourning for someone loved and lost. "I had to go away. When I came back, she was gone. For weeks I searched for her, but to no avail." After a moment, his features tightened, the head came up. "What are you willing to pay me for the ring?"

"Pay?" Matt stared at his father.

"But of course. This is a valuable piece of jewelry. It's been in the de Vega family for almost two hundred years. What is it worth to you?"

"Everything," Matt said. "Unfortunately, all I have is my horse and rifle."

Don de Vega gave a harsh laugh. "And you expect me to take that in exchange for the ring?"

"No, but . . ." The anger and bitterness returned. "The ring is mine!"

Don de Vega spread his hands in a gesture that hinted of compromise. "Why don't you sit down? After your long journey, you must be tired."

Matt accepted the invitation with guarded relief. His head ached miserably and his legs still felt shaky. "Where's Rafael? Why isn't he here?"

"Rafael." Don de Vega spat the name in disgust. "You would be wise to forget your hermano. He's a thief . . . a murderer!"

"Murderer?" Matt rose to his feet. "Rafael may be a thief, but he wouldn't kill anyone."

"Perhaps not with his own hands," Don de Vega agreed. "But if he could find another way—"

The muscles in Matt's chest constricted. "Who . . . and why?"

"My son Felipe, of course. A weak heart prevents him from riding. Rafael knew this, yet he challenged the boy." Don de Vega's voice turned to steel. "I didn't believe my wife when she told me, but when I found Felipe with one of the stallions . . ." Hatred smoldered in the Spaniard's eyes. "I almost took the whip to Rafael myself. After Benito finished with him, I ordered him off the ranch."

Matt looked away. Why hadn't Rafael left the boy alone?

"That wasn't the end of it," Don de Vega continued. "A week after Rafael left, ten of my cattle were stolen. The next week, ten more. It's been going on for a month." Don de Vega rubbed his jaw. "It's Rafael, of course. We've hunted for him and so has the sheriff. When I saw you . . ." The hacendado's eyes narrowed with suspicion. "Do you know anything about this? Did Rafael send you to gloat?"

Matt's brain reeled like a mill wheel. "I haven't seen Rafael since summer. Besides, how do you know it's him?"

"Who else would have the audacity to do it? Rafael knows where the cattle graze, the times they're left unguarded. He won't get away. I think Rafael is using an old Indian trail through the mountains. The jefe has men watching it. He will be caught before he can get the cattle across the border."

"No!" The word slipped out before Matt could stop it. The sheriff's men could be brutal.

"Do you sympathize with a thief?"

Matt lifted his shoulders. "I understand how he must feel. There were times when he almost starved. After living here, Rafael probably figures the cattle are his . . . part of his birthright."

"He has no birthright!" Don de Vega's voice shook with anger. "And neither do you."

The words stung like a slap to the face and sent Matt to the door, both fists clenched, his jaw clamped down tight. He'd been a fool to come, and an even bigger fool to think his father would help him. "You're right. The sooner I leave here, the better it will be."

"Wait!" Don de Vega's voice caught Matt in midstride. "There's a reward for Rafael's capture. If you aren't careful, you'll be mistaken for him."

"I can manage." For a moment Matt was of a mind to join Rafael and help him take more cattle. It was what the arrogant Spaniard deserved.

"Perhaps you can. But just in case . . ." Don de Vega's jaw tightened. "It will be better if you wait until morning to leave. I'll send Benito with you. He'll see you safely back to the Mormones."

"I don't need Benito to protect me."

Something glinted in Don de Vega's eyes. "I'm sure you don't." He pulled a tasseled bell rope. "But since you're a guest at Valle Grande, you will do as I say."

* * *

A servant helped Matt collect his bedroll and put it in the bunkhouse. "It is El Patrón's wish," the boy told him. "It is where

Rafael stayed. The jefe also." He paused to gaze at Matt, shaking his head in wonder. "Who would have thought there were two? It's a miracle. When la patróna hears, she won't be pleased."

"I'm just staying for the night. I doubt Don Vega's wife will ever see me."

"Sí. That is what El Patrón said. But still . . ." He shook his head and edged away. "You can eat in the kitchen with the vaqueros. It's over there." The servant pointed to a whitewashed building adjoining the bunkhouse.

Matt dropped his bedroll onto one of the cots and glanced around. The room was filled with narrow, unmade beds and rumpled clothes hanging over bed rails. Matt's throbbing head clamored for a place to lie down, but he knew he wouldn't rest. The best horses in Mexico were owned by the hacendados, and Matt wanted to see Don de Vega's. Matt had seen one in Casas Grandes, an Arabian with arched neck and prancing hooves. Next to it, his gelding looked like a plow horse. If he didn't have time to see anything else, he meant to see Don de Vega's horses.

Matt paused on the wooden steps of the bunkhouse to get his bearings. There were no arched gates or potted flowers here, only a rail fence, wooden troughs for the horses, and a few chickens scratching in the dirt. The stable was whitewashed like the hacienda, with a grassy pasture flanking the back. When Matt stepped inside, he became aware of the horses, their soft blowing and occasional shifting of hooves. Then he heard a small voice.

"I'm going to take you for a walk. Perhaps later I will ride you. Then Padre will know I'm strong enough to help."

A young boy led one of the horses from its stall. He wore a white shirt and black breeches and looked to be about eight. Unaware of Matt's presence, he started toward the pasture, his face beaming as he looked up at the prancing stallion.

Matt knew who it was. He also knew the boy was too small to control the spirited stallion. "Wait, Felipe!"

Shock registered on the boy's frail features when he saw Matt. "Rafael . . ." Before Felipe could say more, the horse reared and jerked him into the air.

Matt flung himself at the stallion, grabbing Felipe, then twisting sideways to avoid the horse's hooves. Matt's right knee bore the brunt of impact when they hit the ground. Ignoring the pain, he rolled to one side, his body curled protectively around Felipe. He didn't move until he heard the horse gallop away.

The small boy struggled, his frail arms flaying. "You've let Fuego get loose. If Padre finds out . . ."

"I hope he does find out. That stallion almost trampled you." Matt glared down into Felipe's thin face. "You should be spanked."

"You should be hanged. When I get Padre . . ." Felipe struggled for breath.

Seeing the blue-tinged lips, Matt loosened his hold. "Are you all right?"

"Sí." The fire in Felipe's eyes sat at odds with his pallid skin and the uneven heartbeat fluttering against Matt's chest. He pushed at Matt and slowly got to his feet. "You stole . . . our cattle," he accused between breaths. "If I had a gun . . . I would shoot you."

"I didn't steal your cattle."

"You lie—and you tried to kill me." Felipe frowned, the harsh sound of his breathing filling the stable. "Who are you?" he demanded, after a pause. "You look like Rafael . . . but now you tried to help me."

"I'm Matt Cameron. Rafael and I are twins."

"Caray!" The boy's eyes widened, then quickly narrowed. "How do I know you're not trying to trick me?"

"Why would I want to do that?" Not waiting for an answer, Matt got to his feet. Lancets of pain shot up his leg.

"You're hurt." Felipe looked uncertain. "But if it's a trick . . ." This came in a small voice as if speaking to himself. His large, hazel eyes searched Matt's. Seeming to come to a decision, he started for the door. "Wait while I get help."

Matt gritted his teeth and leaned against a stall. First his head, now his leg. Misfortune had dogged him from the moment he set foot on Valle Grande. Before he had time to dwell on his run of bad luck, a vaquero hurried into the stable. Felipe trailed at the man's heels, his breathing labored.

"Go to your room," the vaquero growled. "Maria will be upset when she sees you are sick again."

Felipe placed his hands on his hips. "I will wait until you have helped the señor, then I will go to my room."

The vaquero shrugged and shifted his attention to Matt.

"I'll be all right," Matt said. "Give me a minute."

Just then the vaquero noticed the empty stall. "Where is Fuego? What have you done with Don de Vega's stallion?"

Felipe's olive face grew paler. "I . . ."

"I tried to ride him," Matt cut in. "That's how I hurt my leg."

The vaquero's anger could scarcely be contained. "No one rides El Patrón's stallion. When he hears what you've done, he'll—" The vaquero rushed from the stable before finishing his threat. "Where's Feugo? Where did he go?"

"The pasture," Felipe rasped. He darted a quick glance at Matt. "Why did you say you rode him? Now you're in big trouble."

"I already was."

"Then you *are* Rafael?"

Matt shook his head. "I told you Rafael and I are twins."

"That's what you say." Felipe hesitated, his expression perplexed. "Wait while I get Padre Madrid. He'll know what to do . . . he's good at fixing broken bones."

"It's not broken." Matt attempted to walk. The first step was agony. So was the second. He continued walking, hanging onto the stalls, then a snubbing post, finally the door to the stable.

He saw Felipe crossing the dusty yard, calling in a wheezy voice for Maria. A middle-aged woman hurried from the hacienda. "Where have you been? If you've gone to the stable again . . ."

"Please . . . you must help the señor," Felipe cried. "Send for Padre Madrid."

"The señor?" The woman shaded her eyes against the lowering sun. "Ave Maria! Get the jefe!" She grabbed Felipe and pulled him toward the hacienda, ignoring his raspy protests as she hurried him along.

The retreating figures swam before Matt's eyes while a wave of nausea swirled in his stomach. Feeling faint, he slowly lowered himself to the ground. The nausea increased and he broke out in a cold sweat. Unable to stop himself, Matt retched until there was nothing but bile left in his stomach. He groaned and slumped against the wall. He wished he were in his bed with its quilted coverlet. He could almost smell the sun-freshened sheets, feel his mother's cool hand on his forehead. Why had he ever left Cortéz?

CHAPTER 6

Hushed voices pushed past the gray edge of unconsciousness and nudged Matt toward the surface. He tried to block them out, but the voices persisted, their resonance probing the swirling mist until the sound meshed into Spanish phrases.

"He's been sleeping for hours. How is his leg?"

"The leg is fine, though it will probably keep him in bed for a day or two. As for sleeping . . ." The speaker paused. "The draught I gave him contained laudanum. It should wear off soon."

"You are sure?"

"Sí." Wood creaked as the speaker changed position. "Let your mind be at peace, El Patrón."

"Peace? How can you speak of peace when Felipe gets no better? All the prayers and trips to new doctors have done no good. If he dies . . ." The voice wavered and a hand touched Matt's arm. "Here's the son I've always dreamed of, someone to ride and rope cattle, a child conceived in love rather than duty. Yet I must send him away."

Away. The word seemed to echo as it tumbled through Matt's clouded mind. Someone was sending him away.

"It's the only solution," the resonant voice agreed. "Remember Rafael and all the problems."

"I know." There was a lengthy silence, followed by the sound of footsteps. "Let me know when he wakens."

The click of the door latch stopped Matt as he floated back into the grayness. He sighed and moved his head.

"Are you awake, my son?"

Matt's eyelids flickered open. Dredges of unconsciousness clouded his vision. His eyes slowly focused to carry unfamiliar images to his

brain—the rich grain of a four-post bed, an eagle carved on the door
of the armoire, a heavy crucifix hanging next to the mirror. The sight
of the crucified Christ jarred Matt into full wakefulness. Where was
he? What had happened?

"You are going to be fine."

The resonant voice pulsed like an echo to Matt's pounding heart.
His eyes searched the room. A priest sat beside the bed, his black
cassock melding into the dark leather of a chair.

"Where . . . ?" Memory of the painful meeting with his father
pushed past the panic. He was at Valle Grande. "My leg?"

"Your leg is fine," the priest reassured him. "Fortunately your
knee was only dislocated. In another day or two you should be able to
walk."

Matt closed his eyes and tried to gather his erratic thoughts. He
remembered now—the quick twist as the priest had slipped his knee
back into position. There'd been voices too. One had sounded like his
father's. Then he'd been carried to a room, given a draught, and left to
sleep.

The priest rose and peered down at Matt, the planes of his
bronzed features softening with concern. "You are confused. So much
has happened and most of it not pleasant. First Benito, then your
padre. Even the stallion did his best to make you feel unwelcome."

Matt studied the priest, noting his kindly eyes and patrician
features. He'd never been this close to a priest before. Like the reli-
gious symbol on the wall, the padre's flowing cassock and gold
crucifix made Matt uncomfortable. He'd heard stories about Catholic
priests, how they hated Mormons and called them devils in sheeps'
clothing. Matt searched for any sign of hatred in Padre Madrid's eyes.
He found only concern, though perhaps the padre didn't know Matt
was a Mormon.

"How does your leg feel?"

Matt moved it cautiously, biting his lower lip as the pain intensified, then receded. "Better," he said after a moment. "Much better.
Gracias."

The padre nodded. "I did little. Just a quick twist; it was something I learned years ago at an infirmary in Mexico City. Now my
duties are less demanding, though there are times when my skill is

required with little Felipe." His features lightened. "Felipe told me what you did. How you saved him from the stallion. He's convinced he could have handled Fuego himself, but had the Holy Mother not been watching over him . . ." The priest crossed himself. "And you, of course. I have told Don de Vega and his wife that we are in your debt. Even so . . ."

"You don't have to explain," Matt cut in. "I know my father's anxious to have me gone."

"Perhaps." The priest sighed and looked away. "You mustn't be too hard on Don de Vega. His life is not easy."

"Neither is Rafael's."

"Nor is Isabel de Vega's," Padre Madrid countered. "Your being here adds greatly to her pain."

"If you'll hand me my clothes, I'll leave."

"You're not well enough to travel. The señora is aware of that. You are to stay until you are better."

Matt grimaced and closed his eyes. Hurting his knee was bad enough. To be the unwelcome guest of people who disliked him rankled. His scowl deepened. The whole trip had been a waste. Rafael was gone, his father wouldn't give him the ring, and now he was trapped in bed while a Catholic priest played nursemaid.

"How long until I'll be able to travel?" Matt asked.

Padre Madrid shrugged his rounded shoulders. "Two days . . . maybe three."

"That long?"

The priest nodded. "I will come each day and visit you. Perhaps Felipe will come too. That should help pass the time more quickly."

"Felipe is as anxious for me to be gone as my father is."

"Again you are mistaken. The boy is intrigued with you now that he knows you are not Rafael."

"Why is everyone so willing to think the worst of Rafael? He didn't try to kill Felipe. He couldn't. He's my brother."

"Felipe is your *hermano* too," Padre Madrid insisted. "This blood tie called to you when you went to his aid." A beam of sunlight gilded the top of the priest's balding head. "You are a true de Vega, my son. Which is more than I can say of Rafael. Even so, it is best that you leave."

* * *

Matt's waking was more natural the second time. He looked around the room, noting how sunlight filtered through the grilled window, patterning the tiled floor and glancing off an empty tumbler by the bedside.

"You are a true de Vega." Padre Madrid's parting words circled through Matt's mind. He *was* a de Vega. A *true* de Vega. But he was a Cameron, too—a Cameron who had no business being at Valle Grande.

This thought brought a rush of indignation. But for an accident of birth, Valle Grande would be his. He let his mind drift to how his life might have been—riding over dew-flecked meadows to check on cattle, dining each evening in the sprawling hacienda; he'd always wanted a ranch in the mountains.

Feather-soft thoughts brushed against the daydream. If he'd been born at Valle Grande, he'd never have known Helen's love or the blunt Scotsman who'd given him his name. More than that, he wouldn't be a Mormon. Matt frowned and eased his leg into a more comfortable position. Picturing himself at Valle Grande had been easy. The idea of being a Catholic was more difficult.

A quick knock jarred Matt away from his thoughts. Before he could call, "come in," the door opened to reveal Don de Vega and Felipe. They stood just under the lintel, the boy's face as solemn as his father's.

Don de Vega spoke first. "How are you feeling?"

"Better." Although he strove for nonchalance, Matt felt his heartbeat quicken. Why did he let his father affect him this way? Realizing more was expected of him, Matt added, "The priest did good work with my leg."

Don de Vega nodded. "Padre Madrid is skilled in areas other than religion. He has to be since we're two days' ride from the nearest doctor." The Spaniard put a hand on Felipe's shoulder. "My son has something he wishes to tell you."

Matt studied the heir to El Rancho Valle Grande, noting his thin neck, the blue-tinged lips, and sallow, waxen skin. Standing next to the big bed, the boy looked small and insignificant. He also looked uncomfortable.

"I . . . I confessed my disobedience to Padre Madrid . . . that I took Feugo from his stall." Felipe licked his lips. "Then I told him how you saved me."

Matt met Felipe's hazel eyes. "You didn't have to do that."

"It wasn't fair that you take the blame, especially when I made you hurt your knee."

"The knee was my fault. I shouldn't have been so clumsy." Matt smiled. The more he learned about the boy, the better he liked him. "Gracias."

"It is I who should thank you," Felipe stated. "That's another thing Padre Madrid told me I must do." He cast a swift glance at Don de Vega. The narrow shoulders straightened and the wheezy voice turned formal. "Thank you for saving me, señor. When you are feeling better, Father said I may invite you to dine with us."

At Matt's glance, Don de Vega nodded. "It is my son's wish. Mine also."

"And your wife's?"

Don de Vega's lips tightened. "I have told her how you saved Felipe's life. I also told her how you tried to take the blame for Felipe's disobedience. Like my son, she would be pleased if you would be our guest for dinner."

Matt doubted that. How could a woman who hated him be happy to have him at her table? He searched for an excuse, wishing Felipe had thought of some other way to show appreciation.

"May we take your silence as acceptance?"

"Yes . . . of course. If it's what you want."

"It is." Don de Vega's long fingers tightened on Felipe's shoulders. "My son is very dear to me. I . . . we are in your debt."

Matt looked away, his father's gratitude making him uncomfortable.

"Felipe also wishes to spend some time with you. Unless, of course, you're not feeling well enough for company."

"I'm fine." Matt grinned at Felipe, even as he felt a twinge of disappointment that Don de Vega hadn't voiced a similar desire.

Don de Vega's aristocratic features relaxed into the hint of a smile. "Then I'll leave the two of you to get better acquainted."

After Don de Vega left, Felipe moved closer to the bed. "I told you the padre was good at fixing things. He set Ramon's broken leg and sometimes . . ." Felipe's voice trailed off as he stared at Matt. "Caray! Even your hair is like Rafael's . . . the white spot." Wonder filled his raspy voice. "Madre is afraid you *are* Rafael . . . that you have tricked us so you can get inside the hacienda."

"Why would I want to do that?"

Felipe shrugged. "I don't know. That's just what Madre said. I think she's afraid you'll want to stay."

Matt shook his head. "I already have a home . . . a good home with my family in Cortéz. As soon as I'm better, I'll go back." *Helen wants and loves me.* The words sang through Matt's head. There were others in Cortéz who cared. Joseph Cameron. Matt's adoptive brothers and sisters. Sabra Lindsey and other members of the ward.

"Why are you smiling?" Felipe asked. "And if you already have a family, why did you come here?"

"I asked myself the same question when I hurt my knee." He gave Felipe a rueful glance. "If you'd lived with someone else all your life, called them Madre and Padre, even though they weren't your parents . . . then one day you found out who your real father was, wouldn't you want to meet him?"

Felipe considered the question. "Si, but still . . ." A frown furrowed his forehead. "I wish Madre wasn't so set against you staying. You see . . ." The thin voice turned wistful. "I have always wanted an older brother."

* * *

They talked of many things—Felipe's dream to ride the fiery stallion, a recent trip to the ocean, the telescope mounted on the roof of the hacienda so he and Padre Madrid could study the stars. The boy's fragile health was never mentioned, although his blue-tinged fingernails and frequent pauses between sentences dangled it like a shroud before them.

He's going to die. The words throbbed through Matt's mind and repeated themselves each time Felipe stopped to catch his breath. *The poor kid's going to die before he ever gets a chance to ride Fuego.*

The thought was still with Matt when he entered the de Vega dining room two evenings later. He would rather have stayed in his room. At least there he wouldn't feel self-conscious about his clothes. He wouldn't have to watch Felipe, either. His brother's plucky courage tore at Matt's heart. As for Isabel de Vega . . . Matt took a deep breath and walked toward the señora.

Like her husband, Isabel de Vega was dressed in black. Despite her regal bearing, Matt thought she was plain. Her nose and sallow coloring were not to his liking, but her hazel eyes were striking; they were large and long-lashed like Felipe's. Matt saw scorn as her gaze took in his faded dungarees and slowly moved over his person. She didn't seem to miss a single detail. With a slight incline of her dark head, Isabel de Vega extended her hand.

"My husband told me how you saved Felipe's life. Don de Vega and I are most grateful for what you did." Her plump fingers fluttered impatiently.

Heat rushed to Matt's ears. Was he expected to kiss them? He cleared his throat. His Adam's apple seemed to have grown two inches. "I'm glad I could be of help." Reverting to Mormon custom, he gave the señora's hand a hearty shake.

A stiff smile stretched the corners of Isabel de Vega's mouth as she withdrew her hand.

"I'm glad you were there too," Felipe chimed in. "But I'm sorry about your leg. Is it better?"

"Almost. By the time I get back home, I'll hardly know it happened."

Felipe frowned. "Is home far away?"

"About a three-day ride."

"Three days!" Felipe's frown deepened. "I hoped it was close enough for you to come for another visit."

"You mustn't expect such things of the señor," Isabel de Vega scolded. "Nor should you keep him standing. Have you forgotten your manners?" Seeming to regret the reprimand, the woman's face softened. "If you'll see me to my chair, we can ask Concepción to serve dinner."

An ugly stain crept over Felipe's cheeks. "I'm sorry." He quickly pulled out his mother's chair.

Isabel de Vega gave him a fond smile. "Gracias, my son."

Matt tried to quell his nervousness as he followed Don de Vega to the other end of the table. Although the señora might love her son, she made Matt feel like a gawky cowboy. Any minute he expected to trip and make a fool of himself.

The size of the room and its rich furnishings did nothing to bolster Matt's flagging confidence. The table seemed to stretch for miles, the snowy linen and gilt-edged china taking on a glow from gaslit chandeliers.

The vast array of strange dishes added to Matt's discomfort. He'd never seen so many kinds of food before, all served by hovering servants who whisked them away before he'd had a chance to do more than taste them. Isabel de Vega seemed to watch his every move, smiling each time Matt picked up the wrong fork or forgot to use his napkin. Through it all he was aware of his father's unsmiling presence. From his father's expression, the meal seemed to be an ordeal for Don de Vega too.

It seemed an eternity before Isabel de Vega pushed back her chair. "If you will excuse us, Felipe is looking tired."

"Madre . . ."

Ignoring her son's protest, the woman rose and directed her gaze at Matt. "My husband has made arrangements for one of the vaqueros to accompany you out of the valley. Since you will be leaving, perhaps you should retire early too."

Matt quickly got to his feet. "I appreciate your hospitality."

Isabel's answer was lost in a rustle of silk as she left the room.

Instead of following his mother, Felipe walked around the table and extended his hand. "It has been my pleasure, Señor Cameron." The small body clad in a brown velvet suit stood rigidly erect. Unexpectedly, two thin arms went around Matt's waist. *"Vaya con Dios,"* Felipe whispered.

Felipe's words touched Matt, but before he could recover himself the boy hurried after Isabel, the clatter of his pointed boots echoing dismally behind him. The double door closed, leaving Matt and his father alone.

A tiny silence settled over the room. "Before you retire, will you join me in the study?"

Matt searched for an excuse. He was tired. His leg ached. But the look in his father's eyes, a flicker of something bordering on softness, made him nod his head and follow the hacendado. A lamp was burning and a small fire had been laid to ward off the autumn chill.

"I spend most of my evenings here, going over accounts and reading," Don de Vega told him. "Felipe has much to learn before he can take over the management of Valle Grande." Don de Vega opened a decanter and poured amber liquid into two crystal goblets. "I noticed you didn't drink your wine at dinner. Perhaps my brandy is more to your taste."

Matt stared at the proffered glass. He'd never seen liquor before, though he'd heard many sermons against its use. *"'Tis a sin to drink. A man kinna be in control of himself when he's under its influence,"* Joseph was wont to say. *"I want each of ye lads to give me yer solemn promise that ye'll nae touch the evil stuff. Do I have yer word?"* Joining his brothers, Matt had given his promise, taking the Scotsman's hand to seal the bargain. It had seemed so easy then. Now? How could he refuse without giving offense? "Could I have a glass of water instead?"

"Water?" The Spaniard's eyebrows lifted. "What's this? A de Vega who doesn't like good brandy?"

"I . . . I've never tasted it."

Don de Vega's eyes narrowed. "I think you lie, señor. I think since I won't acknowledge you as my son, you've decided not to drink with me."

"That's not true." Embarrassment heightened Matt's color. What could he say? How could he refuse? Maybe if he just took a sip. The shadowy presence of the Scotsman seemed to fill the room. Matt could almost feel Joseph Cameron's hand on his knee, hear the tremor in his voice when they'd parted. *"Yer mother loves ye, lad. So do I."*

Matt took a deep breath and met Don de Vega's eyes. "I can't drink with you. I . . . I promised someone I wouldn't touch liquor."

"Not touch liquor?" Surprise rather than derision sounded in Don de Vega's voice. "Who would ask such a thing?"

"My father . . . Joseph Cameron. He's a Mormon. I'm a Mormon. Mormons don't drink spirits."

"I see." Don de Vega's expression was thoughtful as he set Matt's glass on the table and walked to his desk. "I've heard of the Mormones and their numerous wives, their industry and thrift. But not to drink?" An amused expression crossed the Spaniard's face. "Perhaps that's why they are so industrious, no?" Taking a sip of brandy, Don de Vega sat down. "Tell me about this man you call your padre. What has he done to command such obedience?"

Matt shrugged. "He's a Scotsman. When he joined the Mormon Church he came to Utah, then Mexico. I told you about his farm."

"Are there other children?"

"Fifteen in all."

The dark brows raised again. "Yet he took you in?"

Matt nodded, not wanting to explain about Joseph's wives unless he had to.

"He is a good man . . . strange too. But what can you expect of a gringo?"

Matt thought it better not to answer.

As Don de Vega sipped his brandy, he continued to study Matt. "A strange man," he repeated. "Did he send you to school? Have you had education?"

"I started school when I was six. That's where I learned to speak Spanish."

"I see." Arrogance slipped back into Don de Vega's voice. "I didn't bring you here to talk about the Mormones. There are more important matters." He opened the drawer and took out the ring box. "What will you give me for this?"

Matt stared at his father, wondering if he were playing a game.

A smile touched Don de Vega's lips. "I believe you said you would give everything. At the time, I thought it was just talk. But now . . ." He removed the ring from the box and held it out to Matt. "You gave everything. Risked your life for Felipe. I am not a man to go back on my word. The ring is yours."

Matt licked his lips, not knowing what to say. "What about Felipe?"

"Felipe will have the ranch and the de Vega name."

Matt still hesitated. The ring was part of the de Vega heritage, something he wasn't sure he wanted. Thoughts of his Mexican mother sifted through his mind. She was the one who'd given it to him. "Gracias."

Don de Vega's fingers closed around his when Matt reached for the ring. "Thank you, my son."

An odd ache gathered in the back of Matt's throat, making him swallow and turn away. Not wanting Don de Vega to see his distress, he started for the door.

"Wait!" Don de Vega's voice cracked with emotion. "You never told me your name . . . who to ask for if I should need you."

"Matt . . . Matthew Cameron."

"And the place where you live?"

"Colonia Cortéz."

Matt shut the door and ran a knuckle across his eyes. The ache in his throat subsided as he put on the ring. It slipped on easily, feeling like it had never left. Strange. Everything he'd experienced at the hacienda was strange. He didn't know what it meant yet, but one thing was certain. He wasn't going to tell anyone in Cortéz about his trip to Valle Grande. Too many people would construe the act as being disloyal. They didn't need to know about Rafael, either. Or Felipe. Most of all, they didn't need to know about his father.

* * *

That night Matt stared at the ceiling above the four-post bed, while the scene in the study paraded across his mind. *What is your name? Where can I find you?* Those weren't the exact words, but the meaning was clear. Like Matt, Don de Vega was afraid Felipe might not live.

Matt sighed and rearranged his pillow. He'd come to Valle Grande prepared to dislike Don de Vega's son. Felipe's spunk and ready grin had wormed their way past his prejudice and wrapped themselves around his heart. *Felipe can't die. He's got to live.* But if he didn't? Matt knew the answer. Why else had Don de Vega asked his name? Valle Grande would be his.

"No!" The vehemence in his voice surprised him. Matt's place wasn't at Valle Grande. One evening with Isabel de Vega had shown him that.

Using his good leg to kick back the covers, Matt got out of bed. Moonlight laid patterned shadows across the room, glinting off the mirror and reflecting onto the crucifix. This wasn't where he belonged. But neither was Cortéz. Not unless he found acceptance.

Matt limped to the window and looked out at the moon. Its pale light bathed the valley with pearly iridescence, turning the branches of the trees to silvered lace and shimmering the grass with diamonds. A quiet feeling of peace slowly stole over him. Discovering his identity didn't lie with Don de Vega, nor could it be found with the Camerons in Cortéz. It would have to come from somewhere deep within himself.

CHAPTER 7

Helen Cameron was drying the last of the supper dishes when Matt opened the kitchen door. Joy suffused her face as she dropped the dish towel and hurried to meet him. "I didn't see you ride back to the barn." She paused and wiped her hands on her apron. "Are you all right? You were gone so long."

Matt nodded and tossed his bedroll into the corner by the door. A breeze ruffled the kitchen curtains, and there was a place set for him at the table. Everything looked just the same, even Helen in her dark shirtwaist dress and crisp apron with fine, graying hair pulling loose from its bun. Grinning, Matt gave her a quick hug. "It's good to be home."

"It's good to have you back. I've been worried."

He held her away from him, noting the fine lines around her blue eyes, the deeper lines etched at the corners of her mouth. If anyone had asked Matt whether his mother was pretty or plain, he couldn't have said. He only knew she was Helen and that he loved her.

Matt was aware that Helen was looking him over too. She had that "just before church" look in her eye, one that made him wonder if his face was dirty or his hair needed combing. "I know I need a bath, and I managed to bang my knee." Her quick frown hurried him on. "I'm fine now. Just a little hungry."

"When aren't you hungry?" Helen went to the stove and dipped hot water from the reservoir into a basin, her movements quick and efficient. "Wash up while I fix your supper. You can bathe later." Neither of them made an effort to talk until after Helen had poured milk gravy over thick slices of bread and handed Matt his plate. Then

they talked of trivialities: the Anderson twins had the measles, Helen
had bottled twenty quarts of pears . . . . It wasn't until Matt finished
the last of the gravy, swirling it around the edges of the plate with a
crust of bread, that Helen spoke of what lay on her mind.

"Did getting away help?"

"Yes, I think so." But had it? The last night at Valle Grande he'd
been certain he'd found the answer. Now he wasn't so sure. The
people in Cortéz hadn't changed. Neither had Joseph.

"Things will work out," Helen said. "Now that the Clawsons are
gone, people will forget. Everyone likes you. Your father was telling
me just this morning—"

Matt pushed away his plate. "Father's as bad as Brother Clawson."

Helen's head lifted. "What a thing to say."

"It's true. Haven't you noticed how he treats us? Don't you care?"

"Your father treats us just fine."

"Does he? Then why do we have the smallest house? How come
we don't have running water? We're not good enough, that's why. You
couldn't have children. I'm adopted and a Mexican. Since Father
treats us like we're second best, no wonder everyone else does too."

"Is that what you think? That we're second best?" When she saw
Matt nod, Helen's eyes filled with tears. "Oh, Matty." She struggled
for control. "If I'd wanted a bigger house, I could have had one. But
for what? You and I would just rattle around in all the empty rooms."

"We could have had one?"

"Before Kate and Lou got theirs. It's what your father had planned,
what he wanted. I was tempted, but when I thought of the extra
scrubbing and cleaning, I knew there were other things I'd sooner do.
You know how I love to garden, the hours I'm away nursing." She
shook her head. "A big house would be a burden . . . unless, of course,
you'd like to borrow my apron and do the cleaning yourself."

Helen's attempt at humor eased the tension. "As for running
water, with fourteen children between them, Kate and Lou need it far
more than we do. Since Kate's so heavy, she has a hard time lifting the
buckets."

"She's got five strong sons."

"And I have you. A family as big as ours has to rely on cooperation. There's give and take. You know that. Our running water will

come. Your father plans to start on it as soon as he finishes the harvest."

Would he? Something would probably come up. It always did.

Seeming to read his mind, Helen put her hands on Matt's shoulders. "Your father loves you. He's been worried. He's stopped by two or three times a day to see if you've come back. Did you know he and Harry rode all the way up to the Steps yesterday looking for you?" Helen's fingers tightened. "He loves you, son. Trying to balance his time, wanting to be fair to everyone, isn't easy."

Although Matt knew Helen hadn't set out to make him feel small and ungrateful, she'd succeeded. He wished he could come in the door again and start all over. This time he'd keep his mouth shut so he wouldn't have to apologize. "I'm sorry. I should have known better."

"And I need to remember you're not a child anymore, that you're eighteen and old enough to be included in the decisions." She patted Matt's shoulder and reached for his plate. "Sometimes life gets complicated."

The faraway look in Helen's eyes told Matt the plate was forgotten. Perhaps he was forgotten too. She was somewhere else, a time and place where he didn't exist. After a moment, Helen went on. "Your father's love has always been here to sustain me. I know he loves me, Matt. Deeply. Completely. And I know he loves you."

* * *

After Matt had bathed and changed into clean clothes, Helen seated him in a chair on the porch and proceeded to trim his hair. "Before long, I'll have to trim your beard, too," Helen teased, rubbing his cheek with her finger.

Matt grinned, then, when Helen was busy cutting the back of his hair, he ran a surreptitious finger along his jawline. He'd shaved before he dined with the de Vegas. Now, just three days later, there were definite signs of growth. Pleased with himself, Matt closed his eyes and gave himself over to the luxury of Helen's ministrations—the soft snip of scissors, the pleasurable sensation of the comb. A sense of peace stole over him. Everything was going to be all right.

"I think I've outdone myself," Helen said when she'd finished. "Would you like to use the mirror in my bedroom and see what an accomplished barber your mother's become?"

Matt grinned and followed Helen into the bedroom. Left-handed, Helen's awkward snipping with her right hand was something they liked to joke about. "It looks like you managed to leave me with my ears this time."

"Your hair, Matty. Your hair. Even your father couldn't have done better."

Matt peered into the mirror. She really had outdone herself. "It looks good."

"You're the one that looks good." Helen leaned her head against his shoulder. "There's not a handsomer young man in the colonies . . . or a better one, either. Tuck that away in your mind and don't forget it."

* * *

Joseph's arrival broke the tranquility of the evening. Matt and Helen were sitting on the front porch, Matt leaning back in a chair, his booted feet propped on the railing and his worries put aside. They sat without speaking, watching the sky soften to pearly saffron as they listened to the birds' last sleepy sounds. Engrossed in the beauty of the evening, they failed to see Joseph until he paused at the gate.

"It's your father." Helen's voice filled with gladness, one that leaped from mother to son. She called to the burly Scotsman, "Matt's home!"

Joseph's purposeful gait slowed. "So . . . he's come home, has he?"

Matt's gladness fled as quickly as it had come. He could feel his father's anger, recognize it in the tightness of his voice. He waited, knowing before Joseph stepped onto the porch that he was the cause of the anger.

"Is something wrong?" Helen's hand stole over and closed on Matt's fingers.

Instead of answering, Joseph looked at Matt. "I hope what I heard tonight isn't true."

Matt's mind leaped to Don de Vega. "I was hoping you wouldn't find out."

"'Tis a small world, Matty. Such things are bound to be found oot."

Matt's heart plunged. If Joseph knew about Don de Vega, Helen would soon hear of it too. The hearing would hurt, tearing her heart when she learned that the son she loved as her own had wanted to find his true father. The very act would be construed as a form of rejection. Weren't she and Joseph enough?

Matt squeezed Helen's hand and got to his feet. "Can we talk about this somewhere else . . . without Mother?"

"Aye." It came as a sigh, as if Joseph had hoped Matt would deny it. "Let's go into the house."

The air was charged with tension by the time the two men faced each other in Matt's tiny bedroom. Matt was glad there wasn't any light, glad he didn't have to watch his father's face when he tried to explain his need to find Don de Vega, though maybe Joseph Cameron wouldn't care. Maybe he'd never cared.

"I thought I'd taught ye better." Anger vibrated through the Scotsman's voice. "Dinna we strike a bargain? Dinna ye take my hand?"

"What are you talking about?"

"There's nae need to play dumb. I heard it straight from the horse's mouth, though I nae thought to hear such a thing aboot one of my own. Carousing with riffraff . . . swearing and drinking."

Matt felt slightly addled.

"I've just come from ward teaching at the Murdocks. When I was leaving, Brother Murdock took me aside and told me what you'd been up to."

"Just what am I supposed to have been up to?" Matt said, then added quickly, "No, don't tell me. If Fred's had a hand in it, it's bound to be bad."

"Do ye deny it?"

"If it's about me drinking, you bet I deny it."

"Fred saw ye coming out of a cantina over in Casas Grandes, and Brig Shumway saw ye a couple of days ago with a bunch of riffraff."

"It's a lie."

Joseph grabbed Matt's arm. "They both saw ye, Matty. If 'twas just Fred, I might think he was lying, but Brig Shumway . . ." His fingers tightened. "Dinna add lying to yer list of sins. The swearing and drinking are bad enough."

Thoughts of Rafael tumbled through his head while his father's voice went on, decrying Matt's lack of respect, the trust he'd broken, and the resulting pain Helen would suffer. The mention of Helen brought Matt's tumbling thought to a skidding halt. "It's not true. None of it's true."

"Brother Murdock said—"

"I don't care what Brother Murdock said. I know where I've been and what I've done. I don't suppose you'd be interested in hearing the truth. You've already made up your mind."

If the room had been lighter, Matt would have seen a change in the older man's expression, a softening of his features, the suggestion of doubt.

"I've been in the mountains, not drinking and carousing with riffraff. Of course, you wouldn't take my word above Fred's or Brig Shumway's. After all, I'm a Mexican. Mexicans lie."

"Nae . . . Matty . . ."

Matt didn't hear Joseph's soft protest. He was out the door, grabbing his bedroll, snatching his jacket from the nail by the back door. Why bother to explain about Rafael and Don de Vega. No one would believe him. They'd all think the worst. And if that's how it was, then he'd darn well give them something to think about.

* * *

Ten days had passed since Sabra had seen Matt, days during which she helped her mother and Aunt Mae pack lemony wedges of pears into glass jars as a guard against winter. Both Elizabeth and Mae noticed that Sabra was unusually quiet while she sat at the kitchen table and peeled the pears. What's more, she did it without complaint. Exchanging pleased glances, they took this as a favorable sign that she was beginning to mellow.

Sabra's thoughts would have surprised the women. Instead of satisfaction in the filled jars, her mind was on Matt Cameron, wondering if he'd found his Mexican father and when he was coming home. Couched between her concern were pockets of disturbing new emotions, which made her envy her oldest brother, Carl, who'd recently married. Sabra felt a pleasurable sensation each time she relived the moment when Matt had run his finger across her nose. Was this how Carl's new wife felt when Carl touched her? If so, perhaps marriage wouldn't be so bad, especially if she could marry Matt.

She daydreamed her way through bushels of pears, scarcely noticing the curling peels that trailed from her knife and ran with juice past her wrists and onto her forearms. Oblivious to the two women, Sabra pictured herself three years hence with a face and figure that cast Rosella's pallid coloring into insignificance. Matt would be smitten with her, gazing at her in the same adoring fashion that Carl gazed at Emma. He'd dance with her, too, not just once, but every dance—he in his black charro suit and she in a gown of emerald green. Later, when he walked her home, his hand would tighten on her waist and he'd pull her into the shadows and kiss her, just like Carl kissed Emma when he thought no one was looking.

Lost in daydreams, she often sat for several minutes, staring out the window, imagining Matt kissing her cheek, perhaps even her lips. In between her daydreams, Sabra urged her father to speak out against Brother Clawson so Matt could return to a town that welcomed him. But her efforts to extract a firm commitment from her father were as elusive as her attempts to understand her new emotions.

Late on an autumn afternoon when trees cast long shadows across the lane, Sabra came out of the chicken coop and saw her mother talking with Kate Cameron. There was a moment of surprise, a quickening of excitement. Did Matt's aunt have news of him? Had he come back?

Her first impulse was to break in on the conversation and ask, but there was something in the women's stance—Mama looking sober and concerned, Kate Cameron's cheeks quivering with agitation, her voice loud enough for Sabra to hear.

"I imagine it's all over town by now. Helen says it's not true . . . that Matt would never run with bandits and get drunk. Joseph said Matt all but admitted it. At least at first, but later . . ." Kate pressed a plump hand to her lips. "Later Matt said he'd been in the mountains, that Fred and Brig Shumway were lying."

Sabra moved closer, the basket of eggs forgotten, her ears straining to hear. She knew Fred Murdock was lying. Hadn't Matt told her he was going to the mountains to try to find his father? But she'd promised not to tell.

"Now that Matt's run off again." Kate paused and shook her head. "It looks bad, Lizzie."

"Poor Helen."

Kate nodded. "I've never seen her this upset. She's been so wrapped up in that boy . . . loving him. He's her entire life. She and Joseph couldn't have done more if Matt had been their own. But he isn't. That's the problem, what we've all feared, though the family loves Matt too. Adoption is such a chancy thing. Who's to say who Matt's real parents were? You know what they say about bad blood."

The women walked away, their heads close together and steps slow. Sabra wanted to hurry after them and ask Sister Cameron to explain, but her legs were frozen by the same terrible iciness that had closed her throat. *Running with bandits. Bad blood.* Surely they didn't believe it. Not about Matt.

They did. Everyone in town seemed to believe it. Matt Cameron had run off, turned his back on the Church and broken his mother's heart.

Sabra felt as if her heart had been broken too. Despair followed her every step, devouring the wispy daydreams before they'd had a chance to take root and flower. How could she grow up and amaze Matt with her beauty if he wasn't there?

Unable to sleep, she stared at the pale square of her window, feeling as empty and desolate as a midnight sky stripped of moon and stars. "He'll come back," she whispered. The fierceness in her voice made it tremble. "He's got to come back."

CHAPTER 8

The new year of 1911 was to be ushered in with a dance followed by a giant bonfire. Anticipation ran high, touching those living in Cortéz with sufficient excitement to subdue their growing worry over the Mexican Revolution.

"Hurry, Sabra. Charlie will be coming any minute now."

"I'm almost ready," Sabra called, though she'd been staring out the window, wondering how to answer Charlie if he asked her to marry him. The proposal was imminent. Sabra sensed it, just as she sensed she wasn't ready for marriage. At least not to Charlie Teasdale.

Remembering the need to hurry, Sabra slipped out of her dress and stood in ruffled petticoat as she bent over the washbowl and splashed water onto her face and throat. "What's wrong?" she asked the damp reflection gazing back in the mirror. Charlie was clearly taken with her, as were half the other young men in Cortéz. He would make a good husband. *But Charlie won't make you happy,* the long-lashed green eyes in the mirror seemed to say.

Sabra reached for the towel. Her popularity had taken everyone by surprise. Young men, who'd been no more than friends, suddenly realized she'd changed from a gangly girl into an attractive young lady. The Lindsey parlor had never seen so many male visitors, all vying for the chance to walk Sabra to church or escort her to the weekly dances. The attention was more frustrating than flattering since she felt nothing stronger than friendship for her numerous suitors, a fact which disturbed her and made her wonder if something were wrong.

"It's likely your glands," Becky said when Sabra confided her concern. "Sister Jones at the academy believes our glands are the root of all our emotions."

If this were true, why did thoughts of Matt Cameron's touch still have the power to fill her with longing? There had to be another reason, one hopelessly entangled with memories of Matt.

The years had clouded her memory of the young Mexican, making it difficult to recall the shape of his face or if his eyes crinkled at the corners when he smiled. Memories were as traitorous as Matt, who hadn't written so much as a letter to her in the four years he'd been gone. Not that she'd actually expected one, but she'd hoped and dreamed with a longing that hadn't diminished over time.

Helen Cameron was the only one who'd received any communication from him. It came in the form of a letter, one opened and read so many times that the words had faded along the creases—or so Sabra overheard Aunt Mae tell Mama. Aunt Mae was one of the few who'd seen the short letter telling his mother he was all right and that she wasn't to worry. One day he'd come to see her, though it wouldn't be more than a visit, not when people were so quick to judge and condemn. There had also been a brief line telling Helen he loved her . . . that he'd always love her.

It was the paragraph that followed that had set the town to wondering. In it Matt said he had an identical twin brother, one with the same distinctive white patch in his hair. *Remember the young man who saved me from the cougar? That was my twin brother.*

"Likely story," Fred Murdock said when he heard of the letter. "Very convenient, too. Matt's just trying to cover up what he's done . . . what he's still doing."

There were others who thought the same, but a few, especially Matt's family and friends, believed him.

Repentant, Joseph Cameron wished he'd waited to talk to Matt until after his anger had cooled. A twin brother. All this time a twin brother. Was it possible? But why hadn't Matt told them about him when he explained about the cougar? Joseph's frustration increased when there was no mention of where Matt was or what he was doing. There were rumors, though. He'd been seen with Mexicans in Casas Grandes. Some even said there'd been a shooting and that Matt was in jail. Anxious to dispel the rumors, Joseph set out for the jail in Casas Grandes.

"Si, there was such an *hombre* with a white streak in his hair. But his name is not Matthew Cameron. This vaquero . . . *bandito* . . ."

The jefe's voice hardened. "Rafael Acosta is this bandito's name. His companions broke him out of jail two nights ago. Where they've gone, no one knows, but if I get my hands on him . . ."

Upset and not knowing what to believe, Joseph set out for home. Had the accusations he'd voiced to Matt been justified? Uncertain, he was left to wrestle with doubt. *Rafael Acosta.* The name wouldn't leave his mind. Had Matt's rejection of Mormonism and his family been so complete he'd changed his name? The thought rankled. More than that, it hurt, though perhaps now Joseph wouldn't have to worry that Matt would tarnish the Cameron name. This last sarcastic remark had come from Helen, who never raised her voice, who'd never spoken ill of her husband.

Sabra heard about this last incident while she was shelling peas with Aunt Mae and Mama. Head bent and thumbnail slitting the pods, she'd listened through the afternoon, scarcely daring to breathe for fear they'd remember she was there and end the conversation. Since then, there'd been no news, only silence, as if Matt had been swallowed by the Chihuahua desert, his name seldom spoken by anyone other than his family; but it tugged at Sabra's thoughts more often than she cared to admit.

This was something she couldn't explain—the hold he still had on her thoughts. How often she had wondered about him and compared him with her suitors. No one who came courting seemed to measure up. Sometimes it angered her, how she would unconsciously compare every young man with Matt, whom she hadn't seen in four years and who probably didn't even remember her.

Determined not to waste another minute on a man who'd turned his back on the Church, Sabra went to the curtained enclosure that served as her closet and took out an apricot-colored dress. It had been given to her for Christmas, secretly stitched by Mama and Aunt Mae on the afternoons Sabra worked at the Teasdale Union Mercantile. The cheery color of the dress and the knowledge that it became her buoyed Sabra's sagging spirits. Smiling a challenge at the slender reflection in the mirror, Sabra ran a tortoise-shell brush through her chestnut hair. Tonight was New Year's Eve. Even though she was going to the dance with Charlie, she was determined to have a good time.

Charlie Teasdale was waiting in the parlor, his long frame dominating the sofa just as his shock of auburn hair dominated his pleasant features. He was the affable son of Cortéz's leading merchant, and he was clearly smitten with Sabra. Maybe that was the problem. Perhaps if Charlie weren't so eager, she'd find him more to her liking. Part of her did like him. His freckled face always had a ready smile, and he was more thoughtful than most young men. The knowing look he exchanged with her mother, however, put a quick damper on her feelings. *Please, Charlie. Not yet!*

Charlie got to his feet, a smile of approval lighting his face. "You look real pretty, Sabra." Charlie's face turned ruddy above his starched white collar and dark suit. "You, too, Sister Lindsey. Your husband and I will both be envied."

"Thank you." Elizabeth glanced at her daughter. "I'm afraid you're going to need a broom to keep the boys away from Sabra tonight. Did you know she had four other invitations to the dance?"

"Mama," Sabra protested, even if it had set Charlie back for a second.

"I'll keep that in mind." Charlie regarded her with the sober, thoughtful look he sometimes took on. "Since you accepted my invitation, I hope you plan to save most of the dances for me."

It was on the tip of her tongue to tell him no, for Charlie was already acting as if they were engaged. "I promised a quadrille and polka to LaMar, and Seth Johnson asked me to save two dances for him. So did Archie Mortensen."

His dismay gave Sabra a fleeting satisfaction that disappeared as soon as they stepped out into the crisp night. Charlie's grip on her elbow immediately tightened and he leaned his head close. Fearing he might try to put his arm around her, Sabra quickened her step and chattered about the bonfire, not stopping until they reached the church. Her actions clearly put Charlie out of sorts.

"Sister Moffit and I were just saying what a handsome couple you two make," the bishop's wife said in greeting. She gave them a knowing wink when Charlie put his hand on Sabra's shoulder. "Do I hear wedding bells?"

Charlie beamed, his good humor restored by Sister Harris's encouragement.

Sabra slipped out of her coat, fuming as she went to the women's side of the hall. Couldn't they see she and Charlie were just friends? Must everyone think of marriage? To cool her anger, she concentrated on the tissue-paper bells that crisscrossed the ceiling, watching them swing each time the door opened. When the dance manager called for an opening prayer, she had difficulty concentrating on the words. Escape filled her mind—escape from Charlie and his plans for marriage.

As soon as the prayer was over, she lifted her head and smiled at Seth, who lounged under a coal-oil lamp with some of his friends. When the fiddles struck up the bars of the opening reel, he hurried across the floor to claim her, his closer position giving him advantage over Charlie. The hurt on Charlie's face pricked Sabra's conscience, but the need to be free was stronger. It carried her through the steps of the reel, making her smile and invite pursuit each time she caught the eye of an unattached male. She knew Charlie disapproved of her recklessness, and he hoped, like her parents, that marriage and the arrival of children would correct the flaw.

I'm not ready for marriage! Sabra wanted to shout. She threw back her head and whirled through the steps of the dance, letting the music carry her along until Uncle Ernie called a change in the dance.

"Circle all. Now right-hand your partners, and right and left around the hall."

The ring the dancers formed filled the room. While fiddles called encouragement, they began to circle, men to the right, women to the left, right hand to one partner, left hand to the next. Sabra touched fingers with Bishop Harris and Rob as she passed them. The clapping hands and stamping feet intensified her recklessness as it shook the floor and shivered the air with noise and excitement. As Sabra whirled, she looked into a pair of dark eyes, felt brown fingers close around hers.

"Matt!" She missed a step, thinking she must be mistaken. Matt's grin and half-questioning, "Nutmeg!" told her she was right. Before either of them could say more, Charlie's sweaty palm swung her along the circle away from Matt.

"I'm sorry if I've done something to offend you," Charlie panted.

Scarcely listening, Sabra looked over her shoulder at Matt. Something deep inside changed when she saw him do the same. A missing portion of her body had been restored, the part filled with warmth and caring and all the exciting, mysterious feelings Becky attributed to one's glands.

Happiness whirled within Sabra, making her forget about Seth and Charlie. All she could think of was Matt. He'd come back, and at eighteen she was confident enough of her charm to know she had a chance of winning his admiration.

When the dance ended, Sabra listened absently to Charlie as he escorted her to the bench, her eyes on the men gathered in the corner near the stove. She squeezed Becky's arm when she spied Matt. "He's back."

"Who?"

"Matt."

Becky looked puzzled.

Sabra had never confided her feelings for Matt to anyone, not even Becky. Striving for nonchalance, she loosened her grip on Becky's arm. "The Cameron boy. Remember Matt Cameron?"

Others seemed to remember him. Now that she was thinking more clearly, Sabra heard snatches of conversation whispered about him on every side.

"I wondered if he'd be here."

"He rode in bold as you please yesterday evening."

" . . . dare show his face."

"Bandit . . ."

"I'm surprised Bishop Harris let him come to the dance." This last came from Becky, whose eyes, like those of the majority of the ward members, were fastened on the dark-headed man standing near the stove.

"Why shouldn't Matt come to the dance?"

"Because he's a bandit."

"Who says he's a bandit?"

"Papa."

"Well, it's a lie." But was it? Matt had been gone so long. Hurt and angry, who knew what he might have done? Did he really have a twin brother?

Sabra's eyes searched for Matt again and saw him shaking hands with Brother Moffit. She scrutinized him for any change in his appearance. Her thirsting gaze noted the breadth of his shoulders, his vitality, the dark eyes that had come to rest on her. She felt her color rise and looked away, knowing Matt still watched her, while half-formed thoughts tumbled through her mind. Where had he been? How to be rid of Charlie? Did Matt find her pleasing? The need for another quick look was rewarded by the slow smile that lit Matt's bronzed features when their glances met the second time.

Sabra was so busy watching Matt she failed to hear Uncle Ernie announce the next dance. Nor did she notice Charlie and Seth lined up like racers ready to dash across the floor to claim her. Charlie got there first, almost tumbling into Sabra's lap as he tried to outmaneuver Seth. She stifled a giggle, excitement throbbing through her, although she was disappointed that it was Charlie, not Matt, who led her onto the floor. But Matt had noticed her—she knew he'd noticed.

"I'm sorry if I've offended you," Charlie began again.

Sabra only half heard the repeated apology, her eyes on Matt, who'd crossed the floor to join his mother.

"You haven't offended me." She strained to see what Matt would do next.

"Well, you're acting like I have."

Charlie. Why couldn't he be quiet or move so she could have a better view of Matt. Would he dance with his mother? She caught a glimpse as she and Charlie touched hands and changed position. Matt was talking with his brother Harry, the two standing by themselves. Sabra whirled to the next partner, her steps automatic, all her thoughts on Matt. Maybe he would ask her for the next dance. Maybe . . .

He didn't, dancing instead with his mother, then his Aunt Lou. Through it all there were questioning eyes, everyone seeming to watch Matthew Cameron amid whispers and an air of constraint. She saw it, felt it. Surely Matt felt it too.

If he did, he didn't show it. Instead, he and Harry lounged near the stove while the dancers went through their antics. Suddenly Matt was there beside Sabra, he and Harry bringing Harry's two sisters to make up a part of Sabra's set.

"First couple lead to the couple on the right, and four hands around," Uncle Ernie called.

Sabra and Charlie joined hands with Matt and his partner. All of her senses were centered on Matt, his voice deep and laughing as he said something to Charlie, the feel of his lean fingers, the quick smile when their glances met. Was he aware of it too, the tingling nerves and senses?

"On to the next, and four hands around," the little Englishman called.

Charlie led Sabra to the next couple, his touch eliciting no more emotion than if she'd been dancing with her father. Instinct took her through the steps of the reel, her mind a fog of conflicting emotion—elation that Matt was home balanced by the fear that what she felt for him was one-sided. He looked so fully in control of himself, not disconcerted like she was.

"Are you feeling all right?" Charlie's voice was anxious.

"Yes . . . of course." Her answer came quickly as she strained to hear what Matt was saying to Elsie Cameron. Something about dinner at their Aunt Lou's and would Elsie be there? Elsie, who still wore her hair in braids, looked both frightened and excited to be with her black-sheep, adopted half brother.

When the reel was over, Charlie escorted Sabra back to the bench. "Are you sure you're all right?"

She nodded, smiled, anything to speed Charlie on his way. In the sudden crush of people, she lost sight of Matt. Where was he? Then she became aware of someone standing behind her and bending to murmur in her ear.

"Sabra."

It was only her name, his voice soft and seeming deeper, as perhaps it was. She turned so she could look at him, savor him—her whole body quickening with delight and joy as she assessed Matt's mustache and the strong angles of his face, which had changed him from boy to man. His eyes were the same deep shade of brown, accented by thick brows, and they did crinkle at the corners when he smiled. Matt's shoulders had broadened though, stretching the fabric of his wide-lapel suit, the one he'd left hanging in his closet all those years ago. How old was he? Twenty-two? Twenty-three?

"Have you forgotten how to talk?"

"No." Sabra smiled, blushed, wished she didn't feel so muddled. There was so much to remember, memorize before Matt left again.

"Can I have the next dance?"

"Yes." She knew her actions wouldn't please her parents. The fact that Matt had come to the dance had upset more than a few. Until Joseph Cameron's adopted son gave a proper accounting of himself to the bishop and disproved the rumors, young ladies would be wise to steer clear of him. But Sabra had never been noted for her wisdom. Without thinking, she smiled and said, "Yes," for the second time.

Matt's easy grin was just as she remembered it, carved into her memory along with his gentleness. "I'll be back."

He came to claim her as soon as Uncle Ernie had determined the ladies were rested enough to go on with the dancing. Perhaps it was a similar consideration, a guard against someone fainting, that led the fiddle and accordion players into the lilting strains of a waltz.

Matt's brows lifted. "Isn't waltzing forbidden?"

"Not anymore." She felt a sweep of pleasure as she explained how Bishop Harris had given permission for them to do an altered version of the waltz, which was done side by side with the lady pivoting under her partner's raised arm. Sabra felt another sweep of pleasure when she saw Matt grin. It seemed there were no bounds to her pleasure now that he was home and they were together.

Matt danced well—too well for someone who had never waltzed before. This observation diminished her pleasure and set Sabra wondering again. Where had he been and what had he been doing?

"Will you be staying in Cortéz?" The question came of its own volition, part of her sensing that the answer to where he'd been must come without her asking.

"Maybe."

They glided around the edge of the floor. Neither spoke. There was no need. Enough was said through glance and fleeting touch.

"You've grown up, Nutmeg."

Joy and delight came again in the use of the cherished nickname and in the timbre of his well-remembered voice.

"When I left, you were young . . . still part child. Now . . ." A smile hovered around his mouth while the soft light in his eyes told her what he'd left unsaid: Matt thought her comely, perhaps even beautiful.

A hundred lamps seemed to surround Sabra, warming her cheeks and filling her heart with radiance.

Neither was aware when Charlie waltzed past with Myrtle Hamblin, jealousy glinting in his pale blue eyes, nor did they see the swift glance Samuel Lindsey exchanged with Elizabeth. *Why hadn't the Camerons left well enough alone?* the glance said. *They never should have adopted that Mexican baby.*

CHAPTER 9

Starlight and a half-moon bathed the bonfire hill in shadows and outlined the faces of the people who climbed the rocky path leading to its summit. Others were already there, calling encouragement and urging them to hurry.

As Matt climbed the hill with Harry, he wondered why he'd come. It certainly wasn't because he'd been made to feel welcome, though there had been a number of outstretched hands and "It's good to see you back," comments interspersed between the whispers at the dance. He'd known how it would be, and giving the Mormons their due, he couldn't blame them. Both his mother and Harry had told him about the continued rumors. The fact that Matt had a twin brother was hard for some to swallow. What else were they to think?

That I am innocent. After living with him all those years, they should know what he was made of and realize he wasn't a thief. Even the hard-bitten cowboys on the Ojo Mandello Ranch had known that, sensed it from the start. Matt Cameron was someone they could rely on. But their friendship and trust couldn't offset the stronger pull of Cortéz. Like a bird winging homeward with the coming of nightfall, Matt had followed its call, love for Helen being the overriding factor. But something else, something so elusive that he couldn't put a name to it, had nudged and pushed him too. There were unknown needs to be met, unknown questions to be answered. Only when it was finished could Matt be free.

He'd gone to the dance telling himself he didn't care what others thought of him. It was what he thought of himself that mattered.

Right now, Matt thought he was crazy. He never should've let Harry talk him into staying for the bonfire.

It wasn't entirely Harry, though. Sabra Lindsey's presence on the path kept him firmly in the group that followed her. He noticed her unsuccessful attempts to put as much distance as possible between herself and Charlie Teasdale. Matt wanted to go to her rescue, tell Charlie to leave her alone, though if his memory served him right, the young Sister Lindsey was capable of handling Charlie without any help from him.

"She sure knows how to give Charlie fits," Harry chuckled.

They were among the last to reach the top of the rocky hill outlined by shadowy spikes of cactus. Harry quickly joined the rest of the crowd, but Matt was content to stay on the fringe, watching and exchanging a few words with those who spoke to him. For the most part they ignored him, which was fine with him. He didn't need their acceptance to validate his worth. Four years in Texas had taught him that.

Matt stood at the back of the crowd, hands in his trouser pockets, his dark head tilted upward, and attempted to observe them with the eyes of a stranger. What would strangers think of a New Year celebration without liquor, all the "brothering" and "sistering," the men with more than one wife? They'd find it strange, comical—sinful too. People called all sorts of things sinful.

The sight of three boys crumpling newspaper for the bonfire hampered Matt's attempt at detachment. Ten years ago it had been he and his friends. Now it was Sabra's brother Willie and the Johnson twins. He watched as the dry desert wood caught flame and sent a shower of sparks up into the crisp winter air.

"*Viva Mexico!*" a voice shouted.

"Viva los Mormones!" another voice added.

"Viva everyone!" Willie's twelve-year-old voice cracked with excitement. "And Happy New Year!"

Acting on cue, Brother Johnson's baritone sang out the opening strains of "Auld Lang Syne." Others joined him, blending their voices in rich harmony that filled the night with song.

Harry moved to stand with Matt. "How come you're not singing?"

He shrugged, not wanting to explain the need for detachment, his vow to keep the members of the Church at a distance.

"Someone else isn't singing, either. Have you noticed how Sabra Lindsey keeps looking at you?"

Matt had, his eyes drawn to her all evening too. The promised beauty he'd glimpsed at fourteen had come to fruition. The bones and sharp angles had rounded—a woman's charm reaching across the leaping bonfire, emerald eyes and shadowy wisps of hair conspiring to ensnare. He was a willing captive and answered her hesitant smile with a grin as he recalled the spunky girl who'd challenged Carlos, the almost woman whose freckled fingers had curled protectively around his. Nutmeg, Sabra, Sister Lindsey. Mischief, beauty, Mormon.

Matt wasn't aware the singing had ended until Bishop Harris began to speak, his rotund body blocking Matt's view of Sabra.

"If he takes as long as he did on Sunday, we'll be here 'til morning," Harry whispered.

Matt smiled. Evidently Bishop Harris's long-windedness hadn't diminished, but at least at the bonfire he couldn't pound on the pulpit.

The lack of a pulpit didn't prevent Bishop Harris from warming to his subject. "I'm sure you're aware of the trouble around us . . . the burning of the railroad bridges north of Chihuahua City. Unfortunately, the trouble will likely continue, perhaps even worsen. This prompts me to bring up the need for continued caution."

Matt moved closer so he could hear the bishop.

"Since the lynching of that poor Rodrigues fellow in Texas last fall, anti-American feelings have increased. Our Mexican friends have remained faithful, however. One came to me yesterday with word that bandits have threatened to kill all white ranchers."

Matt saw covert glances, felt a subtle pulling away. *Is he bandit or Mormon?* they wondered. *Matt Cameron or Rafael Acosta?*

"On my advice, Nate Briggs and Gilbert Johns have moved their families into town for a few days," the bishop went on. "The two brethren have asked me to convey their gratitude to those who've opened their hearts and homes to them."

Matt looked for Nate Briggs, who lived with his wives and children on a ranch ten miles west of Cortéz. The face of his first wife was stern and devoid of expression, but his second wife's mouth trembled as if she were about to cry.

"Hopefully this will be temporary and the bandits will move on. But just in case . . ." He paused. "We must continue to pray for protection. We must continue to be cautious. And we still need men to keep watch along the river."

Matt nodded. He'd seen what complacency had done to some of the ranchers outside of Chihuahua City. He'd hate to see the same thing happen here.

"Our leaders in Salt Lake have advised us to remain neutral," Bishop Harris continued. "This may not be easy. President Diaz has been good to us. But Madero and others want to make reforms . . . take land from the rich and give it back to the poor, a course our better instincts should applaud."

Bishop Harris's eyes traveled over the crowd that looked to him for leadership and guidance. Firelight played on solemn faces. Someone hushed a fretful child. For a second, Junius Harris's shoulders drooped as if the responsibility of so many was a physical weight. Straightening his stocky frame and rocking up onto the balls of his feet, he went on. "Being watchful doesn't mean we have to go around with long faces. The Lord will continue to bless us as He has in the past." Glancing at the chorister, he said, "If Brother Johnson will lead us in another song, I suggest we get on with our celebration. A cheer for 1911, the best year yet!"

The crowd responded with a lusty cheer and raised their voices in a rousing rendition of "Come, Come Ye Saints."

While they sang, Matt studied Bishop Harris, watched the play of firelight on his jovial features, the unconscious rising onto his toes when he sang. He'd always liked Junius Harris. The feeling had been reciprocated. Would that change when the bishop learned Matt had determined to steer a middle course, one that didn't necessarily include the Mormons?

Exploding firecrackers split the air as the final notes of the hymn died away. That would be Brother Hamblin. Matt couldn't remember a New Year's Eve without Brother Hamblin's firecrackers. Taking advantage of the confusion, Matt moved closer to Sabra, who was laughing with the Wilson girl while Charlie hovered by her side.

"I'm afraid that's all," Brother Hamblin apologized after the second rocket. "This revolution has made fireworks hard to come by."

"That's all right," someone said. "The sun's about to come up and I'm ready for bed."

A glance at the setting moon sent most parents down the hill to wagons waiting to transport them back to town. Sabra's parents sought her out before they left. "Willie's going home with us, but I expect you to have Sabra home within the hour," Samuel said to Charlie. When he saw Matt he hesitated. "Rob will be driving one of the teams. I'm depending on the two of you to see that Sabra gets home safely."

Sabra had planned to plead a headache and go home with her parents. Now that Matt had materialized at her side, she was anxious to stay, even if it meant putting up with Charlie.

"Anybody game for a little fun?" one of the Murdock boys asked as soon as the adults left the hill.

"Depends on what you call fun."

"Fireworks that will make Brother Hamblin's firecrackers seem like toys."

"Did you bring dynamite from the mines?" Rob asked.

"Sure did. When me and Fred came home for the holidays, Mr. Conway told us we could bring a stick to liven up the party."

"Dynamite sure ought to do it," Charlie said, "though maybe we ought to unhitch the horses so we don't have a runaway."

"I'll see to 'em," Rob volunteered. "Don't set it off 'til I get back."

Sabra heard the exchange with only half a mind. The other half was centered on Matt, conscious of his close presence, wishing she could get rid of Charlie.

"We hid the dynamite on the other side of the hill. When Rob gets back, holler and we'll light the fuse." For a second, Fred's eyes met Matt's. It was only a glance, one that was far from friendly.

"Let her go!" Rob shouted a few moments later.

A giant explosion rent the air, the ricocheting vibrations making Sabra feel as if she were caught in a shuddering earthquake.

"Look . . . there's a bucket! Fred must've set it off with the dynamite to see how high it would go."

Sabra watched the tin pail hurtle skyward. Reaching its zenith, it hesitated, then, gathering speed like a charging locomotive, it plummeted toward them.

"Look out!"

Everyone scrambled to get out of the way—screams, excited giggles, bumping, and tangled legs adding to the confusion. Sabra struggled to keep her balance, then felt a muscled arm catch and steady her. She knew it was Matt even before she saw his face, felt his warmth and feather-soft breathing. Then Charlie was there, his voice unsteady as he wiped a bloodied palm on his trousers. "I tried to catch you, but I tripped and . . ." Charlie stopped when he saw Matt's arm around Sabra. "She's not hurt, is she?"

"I don't think so."

"Then there's no reason for you to have your arm around her."

The two men measured each other. Charlie was the first to drop his gaze. "Since you've been away, I guess you don't know Sabra's my girl."

"I'm not your girl!" Her protest came out in a tight whisper. "I may have come to the dance with you, but I'm not your girl, Charlie." She turned and smiled at Matt, aware that his hand was still on her waist and that she wanted it to stay there. "Thank you."

"It was my pleasure." Matt raised an eyebrow and grinned. "I see you haven't lost your spunk, Nutmeg." Noticing that a crowd had gathered, he dropped his hand and looked at Charlie. "I'll leave you and Sabra to settle this yourselves."

Sabra wasn't in a mood to settle anything with Charlie. She pushed past him and went to find Becky, her anger warring with unexpected happiness. Matt had been slow to take his hand from her waist. He'd smiled and called her Nutmeg. Her eyes searched the shadows until she found his dark silhouette. There it was again, their glances meeting as if neither could keep their gaze from the other, Matt's eyes reflecting the glow of the dancing firelight. She knew she should look away, but her heart whispered otherwise. Lifting her lips in a hesitant smile, excitement diminished her awareness of anything else.

* * *

Charlie's scraped palm and a torn hem on the Johnson girl's skirt were the only casualties of the dynamite. After the Murdocks had been congratulated, Seth pulled a harmonica out of his pocket and began to play. Voices picked up the plaintive melody, Becky's alto following Myrtle Hamblin's soprano as couple after couple drifted away from the fire, arms interlocked and heads close together.

Matt stood with Harry, making a point to distance himself from Sabra. This didn't prevent him from noticing the soft flush of her cheeks in the firelight, the shadowy wisps of hair lying across her forehead.

"Sabra's watching you again," Harry whispered, then in a louder voice, "So's Charlie. I don't think he's happy with the way things are going tonight. Did I tell you he's got plans to marry Sabra? He said . . ." His voice faltered when he saw Fred and his girlfriend running toward the fire.

"Men on horseback are coming up the hill!"

The singing broke off, and Seth clapped his hand over his sister's mouth.

"Bandits . . ." someone whispered.

Fred pushed his way to Matt and grabbed his arm. "What did you do, invite your friends to our party?"

Matt's jaw tightened around an angry retort. "I don't know any more about this than you do." He brushed Fred's hand away and turned to Harry. "We'd better help the girls down to the wagons. Run for the wagons—fast!"

Sabra picked up her skirt and ran toward the path while Rob sprinted ahead to help them down the steep incline.

"Wait!" Rob held up his hand. "Someone's coming up this side too."

Stunned silence followed his words and one of the girls began to cry.

"Hush, Sadie." Seth put a comforting arm around his sister and looked at Fred. "What should we do?"

"Hide the girls." Fred shot an angry glance at Matt. "Seems strange that as soon as you come back, we have trouble with bandits."

Matt wanted to hit Fred. Harry almost did. "I don't know anything about this." Urgency took precedence to anger. "Someone run for help," Matt said.

"I'll go," Myrtle's little brother said. "I'm small and can run fast."

"I'll go too," Rob said. "That way, one of us is sure to make it."

Rob and the boy were gone before Matt could nod agreement, their dark silhouettes melting into the darkness as they slipped over the brow of the rocky hill.

Matt turned to the girls. "Scatter and hide the best you can." His eyes sought Sabra. "Hurry! We don't have much time."

"Can't I help?"

"Help?" Fred's voice cracked with derision. "Do you know what bandits will do if they find you? A lot worse than they'll do to me. I guarantee it."

A horseman appeared on the far side of the hill. "Run!" Matt whispered. "And keep away from the fire."

When Sabra saw a second rider following, she put aside her notion to be brave and sped over the rough ground, feeling the terror of pursuit. Spying a large mesquite bush, she scrambled under its protective branches.

The young men weren't far behind, a stand of yucca their destination. They crouched, their ragged breathing masking the approach of the horsemen. The mournful howl of a coyote was drowned out by the crack of a rifle.

"What's going on up here?" a voice called.

Harry's fingers closed around Matt's arm. "That sounds like the bishop."

"Is that you, Bishop?" Fred's voice was unsteady.

"Who were you expecting?"

"We thought . . ." Fred began.

"We thought you were bandits," Seth called. "At least Fred did."

"We all did," Harry chuckled. "We're mighty glad it was you."

More than a dozen anxious fathers had mistaken the dynamite explosion for a rebel cannon and had come, rifles in hand, to rescue the young people.

Sabra crawled out of her hiding place and brushed dried mesquite beans from her green coat. She saw relief spread over her father's handsome features when his eyes met hers. She was Samuel's jewel, his bright oasis amid the drab sameness of eight sons. Good though they might be, none had the spark and verve of his daughter. Samuel's delight vanished when he saw her gaze shift to Matt. The shadows hid her expression, but Samuel knew what was there—the softness and barely concealed yearning. He'd seen it at the dance and again at the bonfire. Fear bordering on panic seized him. He had to get Sabra away from that bandit. *Please, God, don't let her do anything foolish,* he prayed, and in the next breath said, "Dad gum it, where is Charlie?"

CHAPTER 10

Matt had only intended to stay in Cortéz for a couple of days, just long enough to visit his mother and Harry and to let them know he was all right and that he'd saved enough money to buy a ranch. The ranch wouldn't be close to Cortéz. He was adamant about that. At least he had been until he saw Sabra Lindsey. Since then, things hadn't been quite as clear.

The uncertainty bothered him. He'd made the decision months before, all the points had been carefully weighed and measured. His life would follow a middle road, neither Mormon nor Gentile, a man who would have the respect of both. The decision hadn't come easy. Matt knew God had restored His Church and that the gospel was true. Even when he'd been the angriest, he'd never doubted that. But since some of its members wouldn't accept him and his brown skin, Matt had chosen not to participate with them. It was as simple as that. Or at least it had been.

He'd followed this middle road for four years. The road had brought him a measure of contentment, and the leather pouch wrapped inside his bedroll with its hoard of cash attested to its success. But the middle road couldn't bring him to Sabra Lindsey. Only full fellowship with the Mormon Church could do that.

Instead of riding out of town at the end of the week, Matt found himself on his way to the church for an interview with Bishop Harris. It was a fine January night, the air just crisp enough for him to see the white puff of his breath as he walked along, the moon a lopsided orb lighting his way through fragile shadows.

As he neared the church, he heard the faint sound of a hymn. It was one he'd heard since childhood at Sunday meetings and a favorite to Helen, who loved to sing as she tended her garden. The hymn was familiar and dear:

O my Father, thou that dwellest
In the high and glorious place

Feelings long repressed surged to the surface. For a moment Matt was a child again, sitting in church between two loving parents with a cloak of security wrapped snugly around him. God made up part of the cloak, God who was there to listen and help if Matt would just ask Him.

The past few years Matt hadn't done much asking. Guilt was part of the reason. He wasn't sure God would listen to a man who no longer attended church. Yet here he was on his way to see the bishop, and even though he knew it was just the choir practicing, the hymn made him feel like he was back in the fold. With an unconscious straightening of his shoulders, Matt walked past the meetinghouse and on to the tithing building where Bishop Harris conducted his business in a room added to the back.

The door to the bishop's office swung open in response to his knock. The years on the Ojo Mendello Ranch had done much to build Matt's confidence, but they couldn't erase his nervousness as Bishop Harris offered his hand. Matt took it and gave a stiff smile as he seated himself on a wooden chair.

Guilt was there again. Junius Harris had given his life to the Church, while Matt's main focus had been on earning money to buy a ranch.

"We've missed you, Matthew. It's good to have you back."

"Thank you." Not *It's good to be back,* for that would be lying. There would be no lying tonight. Bishop Harris would be told about Rafael and Don de Vega. If Matt wanted his name cleared, he would have to submit to the Mormon leader's questions.

* * *

Junius Harris took a deep breath as he approached the pulpit on the following Sunday morning, knowing that the next few minutes would be difficult. There'd been too many rumors, too much talk about Matthew Cameron. At times Bishop Harris had wondered about him too. He'd wondered again as he'd listened to the young man's explanation about his father and twin brother. Years of observing those who sat across from him had honed Junius's ability to judge if a person was lying. All his instincts told him Matthew spoke the truth. Fervent prayer had confirmed it. Even so, the next few minutes were going to be difficult.

"Brethren." The bishop's voice boomed over the heads of fifty men and older boys in attendance at priesthood meeting. They were his friends, men he respected, and sometimes they were even saints. But other times . . . Junius didn't like to think about the other times. He took another deep breath.

"Gossip is a terrible sin. There's nothing that spreads more discord among an otherwise good group of people. Satan knows this and uses it well. He's using it now." He pounded the pulpit for emphasis. "Right . . . here . . . in . . . Cortéz."

Gathering confidence, Bishop Harris launched with full force into the uncomfortable subject. "Most of you are aware that Matthew Cameron has returned to our ward after a lengthy absence. You're also aware of the numerous rumors . . . the out-and-out gossip that has circulated about him while he's been gone."

The mention of Matt had gained everyone's attention. Heads lifted, eyes were alert.

"To fulfill my duty as bishop and judge in Israel, I've had a long and searching interview with Matthew. This interview has convinced me the rumors about him are false. After prayer, the Lord has confirmed this. Matthew Cameron is a worthy Latter-day Saint and priesthood holder, one who deserves your support and hand of friendship."

Bishop Harris's eyes rested briefly on Matt. Respect and understanding flowed between them. *I believe you,* Junius's gray eyes said. He rose onto the balls of his feet. "This is all I intend to say about the matter. But I exhort each of you to search your hearts and do as I have done—offer Matthew your hand and extend your love and brotherhood."

From his place on the back bench next to Harry, Matt watched the heads of the men, some bald or graying, others youthful, turn and look at him. He saw doubt and skepticism. Hadn't Fred Murdock seen him coming out of a cantina? Why, Matt's own father had even talked to the jailer in Casas Grandes. Were they to believe he really did have a twin brother? The men's reliance on Bishop Harris's wisdom, their belief he received guidance from God, warred with the skepticism on their faces. What should they do?

Matt sensed their indecision as he left priesthood meeting. He stopped to talk to those who extended a hand, and he tried to ignore the others. Samuel Lindsey's handshake was less than enthusiastic as was Charlie's. Even so, Matt was square on the side of the Mormon Church again, the Church and Sister Sabra Lindsey.

If the bishop had been less understanding, perhaps Matt only would have explained about Rafael. As it was, he'd ended up telling Bishop Harris about his time of rebellion and the trip into town with the cowboys. Matt didn't know exactly how it had happened—this need for confession, the desire to set things right between himself and God. He'd gone into the room believing he was doing it for Sabra. By the time he left, he knew he'd done it for himself. It was as if a heavy, invisible load had been lifted from his shoulders. He felt clean. Whole.

Matt pondered this as he sat with his family in sacrament meeting that evening. His eyes kept straying to Sabra. Although he didn't remember all the speaker said, he could describe in detail the blue pattern on Sabra's high-collared blouse, the proud tilt to her head with its mass of chestnut curls, her flushed cheeks when she became aware of his gaze.

Through it all was the grim presence of his adoptive father. The Scotsman's stiffness was more uncomfortable than the wooden bench, and the knowledge that he still hadn't taken Matt's hand was a sermon in itself. Family loyalty decreed that he act his part. Love for Helen kept him seated at the young man's side, but it couldn't make either of them like it.

Despite this, Matt felt a sense of homecoming as he joined his voice with the congregation for the opening hymn, felt a sense of reverence and belonging as bread and water were passed by young deacons. There was much to be thought upon, more to be decided. Rather than do either, Matt gave himself over to the luxury of admiring the high color in Sabra Lindsey's flushed cheeks.

* * *

Like skeins of bright silk woven through a muted tapestry, feelings of expectancy followed Sabra through the sameness of the next week. The feelings were tangled around Matt's name, which slipped into her mind a hundred times a day, interrupting her concentration and causing her to flit around the house like a summer moth. She was no better at the Union Mercantile where she worked three days a week. Her head jerked up each time the bell tinkled over the doorway, her pulse quickening with anticipation.

It was Wednesday when Matt finally came. A shaft of winter sunlight streamed through the door behind him, outlining his lean figure and accenting the white hair near the crown of his head. Sabra thought the hair gave him an air of distinction and added to his good looks, but she knew there were others, her parents among them, who remembered a bandit with the same distinctive feature, one described in detail by Brig Shumway and the sheriff in Casas Grandes. Did Matt Cameron truly have a twin brother, or had he ridden with outlaws before he'd repented and come back to the Church? It was an oft-debated question, one Sabra did not like to wonder about. Like the bishop and Matt's mother, she believed in the twin brother.

When Matt's brown eyes rested upon her, their warmth drove all other thoughts from her mind. This was the man whose favor she intended to win, the man she cared for. "May I help you?" It was a question Sabra asked a dozen times a day, but never to Matt and never with a tremor of excitement in her voice.

"I hope so. Someone told me you carry different kinds of spices."

"We do. They're right over here." Sabra glanced at Matt as she came around the counter. His appraising look made her drop her gaze. "We have eight different kinds. There's cinnamon and cloves and . . . What kind would you like?"

"Nutmeg. I've always been partial to nutmeg."

The sunlight streaming through the display window seemed to leap to Sabra's cheeks. She lifted her eyes, saw Matt's grin, and couldn't stop the laughter. The easy camaraderie was still there, wrapping itself around them like a warm quilt—soft and comfortable, but with little undertones of excitement.

"Freckles, too." Matt's grin widened as he took in the dusting of freckles on Sabra's nose. "I was afraid they'd be gone."

"No." Sabra forgot about Charlie's parents, who were straining to hear their conversation. Matt liked her freckles, dreadful things that they were—or had been until now. With one sentence Matt had changed them into something beautiful.

"Have you worked here long?"

"Just since summer." Realizing how working for Charlie's family looked, and not wanting Matt to believe the talk about her and Charlie, she hurried on. "Del just left on a mission. With all the expense . . ." She looked away, suddenly embarrassed. Supporting a missionary wasn't going to be easy, especially when Del had been called to serve in far-off Pennsylvania. Sacrificing for the Church was nothing new to the Lindseys. All that the family produced or earned was tithed, every tenth egg going into a special basket, each tenth pound of butter put into a designated crock. Once a week this was carried to the tithing office, their sacks of wheat, potatoes, and slabs of bacon joining similar offerings from their neighbors. "When the Teasdales offered me work here, it seemed the perfect solution," she ended lamely.

"Aunt Kate cooked and did laundry at a railroad camp to help keep Orson on his mission," Matt said.

Suddenly everything was right again. He understood why she was working for the Teasdales, and they were talking, his face just inches from hers, with sunlight rather than shadows playing over his handsome features and no one to jostle or block her view as there'd been on New Year's Eve. She could admire at her leisure—his dark mustache outlining full, firm lips, the way his head bent toward her, the bronzed, muscled cords in his neck. The tinkling of the bell reminded Sabra of her duties. "Can . . . can I help you with anything else?"

Matt shook his head, though his eyes remained fixed on her face. "I'll just look around for a few minutes."

She sensed Sister Teasdale's disapproval as she hurried to wait on the customer. Like Charlie, Sister Teasdale acted as if he and Sabra were already engaged, and she frowned on anything that bordered on unfaithfulness to her son. *I'm not married to him,* Sabra wanted to say as she measured a yard of ribbon for Sister Patton. The simple purchase took twice its usual time as her eyes strayed to Matt while he examined a shovel, followed him as he paused to exchange a few words with the Teasdales.

There was an awkward moment when Charlie came in from the back room. As the two men nodded to each other, the awkwardness seemed to leap to the others and charge the air with tension. The tension didn't ease until it was revealed that Charlie had just gotten back with a wagonload of goods from the railroad station in Pearson and Matt asked for the latest news.

"They say Madero plans to slip back into Mexico," Charlie told them.

Animosity was forgotten as the newest rumor was discussed. What did it mean? Did Brother Teasdale think there would be fighting? Sabra listened to the men—Charlie's face solemn like his voice, Brother Teasdale's finger pointing for emphasis, Matt's dark brows lifting as he asked a question. She noted his concern and wondered how anyone could doubt Matt Cameron's loyalty.

When the subject of Madero had been exhausted, Matt excused himself and walked over to Sabra. "Are you going to the dance Friday night?"

She nodded.

"Will you save me a waltz?"

Her heart skipped as she wound the ribbon back onto the spool, and she had to wait for its beat to steady. "Yes," she answered, aware that others were listening.

Tension returned, manifest in Sister Teasdale's pursed lips and in the sullen look on Charlie's face. Sabra's eyes locked with Charlie's, daring him to say anything.

After Matt left, Brother Teasdale reminded Charlie that the wagon needed to be unloaded. Sabra saw Charlie nod as he and his mother followed Brother Teasdale to the back of the store, sighing in relief that a confrontation between Matt and Charlie hadn't occurred.

She picked up a feather duster and absently moved it over the shelves, smiling when she remembered the ruse about the nutmeg. She recognized it as a prelude, a foretaste of what was to come—the knowledge borne to her by the look she'd glimpsed in Matt's dark eyes.

Engrossed in her thoughts, Sabra climbed a ladder to clean the upper shelves. Charlie and his parents were forgotten as she lost herself in a world of dust motes, cans of baking powder, and images of Matt. She didn't see the whispered exchange between Charlie and his father, nor did she notice when his parents left the store.

"Sabra."

She jerked and almost lost her balance.

"I'm sorry. I didn't mean to startle you." Charlie's face turned ruddy as he waited for Sabra to get down from the ladder. The moment her foot reached the bottom rung, Charlie's hand took her elbow. "Father asked us to lock up. He and Mother have an early meeting tonight. I've put up the closed sign and locked the front door, but . . ." Charlie's arm went around her and his red head bent close.

"No . . ." She twisted her head and pushed Charlie away.

He immediately dropped his arms, his apologetic expression at odds with the longing in his eyes. "I'm sorry. I shouldn't have done that."

"No, you shouldn't have." Sabra used the ladder as a barrier between them.

"Don't be mad. Let me explain."

"You don't need to explain. Just forget it happened and finish locking up."

"No." His voice was resolute. He came around the ladder and grasped her hand. "We've got to talk, Sabra." He smiled at her. "Please. We can sit by the fire. It won't take long."

Realizing the inevitable was about to happen, Sabra followed Charlie to the stove at the rear of the store. When she was seated, Charlie cleared his throat. "I . . . I've been wanting to talk to you. I've spoken to your father. He's given me permission to . . ." Charlie paused and swallowed, " . . . to ask you to be my wife."

Sabra didn't want to hurt Charlie, but she certainly didn't want to encourage him. Before she could do either, he hurried on.

"You don't have to give your answer. I know you'll want time to think it over . . . I want you to think it over. Marriage is a big decision." He took a deep breath and smiled. "Did I tell you Father's made me a partner? I'll be able to support you . . . our children too."

His freckled face turned ruddy again. "Dad gum it, Sabra. I love you." His blue eyes looked into hers. "I love you. I'm hoping you'll come to feel the same."

"Thank you, Charlie." She was on her feet. "I appreciate the effort it took to share your feelings with me, but . . ."

"I know you don't feel as strongly as I do." Charlie's angular frame blocked her retreat. "And I know how popular you are. A man would have to be blind and addled to not want to marry you." His voice softened and the grin was back. "It's the chance I want, Sabra. Just the chance."

She gazed at the brass button on Charlie's blue vest. It was the same shade of washed-out blue as his eyes, one he'd pass on to his children . . . their children. Sabra took a deep breath. "It would be wrong to get your hopes up."

She brushed past a speechless Charlie to get her coat.

"It's Matt Cameron you like, isn't it?"

"I like lots of people." Sabra slipped her arms into her coat. "That's why I'm not ready for marriage."

"You're attracted to him. I can tell. And I saw how he was lookin' at you at the bonfire . . . how he couldn't keep his hands off you. He came into the store to see you today."

"Everyone in Cortéz comes into the store."

"Not to see you."

"Can I help it if Matt has good taste?"

"Sabra!" Charlie's exasperated chuckle rippled through the tension. "Look, I don't want to say anything bad about Matt. We used to play together. I shook his hand in a show of acceptance on Sunday. Just don't be setting your cap for him."

"I'm not setting my cap for anyone." The heels of Sabra's shoes drummed an angry staccato as she hurried to the back door.

"Maybe not, but don't let Matt's good looks make you forget what Brig Shumway saw him doing. Besides, he's a Mexican. White people don't marry Mexicans."

"Some people may think that way, but I don't. And I'll marry whoever I please." Sabra's words vibrated through the store as she slammed the door and stepped out into the gathering dusk. "At least I will if Matt asks me."

What if he didn't? Doubt pricked at her earlier optimism, and the Friday night dance seemed as far away as the distant Sierra Madre.

* * *

The longer Matt stayed in Cortéz, the easier it became. It wasn't that the people in the ward had actually changed, but there was certainly a visible thawing. Matt could tell people were wondering. After all, this was Matthew Cameron, the boy who'd lived among them most of his life, the young man who'd rescued the Patton baby from the river. All the good things about Helen's son were recalled, the recent rumors about him downplayed. But there were a few who persisted in thinking the worst.

"We've had the wool pulled over our eyes," Brother Murdock grumbled as he helped his neighbor haul a load of logs from the river bottom. "Fred says—"

"Forget what Fred says," Jesse Moffit interrupted. "Have you ever known Bishop Harris to be mistaken about a man's character?"

"No, but . . ." Burt Murdock paused and leaned his ample frame against the side of the wagon. "The sheriff in Casas Grandes described Matt to a tee. Just because he says it wasn't him, are you going to believe it? Where's his proof? Why did he wait so long to come back and deny it . . . say he had a twin?"

"I don't know," Brother Moffit conceded, "but I've lived around the block from Matt for years. I'll admit I've seen him get into a fair amount of mischief. There was that time he and his friends fed onions to the Patton cows before milking, and I remember how he nailed the door shut on the Anderson's outhouse, but I've never known Matt to do anything mean. I've never known him to lie, either. If he was caught doing something wrong, he was quick to own up to it . . . not to fib or try to weasel out of it like some boys I know . . ."

All of the criticism didn't come from the Murdocks, however. Although the Camerons closed rank around Matt in public, there were members of the family who wondered and questioned in private, the most notable being Joseph himself.

The last four years had been difficult for the Scotsman. Proud by nature, wanting the best for his children, the scandal surrounding

Matt had cut close to his heart. Looking back, Joseph didn't believe he'd failed as a father, though when he was being completely honest, he admitted there were times he'd shown partiality to his natural sons. Doing so didn't mean he hadn't loved Matty. He'd loved the boy more than he'd realized, given him responsibility, felt pride when Matt measured up. Perhaps that's why it hurt so much, why he felt betrayed. The betrayal rankled. Where would Matt be if he and Helen hadn't taken him in? Dirt poor and living in some one-room adobe shack, perhaps even dead.

Joseph's insides twisted each time he thought of how they'd been repaid, especially when he saw what it had done to Helen. He'd never known a woman with more patience and kindness, and all of it poured out on her adopted son. Although she continued to cling to Matt's story about his twin brother, all the talk and scandal had taken a toll. For a time she seemed to have shriveled and turned colorless, like leaves in the bleakness of winter, never singing or smiling. Each time he'd looked at Helen, his anger increased. Helpless to change what had happened, he could only blame others. The blame fell squarely onto Matt and his Mexican race. Where else had he learned to steal?

Joseph might have believed Matt as well. If his son had mentioned his twin when he'd told them about the cougar, Joseph would never have doubted him. But after so much time . . . Joseph shook his head. That night when he'd confronted Matt with the rumors, hadn't Matt's response been "I'd hoped you wouldn't find out"? It was only when they went into the house that Matt had back-tracked and said the rumors about him were lies. Now, watching Helen and Matt as they sat across from each other at the kitchen table, he could only clench his fists and leave the room.

Love for Helen prevented him from speaking his mind. One false word and Matt would be out the door. The Scotsman knew this as surely as if Matt had spoken it. The knowledge lay just under the surface next to their shared animosity, each knowing how the other felt—mistrusting and disliking while they strove to weave a veil of normalcy for Helen's sake.

"Won't you stay and have a bowl of rice pudding with us?" Helen called.

The lilt was back in her voice, and because Joseph loved hearing it, he turned and came back into the kitchen.

Helen ladled spoonfuls of the steaming pudding into three matching bowls. As she placed them on the table, a knock sounded on the back door. It was the oldest Anderson boy, bundled with coat and scarf against the January wind blowing down from the mountains.

"Mama sent me," the boy panted. "It's Lavena. She's got bad croup."

Helen reached for her coat. "I'll be right there." Seeing Joseph and Matt rise, she added, "There's no need for you to go. Stay and eat your pudding while it's hot." *And try talking to each other,* her eyes pleaded. *I'd sooner have you quarrel than this stiff politeness.*

An uneasy silence settled over the kitchen with the closing of the door. The men ate with lowered eyes, spoons clinking against bowls, neither one enjoying nor tasting the steaming pudding.

"Why don't you just come out and say you wished I hadn't come back?"

Joseph's head jerked, surprise warring with anger. "'Tis a waste of breath ta say what should be obvious."

"Why don't you want me back?"

Joseph's spoon paused on its journey from bowl to mouth. "Ye oughta ken the answer to that without askin'."

"But I am asking."

A pounding began in Joseph's ears. He wanted to strike Matt. Who did he think he was, challenging him like they were equals, forcing him to answer? When the words came, they were shouted, the years of festering hurt pouring from his mouth without thought of the consequences. "Because yer a hypocrite. Because ye lied to yer mother and the bishop aboot havin' a twin brother." Once he started, Joseph couldn't stop. He wanted to hurt Matt back, make him pay. Joseph's brogue thickened as he spoke. "Ech, yer nae but a lying thief. Should ha' left ye with yer own kind. Should ha' ken how 'twould turn out . . . breaking yer mother's heart." It was the mention of Helen that stopped him, his gray eyes glaring, a hand gripping the spoon.

Silence hummed with taut strings through the clock's loud ticking and the sound of the wind as it rattled the shingles. Where was the bairn who'd followed Joseph into the fields, a hoe balanced over his thin shoulder? Where was the laddie learning to drive a team? *"Tis a firm and steady hand they need, Matty. If ye'll remember that, ye'll nae ha' any trouble."* And the boy's quick smile. Always the smile, his brown eyes worshipful as they looked up into Joseph's. Now they were cold and filled with anger.

"I'm not a thief, and I've never lied to you . . . even when I was little and knew it meant a licking." Matt shoved back his chair and got to his feet.

Joseph continued to spoon the tasteless pudding into his mouth, eyes on the brown crockery bowl, his unsteady hand the only sign of his turmoil. A cold draft swept over him when the door opened, and he felt the vibration as it slammed shut.

Joseph dropped his spoon and half rose from his chair. "Dinna go, Matty." The hoarse words were drowned by the clatter of his spoon. The Scotsman's gnarled hands grasped the edge of the table, shoulders hunched, his head bowed. Was it possible his son was telling the truth?

CHAPTER 11

Two weeks passed, then a month, the days slipping by in a pleasant pattern of chores, farm tasks, and long talks around the stove in the evening with Helen and Harry. Since Matt had come back, Harry spent as much time with them as he did in his own home. He was glad to have Matt back, and neither he nor Helen wanted to see Matt go again. But they could see the wisdom in his leaving. Having both Matt and Joseph sitting at the same table put a terrible strain on them all.

Matt was surprised at how easily he picked up the threads of his old life—kneeling with Helen and Joseph before meals when it was Joseph's turn to be with Helen, reading scriptures after supper, Joseph's rousing him before dawn to get an early start on the chores. There were no slackers among the Camerons, though the number of boys had dwindled since Ted and Orson had joined Peter and Jake among the ranks of the married.

The years had taken their toll on Joseph. The Scotsman's mustache was grizzled, his step less vigorous. Even so, he banged on Matt's door each morning to tell him what to do. *If yer going ta eat my food, ye'll have ta work for it,* the knock said.

Matt prided himself on earning his keep, in doing more than his share. His share was taking up the slack left by his brothers who'd married and moved away. Sometimes while Matt and Joseph worked, the tension slipped away as muscled arms worked in unison with a two-man saw, or booted feet braced side by side as they pulled the top wire on the new fence they were stringing. Even so, it galled Matt to take orders from the Scotsman when the mountains were calling to him. But a girl with a dusting of freckles across her nose kept Matt firmly in Cortéz.

* * *

Matt was waiting for Sabra when she left the Union Mercantile on a February afternoon. The breeze tousled his dark hair as he took her elbow and matched his step with hers. "Sister Lindsey." The mischief in his eyes belied the formality of his tone. "Or may I call you Sabra."

"You may."

"And Nutmeg?"

"You're the only one who calls me Nutmeg."

"Do you mind?"

"No."

Matt's hand tightened on her arm as he helped her over the ditch and onto the path. His touch seemed to radiate through the heavy fabric of her green coat.

"May I walk you home?"

"If you'd like."

"What I'd like is to take you to the dance on Friday. Am I too late to ask?"

"No." Although her answer was demure, Sabra's face betrayed her delight. She'd waited weeks for the invitation, counting the days until the Friday dances. Whether she was at the dance or at meetings, she was aware of Matt's presence, her eyes constantly searching for the dark head, her ears listening for the deep timbre of his voice. And Matt had done the same with her. Each sought opportunity to talk and be together. "I'd like to go with you," she added.

A slow smile spread over Matt's face, lifting his mustache and crinkling the corners of his warm eyes. "I'll be by to pick you up a little before eight."

He arrived fifteen minutes before the hour, dressed in a dark suit and white shirt with a freshly starched collar. Sabra hurried down the stairs to meet him. She paused on the bottom step, aware of Matt's approval, knowing the emerald-green dress she wore became her. The dress was inspired by her long-ago daydreams.

Elizabeth's unsmiling presence at the bottom of the stairs cut at her happiness. Her mother had been upset when she found out Sabra was going to the dance with Matt.

"I wonder why Charlie isn't here?" Elizabeth had asked.

"I'm not going with Charlie."

"Oh . . ." Elizabeth's eyebrows raised. "Then who?"

"Matt Cameron."

"Matt . . ." Elizabeth's usually placid voice cracked and her mouth tightened. "You know how your father feels about him. He's not what we want for you. Besides, what will Charlie think?"

"I really don't care what Charlie thinks."

Elizabeth clamped her lips shut and turned to leave. "You're not to accept any more invitations from Matt Cameron," she called over her shoulder.

"Why are you so quick to think the worst of Matt? Why can't you believe he has a twin brother?"

Instead of answering, Elizabeth hurried to alert Samuel before Matt arrived.

Sabra watched the two men shake hands. *Please don't let Papa say anything rude,* she prayed. Thank heaven he hadn't. At least not out loud, though the rigid set of his jaw spoke volumes. *What's wrong?* she wanted to cry. *Can't you see anyone but Charlie?* Sabra handed Matt her coat while imploring her father with a look not to lecture Matt about how soon he should have her home.

Samuel ignored the look, his anger manifest in his brusque voice. "Sister Lindsey and I will be leaving the dance when it ends at midnight. We expect you to have Sabra home by twelve fifteen . . . not a minute later."

"I'll see that she's here." Matt's eyes held Samuel's in a steady gaze. "Harry and Myrtle Hamblin will be riding in the buggy with us, so we won't be alone."

He nodded, respecting Matt's honesty even as he tried to put the memory of how Sabra had defended Matt out of his mind. He'd sensed her attraction for the Mexican all those years ago. And now . . . his chest constricted when he saw the glow in his daughter's eyes. Why hadn't Matthew Cameron stayed away?

"Don't worry, Papa," she whispered, kissing him on the cheek. Then she felt Matt's hand on her arm and forgot everything else.

Neither of them spoke as they walked down the front path to the waiting buggy. The easy camaraderie had disappeared, replaced by an awareness of each other that was both exciting and disturbing. The awareness increased when Matt helped Sabra into the back of the buggy and took his place beside her on the wooden seat. She could hear his soft breathing, the quick rasp of his shoes as he shifted to keep his balance when Harry started the team.

"Are you warm enough?"

Sabra nodded and tried to control the nervous shivers racing up and down her spine. Was Matt as excited as she was?

Harry grinned and looked back at them. "Charlie wasn't pleased when I told him Matt was takin' you to the dance. He seems to think you're his girl."

"Well, I'm not. I'm not anyone's girl."

"Seth will be happy to hear that. So will Matt. Has he told you about the ranch he's plannin' to buy? Ol' Charlie better watch out." Harry chuckled and winked at Sabra.

Sabra stole a glance at Matt. By the set of his jaw, he'd probably have a few choice words with his brother when they got home. No one spoke until they reached the Hamblins.

"I'll be back in a minute," Harry said. He gave them a quick grin, clearly enjoying himself.

Matt grimaced as he watched Harry's retreating figure blend with the shadows. "Unfortunately my brother likes to talk."

"So does Charlie."

"You can't blame him. When a man finds the right woman, he doesn't want anyone to steal her away." There was a long pause while Matt gazed at Sabra. He reached over and took her hand.

Instead of snatching it away as Sabra had been taught, she let it stay in the warmth of Matt's slender fingers. She knew that by doing so she might be considered "fast," but her pleasure overrode any thought of censure.

"I need to talk to you . . . explain about where I've been," Matt began. He covered her fingertips with the palm of his other hand. The few minutes he'd spent in the Lindsey parlor had told him it wasn't going to be easy finding time alone with Sabra. And Harry and Myrtle were already on their way out to the buggy.

Neither spoke while the couple climbed into the buggy, but Sabra focused only on Matt. Was she wicked for letting him hold her hand?

All her thoughts, everything she did, had taken on new life since Matt's return. How could anything so wonderful be wrong?

* * *

The rest of the evening passed to the sound of stamping feet and clapping hands. "Bow to your partner, then circle all," Uncle Ernie called in his familiar voice.

Their fingers touched and parted as they passed each other in the reel, Matt's dark eyes smiling at Sabra. Now that he was back, life was good, so very good. If only Papa and Mama would smile. She saw them standing just outside the circle of lamplight, their pensive expressions gnawing at her happiness.

Matt saw them too. By unspoken agreement, they strove to hide their interest in each other. He danced with his mother and a bevy of other matrons and young cousins while Sabra made a show of enjoying herself with Charlie and Seth. She even flirted with Charlie, hoping to erase the hangdog expression from his face.

It seemed an eternity before Uncle Ernie announced a waltz. Sabra watched Matt come across the floor to claim her. All her daydreams meshed in the lithe figure walking toward her, meshed again as he extended his brown hand and smiled. She pushed thoughts of her parents and Charlie out of her mind.

They moved through the dance without speaking, Sabra pirouetting under Matt's arm, their glances meeting and holding each time she began her turn. She wanted to tell Matt of her happiness. Instead, she found herself apologizing. "I'm sorry about my parents . . . that they weren't more friendly tonight."

Matt was aware of Sister Lindsey's stiff expression, the questioning look on Bishop Harris's face, the glare on Charlie's. Sabra's parents weren't the only ones he'd have to deal with. He'd have to go slowly, give everyone in Cortéz time to get used to the idea. It wasn't going to be easy. Not with Sabra looking at him that way. "They'll come around," he promised her.

"I know, but . . ." She licked her lips and hurried on. "It's just that Charlie's already spoken to Papa. I think my parents have kinda settled on him."

"But you haven't?"

"No." Matt's hand was on her waist, leading her into a pirouette, its pressure letting her know he was pleased.

The dance ended far too soon. Sabra's parents were waiting when she went to get her coat, the expression on Sam Lindsey's face as stern and unfriendly as Brother Clawson's had been years ago.

"I expect you to be home in fifteen minutes," Samuel said as he and Elizabeth left the hall. He glanced at Matt, his voice commanding obedience.

"We'll be there." Matt looked around for Harry and saw him coming with Myrtle and her two sisters.

"Myrtle's mother wasn't feeling well, so her parents went home early. Is it all right if her sisters ride home with us?"

Matt had hoped to have some time alone with Sabra so they could plan a way to meet and talk. But there were advantages to the inconvenience too. Lucy Hamblin's ample frame took up half of the backseat and gave them an excuse to sit close. Matt slipped his fingers under the cuff of Sabra's coat sleeve and found her hand. Lucy began to chatter the moment they left the church and didn't stop until the buggy pulled in front of the Lindsey home.

"That girl has more stamina than brains," Matt whispered as he swung Sabra down from the buggy.

Her giggle was cut short when she saw the front door open, spilling a shaft of lamplight onto the porch.

"It's time to come in, Sabra," Samuel called.

"We need to talk," Matt whispered. "I'll figure a way for us to meet." Then he nodded to Samuel and strode down the moon-washed path to the waiting buggy.

* * *

They met under the acacia tree on the bluff, the one whose hanging branches had shared Sabra's daydreams and her longing for freedom all those years before. She tried to control her excitement as she watched Matt dismount and walk toward her. They'd come from opposite directions—Matt from the farm, Sabra from town, neither telling anyone of their meeting.

"You've come." Gladness sounded in Matt's voice. He'd been afraid she wouldn't be there, that someone or something would prevent her from getting away.

"Yes."

Matt sensed her shyness, saw hesitancy warring with the joy shining in her green eyes. He'd told her they must talk, and talk they would, but not before he'd had a moment to savor her beauty and nearness.

She wore a white, high-collared blouse and black riding skirt, a green ribbon fastened around the collar and a matching ribbon in her hair that hung in curls past her shoulders. Matt only meant to look at her, savor, but before he realized what he was doing, his fingers brushed a wisp of chestnut hair away from Sabra's cheek. Everything was quiet, with only the wind for company; all thought of talk had vanished. He wanted to pull her into his arms and tell her what he was feeling. Instead, he took both of her hands in his.

"I brought a quilt so we can be more comfortable while we talk." Matt's cheeks warmed when he thought of what the cowboys on the Ojo Mendello would have said to that. But this wasn't the Ojo Mendella. And Sabra wasn't Maria.

Matt spread the blanket on a patch of brittle grass near the base of the tree. They sat with a small space between them, knowing distance was wise. He hesitated, unsure of how to begin. What should he say? How much should he tell her? Whatever he said, it must be the truth. "I want to tell you where I've been . . . what I've done," he began. And then he was into the telling—of his twin brother and Don de Vega, the fight with Joseph, and his decision to leave Cortéz. He paused, his heart lifting when she smiled.

"Your mother said a few things about your twin brother." Gladness sang in Sabra's voice. Having him tell her himself, watching the steadiness of his gaze, added substance to her belief. "But some people thought . . ." Matt knew what they'd thought. "I didn't want to believe the rumors, but I knew how angry you were . . . maybe angry enough to do what people were saying."

"That's what I set out to do. I even planned to join up with Rafael." Matt didn't like to remember the two days he'd spent with his brother. Rafael had changed, the affable Mexican he'd met in the mountains was so hardened by hatred and bitterness there was no room for reason. No room for trust, either.

"A couple of days with Rafael were enough. The men he rode with were pretty desperate. That's when I decided to go north."

He told Sabra about the Ojo Mendello Ranch in Texas, his first tentative steps into manhood, the razzing and teasing. "I didn't let anyone know I was Mormon. After the way I'd been treated, I decided I wasn't . . . at least I thought so. I tried a few of the Gentile ways." The troubled look on her face made Matt hesitate. What if he'd misjudged her? What if she wouldn't understand? "I tried a few smokes. Coffee, too. I even got drunk once."

"I thought you might have." The quiver in Sabra's voice cut at Matt's heart. She leaned toward him, her expression earnest. "I understand why you did it . . . your need to find your own way. Sometimes I feel it too—the restlessness, not always wanting to conform, but . . ." There was a pause, a moment of awkwardness. "I guess what I'm trying to say is . . . do you plan to keep your new ways?"

He shook his head "I gave them up a long time ago." After his first trip into McNary, in fact. Matt didn't want to burden Sabra with a description of that outing, his excitement as he rode into town with the other cowboys, money jingling in his pocket, a chance to celebrate. Cowboy celebrating wasn't anything like Mormon celebrating. Music from saloons beckoned, liquor flowed, there were card games and women. Except for the women, Matt had tried them all, matching Luke drink for drink, laughing and swearing as loud as the rest. His head was swimming by the time he made an unsteady trail to the card table. Luke and Bernie had taught him a few tricks. Now was his chance to win some money, maybe a nest egg for a ranch.

Two hours later Matt sat in the dust by the hitching rail, water dripping from his head after he'd doused it in the water trough, pockets empty. What would Helen think if she could see him now? It was a long, lonely ride back to the Ojo Mendello, one that had given him plenty of time to think. After that, he'd stayed at the ranch on payday.

"Can you forgive me?" he asked.

"There's nothing to forgive." Sabra was smiling again, the sight of it loosening the tightness in his chest. She understood that he'd changed.

Understanding didn't prevent a sudden constraint to settle around them. Matt sensed it even before he saw her smile fade, sensed it again as he watched her clasped hands tighten.

"Were there . . ." Sabra's tongue flicked over her lips. "Were there any girls at the Ojo Mendello?"

The tightness returned. Matt didn't like to remember Maria, but he'd promised to tell Sabra the truth. "There was a girl who worked in the kitchen."

Sabra's mouth settled into a tremulous line, her green eyes clouded. "What was her name?"

"Maria." Maria with liquid brown eyes and swaying hips, who'd tempted Matt almost past bearing—teasing, provoking. The cowboys thought Matt a fool for not taking what was freely offered. Now, as he looked into Sabra's questioning eyes, he counted himself fortunate. "I kissed her a few times. That's all."

Sabra sat without speaking, her gaze on her clasped hands. She hadn't expected that hearing about Maria would hurt so much. What had she looked like? Was she pretty? Part of her wanted to know, ferret out all the painful details, picture it in her mind. The need to protect won out. "Did you love her?" This last slipped out before she could stop it, her voice low, lips trembling.

"No."

She gathered his answer to her heart, held it close, needing its reassurance.

As if he knew her need, Matt took her hand. "Those I love are here in Mexico, not in Texas."

The hurt vanished like frost in April sunshine. Sabra lifted her head to look at him. When she did, she knew he was going to kiss her, knew it as surely as she knew she loved him. It was in his face, in the shimmer of his dark eyes, in his parted lips. She closed her eyes when Matt's fingers caressed her cheek, his touch soft as velvet, soft as his lips when they reached her mouth. Without knowing what she did, and with the words of caution taught by her mother forgotten, her hands found their way around his neck as he pulled her close and his mouth firmed against hers.

The kiss ended far too soon. For a moment Sabra felt bereft, as if all she had longed for had been taken away. Then she felt Matt's brown fingers cup her chin, heard the sound of his voice as he whispered her name. She slowly opened her eyes, and the day became complete when she saw her own happiness reflected in Matt Cameron's face.

CHAPTER 12

The days lengthened with the coming of early spring. Leaf buds swelled and winter-browned lawns took on suggestions of green. Sabra gloried in each change, stopping to touch the hopeful buds, lifting her face to the warmth of the sun as she walked to the Union Mercantile. There were other changes that had nothing to do with the weather. Nor were they as pleasant. Since she'd refused Charlie's proposal, the atmosphere at the store was charged with tension. Sister Teasdale scarcely spoke to her, and Sabra never knew what to expect from Charlie. Some days he was his old self, eager to please and smiling, but on mornings after she'd danced with Matt, he looked hurt and his face was stiff with disapproval.

Home was no better. Lately her family seemed to be joined against Matt. Although he wasn't exactly courting her, the two of them managed to be together—parties at the Shumways', a taffy pull at Becky's . . . even with others around, she and Matt always found time to talk and share ideas. These times together reinforced Sabra's knowledge that Matt held all the qualities she wanted in a husband.

One evening as they finished supper, Samuel pushed back his chair and directed a stern gaze at Sabra. "Your mother and I would like a word with you."

"Me? But why?"

Instead of answering, Samuel led the way into the parlor and waited while Sabra and Elizabeth seated themselves on the sofa. When he closed the tall, double doors against her brother's inquisitive ears, Sabra knew she was in for a lecture.

Samuel paced the length of the parlor floor, pausing to adjust the wick on the lamp, then going to stand by the fireplace. She watched with growing unease, the rhythmic ticking of the mantel clock emphasizing the silence. She glanced at her mother, whose eyes were averted as she rolled the corner of her gingham apron between work-worn fingers.

"Has Charlie asked you to marry him yet?" Samuel finally asked.

"Yes."

"Did you accept?"

"No."

The quick release of her mother's in-drawn breath seemed to fill the parlor. Sabra stared at the pink roses on the wallpaper and willed herself to be calm. *They won't make me marry Charlie. They can't.*

"Charlie's a fine young man. He'll make a good husband."

"I know. I like Charlie too. But . . ." She lifted her green eyes to meet her father's. "I don't love him, Papa."

"Love . . ." Samuel's bristly mustache tightened. "There's more to marriage than love. You've said you like him. That's how love begins. Please, reconsider."

Sabra bit back a protest. *Wait,* she told herself. *Give them time to get used to Matt.* "I'll think about it."

The muscles in Samuel's jaw relaxed. "You know we're only thinking of your future . . . your happiness. Charlie's a good worker. He loves you and he's strong in the Church."

Samuel's voice droned on. Everything he said about Charlie was true. But none of it changed her feelings. "Please . . . may I go?"

Her father stopped in mid-sentence.

"May I be excused? Becky invited some of the crowd over to play charades tonight. I'll be late if I don't hurry."

"Will Matt be there?"

Sabra had never lied to her father. She didn't want to start now. "I don't know for certain." Then in a stronger voice. "Yes."

She watched her father's features tighten with indecision. Would he forbid her to go, or would fear that she'd secretly meet Matt cause him to be more cautious?

"Please, Papa."

At his nod, she started toward the door.

"Sabra." Elizabeth put out a detaining hand. "I understand why you're drawn to Matthew. He's handsome and he has many good qualities. But don't forget that no one except his family and the bishop knows what he did while he was away."

"I know what he did, and it's not what you and everyone else think." She lifted her head and met her mother's gaze. "I know he has a twin, and I don't care about the silly rumors. Neither should you. After the way Matt was treated, wouldn't you want to leave? The important thing is that he came back. He talked to the bishop. That's all that should matter."

Elizabeth's only answer was a quick shake of her head.

Samuel wasn't so reticent. "It can't be, Sabra. Your mother and I have talked it over and it can't be."

She wanted to ask why, to force her father to admit to his prejudice. Caution held her back. "We'll only be playing charades. Everyone will be there. Becky and Seth and Ralph . . ." But she'd only see Matt, who was never far from her thoughts. All she did, all she saw, was colored by her feelings for him. She loved him and was loved in return, though he'd never told her so. He didn't need to. She knew it, as every woman knows—by his look, in the tone of his voice—even as she sensed his restraint and recognized the need for caution. Her parents needed time to get used to the idea. The whole town needed time. And she must try to learn patience. Her father looked cautious, but also relieved, and Sabra nodded as she hurried from the room.

* * *

The drabness of the desert brightened with the coming of spring. Tender shoots of grass pushed through the rocky soil, and the barren bluffs took on shadings of red and yellow as cactus and mesquite came into bloom.

Seeking release after a week of plowing, Ralph Shumway invited his friends out to the grove to celebrate his twentieth birthday.

Sabra's heart was light as she climbed into a wagon filled with quilts, picnic basket, and giggling girls. Her excitement increased when she looked for Matt and saw him following on horseback with Harry and the other young men. Unfortunately, Charlie was there too. So was Rob, though he was so besotted with Clara Mortensen that Sabra hoped he'd forget to try to keep her and Matt apart.

The grove lay in a grassy hollow carved by the Casas Grandes River. Situated five miles south of town, it was a favorite place for picnics and outings. The young people converged on it with high-spirited shouts and laughter. Quilts and picnic baskets were left with the wagon as Ralph and his friends climbed the giant cottonwoods to fasten long ropes to their branches. The results gave the grove a carnival air, and the young women quickly lined up for a turn on the swings.

Sabra chose the swing closest to Matt, but Charlie was there too, stubbornly keeping close to her side. She caught a fleeting glimpse of Matt as she flew into the air, saw his blue chambray shirt framing his face, his smile widening when she squealed with excitement.

Charlie continued to follow her, sticking like a troublesome burr and making it almost impossible to talk with Matt. It wasn't until they'd finished eating and Harry challenged Charlie to a game of horseshoes that they had their chance. Matt slipped away first, and Sabra was quick to follow, hurrying so Ralph's parents wouldn't see.

They ran hand in hand along the riverbank, laughing and looking back over their shoulders like two errant pupils playing hooky from school. When they finally stopped and turned to face each other, their laughter faded, and Sabra's eyes were bright like sun glints on water as Matt's finger slowly traced the contour of her flushed cheek.

She closed her eyes as Matt's arms went around her, memorizing the feel of his lips on her cheek, the catch in his voice as he whispered. "I love you." It was everything she'd dreamed of—the three small words and her own given in quick reply, a promise like her kiss had been under the acacia tree, a giving of herself and the knowledge she would never be complete except with Matt.

"I guess you know I want to marry you," Matt said.

"No . . . but I hoped you did."

"I do."

It took great effort for Matt to pull away, to move his hands to her arms and keep her at a safe distance.

"We need to talk."

They sat side by side, hands interlocked, backs resting against the trunk of a cottonwood.

"I have to go away for a few days. Probably for a week or two," Matt began.

Sabra's heart plunged. "Why?"

"To buy a ranch. It's what I was saving for while I was in Texas. If we're to marry, we'll need a home." This last stilled her protest. "I planned to leave right after New Year's, but then I saw you." He smiled and tightened his fingers on hers as he added, "I think it will be better if we live away from the colonies."

Sabra's eyes widened. "Do you think things in Mexico are that bad? Papa says if we continue to keep to ourselves, the revolutionists won't hurt us."

It took Matt a second to realize where Sabra's thoughts had flown. It was always just under the surface, the fear of being caught in the middle of the burning and carnage of the revolution.

"Do you think things are bad enough for us to leave?" she repeated.

Matt thought of sturdy homes set behind greening lawns, homes built with the idea of living in Mexico indefinitely, perhaps forever. Now with the revolution, some Mormons were having second thoughts. Since the Church no longer sanctioned new plural marriages, the doors to the United States were opened again. "It's better to give up a farm and comfortable home than risk harm to our wives and children," some of the colonists argued. But most had taken a wait-and-see attitude.

"I think the Mormons will be all right," Matt answered. "That's not why I want to move away."

"Oh." Sabra's eyes were on his face, her expression questioning and a little fearful. "You said *Mormons,* as if . . ." Her voice broke. "Aren't you one of us?"

"I am." His determination to follow a middle course separate from the Mormons had ended after his talk with Bishop Harris. It hadn't been the gospel he'd rejected, only the prejudice. "You must know I'm not the most popular man in Cortéz right now. It will be easier for us if we live somewhere else."

Sabra nodded. A fresh start away from Cortéz with its veiled innuendoes about Matt was a good idea. She hoped it wouldn't be too far away, though. She'd miss her parents, her brothers too. "Where do you plan to look?"

"In the mountains." Matt lifted her hand to his lips. "You'll love it up there. Bishop Harris says Brother Whiting wants to sell. He has a place above Garcia. I plan to ride up there as soon as I finish helping fa . . . Joseph with the plowing."

"I've always wanted to see the mountains." Her voice turned pensive. "How is it with your . . . with Brother Cameron?"

"Not good. He's thawed a little, but in his eyes I've sullied his good name. Even though Mother told him about Rafael, he's afraid I'm lying." Matt turned to Sabra. "It's a good name I offer you, Nutmeg. You won't ever need to be ashamed of being Matthew Cameron's wife."

"I know." Her eyes glowed with love. "But must you leave so soon?"

Matt nodded. "If I can settle on a fair price with Brother Whiting, we can move up to the ranch this fall. I heard Mother say two couples from Juarez are planning to make a wedding trip up to the St. George Temple in June. We can go with them." Matt's eyes looked steadily into hers. "Our marriage won't be easy. Your family . . . the members of the ward. A lot of people aren't going to like it."

"So?" Seeing the concern in Matt's eyes, she added, "Don't fret about my parents. When Papa and Mama see how happy we are, they'll come around." *And if they don't?* Sabra refused to consider the possibility. All her life she'd struggled with the need to conform; the love she felt for her parents balanced in a delicate tug-of-war with her need for freedom. This time her deep feelings for her family had come up short. Nothing could keep her from marrying Matt Cameron. Nothing.

* * *

It was Harry who interrupted their interlude—grinning, irritating Harry who led two horses and a flustered Becky by his side. "When I saw Becky looking for Sabra and I couldn't find you, I figured you'd gone off together." Harry's grin widened when he noted Sabra's flushed cheeks. "Someone else is a mite upset about your where-abouts. To avoid Charlie, I suggest we all go for a ride."

"Why a ride?" Matt asked.

"A little distance between you and Charlie might be a good idea, especially with Charlie's temper. Then, when we come ridin' back together, there's not much he can say. Rob, either. The four of us spent the afternoon together. No one went off alone. That should take care of the gossips."

Since there were only two horses, they had to ride double. As Matt urged the horse into a canter, Sabra savored the feel of her arms around Matt's waist, her face resting against his muscular shoulders. She liked the clean smell of him and the feel of the coarse chambray shirt and dark blue bandanna knotted around his neck.

They followed the course of the river, their voices low so no one would hear. The day seemed to mirror Sabra's happiness. Sunlight danced off the water and played through spring-tender grass. She watched a mother quail hurry her newly hatched chicks into the undergrowth while a white-faced steer drank from a shallow pool. There was only sunlight, Matt's closeness, and the knowledge of his love.

The crack of a rifle shattered the quiet. For a heart-jerking second, Matt knew panic. Had Charlie and Rob gone mad? A pitiful bellow and a splash drew his eyes to the river where the steer floundered in bloody water.

"What the . . ." Before he could say more, a group of Mexicans rode into the river. They stopped in midstream, hands moving to rifles when they spied Matt and Harry. Matt dug his heels into the gelding's sides as a bullet sang past his head and slammed into the trunk of a tree.

"Alto!" a harsh voice ordered.

Fearing the next bullet would plow into the soft flesh of Sabra's back, Matt swung the horse to face the Mexicans. Over a dozen men with bandoliers crisscrossing their chests had rifles trained on them. Their grubby white shirts and pants told Matt they weren't government soldiers. He could feel the rapid beat of Sabra's heart through the cotton fabric of his shirt. "Keep your head down and stay behind me," he whispered. He snatched a quick look at the other couple. Becky looked ready to cry, and a tight-lip grimace had replaced Harry's ready grin.

"Put your hands up," one of the Mexican's ordered in Spanish. When Matt didn't move, the soldier brandished his gun.

"Please, Matt. Do what he says," Sabra whispered.

Keeping a wary eye on the men, he slowly raised his hands.

"That's better." A burly rider with his gun trained on Matt urged his horse past the steer and up the riverbank. "An army must have food," he explained.

"It should pay for what it takes," Matt countered. "Señor Schmidt will come after you when he sees what you've done to his steer."

The rebel soldier shrugged, his eyes intent on their horses. "An army also needs caballos."

Matt's hands dropped to the reins. "No, you don't."

"Get your hands up."

As Matt reluctantly complied, another soldier rode out of the trees and spurred his horse across the shallow river.

"Villa has found a place where we can get food and more caballos. He wants us there. *Rápido!*"

The burly soldier kept his gun on Matt and Harry. "What about these gringos and their caballos?"

The other soldier sat on his mount with a ramrod back while his eyes darted over them, seeming to take in each detail of their person. Matt's stomach tightened when the soldier's gaze lingered on Sabra.

"Leave the beef. There's plenty more where we're going. But the gringos . . ." The soldier rode his horse close and jammed his rifle into Matt's side. "What is a Mexican doing with gringos?"

"They're my people," Matt replied. "They raised me after my madre died."

The rebel's cold eyes shifted to Sabra, his lips lifting at the sight of her bunched-up skirt. "So you intend to sample the *señorita*'s charms? A smart man, amigo." His chuckle rippled the air as he ordered his companions to surround the prisoners. "The gringos go with us. Villa can decide what to do with them."

Knowing escape was impossible, Matt placed his hand over Sabra's. "Stay calm," he whispered. "Don't let them know you're scared."

"Who's scared?" Sabra's voice was unsteady. Using a rock against Carlos was one thing. Being captured by rebel soldiers was quite another matter. Thank heaven Matt was with her . . . and Harry— exasperating Harry who never seemed to have anything on his mind except a good time. Now his teasing blue eyes were watchful, and tense lines tightened his jaw.

"Are they really taking us to Pancho Villa?" Sabra asked.

"Silence!" the leader ordered.

A similar question raced through Matt's mind. Rumor said the famous bandit had joined the revolution, rallying other bandits and calling on the peóns to help return the land to the villagers. Although the cause Villa espoused might be just, Matt wondered if such a man could be trusted. More than that, bandits did not have a reputation for kindness.

They rode for more than a mile, the horses splashing across the river and up an incline bordering the ranch owned by Wilhelm Schmidt, a wealthy German whose thrift and industry rivaled that of his Mormon neighbors. Herr Schmidt had staked his claim on land along the Casas Grandes River. Now his ranch was stocked with the finest horses and cattle in northern Mexico, and his barns were filled with grain and hay. A section of barbed wire fence had been cut. The trampled earth and fresh horse droppings gave evidence that a large party of men had recently passed through the opening.

The leader urged them on. Surrounded by stern-faced rebels whose expressions only lightened when someone made crude remarks about the girls' exposed legs, Matt was forced to suffer in silence. If only he had a gun. If only they'd stayed at the picnic with the others. If only . . .

The man in command lifted his hand when they crested a ridge overlooking Wilhelm Schmidt's ranch house. The area between the house and barns swarmed with men, a ragtag army whose threadbare clothes and wide-brimmed sombreros served as uniforms. Matt saw guns and heard voices followed by bursts of laughter. Herr Schmidt's ranch had been taken over by the rebel army.

Sabra peered over Matt's shoulder. "There's so many," she whispered.

Matt nodded. "Hopefully all they want is food and a few horses."

"They can't just take his horses." Sabra's voice was indignant. The sight of a portly figure being dragged from one of the barns forced her to silence. Of course the soldiers could take Herr Schmidt's horses. So many armed men could take anything they had a mind to.

Even though Wilhelm Schmidt wasn't a Mormon, he'd often traded at the Union Mercantile, his broken English punctuated with gestures as he strove to make himself understood. Sabra saw Herr Schmidt's arms waving now as he argued with the soldiers. Her heart went out to the rotund German whose Spanish was probably as atrocious as his English. He had no chance against so many. Like them, he must bide his time for a chance to escape.

Their progress into the yard was scarcely noted. Everyone's attention was centered on the German, who suddenly broke from his captors and scrambled under a wooden manger.

The afternoon air was peppered with ribald shouts as two soldiers snaked Wilhelm out of his ineffective hiding place. "Look at the fat little pig I've caught . . . just the right size to skewer on the end of my sword," one of them chortled.

Several pretended to do just that, poking Schmidt's generous girth with the points of their bayonets. The German cried out when he was thrust toward a horseman who laughingly watched the spectacle from an area apart from the others.

Sabra studied the horseman's round, almost handsome face, watched his mustached lips lift in amusement. Authority sat on the man's broad shoulders as casually as he sat his horse. "Is that Villa?"

"It must be."

"Perhaps we should butcher the German instead of one of his beefs," Pancho Villa chuckled.

"Nein . . . nein." Herr Schmidt's quivering protest ended in a squeak when the prod of Villa's scuffed boot sent him sprawling into the dirt.

"On second thought, we'll take your horses and a few beefs instead. My men are hungry." Pancho Villa's eyes glinted with pleasure as he surveyed the pasture where Wilhelm's prize stallion grazed. "Round up all the caballos," he called.

"Nein ...." Wilhelm swallowed his protest when Villa's hand moved to his pistol.

"I'm tired of playing games, *Gordo*. I need caballos and food for my men." Villa wheeled his horse and called to the soldiers rounding up the horses. "Don't forget the ones in the barns. Rápido! We don't have all day."

The army came to life, opening the barn doors and hurrying to empty the chicken coop, Spanish oaths accompanying the frantic squawks of chickens. Only then did the bandit turn his attention to the new arrivals. "What have we here?"

Their captor saluted, his chest expanding with importance. "We found these gringos when we were scouting for food. Their caballos look good. And the señoritas . . ." His smile widened.

Matt urged his horse toward Villa. "The señoritas are daughters of American citizens. If anything happens to them, you'll have the American government after you."

"Americanos," Villa spat the word. The bandit was astute, however. If he and Madero won their fight against Diaz, they needed American support and sympathy. His wide-spaced, brown eyes moved from the girls to Matt, and a look of speculation flitted across his face. "I thought I recognized you." The dark head and felt hat nodded. "How long has it been? One year? Two? We must have another talk sometime. But now . . ." He turned a harsh look on their captor. "Set the gringos free. We don't want trouble with Americanos."

The soldier's jaw dropped. "Their caballos . . ."

"Gordo has given us his. The gringos go free."

Hearing his words, Matt dug his heels into the gelding's side and sent them through the melee of men and back up the ridge. Sabra tightened her grip on Matt's waist, the sharp staccato of her heart melding with the horse's hoofbeats. She glanced back and saw Harry and Becky following. Villa was letting them go! Relief smothered the dredges of fear as she laid her face against Matt's broad shoulders. *Thank you, Father . . .*

No one spoke until they neared the river. "What was that all about?" Harry asked in an unsteady voice. "Villa acted like he knew you."

"Knew my twin brother," Matt said.

"Well, I'll be a horny toad." Harry shook his head. "I don't know about you, but meeting up with Charlie doesn't seem half bad after what we've just been through."

Instead of answering, Matt set the gelding on a course back to the grove. It wasn't Charlie who worried him. It was Rafael. When was his twin brother going to stop being a problem? More important, what were Rafael's connections with Pancho Villa?

CHAPTER 13

The incident at the Schmidts' ranch brought the reality of the revolution more forcibly into the colonists' minds. Perhaps their policy of minding their business and treating the Mexicans fairly wouldn't guarantee that they would be left alone. Although Wilhelm Schmidt wasn't a Mormon, Villa's high-handed manner with the German served as a warning to all. In time of war, no one was safe.

The next few days seemed to bear out this conclusion. A Mexican farmer was hit by a bullet when Villa's men encountered a government patrol near Colonia Diaz. Then word arrived that Madero had attempted to take control of Casas Grandes. Several lives had been lost and parts of the town damaged. The news put match to rumor. Some claimed Madero had been wounded. Others said it was the *federale* General Cuellar. The rumors had an unsettling effect on Cortéz. Although the Mormons governed themselves ecclesiastically, politically they were under the jurisdiction of Mexican authorities in Casas Grandes. But who were the authorities? Madero, the revolutionist, or the federales under Diaz?

Wilhelm Schmidt didn't wait to find out. Badly frightened, he offered Martin Cluff ten dollars to take him and his wife safely across the border into Texas. Schmidt's departure served to increase the tension. Maybe they should all leave.

"We haven't been hurt yet," Bishop Harris advised the men on Sunday morning. "Church authorities in both Salt Lake and Juarez have advised us to remain calm. Unless things take a decided turn for the worse, I think we should stay put and continue to go about our business."

Most agreed. Agreement didn't mean they weren't going to take precautions, though. Harry and Matt hid a rifle in the hollow of a willow tree out on the farm. Another rifle was kept in readiness at home.

"Just in case," Joseph said. "'Tis better to be prepared than sorry."

Sam Lindsey's only gun was taken out and oiled, and Sabra was admonished to stay close to the house.

"No more riding out to the bluff," her mother told her. "When I think of what could have happened." Elizabeth's lips compressed into a tight line. "You're lucky you weren't killed. If you'd stayed in the grove with Charlie, you wouldn't have been seen by Villa's soldiers."

"No one was hurt," Sabra argued.

"But you could have been. Matt had no business taking you off like that. Remember what your father said. No more, Sabra. We can't have you seeing Matthew Cameron anymore."

"Please, Mama, we've been over this a hundred times." *More like a thousand,* Sabra thought, as she cleared dirty dishes from the table. And they'd probably go right on quarreling about it. That's all they did anymore. Anger welled up in her throat. Instead of accepting Matt, her parents seemed to hate him. Even Willie had taken to saying mean things about Matt. Tranquility, the lodestone of the Lindsey home, had vanished, taking Sabra's safe, familiar world with it. If only her parents would listen and try to understand. If only she could be with Matt.

Scarcely aware of what she was doing, Sabra ladled hot water into the dishpan, then added a dipper of cold. Everything was such a tangle—all the wrangling, love warring with hurt, the ultimatums. Thoughts of Matt were all that brought Sabra any pleasure. Her mind flew to him now, folding around him like fingers clinging to a talisman. Now Matt was her lodestone, her world.

Sabra wondered how this could be, how in the midst of sorrow she could also know happiness. It was as if she had become two people, one torn and battered by the bickering, the other drifting just beyond the contention, eyes turned inward, thinking only of Matt. Since they'd kissed, Sabra's senses had intensified, her awareness sharpened. The beauty of familiar things was viewed through new eyes—the warm tones of the desert, a pattern of clouds against a cobalt sky, even the leafing trees took on beauty, their branches intertwining like the delicate, tatted lace on her mother's best pillowcases. Love for Matt pulsed and radiated around her, making everything look beautiful and new. There were times when she sat, hands idle, staring at nothing. Other times, she drifted around the house with a bewildered smile on her face, one she found difficult to hide from her parents.

When the weekly dance arrived, Sabra noted the wary look in her father's eyes as they approached the church. A line had been clearly drawn with Sabra on one side and her parents and brothers on the other, but tonight they would pretend it didn't exist. Politeness was as deeply ingrained into the fabric of Cortéz life as keeping the commandments. If Matt asked her to dance, then of course Sabra must accept. Matt would ask her. She knew he would. And she would accept, but not for politeness's sake.

It seemed an eternity before Uncle Ernie announced the first waltz. When Matt bowed and reached for her hand, everything suddenly seemed right again.

"Harry's getting to be an expert at diverting Charlie," Matt confided. His dark eyes turned serious. "I've had a dickens of a time trying to see you. Your father . . ." His jaw clamped down on the word. If looks could kill, Matt would be in his grave. It wasn't just Sabra's family either. Others who'd given their hand in support were treating Matt with coolness, and yesterday, Matt's mother had suggested that now might be a good time to look over the Whiting property. Even the bishop had taken him aside.

"Do you think you're doing the right thing seeing so much of Sabra Lindsey?" the bishop had asked.

"I didn't know I was seeing that much of her. Sabra's father . . ."

"It's her father I'm worried about," Bishop Harris cut in. "Although this is a good ward with good people, once in a while feelings get stirred up. Sam Lindsey's are a mite warm right now. He's not pleased you've singled out his daughter. I'd hoped that speaking to the brethren would solve the problem, but . . ." Junius searched for the right words. "Brother Lindsey asked me to speak to you. He wants you to . . ." The words seemed to stick in the bishop's throat. How could he tell someone he liked and respected that he wasn't wanted, at least not as the suitor of Sam Lindsey's only daughter. Junius had knelt in prayer before he came to talk to Matt. He found himself praying now. *What do I say, Lord? I don't want to hurt Matthew. But marriage between him and a white girl? It just isn't right. At least I don't think it's right. Please, help me.*

In the twelve years Junius had been bishop, he'd had numerous conversations with the Lord. God was Junius's close friend, someone with whom he could talk over his problems, a mentor who listened and often gave Junius advice. Tonight, no matter how hard he'd prayed, there had been no clear-cut answer—only emptiness and wisps of doubt. Could he and others be wrong? Since God looked to a man's heart, maybe they should learn to do the same.

Instead of telling Matthew it would be unwise for him to continue seeing Sabra, Bishop Harris placed a hand on his shoulder. "You know I think highly of you, Matthew. You must be the one to decide about Sabra. As your bishop, I advise you to make it a matter of prayer."

"That's what I'm doing," Matt had told him.

Now, as Matt looked down into Sabra's shimmering green eyes, he knew his decision to marry her was right. But from the number of frowns directed at them, it seemed that God hadn't let others know it. When Matt had told Sabra things wouldn't be easy, he hadn't known the half of it.

"I'm sorry the way things have turned out. If I'd had any idea it would make so much trouble between you and your parents, I wouldn't have taken you away from the grove."

"How can you be sorry?" Sabra asked. "If we hadn't slipped away, you couldn't have proposed or kissed me." Thinking about Matt's kisses brought heat to her cheeks, a return of the deep, half-frightening feeling. Here he was at last, bronzed and clean with his crisp hair combed back from his forehead, his dark eyes looking down into hers. There it was again, the desire to touch him. She put a hand on Matt's arm for the pleasure of feeling his muscled strength through the fabric of his coat while she pretended, for the watchful eyes, that it was only to follow him through the intricate pattern of the waltz. Did Matt have any idea how many times she'd relived their time together, savoring the memory of his lips on hers, the look on his face when he'd asked her to marry him? How could she be sorry about anything so wonderful? "Don't ever be sorry," she repeated.

The fervor in her voice erased Matt's doubts. He'd been afraid the commotion over their capture might make Sabra regret her decision. It couldn't be easy with her family closing ranks against him. Against them. From now on they must act as a team. "I'm leaving for the mountains on Monday," Matt went on. "I planned to stop by and tell you good-bye, but the way things are going . . ." He glanced at the row of benches where Sabra's parents sat.

Sabra's gaze followed, saw her father's pensive expression; Samuel was usually so jovial. And poor, sad Mama. Why couldn't they see they were wrong? She must use the time while Matt was away to convince her parents of their error. After that, things were sure to be all right again.

Her mind quickly jumped ahead to Matt's journey and possible danger. "Do you think it's safe? Papa heard Madero and Pancho Villa might join forces. Maybe you should wait."

"I'll be all right. The mountains should be safer than here in the valley. It's the towns Madero wants to control, not isolated ranches."

Sabra swallowed the impulse to argue. The memory of Villa's ruthlessness wasn't easy to dislodge. What if the bandit swooped down on Matt while he rode across the flats? The rebels needed horses. A lone man would be easy prey.

"Smile," Matt said. "I don't want Charlie thinking you've tired of me."

"I'll never tire of you." She let his teasing override her worry. "How long will you be gone?"

"Probably a week or two. A lot will depend on how quickly Brother Whiting and I can agree on a fair price for his ranch. I heard that since his wife died, he's anxious to sell. Maybe news about the fighting will make him even more eager. If everything works out . . ." Matt tightened his hold on Sabra's waist. So what if a hundred pair of eyes watched them. By the time he got back from the mountains, the gossips would have found someone else to talk about. "If Brother Whiting agrees to sell, we can be married and moved in by fall."

* * *

The days while Matt was away seemed to stretch on forever. One week. Two. Impatient for news, Sabra searched for an excuse to talk to Matt's mother. Maybe Helen Cameron had heard something from Matt.

It was Sunday before the opportunity presented itself. Sabra lingered by the church door until she saw Helen coming. "How are you, Sister Cameron?"

Helen paused and smiled. "Fine, Sabra. And you?"

"Just fine." She tried to remember the words she'd rehearsed.

"I don't suppose you've had any word from Matthew?" Helen asked.

"No . . . have you? I mean . . . I thought maybe Harry or someone might have gone with Matt and come back early."

Helen shook her head. "Matthew went alone. Buying the ranch is something he wants to do himself." As Helen searched Sabra's face, her features softened. "Why don't you stop by and visit with me sometime? With Matt gone I get lonesome for young voices."

"Thank you, I will."

* * *

Three days later Sabra gathered her courage and stopped at Sister Cameron's little house on her way home from the mercantile. The heady fragrance of a blossoming peach tree, its heart-shaped petals scattering the grass like a froth of pink snow, greeted her as she walked up the dirt path to the gray stucco house.

Helen opened the door before Sabra could knock. "I was watering my geraniums in the front window and saw you coming." Sensing Sabra's hesitation, she added, "Come on back to the kitchen so we can talk."

She followed Sister Cameron through the parlor and into the cheery kitchen where the smell of fresh-baked cookies filled the room.

"Excuse the mess." Helen indicated the clutter of unwashed dishes on the sideboard. "I've been out to the Johnsons' helping Sadie with her new baby. When I got home, I decided to bake molasses cookies. They're Matt's favorite . . . in case he comes today."

Sabra nodded, her eyes taking in the cheery kitchen. Everything from the gingham curtains to the scrubbed pine floor scattered with braided rugs spoke of love and care.

"Won't you sit down?"

"Yes . . . thank you." What was wrong with her? Why couldn't she think of something else to say?

Helen didn't have difficulty making conversation. She spoke of the Johnsons' latest addition—a little boy with coal-black hair—as she pulled out a chair and sat down. "This is my favorite place to talk. There's something about the parlor. Have you noticed how it seems to put people off? But here . . ." Her voice and eyes warmed. "This is where Matthew and I have our best talks."

Sabra looked at the kitchen with new eyes, wondering which chair Matt sat in for supper and if he had to be reminded to fill the wood box.

Seeming to read her mind, Helen spoke. "He's a good son. I couldn't ask for better."

"I know." When they smiled, the barriers melted. Instead of a woman with uncanny skill for easing pain, Helen Cameron became a listening ear for Sabra, one with whom she could share the story of her rescue from Carlos. "Matt told me how he tried to scrub off his brown skin," she ventured as she finished.

Helen studied Sabra with new understanding. If Matt had shared this experience with Sabra, his feelings for the girl were deeper than she'd suspected. Helen's mind traveled over the years, recalling the numerous slights Matt had suffered because of his race. "Acceptance is what Matthew has always wanted, and the one thing I could never give him."

Sabra saw the hurt in Helen's blue eyes, heard the pain in the long, drawn-out breath. "What's wrong with people? Can't they see how good Matt is?" she asked in frustration.

"They see it. At least they did until those rumors about him began. Now people aren't so sure. As for the prejudice . . ." Helen's mouth tightened. "I could preach a sermon on its evils, one that would scorch more than a few pious faces, but I doubt it would change anything. The judging is just there. Don't ask me why. As Mormons they should know better. Perhaps if everyone had been given a brown baby to raise . . . had loved and cared for it as I did for Matthew, things would be different." She looked at Sabra. "Because I love him, I never think about the color of his skin. But there are others . . ."

"Matt's skin is beautiful, like his hair and eyes."

Helen rose from her chair to get a plate of cookies. She'd been right about her son and Sabra. "What about your parents. Do they feel the same as you do about Matt?"

The memory of the scene in the parlor and the strained atmosphere of the past few days made her look away. "It's . . . they . . ."

"You don't have to tell me." Helen knew it all too well. Matthew was a good boy . . . a fine man, as long as he didn't try to court someone's daughter. Although it had shattered her dreams, Helen had finally accepted the fact that Matthew's place was with the Mexican people, not with a white girl . . . not with Sabra. Helen tried to swallow the tightness in her throat. The impulse that had prompted her to invite Sabra over had been as foolish as her dreams of her son marrying a girl from the colonies. There were several Mexican families in Chihuahua City who had joined the Church—some in Mexico City too. Hopefully one of them had a daughter, someone Matthew could come to love and marry.

Helen looked at Sabra, not liking to think what prejudice and narrow minds would to do to her. She wished the young woman's eyes weren't so wide and trusting, her mouth so youthful. Helen forced a breath past the tightness. "Even if there weren't rumors about Matthew, your father wouldn't let you marry a Mexican. Neither will any other father in the colonies . . . especially now. Like it or not, Matthew's reputation has been sullied. Even though he's active in the Church, people will always wonder. I know he never rode with bandits or rustled cattle. I think you do too. But others . . ."

Sabra got to her feet. "Others don't matter."

"Yes, they do. You and my son, Sabra. It can't be."

"Matt has asked me to marry him. We're planning to join the next wedding party going up to the St. George Temple. You're just trying . . ."

"Trying to do what's best for my son," Helen finished for her. Seeing the pain in Sabra's eyes, Helen took her hand. "Do you think I like this any better than you do? All my life I've dreamed of him marrying a girl from the colonies, living close so I can enjoy his children. If I could pick his wife, I'd choose you. I've always admired your spunk and the way you speak your mind. That's the kind of wife Matthew needs. One who'll stand up to the narrow-mindedness."

"Then why do you say it can't be?"

"Your parents. I've lived with them too long, cared for them . . . saved your mother's life. How can I let my son cause them heartache?"

"They'll get over it. If we give them time, they'll . . ."

"Time." Helen's voice hardened. "I've given them twenty-two years. They haven't budged. They'll never budge."

"Then we'll run away. Once we're married, no one can do anything."

"Oh, child." Helen's fingers tightened on Sabra's. "Don't you realize they can refuse to speak to you . . . refuse to sit by you in church. Even though we call ourselves Saints, Mormons are human. We can be cruel too. What if Charlie's parents refused to sell you goods from their store?"

"They wouldn't." Even as she spoke, Sabra recalled Sister Teasdale's recent coldness and the woman's penchants toward pettiness. Matt was right. It would be better if they lived someplace else. "I'm not worried about what others might do. It's Matt I care about. Matt and our happiness."

"What about other people's happiness? Think about your children. Will they like being called half-breed? And your poor mother. It would break Lizzie's heart to see you and your children mistreated."

Sabra didn't want to think about her mother. Lately, the specter of Mama's sad face seemed to follow her everywhere. Why couldn't her parents see they were wrong? Why couldn't they love Matt? She stared down at the floor, noting the cracks in the wooden seams, the torn edge on the braided rug, her frustration increasing. "I know you mean well, Sister Cameron, but it doesn't change my mind." Sabra's chin lifted, her emerald eyes flashed. "I'm going to marry Matt. No one can stop us. Matt and I have prayed about it. We know it's right."

Helen remained silent. She hoped Sabra was right. But the prospect of their marriage filled her with foreboding. Not that Helen believed God would lead anyone astray. He couldn't . . . wouldn't. It was the young people who frightened her—a love-struck couple that might mistake their wants for those of God's.

* * *

Matt brought his horse to a halt on a bluff overlooking Cortéz. Evening shadows stretched across the valley, touching newly plowed

fields that formed patchwork patterns with the greening wheat. The
sight never failed to raise his spirits. Like it or not, this was his town,
these were his people. He watched a trail of cows being brought in for
milking, saw a lazy spiral of smoke drift skyward from a chimney.
Supper would be cooking, families called together for evening prayer.
Somewhere Sabra was waiting. Matt could hardly wait to tell her the
news. The Whiting ranch was his, all four hundred acres with enough
money left over to buy new stock and a team and wagon.

Digging his heels into the gelding's sides, Matt pulled off his
Stetson and waved it over his head. The startled horse set off with a
burst of speed that sent them down the bluff and across the flats in
record time. He'd done it! He'd worked out an agreeable deal with
Brother Whiting. If all went well, by fall he and Sabra could be
married, then the temple in June.

Eager to get home, Matt took a shortcut across the community
pasture, then along the back of Brother Moffit's orchard and on to the
Cameron barn. After he rubbed down the gelding and put it into the
corral, Matt started for the gray stucco house with its broad side
porch where he and his mother sat on summer evenings. Like Helen,
it was solid and dignified, a home designed for utility instead of
pretense. Matt cut past the grape arbor and across the backyard,
ducking his head to avoid the clothesline.

"I'm home." The sharp slam of the back door vibrated behind
Matt as he set his bedroll in the corner and looked around the
kitchen. The loud ticking of the clock in the parlor called through the
silence. It, and Helen's gingham apron hanging over the back of a
chair, told him she was gone. Disappointed, Matt went back out to
the barn. After feeding the chickens and milking the cow, he carried
the bucket of foaming milk into the back room, strained it, and set it
to cool on a shelf in the dark pantry.

Since Helen still wasn't home, Matt ladled beans into a bowl from
a steaming pot on the back of the stove, cut a thick slice of bread, and
sat down to a solitary meal by the window. It was after seven o'clock
before Matt started for the Lindseys. He was freshly shaved, the dirt
and grime from the mountains washed off in a tin tub set next to the
stove. The moon was just coming over the bluff, and a slight breeze
made him glad he'd decided to wear his Sunday suit.

It took less than ten minutes to walk across town. Matt tried to quell his nervousness when the gabled, two-storied home came in sight. The upcoming interview wasn't going to be easy.

Elizabeth Lindsey answered Matt's knock, a startled, guarded look crossing her face.

"Good evening, Sister Lindsey. Is Sabra home?"

"Y . . . yes, but I'm afraid she can't see you." Elizabeth moved to close the door.

Matt caught the edge of it with his fingers. "Please, I need to talk to her . . . to your husband too."

Elizabeth hesitated, her pale eyes darting over Matt's face. "I'll tell Brother Lindsey you're here."

Matt waited in the parlor. This was worse than he'd expected. If he didn't talk fast, Brother Lindsey would throw him out before he'd had a chance to tell him about the ranch. He heard anxious whispers in the next room, the scrape of a chair, then Sam Lindsey came through the tall, double doors. Sabra's father still wore his work clothes, the cuffs of his faded cotton shirt rolled up, the knees of his overalls stained with red-brown earth.

Samuel ignored Matt's outstretched hand. "My wife says you want to see Sabra."

"Yes, sir."

"May I ask why?"

The muscles in Matt's throat tightened. "I wanted her to know I was back . . . that I was able to buy the Whiting place up by Garcia. I hope you don't mind that I'm calling on her."

"I do mind. Sabra and Charlie are . . ."

"No, we're not, Papa." Sabra's voice cut past her father's as she hurried into the parlor. Her green eyes were anxious when they met Matt's, then she turned her full attention to Samuel, her chin lifted, the knuckles of her hand tightening around a damp dish towel. "I've done what you and Mama asked. I've reconsidered . . . I've prayed about it too. My answer's still the same. I don't want to marry Charlie. I won't marry him."

Samuel's eyes narrowed. "You may not have any say in the matter, young lady. Your mother and I will be the ones to decide what's best for you."

"That's not fair."

"Maybe not, but that's how life is sometimes." Samuel pointed to the door, anger and frustration tightening his handsome features. "Go to your room."

"No!" Sabra's heart pounded through her breathing. She couldn't believe this was happening. Not between her and Papa. Not after all the years of closeness. "It's my life you're planning . . . my life you're throwing away." Her voice broke when Matt's hand closed around her shoulder.

"Do what your father says. This is between your father and me. You and I can talk later."

Sabra turned to face him, tears filling her eyes. "There won't be any later. Can't you see, Matt? Papa's already made up his mind. He . . ."

Matt's fingers tightened. "Your father's a reasonable man. Please, do as he says."

For a second Sabra was of a mind to light into Matt too. They were both treating her as if she were a child. Anger fought with logic. Matt was right. It was between him and her father. At least the asking. But after that, after Papa said no, it was something she and Matt would face together.

Matt waited until Sabra had left the parlor before he spoke. One glance at Brother Lindsey's set features told him he'd have to talk fast. "I . . . I love your daughter, Brother Lindsey. I've come to ask your permission to marry her."

"Marry her!" Samuel's mouth clamped shut. Why hadn't the bishop spoken to Matt like he'd promised? Now there was no way out of it except to speak his mind and, by George, Samuel intended to speak it. Tactfully, of course, but emphatically enough that Matthew Cameron would never bother Sabra again.

"Yes, sir. I just bought the Whiting ranch up above Garcia. With the experience I had on the ranch in Texas, I know I can make a go of it. I promise you Sabra won't want for anything."

"I don't care how many ranches you buy. You still can't marry my daughter."

"Why?"

"Do you have to ask?"

"Yes, I do." Matt waited, knowing what Brother Lindsey was going to say.

"Because you're a Mexican. No daughter of mine is going to marry a Mexican." There, it was said, though the saying left a putrid taste in Samuel's mouth. He hurried on. "I don't have anything against you personally, Matthew. I believe in the principle of repentance as much as the next man. But how do I know that what you told your mother and the bishop is true? Even if it is, you should know by now that God doesn't hold with the mixing of races. Some of our Church leaders have said the same. You need to stick with people of your own kind. People who . . ."

Matt had ceased to listen. He'd known what Samuel was going to say. What he hadn't known was how badly it would hurt, twisting deep inside, numbing and tearing like a knife heated in hot coals. He balled a hand into a fist, his tight control all that kept it from smashing into Brother Lindsey's pious face. His mouth pulled into an angry grimace. Why had he bothered to come back?

Matt hurried out the front door, slamming it behind him. The crisp evening air seared at his lungs as he hurried down the street, his awkward steps stiff and stumbling. The ragged sound of his breathing wretched from his throat in a painful sob, the tearing rasp filling the air. Anger drove back the sobs. He hadn't cried in years. He wasn't going to start now. He should have known better than to ask to marry a white girl. Hadn't Bishop Harris tried to warn him?

Halfway across town he leaned against a fence post to catch his breath, anger and frustration warring with his pain. His head jerked up when he heard footsteps stumbling behind him, a voice calling.

"Matt! Wait! Please, wait . . ."

He recognized Sabra's voice before he saw her. She rushed out of the night, her voice breaking with little sobs. "Matt . . ."

She was in his arms, clinging to him as she buried her face against his shoulder. For a moment Matt wanted only to hold her, needing her touch, the fragrance of her hair, her warmth to soothe away the hurt and anger.

"I was listening by the stairs. I heard what Papa said. I never thought he could be so cruel. Not Papa." She paused and took a shuddering breath. "I should have known. Your mother tried to warn me." Sobs jerked through Sabra's body. "I'm sorry, Matt. I know how it must hurt you."

Matt lifted her face from his shoulder and wiped her tears with the palm of his hand. "Please don't cry. I'll be all right."

"How can you be all right after what happened?" Not giving Matt a chance to reply, she hurried on. "I love you. I don't care what Papa said. I'm still going to marry you. Even if we have to run away."

His arms tightened around her shoulders. It would serve Sam Lindsey right if they did run away. His mouth tightened into a grim smile as he pictured her father's chagrin—the town's chagrin, especially Charlie's. His euphoria only lasted a few seconds. If they ran off, there'd be no temple wedding, no celebration and dance to send them off to their home at the ranch with gifts and well wishes. There'd only be him and Sabra standing in a dusty, fly-filled room while a Mexican authority rattled off the marriage vows in Spanish. Matt closed his eyes against the dismal picture. He wanted better than that for Sabra . . . for his wife.

"No." Matt set Sabra away from him. "We're not running off. I don't want that kind of wedding and neither do you."

Sabra stared at Matt. What was wrong with him? Hadn't he heard what she'd said? "I don't care two pins about that kind of a wedding. It's being with you that matters. I want us to be together."

"And just how long do you think we'd stay together? As soon as your father realizes you're gone, he'll come after us with a posse. Since the bishop is also the sheriff, he'll be with him." Matt's lips twisted. "Even though the bishop's my friend, I know whose side he'll be on."

Sabra wrapped her arms around him, her nearness sending the blood pulsing to his head. Matt lifted her face to kiss her, forgetting for a few wild moments all the problems that faced them as he lost himself in the eager, astonishing softness of her lips, the warmth as she melded her body with his. Then he gently untangled Sabra's arms from around his neck and framed her face with his hands. Unable to end it so quickly, he kissed her softly on the mouth, then her eyelids, tasting the salt of her tears and knowing he couldn't bear to lose her.

"I'm not giving up on us getting married. But I need time to think this through . . . figure a way around your father. And you need to get back home. If he finds out you've gone . . ."

Sabra nodded, one hand to her lips as if she were trying to hold his kisses there, her face a pale oval in the watery moonlight. "I'm not going to let them stop us, Matt."

"Neither am I." He brushed her cheek with his fingers, letting his touch bind like a promise. No one was going to stop him from having Sabra for his wife.

CHAPTER 14

The next week Harry slipped a note from Matt into Sabra's hand as he left the Union Mercantile, giving her a broad wink as he hoisted a sack of beans onto his narrow, muscled shoulder.

She surreptitiously put the scrap of tightly folded brown paper into her pocket. She wanted to read it, but she couldn't. Not with Charlie's mother looking on, her sharp eyes darting from Harry to Sabra, then back again. Her hand went to her pocket a dozen times that afternoon, the rough texture of the paper filling her with happy anticipation each time she touched it.

It wasn't until she was home and in her room that she had a chance to read the hastily scribbled message. Matt's plan was simple, at least in theory. He was going to the ranch until things cooled down a bit. A lot needed to be done before they moved in. After tempers had quieted down and Sabra had allayed her parents' fears, Matt would come back and they would be married.

Don't ask me how we'll do it. I haven't had time to figure it out yet. The bishop in Garcia seems like an understanding man. So maybe . . .

Matt had scribbled out the rest of the sentence and added,

Watch for Harry. I'll send word to you with him. Hang on to your temper, Nutmeg, and remember you have my love. All of it.

—Matt

Sabra pressed the coarse paper to her lips before tearing it into little pieces and putting them into the stove when Elizabeth wasn't looking. If Mama found out Matt had written to her, who knew what might happen? Everything was going to work out. Hadn't she and Matt prayed about it? Hadn't they both received the same answer? Their marriage was right. Their love was right. All she had to do was bide her time until Matt came for her. A simple thing, really.

But it wasn't simple, not when feelings were so strained and uncomfortable between her and her parents. There'd been a terrible row after she came home that night, one so heated Sabra had lost her temper and called her father a hypocritical bigot. She'd held her breath, watched his mouth twist with rage, followed the upward move- ment of his hand, certain he was going to strike her. He didn't, but she knew he'd wanted to, just as she knew he wasn't proud of the things he'd said to Matt. Such feelings didn't mean Papa was about to change his mind. He'd made himself clear on that point, but Sabra had glimpsed the shame in his eyes, noticed how he left his breakfast untouched the next morning. Then she felt sorry for him, sorry and mad at the same time. Sorry for Mama too, because she knew they both loved her. Knowing didn't heal the hurt. All the laughter between them had died, and no one seemed to know what to say anymore.

The members of the ward were another matter. Not only did they know what to say, they were saying it. Sabra never learned how the incident between Matt and her father became common knowledge. Perhaps Samuel had confided it to one of his friends, or maybe Mama had let something slip to Aunt Mae. Whatever the case, the story was out and she was forced to suffer the knowing glances with pretended indifference.

In ways this was more difficult than the widening breach between her and her parents. Sabra wanted to rail at the whole ward, stand up in sacrament meeting and let them know what she thought of their hypocrisy. But prudence kept her tongue in check. *Make them think you don't care,* she told herself. *The sooner things calm down, the sooner Matt will be able to come for me.*

Through it all, Charlie's attentiveness never wavered. He'd let Sabra know he disapproved of what had happened, though. After all, Matt would never have spoken to her father if Sabra hadn't encouraged him. Once Charlie had his say, he was his old self again, dropping by to see her, smiling his little-boy smile.

Brother Teasdale was like his son, quick to forgive and eager to please, but his wife never missed an opportunity to let Sabra know how she felt.

"I can't believe Matt would be nervy enough to speak to your father," Sister Teasdale said as she helped Sabra arrange a new shipment of calico. "He should've known what Sam would say . . . what any father in his right mind would say. It isn't right. Mexicans marrying whites. God set the distinction between the races for a purpose. We have no business interfering with God's plan."

Sabra managed to hold her tongue, though it took effort. *How can you be so sure about God's plan?* she wanted to ask. *Aren't we all His children?*

Her refusal to comment seemed to have an unsettling effect on the heavyset woman. "Mind, I don't have anything against Matthew personally. Brother Teasdale and Charlie both offered him their hand that morning in priesthood meeting. But you can't just ignore what Brig Shumway saw . . . what happened in Casas Grandes. I knew when the Camerons first brought that boy to Cortéz there'd be trouble . . . a Mexican being raised by whites. Not that it wasn't commendable of Helen and Joseph to take him in and offer him the chance to have the gospel in his life. Still . . ." She turned her slightly protruding eyes on Sabra. "You should've known better than to encourage him. You're as much to blame in this incident as he was. Even though I promised Brother Teasdale I wouldn't say anything, I want you to know I have serious doubts about you being a suitable wife for Charlie."

"I have serious doubts about it too," Sabra cut in. "Now if you'll excuse me, it looks like Sister Durfee needs help with the sugar."

The rest of the morning passed in uneasy silence, though Charlie's mother acted as if nothing were amiss each time a customer came into the store. When it was time to go home, Sabra all but ran out the door, knowing where she must go, where she'd wanted to go ever since Matt had left her.

The gray stucco house warmed itself in the late spring sunshine, its multipaned windows seeming to call a welcome to her as she walked up the dirt path.

Helen's welcome was hesitant. "Why, Sabra . . ." Her voice trailed away and she looked a little uncertain.

"I hope you don't mind that I've come."

"Of course not." Helen stepped back so she could come inside. "But I suspect that if the gossips are on their toes it will be all over town before suppertime."

Noticing the unshed tears shimmering in Sabra's eyes, Helen led her back to the kitchen, pulling out a chair and offering her a handkerchief.

"I didn't come to cry." Sabra sniffed as tears rolled down her cheeks. "Everything's been so awful. There's no one to talk to. Not even Becky." She felt Helen take her hand. "Becky's parents have sent her to her aunt in Juarez. They think I'm a bad influence on her . . . that she wouldn't have been captured by Villa's soldiers if she hadn't been with me. And now this." Sabra straightened her shoulders and gave her freckled nose a lusty blow. "I'm sorry."

"You've nothing to be sorry about. I just wish I'd been here to talk Matt out of going to see your father. If I hadn't been out nursing the Hawkins's baby . . ."

"I'm glad you weren't here to stop him," Sabra cut in. "Now there's no more pretense. They can't skirt around the prejudice since it's out in the open."

"I suppose that's true." Helen went to put more wood into the stove, rattling the metal handle, then banging the door closed. "I'm just so tired of it all . . . of being made to feel my son isn't good enough." She sighed and wiped her hands on her apron. "What's wrong with them? They're good, honest people who should know better, but there are some who try to twist the scriptures. They justify their prejudice against dark skin by quoting—"

A loud pounding on the back door drowned out Helen's words. Startled, Sabra glanced at Helen. The knock repeated itself, its urgency clanging like an alarm bell. *Don't go,* Sabra wanted to say, sensing even before Helen opened the door that the knock was a harbinger of bad news.

One look at Danny Johns's distraught face confirmed her premonition. She saw a trickle of dried blood on his cheek, heard the desperation in his voice. "Please . . . you gotta help Pa."

Helen reached for her shawl hanging by the door. "What's wrong?"

The boy pointed up the lane. "Ma and Aunt Nellie are bringing Pa in the wagon. He's been shot, Sister Cameron. He's hurt bad and bleeding."

"Shot?"

Danny's chin quivered. "Bandits raided our ranch this morning. When Pa tried to stop them from taking the cattle, they . . ." He paused and swallowed.

Helen and Sabra hurried out the door. A wagon driven by Gilbert Johns's widowed sister and filled with mattresses and children was coming up the lane. Helen went to meet it, clutching her blue shawl with one hand. "Pull the wagon up to the gate, Nellie. It'll make it easier to get him inside."

Sabra heard the murmur of the women's voices, the wails of the frightened children. The sight of blood always unnerved her. Something—perhaps the desperation in the boy's voice, maybe the knowledge that she was needed—impelled her forward.

Gilbert Johns lay on a mattress in the back of the wagon, his head pillowed by his wife's ample lap. Horror rose in Sabra's throat when she saw the still form, the waxen face bristling with the dark stubble of unshaved whiskers, his closed, sunken eyes. Was he dead?

Helen climbed into the wagon. "Where was he hit?"

"His shoulder. It went clear through. There's so much blood . . ." Emma Johns bit down on her lower lip. "Nellie packed it tight, but he's still bleeding."

Helen nodded and lifted the blanket. Blood-soaked towels swathed Brother Johns's upper body. She felt his pulse and tested the bindings. "We've got to get him inside. With four of us to lift, I think we can manage."

The women and children scrambled out of the wagon.

"Run and open the back door," Emma called to Danny. "Then take the little ones down to Aunt Sarah's."

Danny ran ahead while the women struggled with the wounded rancher. The deadweight of the unconscious man dragged at Sabra's hands and shoulders. She tightened her grip and counted each step, willing herself to hold on.

"Clear the dishes off the table," Helen instructed. "We can lay him there."

They managed to get Brother Johns through the door and onto the table. A low moan escaped his lips. His eyelids fluttered and closed.

"Do you think he'll be all right?" Nellie asked.

"Hard to say. He's lost a lot of blood." Helen removed the red-soaked towels. "I'll need hot water and clean rags." Her eyes sought Sabra's. "My medicine bag's in the bedroom. Get it for me, then go for Brother Cameron and the bishop. It'll take more than my skill to get him through. Brother Johns needs a blessing."

Glad to escape, Sabra hurried to get Helen's bag from the bedroom, then ran through the block for Brother Cameron. Dusk was falling by the time she found the bishop. They walked quickly, Sabra answering his questions even as she worried they'd be too late. What if Brother Johns was already dead?

"How's he doing?" Bishop Harris asked when they reached the house.

"A little better now that the bleeding's stopped."

Gilbert Johns's eyelids flickered. "Emma . . . ?"

"I'm right here, Gil. Nellie too. So's the bishop and Brother Cameron. They've come to give you a blessing."

Gilbert's lips curved into a weak smile. "Good."

Not wanting to be noticed and sent away, Sabra eased back into a corner while Bishop Harris took a vial of consecrated oil from his coat pocket. She bowed her head and concentrated on the solemnity of the moment. If Brother Johns was going to be healed, it would take the faith of everyone in the room. *Please, help Brother Johns to get better,* she silently prayed as Brother Cameron anointed Brother Johns's head. But what if it wasn't God's will? What if it was Brother Johns's time to die? By the time she could rid her mind of the negative thoughts, Joseph Cameron had finished anointing the wounded man's balding head with the oil and Bishop Harris was well into the blessing. *Help me have more faith,* Sabra prayed. *Help all of us to have more faith.*

Bishop Harris didn't lack the attribute, nor did he doubt the power of his priesthood. Not only was Gilbert Johns told that he would live, he was promised a speedy recovery.

"Thanks . . . Bishop." Gilbert Johns attempted another weak smile that faded when his eyes focused on Helen. "It was your son . . ."

"What?" Helen stepped closer to the bed.

"Matt . . . was ridin' with the bandits that shot me."

A terrible weight settled into Sabra's stomach.

Helen looked as sick as Sabra felt. "You're mistaken. Matt's not a bandit. Besides, he's up at his new ranch."

Brother Johns's pasty face moved on the pillow. "It was Matt."

"Gilbert's speaking the truth," Nellie interrupted. "Me and Emma saw him too. I know the tale he told you about havin' a twin brother. But this was Matthew, all right. He rode up to the house as bold as you please, laughin' and actin' like he didn't know us. He even pointed his rifle at Emma when she wouldn't give them another cheese."

Joseph Cameron's face was stricken as he put a protective arm around his wife's shoulder.

"You don't understand . . ." Helen began.

"That's what I thought at first." The rail-thin woman looked imploringly at Helen. "You know I wouldn't say anything to hurt you. Not after you saved little Cora and tried so hard to save my Peter. All the way in I kept tellin' myself . . . it can't be. Not Helen's son. I'd like to pass it off as a mistake, but . . ." Nellie came around the bed and took Helen's hand. "When the bandits were leaving, Matt's sombrero fell off. I saw the white steak in his hair. All three of us saw it. This ain't no mistake, Helen. In spite of what Matthew told you and the bishop, the rumors about him are true."

The silence that settled over the tiny room seemed to press against Sabra's heart, squeezing and making it difficult to breathe. Why didn't Matt's mother say something? Explain?

Bishop Harris broke the silence. "The man you saw wasn't Matthew. If you knew the facts, you'd understand."

"The bishop's right," Helen added. "Matthew can explain."

"Tell more lies ye mean," Joseph said. "He's usin' the story aboot a twin brother to cover the looting he does when he leaves town. Most likely that's how he got the money to buy his ranch. Can't ye see, Helen? The laddie's nae good. In spite of all ye did . . . all the lovin', he's hoodwinked ye. The bishop too."

"No." Bishop Harris's voice was emphatic. "Matthew's not a liar." Junius put a hand on Joseph's shoulder. "You've got to have faith. You have to trust." Bishop Harris turned to the others. "I want you to keep quiet about this until I've had a chance to talk to Matt. Until then, the less said about this, the better."

Emma was of a different opinion. "I don't mean to sound disrespectful, Bishop, and I don't like saying things that'll hurt Helen and Joe. Talking to Matt won't change a thing. I saw him. He was enjoyin' himself . . . laughin' with his friends and pretendin' he didn't understand English. Don't forget he pointed his gun at me. You've seen what his friends did to Gil." She paused to catch her breath. "I saw what I saw. As for keeping quiet . . ." Emma shook her head in sympathy. "I'm afraid it's too late for that, Bishop. I sent the children over to Sarah's when we got here. They saw what happened too. I imagine it's all over town by now."

Sabra pressed trembling fingers to her lips. What chance would Matt have with the whole town talking against him? Someone had to explain.

"Do you know when Matthew will be coming home?" Bishop Harris asked.

Helen shook her head. "He's up at his ranch. He was worried about the new calves." Her usually stoic face crumpled. "Oh . . . Joseph."

The Scotsman patted her shoulder. "I'm sorry, Helen."

The bleakness in his voice echoed in Sabra's heart. Anger pushed past the bleakness. "Matt didn't do it," Sabra blurted. Helen ceased crying and the others turned to stare. Someone besides the bishop and Sister Cameron had to speak up. "Matt does have a twin brother. He's known about him for years. His twin brother's the one who's doing these terrible things. Rafael . . ."

"Likely story."

Sabra wasn't sure which of the women spoke, but she could see disbelief on both faces. "It's not a story. It's the truth."

"He's got you hoodwinked too."

Sabra wanted to shake Sister Johns. "What would be the sense to it? What would Matt have to gain by robbing his own people?"

She saw Emma exchange a look with Nellie. "He wants revenge. Everyone knows about him wantin' to marry Sabra . . . how upset he was when Sam sent him away. I kept thinkin' about it on the way in. Sam's farm is too close to town for Matt to risk making a raid. But our ranch . . ." Her eyes locked with Sabra's. "He raided our ranch to get back at us. All of us."

CHAPTER 15

Sickness slowed Sabra's steps as she left the stuffy bedroom, then walked through Helen's kitchen out into the cool evening air. She leaned against the pillar of the side porch, needing its support for her shaky knees. She couldn't believe what Emma Johns had said. It wasn't true.

The sound of Bishop Harris's deep voice spilled from the back door as he said a subdued good-bye to Helen. Joseph followed him out onto the wooden step. They stood without speaking, Joseph's shoulders hunched against the coolness of the twilight air, the bishop frowning. Sabra drew back into the shadows under the porch. She'd said enough. It would be best if they thought she'd gone home.

The bishop spoke first, his voice hesitant and heavy. "I meant what I said about Matthew . . . about trusting, but these new charges against him can't go unanswered." Junius paused and looked up at the first of the evening stars. "Much as I hate to do it, as bishop and sheriff I've got to find your son and bring him in."

Joseph Cameron sighed and lowered his head.

"You understand why I've got to do it, don't you?"

"Aye, bishop. What I don't ken is how it could happen. I thought we'd taught him right. Four years ago I would ha' staked my life on the laddie. Now . . ." Joseph rubbed his hand across his forehead. "'Twill be hard on Helen . . . on me too. I'd not admit it to anyone except ye, Bishop, but these last few weeks, working with him and all . . . I was startin' to believe in Matty again."

"You can still believe in him. But I've got to bring him in."

Sabra's thoughts reeled. If the bishop went after Matt, it must mean he half believed what Sister Johns had said. Too stunned to move, she could only listen.

"I'd like you to come with me, Joe."

The Scotsman nodded. "'Tis what I was plannin'. Matty's got to answer the charges." Joseph turned to go back into the house, his gnarled hand resting on the doorknob. "I'll be ready to go at sunup."

Sabra watched the bishop walk up the path. She heard him sigh, saw the droop of his shoulders. But the sight didn't erase her anger. If the bishop brought him back to Cortéz, what chance would Matt have? She knew the answer, just as she knew Matt had to be warned. Sunup was only a few hours away.

* * *

They rode across the flats in the gray hours before dawn, the horses picking their way through the prairie-dog infested grassland. Getting Harry to go with her had required Sabra's best powers of persuasion.

"Look, I've told you I'll go. I can leave in less than an hour, but I'm not taking you," Harry had said.

"Then I'll go alone." She'd turned as if she meant to leave.

"You can't go alone. If Mexican soldiers see you, they'll—" Harry broke off and scratched his neck. "Besides, you don't know how to get there."

"That's why I'm asking you to come with me." She paused before going on. "Please, Harry, say you'll come. We can go together."

Harry's reluctant nod was quickly followed by instructions. They'd need horses, a rifle, and must travel light if they wanted to get to the ranch first.

They'd left at midnight after Sabra climbed out her upstairs window with a bedroll and food tied in a pillowcase. Now, as dawn colored the sky with streaks of gold, they found the road leading to Pacheco. Seeing the familiar road lifted Harry's spirits.

"There they are," he called, relief tingeing his voice as he pointed to the first of the foothills protruding onto the flats.

Sabra looked past the foothills to the mighty thrust of the sierras. Matt was somewhere in the plunging canyons, mending fences or checking on cattle, unaware of danger or that they were hurrying to warn him.

Urgency drove them up the steep grade below wind-carved ridges where they camped the first night, building a fire in a grove of oak where spring water seeped between tumbled boulders. They were up before dawn, saying little as they ate stale biscuits and slaked their thirst from the spring. Harry led the way after they broke camp, a worried frown puckering his forehead, the enormity of what he'd undertaken gnawing at his usually high spirits. He must be crazy, and if he didn't stop thinking about getting caught, he was down-right stupid.

Harry let memories and loyalty to his brother serve as his goad up the steep road past the sawmill and on to Little Park Hill. He couldn't remember a time without Matt. He let his mind take him back to the day when Matt had pushed him out of the way when they'd met up with a rattlesnake, the time he'd taught Harry how to carve willow-branch whistles, and how he'd kept the older, bullying boys at a safe distance. But each time Matt's brown skin was mentioned, the roles had reversed with the smaller Harry flying to the older boy's defense, blond head lowered, skinny arms flailing at any who made fun of his brother. Harry's loyalty had never wavered. He meant to stand by Matt now, even if it meant incurring their father's wrath; love and loyalty demanded that Harry ask no questions, harbor no doubts. It was all a big mistake, but until Matt could prove otherwise . . . he wouldn't let the thought travel further, just like he wouldn't let himself dwell on the flick of unease he'd glimpsed in Matt's eyes when Pancho Villa had acknowledged their meeting. What if Matt's story about his twin brother wasn't true? *Please, God, let it be a mistake about Matt and Brother Johns. And please help us get to the ranch before the bishop.*

* * *

It took them two and a half days to reach the ranch—dusty, grueling days of hard riding with no stops except to rest the horses and sleep. Sabra couldn't remember when she'd been more tired. Every muscle in her body ached, and the insides of her thighs were raw from constantly rubbing against the saddle.

Sabra tried not to let Harry see her discomfort. She bit her lip when she dismounted and awkwardly walked to the stream, hoping her raised chin and defiant eyes would stop him from grinning and saying, "I told you so."

She needn't have bothered. Harry scarcely looked at her. In fact, he'd hardly spoken after the first night. Now she could sense a change, a subtle lifting of his thin shoulders, as if he'd been relieved of some heavy burden.

"We're almost there." Harry grinned back at Sabra as he pointed to a valley opening through the pine trees. "That's Garcia up ahead. Matt's ranch is only a couple of hours away. It'll be better if we circle around Garcia so no one sees us." Harry's grin faded on this last thought. Heaven forbid if some gossiping biddy saw them. It would be the end to Sabra's shaky reputation, probably the end to his too.

Harry's growing elation wouldn't let him dwell long on the gloomy scenario. They'd made good time. Darn good time. They'd be with Matt by late afternoon. The thought of Matt carried them over the last miles to the ranch house with its barn and granary nestled against the side of a hill.

"What if he isn't here?"

Sabra scowled at Harry. "What do you mean?" She knew very well what he meant. What if Matt really had raided the Johnses' ranch? What if the story about Rafael was a lie? She shook her head while her eyes searched the meadow. Seeing a movement by the barn door, she urged Buttons across the grassy meadow and slid from the mare to run, half stumbling into Matt's arms.

"Matt . . . Oh, Matt."

She felt Matt's muscled arms tighten around her, heard the quick intake of his breath. "What are you doing here? Is something wrong?"

Sabra and Harry both answered, their words tumbling and tangling together.

"You've got to get away. The bishop . . . the sheriff's coming!"

"It's true, Matt. He and Father are coming to take you in."

"Bandits raided the Johnses' place. Brother Johns was shot and . . ."

"Now he's sayin' it was you . . . that you were riding with the bandits who did it. His wife's sayin' the same thing."

Sabra pulled on Matt's arm. "I told them about Rafael, but they wouldn't believe me. You've got to hurry. They'll be here soon."

"Rafael!" Matt's lips tightened around the name, forcing it out in an angry rasp. He started toward the house with Sabra, Harry right behind him. He had to get away and find Rafael so the whole sorry business could be proven and explained.

The sound of their boots echoed through the sparsely furnished front room when they entered the house. Still not speaking, Matt took his rifle from the rack over the fireplace.

"I sure wish you'd told people about Rafael four years ago," Harry said. "If you had, you wouldn't be in this mess."

"I know."

As Matt put his arm around Sabra's shoulder, he noticed the streaks of dirt on her face, the fatigue in her eyes. Harry looked no better, though he managed a tired grin. "You look tired. Let me get you something to eat."

"We did push a bit," Harry admitted. "Sabra was a real trooper. She . . ." The sound of galloping hooves was faintly discernible. "Cripes . . . they're here!"

Matt ran to the window and saw three horsemen approaching the house. He recognized his father and the bishop, but his heart plummeted at the sight of the third rider. "It's your father," he said to Sabra.

Sabra joined Matt at the window. Dear heaven, it was her father. His black hat and the erect manner with which he sat his horse were hard to mistake.

"I knew they were hot on our trail," Harry said. "But I didn't think they were this close." He paused. "Why did they bring Sabra's father?"

Sabra knew the bishop hadn't had a choice. Papa must have discovered she'd run away. She clutched Matt's arm. "What shall we do?" In the next breath she added, "You should have gone as soon as we got here. If you slip out the back door . . ."

"I'm not running away."

As he spoke, Joseph Cameron's deep voice thundered across the ranch yard. "Matthew!"

"Wait here." Matt loosened Sabra's fingers from his arm.

"No."

Matt paused and looked down at her.

"It's not just you, Matt. They're looking for both of us."

"True." A ghost of a smile crossed his face, and faint though it was, it replenished Sabra's strength. By unspoken agreement they went through the door together, standing side by side on the uneven planks of the porch, not touching, though their thoughts intertwined and gave each other courage.

The men paused when they saw Matt and Sabra, the anger on Sam Lindsey's face leaping across the dusty red dirt of the dooryard.

Bishop Harris spoke first. "I guess you know why we're here."

Matt nodded and kept a wary eye on Brother Lindsey. "Harry and Sabra were just telling me."

"The charges against you are serious, Matthew. I guess you know that too."

"Yes, sir, though I hope you know it wasn't me that raided the Johnses' ranch."

"Who was it then?" Samuel strode across the yard to confront Matt from the bottom step of the porch. "And don't give me some cock-and-bull story about a twin brother."

"Why don't you come inside and I'll explain."

"You can explain right here."

"Papa!"

The cold eyes Samuel turned on Sabra were those of a stranger. "You stay out of this, young lady. I'll deal with you when I get you back home."

"You'll have to deal with both of us. We're . . ." The quick pressure of Matt's fingers stopped her. Matt was right. Arguing would only worsen matters. She bit her tongue and listened while Matt explained about Rafael and the trip to Valle Grande where Matt had met Don de Vega and little Felipe. "I know I should've told you as soon as it happened," Matt concluded, this last directed to the burly Scotsman. "I was afraid of hurting Mother. Besides . . ." Matt shrugged. "I didn't want everyone to know I was illegitimate. Being Mexican was bad enough. Then afterward . . ." Matt waited, searching the Scotsman's craggy face for any sign of softening.

"I wish ye'd told me when it first happened. Comin' so late, it sounds like some story ye've concocted to cover what ye've done. And now this with Brother Johns . . ."

"Is that what you think? That it's just a story? That I could have done such a terrible thing to Brother Johns?"

Joseph Cameron looked away, his mouth working as he shook his head. "I dinna ken, Matty. I dinna ken."

Sabra's voice shot through the emotion-charged silence. "I know Matt would never raid and hurt people. I believe what he says."

Harry stepped closer to Matt. "So do I."

"And I." Junius Harris removed his hat and wiped beads of sweat from his forehead. "Some things in life have to be taken on faith, Joseph. Think of the Matthew you knew four years ago. Had he ever lied to you?"

"Nae."

"Then what makes you think he'd lie to you now?"

Unable to answer, Joseph looked down at the red dirt of the dooryard. How could he explain his stubbornness, his difficulty in admitting he was wrong? The muscles in his throat tightened, making it impossible to speak.

"The only way to clear this up is for me to find Rafael."

Sabra's fingers tightened on Matt's arm. "That could take weeks . . . months. Can't you just show everyone the ring?"

"I doubt that would change many minds. I've had the ring since I was eighteen."

"Then go to Don de Vega. Ask him to tell people about Rafael. If he doesn't want to come to Cortéz, he could write a letter."

"Maybe . . ." The hard glint in Sam Lindsey's eyes told Matt he'd need something stronger than a maybe. The only answer was to find Rafael.

CHAPTER 16

May sunshine warmed Matt's shoulders as he rode across the barren flatlands north of the Mormon colonies. It had been a long day, a long week with nothing but tiredness and growing frustration as payment for the hot, dusty hours. Matt had known finding Rafael wouldn't be easy. With the revolution, hundreds of peóns were joining Pancho Villa—Chihuahua's number-one bandit now turned revolutionist. They were also flocking to Madero and Pascual Orozco, anxious to be a part of the fight to regain their sacred land. *"Tierra y Libertad"*—land and liberty—had become their slogan. Where, among all these men, was Matt to find Rafael?

He'd started his search close to the colonies, visiting poorly lit cantinas, stopping at a town, then a farm, then an isolated hut with dirt-packed floor, adobe walls, and flat mud roof housing a dozen poorly fed Mexicans.

"Someone who looks like you? A twin hermano? No, señor, we are sorry."

The answers were all the same. Some spoke the truth, their dark eyes warm and guileless. Others merely shrugged, shutters closing over crafty features. The latter were usually in dark cantinas, their darting glances filling Matt with worry that he'd be knifed as he walked out the door.

Matt's anger increased with each passing day. When frustration became too much, Matt set his thoughts on more pleasant paths, remembering Sabra's face, her whispered promise that she loved him and that she'd wait.

Thoughts of Joseph Cameron filled another path—the stocky, taciturn Scotsman who'd left Matt to wonder if he was loved for most of his twenty-two years. Memories of their last parting warmed Matt as he lay in his blanket and looked up at diamond-sharp stars. "Take care, Matty." Joseph had paused and put a calloused hand on Matt's shoulder. "I'll have Harry and George look after yer ranch and cattle." All this when Joseph was short-handed too. It had been Joseph who'd vouched for Matt when Sabra's father had objected to his going off by himself to find Rafael. "If Matthew gives ye his hand and says he'll be back, ye can rely on him."

A lump swelled in his throat when he thought of Harry, recalling his entreaty to go with him, and after Matt declined, Harry's firm grip as they'd parted. It was for them—Sabra, his parents, and Harry—that he continued his search. He must reward their loyalty, match their love with persistence, and find Rafael.

Loneliness followed him as he wandered the Chihuahuan desert. There was a forsaken quality about the land, a sense of desolation with only the dry, broken earth, the endless sand and cacti, and the hot, brassy sun pouring out of the sky.

As he journeyed to the northeast, Matt narrowed his eyes against the glare of the sun to follow a trail of dust. At first he thought it was a burro train carrying supplies, but when it drew closer, he realized it was Villa's army. He'd never seen so many horses and men before. The army had grown to over a thousand ill-equipped soldiers. Matt waited with his hand on his rifle.

They swarmed toward him, a horde of men, horses, and wagons moving over the uneven terrain. The revolutionists were always looking for new recruits. If Matt pretended to be one, perhaps he'd be able to find Rafael among the soldiers. Quieting the gelding, he grinned at the soldiers and asked for Pancho Villa, silently praying he wasn't making a serious mistake. Instead of being taken to Villa, Matt was told he must travel with the soldiers. Villa was very busy. A new recruit must stay with his captain. Maybe tonight . . . maybe mañana.

Matt rode with Villa's army for three days, sharing their dust and their company, his eyes watching for Rafael. Each day his impatience increased. Where was his brother? Was he ever going to find him?

That night Matt was summoned to Villa's campfire. Four of Villa's men were with him, friends who'd ridden with him as bandits, their guns close, eyes carefully noncommittal as they took stock of Matt.

"So, amigo, we meet again."

Villa caught him in a hearty *abrazo,* clapping him on the back after the hug and saying how good it was to see him. Matt looked into the amber-flecked brown eyes of Chihuahua's notorious bandit, took in the round, handsome features and drooping mustache, the thick-necked, broad-shouldered body that smelled of sweat and smoke and coffee. Although he was dressed much like his soldiers, instinct warned Matt the bandit would make a better friend than enemy.

"I expected you to join me before now. How long has it been? One, two months? But I forgot the pretty señorita. Perhaps she is the reason you delayed, no?"

"I plan to marry her."

"Marry a gringa?" Pancho laughed, but his expression was speculative. "Tell me what you've been doing. Are you still riding with Ignacio?"

Matt couldn't see any way out of it. He took a deep breath and felt his heart pound. "I'm not Rafael Acosta."

"Not Rafael?" The amber-flecked eyes narrowed and Villa's hand moved to his gun. "Who are you?"

"I'm Rafael's brother . . . his twin brother."

Villa studied Matt, his hand fingering his pistol, the guards moving closer. Using the toe of his boot to pull a saddle over to the fire, Villa sat down and indicated that Matt do the same. "I think you'd better explain."

Matt quickly recounted the circumstances of his birth, his meeting with Rafael, and the subsequent trip to Valle Grande.

Pancho nodded when Matt finished. "Your hermano told me about Don de Vega. Rafael had big plans to rid the hacendado of his cattle. Unfortunately, he was caught and thrown into jail before he could succeed."

"Is Rafael in jail?"

"Not anymore. The *rurales* would sooner kill a man than jail him. The jails are only holding pens, part of the law of the fugitives, where a man is freed from jail then shot in the back while he tries to escape." Villa gave a brittle laugh. "Maybe you don't know about such things, but your twin hermano did, though in his case, he was kept in jail for two years. Strange, no? Perhaps your padre, this hacendado grande, didn't have the stomach to order his own son shot in the back."

Villa motioned for his friends to leave. "It is better to talk alone. Sometimes there are too many eyes . . . too many ears." Villa's eyes were busy gauging and assessing. "You haven't told me why you are looking for Rafael."

"I've been working on a ranch in Texas. Now that I'm back, I'd like to find him again, see what he's doing." Matt's heart accelerated. What if Villa didn't believe him? If half the tales about Villa were true, the bandit had no patience with liars. Men suspected of treachery were quickly hanged or stood against a wall and shot. "When you said you knew me, I figured you meant Rafael. So I came looking . . . hoping you'd know where I can find him."

Villa shook his head. "I'm sorry, amigo. I haven't seen Rafael in more than a year. The last I heard, he was riding with Ignacio Reyes, an old bandito who was once my *compañero.* Ignacio doesn't like the desert. But the mountains . . ." He paused. "I doubt there's a cave or canyon in the sierras Ignacio doesn't know. If you wish to find Rafael, you must look for him there."

"Gracias."

"De nada." The dark eyes held Matt's "I think you didn't tell me everything. That is sometimes what a man must do. Because I like you . . . trust you, I have told you what I know." Pancho touched Matt's shoulder. "Is there any way I can persuade you to forget about finding Rafael? I could use a man such as you."

"Maybe later."

"Later." Villa got to his feet. "This has gone on too long . . . the rape of our women . . . the rape of our beloved land. We have been at the mercy of the hacendados too long. While they grow fat, we starve. While they grow rich, we work like slaves and die." Villa paused and spread his arms, his short, blunt fingers pointing to the desert. "The land belongs to us. It is time to take it back."

The rising timbre of Villa's voice brought a thrill to Matt. Here was a man born into oppression who now led the oppressed. But he was also a bandit, a murderer of many. Villa was like his beloved desert—warm and generous, harsh and cruel.

Villa continued to regard him. "It isn't too late to change your mind, amigo."

"I have something to do first." Matt extended his hand. "I wish you luck."

"We will need it. Navarro is a smart general. He has beaten me twice, but I am learning." Villa clapped Matt on the shoulder. "I know. You want to find your hermano. Leave the desert and look for him in the sierras."

Villa's words followed Matt as he walked back to the soldiers. He'd wasted two weeks looking in the desert when he should have been searching the mountains! He wanted to shout his frustration. The next morning he left Villa's army.

* * *

Matt stopped briefly in Cortéz to let his parents know of his failure to find Rafael. Helen confided the disappointing news to Sabra as they rode in Helen's little buggy past fence-bordered fields and on to a Mexican home to check on Lupe.

"Matt's going back to the mountains to look for Rafael. If he doesn't find him, he'll go to Don de Vega and ask him to write a letter. He wanted to tell you himself, but Brother Cameron and I thought it wouldn't be wise. Not with all the talk and your father feeling like he does."

All the talk had commenced before Sabra got back from Matt's ranch. Willie had told his best friend that she had run off to warn Matt. Willie's friend had promptly told his mother, who told her neighbor, and so it had gone. The scandal had kept the gossips busy for days. Even the more charitable had shaken their heads and wondered what the younger generation was coming to—the Lindsey girl off with Harry Cameron for three days while the bishop and Sabra's father looked for them. There hadn't been this much talk since one of the Pace girls ran off with a drifter.

Sabra overheard snatches of what was being said, saw the judging and the excited whispers of girls who'd once been her friends. Only Myrtle Hamblin had anything nice to say, but since Myrtle was in love with Harry, she'd naturally think the best.

Some good did come of the gossip. It rid Sabra of Charlie. He came to see her two nights after she returned. "In view of what's happened, I think it's best if we discontinue our courtship." There was a white area around Charlie's mouth and he kept his eyes pinned on the wallpaper just above her right shoulder.

She knew he'd been deeply hurt, just as she knew they'd have been miserable if they'd married. Poor Charlie. Poor Harry. Poor everyone, especially her parents who suffered through the gossip, pretending not to notice or hear. Although her parents' hurt tore at Sabra, it failed to diminish her love for Matt. It consumed all her waking hours and embroidered her dreams at night. Things would work out. Matt would come for her. One day soon they'd be married.

Sabra clung to her dream during the long weeks while she waited, meeting the critical glances and accepting the termination of her employment at the Union Mercantile without once losing her temper.

The talk and speculation about Matt was just as bad. There seemed to be three opinions on the matter—those who believed he had a twin brother, those who weren't sure, and those who flat out called Matt a liar.

"He's always been a Mexican at heart," Fred Murdock argued. "Didn't I see him coming out of a cantina in Casas Grandes? This story about a twin brother is just a cover for what he's been doing."

Bishop Harris had done his best to silence the tongues. He spoke to the men in priesthood meeting, cautioning them against judging, and reading to them from the scriptures. "I feel confident that Matthew Cameron will return with evidence to prove his innocence. As for this other . . ." Junius waited until every eye was on him. "I've talked privately with the people involved and I've been assured that nothing more sinful than youthful impetuousness was involved. As far as I'm concerned, the incident is closed. Forgotten. It should be the same for you. As holders of the priesthood, you should be striving to follow our Savior's example. You're also heads of your households . . . family patriarchs. As such, you're responsible for controlling the tongues of your wives and children."

No one had much to say after that. Samuel was grateful. The last month had been pure torture, Sabra's stubbornness turning his life into a maelstrom of hurt and frustration. Sometimes his mind hearkened back to the good times when Sabra was small, remembering how she'd toddled to meet him, smiling and calling his name. Now there was only silence broken by an occasional brusque request for her to pass the bread or include a jar of peaches in his lunch. His world had turned upside down. Why must Sabra be so impulsive? Why had she fallen in love with a Mexican?

Samuel sighed. Nothing was clear anymore. Lately, he'd even begun to doubt his own judgment—Sam Lindsey, one of the most respected men in the colonies, a man whose counsel was constantly sought, who governed his wives and children so effectively there had seldom been discord. Until now.

If the truth were known, Samuel liked Matt Cameron. He'd always liked him. He was someone to depend on—good, steady. That's why swallowing the rumors had been difficult and why his explanation was believable. Deep in his heart, Samuel knew Matt had told the truth. He'd watched Matt's eyes during the telling, listened to each inflection in his voice. While his mind searched for holes in the story, Samuel's heart had whispered, *It's true.* If only Matt weren't a Mexican.

Samuel rubbed his eyes, trying to blot out the memory of the last painful scene. Sabra had come into the parlor, knocking softly before she entered, her expression contrite. "Papa . . . Mama. Can I talk to you?"

Samuel exchanged a quick look with Lizzie, certain Sabra had come to her senses. Maybe the breakup with Charlie had done the trick. *Maybe* . . . He should have known better.

"I'm sorry about what's happened . . . everyone saying things about me. I know it's been hard for you." Sabra's voice quivered. "I love you both and I hate seeing you hurt, especially when I know I'm the cause of it." There were tears now, her green eyes overflowing, a pause while she regained control. Samuel's throat constricted. "But I love Matt more . . . more than I thought it possible to love another person. I'm sorry. I can't stop it . . . the love, I mean. I don't want to stop it. But I do want your blessing." Her chin lifted. "I'm going to marry Matt, Papa. How . . . when, I don't know yet. Only that I'm going to marry him. I don't want to be alone at the wedding. I want you and Mama with us. All of us together, like it's always been. But if you can't . . ." Sabra's tears became profuse, her mouth quivering. "If you can't bring yourselves to acknowledge our marriage publicly . . . please, Papa, say you'll give us your blessing. Say you'll . . ."

"No!" The sound with its pain came from deep inside. It impelled Samuel to his feet, his fists doubled, his mouth working.

"Then we'll have to do it without your blessing."

He watched Sabra leave the room, heard the door close, the quick sound of her footsteps as she ran up the stairs. He was aware that his hands were still clenched, his mouth still working. What she asked was impossible.

He and Elizabeth sat in the parlor without speaking until long after their usual bedtime. No one had the inclination or energy to light the lamp. Samuel's thoughts and emotions writhed like an animal in a steel trap, his love and beliefs caught in a battle with no way out of the deadlock, no relief from the pain. Unable to bear it any longer, he left the room, the front door slamming behind him as he strode into the cool night air. How could he let his daughter marry a Mexican?

He began to walk—the need for action, even if it was only to move his arms and legs, a welcome release. Past experience told him he couldn't sway Sabra from her decision, and since God placed such high store on His children having the right to choose, it was doubtful He would intervene.

Samuel jammed his hands into his pockets and looked up at the pinpoints of light scattered over the night-blackened sky. The stars were only a small part of God's creations. There were millions Samuel couldn't see, other galaxies greater than this one. Weren't Jehovah's creations without end, His greatness unfathomable? Surely God could lead him out of the dark maze and into the sunlight again.

Carrying this thought, Samuel returned to the darkened house and quietly undressed so he wouldn't disturb Elizabeth. She'd looked tired tonight, more tired than Samuel had ever seen her, worn down with worry, tossing fitfully as he knelt to say his prayers. While he prayed, his mind veered to Sabra, wondering if she was praying too, asking for blessings that contradicted those for which he prayed. It was a good thing God was wiser than him and his daughter. Sighing, he climbed into bed and pulled the sheet up to his chest, leaving his shoulders exposed to the night breeze blowing through the window. As he closed his eyes, his mind slipped into the familiar trail it had followed for weeks, an endless circle that brought no peace, no answer, only emptiness and pain.

* * *

From her upstairs bedroom, Sabra heard the soft slap of the front door when her father returned to the house. Hearing the creak of the wooden floor as he walked through the parlor, she trembled as she relived the painful scene that had taken place there. Her father's refusal to give his blessing hadn't been entirely unexpected, but she'd hoped, hoped and prayed, just as she was doing now, her head bowed as she knelt by the bed in fervent supplication.

Prayer was as much a part of the fabric of Sabra's life as eating and sleeping. There were morning prayers, prayers at supper and again at bedtime, prayers at meetings and socials. Sacred communication with God wasn't taken lightly. Anyone showing irreverence was soundly reprimanded. The one and only time Papa had spanked Sabra had happened after prayers.

It had been on a winter morning when Papa and the boys had trooped in from chores, their cheeks ruddy from cold, everyone eager for bowls of mush and hot biscuits. They'd knelt around the table, chairs turned outward while they prayed. She'd hoped Papa would call on one of the boys. Their prayers were short and Sabra was hungry. She inwardly groaned when Papa called on Mama. Ordinarily a woman of few words, Elizabeth sometimes outdid Samuel when it came to praying. Sabra closed her eyes and resigned herself for a long wait.

All would have been fine if Rob hadn't crawled the length of the table to join her—Rob who laughed as easily as he rode a horse, who set off Sabra's giggles with his outlandish faces. He was pulling one now. She knew it, even though her eyes were shut tight. She heard his movement, sensed his pent-up laughter. A giggle started to form. *That imp.* Just wait 'til they got outside.

The need to giggle swelled while Mama's soft voice went on, "Turn us from evil, O Lord, as Thou didst with the children of

Israel." Mama's knees cracked as she rose and walked to the stove to check on the biscuits, the soft cadence of her voice never varying. The fact that Mama sometimes got up to stir the contents of a pan or rescue the biscuits while she prayed was so commonplace Sabra didn't give it thought. To waste food was a sin. So was shortening morning or evening prayers. Quiet trips to the stove were Mama's solution.

Rob used the sound of Elizabeth's footsteps to mask his movement. His fingers skittered across Sabra's ribs. Her giggle leaped out of its own accord, rippling through the kitchen to collide with Mama's prayer. Sabra clapped a hand to her mouth just as Samuel's broad palm hit her bottom with a resounding smack. Tears of humiliation replaced the giggle, the pain of the spanking hardly noticed as she looked up into her father's angry eyes—Papa who'd never spanked *her*, though he'd taken the razor strap to the boys on more than one occasion.

Papa believed women were the Lord's handmaids, sacred vessels for creating life and objects to cherish even while still girls. Men, on the other hand, were prone to the buffeting of Satan, the lusts of the flesh lurking just under the surface; such temptations a man must learn to subdue. The training began as boys, discipline and obedience in small things the cornerstone upon which later control would depend.

Elizabeth's prayer was cut short, Sabra was sent to her room, and Samuel, with razor strap in hand, took Rob out to the barn. At first Sabra was mutinous. She was hungry. Now her breakfast would be fed to the chickens, the mush thinned into a gruel and mixed with grain to tempt the chickens into laying more eggs. Then she remembered Rob. Two years her elder, he was her favorite brother, always teasing and laughing, her ally in trouble. The little willow switch Mama kept behind the kitchen door stung the back of Rob's legs as often as it stung Sabra's. Poor Rob. The willow stick was their private joke. The razor strap was another matter.

After that, Sabra schooled herself to endure the long prayers by concentrating on the words—Papa and Mama vocally poured out their hearts for all of their children. Lately Sabra had taken up more than her share of space in the daily prayers, her parents' worst fears carefully couched in familiar phrases: *"Bless Sabra to live so as to be worthy to enter thy holy temple, to choose a husband who honors his priesthood.*" Masked behind the phrase was their silent plea, *"Bless our daughter to choose wisely . . . not a man with a sullied reputation . . . and not a Mexican."*

Although there were times Sabra thought church meetings tedious, she'd never doubted God. He was her friend, her only confidant since Becky had been sent away. Now as she knelt beside her bed, she prayed aloud, hoping Samuel as well as God would hear her, the words penetrating down through the boards of the floor and into her parents' hearts. *Please soften Mama's and Papa's hearts. Help them to see Matt's goodness and forget about the color of his skin.*

It was a prayer she repeated many times a day. Heavenly Father had answered her prayers in the past, healing Mama when Sister Cameron said there was no hope, helping Sabra find Willie the time he'd wandered into the desert, bringing Matt back to Cortéz. Matt's return was the answer to a prayer Sabra hadn't known she'd been praying. God had known she couldn't be happy with Charlie just as He'd known she and Matt were right for each other. If only her parents knew.

"Please soften Papa's heart," she repeated.

But what if the answer was no? The thought struck like terror, causing Sabra to spring to her feet, conscious of her pounding heart. What was it Aunt Mae had told her years ago when her baby cousin died? *"God always answers our prayers, Sabra. But sometimes the answer is no."* Heavenly Father wouldn't tell her no, not when He'd gone to the trouble of bringing Matt back to Cortéz. Would He?

She fumbled for her clothes, dressed, and hurried to Aunt Mae's house, stumbling on the uneven path in the darkness, sobs choking her throat. Aunt Mae had always offered a haven, her ample body pillowing her head while she poured out her frustration. Never taking sides, Aunt Mae mostly just listened. Always, even though the situation hadn't changed, Sabra had returned from her second home with a quieter heart. Aunt Mae wouldn't let her down.

CHAPTER 17

Mae Lindsey hadn't slept well. In fact, if the truth were known, she hadn't slept well for more than a month, the situation with Sabra and Matt throwing her usually placid life into turmoil. Mae knew the problem wasn't her business, just as she knew any advice she gave Sam and Lizzie wouldn't be welcome. But couldn't they see what they were doing, how they were driving Sabra further away?

Mae mulled the situation over while she scrubbed a stain from Samuel's best shirt, held it up to the sunlight, then rubbed it vigorously between her hands. Although Sabra was Mae's niece and the child of her shared husband, Mae considered the girl her daughter, one she shared with her sister—cosseting and spoiling the perky mite, watching her grow, loving her. To see Sabra's longing and love for Matt and to watch her unhappiness since Samuel had refused to let them marry was almost past bearing. Especially after the long talk she'd had with Sabra the night before. Particularly when Sam and Lizzie were being so pigheaded.

Sabra's parents weren't all that bothered Mae. There was more, though the crux of it had been buried for years, not to be thought of or looked at like the faded photograph and the lock of brown hair Mae kept in a box tied with blue ribbon.

"Porter." It was a name Mae hadn't allowed herself to speak in over twenty years. She whispered it now, her mind flying to her girl-hood while water dripped from Samuel's shirt to run in soapy trails over the washboard. The rangy cowboy had stolen Mae's heart the summer she turned nineteen, his hazel eyes crinkling at the corners, his lips raised in a rakish grin. Everything about Porter whispered mischief, but there was strength too, one honed to lean hardness from herding cattle on the harsh Nevada desert.

When Porter had ridden into the little town of Honeyvale, Utah Territory, he'd immediately attracted attention. Unfortunately, most of it wasn't good. Strangers weren't welcome in the close-knit Mormon community, especially strangers who cussed and smoked tobacco and drank hard liquor. Porter had only intended to stay for a day or two, just long enough to attend his grandfather's funeral. It had been a somber affair, one Porter had been anxious to put behind him along with all his strange Mormon relatives. He'd sat stiff and uncomfortable in the tiny rock church only half listening to the long funeral sermon and wishing he were somewhere else. His yearning to leave vanished when he caught sight of Mae.

Porter had shared this with Mae after he began walking her to that same church, sitting on hard wooden benches with his cousins, trying to make sense of a religion precious to the girl he loved. He'd been baptized when he was eight. "Dunked," Porter told her, while mischief danced in his hazel eyes. He hadn't been back to church since, a black-sheep uncle having taken Porter to his Nevada ranch after the boy's parents died. Now anxious to win Mae's affection, Porter had given up smoking and drinking. Refraining from cussing was more difficult, but he tried.

After two months, Mae's Swedish father had reluctantly given permission for Porter to court his daughter. Oh, what a courting! Glorious summer evenings riding with friends in the back of a hay wagon, giggling, dancing, and surreptitiously holding hands.

Remembering, Mae let Samuel's shirt slide back into the tepid water. Why hadn't she stood up to her father when Porter had admitted he didn't really know if the Church was true—didn't really know if Joseph Smith had seen an angel? Instead, she'd listened as their voices rose with angry accusations, fighting back tears, wishing they'd stop. They finally did, but only after Porter left, shouting that he wanted no part of such a stiff-necked religion, vowing he wouldn't be a hypocrite and pretend to believe so he could marry Jorgen Jorgensen's pretty daughter.

Mae had waited through the long autumn, certain Porter would return, certain he loved her as much as she loved him. After a long, miserable winter, her parents had begun to hint of another marriage. In a solemn, heavily accented voice, Jorgen Jorgensen told Mae that Elizabeth's husband had been asked to take a plural wife and that after prayerful consideration, Samuel and Elizabeth had decided on Mae.

Mae listened in a stupor, scarce believing what she heard. Marriage to a man ten years her senior? That was old. *Old!* Marriage to the handsome husband of her only sister? *No!* then, *no,* again.

Mae held out through the spring and into the summer, Porter's failure to return changing her into a shadow of the lively girl she'd once been. When talk about marriage to Samuel had become more pointed, she had prayed for guidance, but no clear-cut answer had come. Finally, worn down with disappointment and endless urging, Mae had agreed to the marriage.

The years since her marriage to Samuel had brought her a measure of happiness. There'd been the babies, coming at regular intervals to swell her shriveled heart as she snuggled them close. They'd almost made her forget the hurt, and in time, she even became content. Samuel was good to her, meticulously fair, always seeing that he divided his time equally between the two women. Little by little, Mae came to care, welcoming Samuel to their little home out in Rabbit Valley. Patient and good as Samuel was, Mae knew most of his heart belonged to Elizabeth. She watched when they were together, saw how his blue eyes followed Elizabeth as she moved around the room, noted how his hand lingered on her slender shoulder.

How could she know Porter would return two months after she'd married Samuel? He'd given himself a year to read and ponder the Book of Mormon so he could look Mae's father in the eye and tell him he believed. He'd come back a true convert, planning to marry Mae, take her to the temple, love and cherish her.

Mae didn't learn about Porter's return until five years later, a chance sentence let slip while visiting with her parents. She'd listened in stunned silence before she ran out the door, stumbling in her haste to get away. Mae had walked for hours, past well-tended fields and into the bleak desert—walked on, not seeing the chaparral and sage brush, ears deaf to buzzing cicadas and the scrape of her shoes on the rock-strewn sand. Like her heart, her senses were saturated with anger and grief. When she couldn't bear the hurt any longer, Mae opened her mouth, her cry crashing through the stillness, rising into a scream as terrible as her pain.

When Mae didn't return by evening, Jorgen went to look for her, driving over the bumpy terrain, his eyes searching for any sign of the daughter he loved, whose feelings he'd failed to consider. He found her just before dark as she sat on an outcropping of rock, staring into the distance. Jorgen helped Mae into the wagon, wrapped his coat around her shoulders, and set off for home. By the time Samuel came to Honeyvale to take her back to Rabbit Valley, Mae knew she was pregnant with their third child. She spent many sleepless nights, said many humble prayers. In time peace and acceptance had come, the sweet warmth of her answer like a swelling breath in her bosom. But it could not change the fact that she was married to a man she had come to care for, but could never love. Not like she loved Porter. Never like she loved Porter.

Now Sabra was being consigned to the same fate. At least, she was if Sam and Lizzie had their way—if Mae remained silent. Mae pondered what she should do while she finished the wash, silently praying for wisdom and courage, then carefully rehearsing what she would say. Later, after bread dough had been mixed down and left to rise in a sunny spot on the kitchen table, Mae took off her apron and walked through the block to have a talk with her sister.

* * *

Elizabeth was finishing the last of the ironing when Mae knocked on the back door. She called for Mae to come in and nodded a welcome as she deftly moved the flatiron over the ruffles on Sabra's green print dress.

"It's a hot day for ironing," Mae ventured after they'd exchanged greetings. "Isn't that one of Sabra's chores?"

The mention of Sabra set Elizabeth's mouth into a hard line. "It's supposed to be, but she rode out to see a new Mexican baby with Helen Cameron." Her eyes slid away from Mae's. "Samuel won't be pleased, but have you any idea how uncomfortable it is around here? The stiffness? My own daughter scarcely speaking to me? When we finally do talk, we're both so polite I can hardly stand it. Or else we're quarreling." Elizabeth's mouth quivered and her eyes filled with tears. "Remember how Sabra used to run to me with everything . . . the first of the yellow poppies, a stray kitten? And she was always laughing. Now . . ." Elizabeth exchanged the cooling flatiron with one warming on the stove.

"If you don't change, Lizzie, you're going to lose her."

Elizabeth lifted her head to look at Mae, the wooden handle hovering over the waiting flatiron. Her face was a study in consternation. "What do you mean?"

"Just that. She'll leave you."

Elizabeth fit the metal covering over the iron and snapped it shut. "Don't you approve of what Sam and I are doing?"

Mae shook her head and made it a point to meet and hold her sister's gaze. "It's wrong to keep Matt and Sabra apart. Let Sabra marry him."

"What a thing to say. I thought you loved Sabra as much as I do."

"I do. That's why I want you to change your mind."

Elizabeth plunked the hot iron down onto Sabra's dress and moved it in quick, angry strokes. "Sabra's been talking to you. She's got you on her side."

"I'm not on anyone's side. I just want to help."

"By siding with Sabra? You can't want her to marry a bandit . . . a Mexican?"

"Matthew Cameron isn't a bandit. You know that as well as I do, Lizzie. As for being a Mexican, what's so bad about that?"

Elizabeth grimaced as she rearranged the dress and set to work on a new area of wrinkles. "I shouldn't think you'd need an answer. You know it's not right. Mixing races . . . all the problems. Their children will be neither brown nor white."

"You're right. They'll be children. Your grandchildren, Lizzie, and you'll love them just like you do your own . . . and mine too, 'cause we've loved each other's children, tended, and fed them. What difference did it make whose they were? What difference should it make now, all this business about brown skin? It doesn't hold water. Not with God, anyway. You'd just as well say Sabra can't marry Charlie 'cause his hair's red. Or the Mortensen boy 'cause his teeth are crooked. Do you think God cares about such things? It's what's inside a person that counts. You won't find a better young man than Matthew Cameron."

Silence settled over the kitchen, one broken by the plunk of the iron, the soughing of the wind as it hurried around the corner of the house. Mae waited, hoping and praying she'd said the right things. But her mind couldn't block out the quick angry strokes Elizabeth made with the iron.

"I know this isn't easy for you, Lizzie, but I can't sit by and say nothing. It's been tearing at me for weeks. Sabra's not like I was. She won't let you spoil her dreams and push her into marriage with someone she doesn't love."

Elizabeth looked up, the iron still, her expression incredulous.

"You must know how it's been. Mind, I'm not faulting Sam. He's a good man . . . a good husband, but he's not Porter. He'll never make me feel like Porter did. I'm sorry. It's something that's needed saying, just like something's needed to be said about Matt and Sabra. I won't stand by and watch her be cheated out of love like I was, though knowing Sabra, she won't let herself be cheated. If you and Sam don't change, she'll run off with Matt and you'll never see her again."

Having had her say, Mae came around the ironing board and kissed her sister on the cheek. "Think about it, Lizzie. Pray about it." Then she quietly left.

* * *

Elizabeth watched Mae's plump figure cross the yard and go through the gate that separated the two homes. She lifted a hand to her mouth while she set the iron onto the stove, tears welling up in her eyes, her legs going weak as if they'd suddenly turned to water. For a second she felt like a stick in a raging torrent, dizzy and bruised on the rocks and debris. She shook her head in a vain effort to still the dizziness. Did Mae think she wasn't a good mother, that she was failing Sabra?

Elizabeth sat down and covered her face with her hands, letting the tears come as she struggled with pain and guilt. If she didn't give in, she was going to lose Sabra. The knowledge had been there for weeks, pushing into her thoughts while she tried to ignore it. But it couldn't be ignored any longer. Not if Elizabeth wanted to keep her daughter. Losing Sabra would be like tearing away the best part of herself. But Mae said Elizabeth was failing her, at least she was if she continued to stand in the way of Sabra's marriage to Matt.

Her mind leapt back to her girlhood, to the day Samuel spoke in church, a young man just returned from a mission, his handsome features alight with enthusiasm for his faith. She'd lost her heart to him, just as Sabra had lost hers to Matt.

Elizabeth had supposed it was the same with Mae, though the thought had caused her lost hours of sleep and a jealousy she often found hard to subdue. Settling on Mae for Samuel's second wife had been both relief and torture. If Elizabeth must share her husband, then let it be with someone she already loved, one whose ways were almost as familiar to Elizabeth as were her own. If only Mae weren't so pretty, so clever with her hands, so cheerful. The fact that Mae loved Porter had quickly been forgotten. At least by Elizabeth. How could anyone not want Samuel and love him as much as she did?

Apparently Mae didn't . . . hadn't for all these years. This astonishing knowledge made Elizabeth's head swim again as she wondered how it had been for Mae. It was something she'd never considered. The pain of it filled her with additional guilt along with fleeting satisfaction in her own fulfilled love. But poor Mae—poor, sweet Mae.

And now it could be Sabra. It was now that rankled. If Elizabeth wanted to keep her daughter, she must let her go. It was as simple as that. Let her go to the man she loved. But first Elizabeth had to figure a way around Samuel.

* * *

It was late July when Uncle Hans arrived, a day Sabra would always remember—a golden afternoon that suddenly grew dark as angry thunderheads rolled down from the sierras and pelted the desert with rain. Sabra had run out to rescue the wash, hastily gathering the fresh-smelling clothes into her arms while the wind gusted and tangled her hair. She ran into the house just as the first drops fell.

She stood inside the door to watch raindrops the size of coins pit and freckle the dry soil, listening as wind rushed through the cottonwoods, lashing branches into a frenzied dance. Sabra loved rain, especially the rain that came in the hot months of summer, its arrival heralded by dark clouds split with lightning and ear-shattering thunder. The smell of summer rain was as exhilarating as the storm, the wet leaves, parched earth, and desert greasewood creating a delicious fragrance Sabra wished she could bottle and save like Mama did with fruit.

Once Sabra and her father and Willie had been caught in a summer rainstorm. They'd been hoeing corn, their backs aching, sweat running in little trails over their faces when sudden rain came blustering over the valley, the drops stinging their arms and backs. When Willie looked ready to cry, Papa had taken them by the hands and ran to crouch in an empty ditch where spikes of thick-growing johnsongrass formed a canopy over their heads. She had felt safe then, safe and warm with Papa's arm around her and Willie begging for a song. Sabra couldn't remember what Papa sang, but she hadn't forgotten the sense of adventure, or that Papa had seemed to enjoy hiding in the ditch as much as they did. *Oh, Papa . . . Papa.* Why did things have to change?

The sound of someone closing the parlor window reminded Sabra of where she was. It must be Mama, for Rob and Willie had gone to Juarez with Papa to get a load of fruit from Uncle Ed. The trip was an annual affair, and Elizabeth and Sabra had been left at home with the silence. That's all there was anymore—work and the terrible silence that no one knew how to break.

Mama's footsteps sounded through the stillness. She took the clothes from Sabra's arms and laid them on the freshly scrubbed table. Neither of them spoke while they sorted the wash, folding and putting the sheets in the upstairs cupboard while sprinkling and rolling the pillowcases and dish towels for ironing.

Twice Elizabeth went to look out the window. Mama had been doing this all day as if she expected Papa, though he wouldn't be home until the end of the week. When the rain was letting up—the last drops an erratic drizzle from the eaves and the sun pouring through a hole in the clouds—a wagon turned into the lane.

At first she thought the blanket-shrouded driver was Matt. She ran out the kitchen door, shading her eyes against the dazzle of sunshine—hoping, praying. Disappointment knifed through hope when she saw Uncle Hans with his merry blue eyes. He was her mother's baby brother, a welcome visitor and everyone's favorite. Even Mama was more cheerful when Uncle Hans was around to tease her and tell her she was getting fat or to rave about her cooking.

Sabra's disappointment couldn't last long under Uncle Hans's merry onslaught. He brought the vigor of the thunderstorm into the kitchen, shaking rain from his hat before dropping it on the back step with the sodden blanket. He twirled Sabra around the kitchen, asking about his beautiful niece and, before she could answer, leaving her to drop a warm kiss on Elizabeth's cheek.

Hans Jorgensen had been sixteen when Samuel took his plural wives and his children to Mexico. Restless and at odds with his father, Hans had asked if he could go too. It was a decision he had never regretted. Hard work didn't scare him, nor did he let it interfere with having a good time. He'd worked with Samuel for six years, helping him build two new homes in the stark Chihuahua desert, plowing and setting his stocky Swedish shoulders to any task. When restlessness overtook Hans the second time, he married one of the Payne girls from Dublan and moved his new wife to a farm in the mountains above Garcia. He'd been there ten years, never really prospering—the growing season in the mountains was too short for that. Hans didn't mind. He had his Anna, four sturdy sons, and an almost untouched wilderness at his back door where he could hunt and fish when he wasn't farming. His only regret was that his two sisters lived so far away. There were visits, of course, and occasional letters—the last received from Elizabeth just the week before. *"Come,"* it had said. Hans had come.

"How long will you be staying?" Sabra asked.

"Just long enough to pick up a few supplies to get us through until harvest. And to see my two favorite sisters, of course." Uncle Hans winked at her. Everyone knew Elizabeth and Mae were his only sisters. "I have a favor to ask, though."

Elizabeth's hand jerked, spilling the hot water she was ladling from the reservoir so Uncle Hans could wash and have a bite to eat. *Goodness, Mama is nervous.* She was more nervous than Sabra had ever seen her, jumping at the slightest noise, forgetting to eat her breakfast.

"What's that?" Even Elizabeth's voice sounded nervous.

"Anna's not feeling well. You know how it is when another baby's on the way." His cheeks turned ruddy. "We hoped you'd let us borrow Sabra for a while. The boys can be a handful, and with Anna not feeling good . . ." He paused and looked at Sabra. "How about it? Would you like to come?"

"Yes." Sabra's eyes flew to Elizabeth, her chin lifted. "Mama . . . ?"

Mama poured hot water into the wash-up basin and tested it with her finger, her back to Sabra, her voice sounding strange when she spoke. "Of course you can borrow Sabra. That's what families are for . . . to help."

"Good." Uncle Hans grinned, his embarrassment forgotten. "Can you be ready by the time I get back from the store?"

"Yes, though we'll have to hurry," Elizabeth answered.

Sabra stared at her mother, doubting her ears and feeling as if she were dreaming. Didn't she know Uncle Hans's farm was just a few hours ride from Matt's ranch? In case Mama had forgotten, she wasn't about to remind her. Nor was there time to wonder at her mother's ready acquiescence. There was a lunch to make, her clothes to pack.

For the first time in weeks, the two of them talked. Mind it was only about trivialities—what Sabra should take and if she should wear her riding boots. "It's a rough trip, so you'll probably need them," Elizabeth concluded. "But I expect you know that."

Sabra nodded. The hurried trip to warn Matt had never been discussed.

"Be sure to take your apricot-colored dress. There'll be church to go to, probably a few dances." Elizabeth's voice shook. "You'll want to look nice."

Sabra's mind raced as she wondered how to let Matt know she'd be staying at her uncle's farm. In the end, she wrote a note and folded it inside one of Rob's shirts. After she bundled it with string, she hid it in the box with her dresses. If she told her uncle the shirt belonged to one of the Cameron boys, maybe he'd take it to the ranch himself.

Before she knew it, Uncle Hans was back, telling her to hurry so they could make it to Alma Whipple's ranch before dark. "We can spend the night there and get an early start in the morning." He hoisted the box with Sabra's things onto his broad shoulder.

There was an awkward moment when it came time for good-byes. Neither Elizabeth nor Sabra knew what to say. There'd been too many days of silence, too much reproach to make the leave-taking easy. Elizabeth gave her an awkward hug while Sabra's lips slid over her mother's cool cheek in a hasty semblance of a kiss.

Touching her mother, feeling her thinness, smelling the tincture of roses she sprinkled on each morning unlocked a wellspring of emotion. "I love you, Mama. Papa, too . . ." Sabra's voice broke.

"I know."

Uncle Hans helped her onto the seat of the wagon. With the flick of the reins and a wave, the wagon bumped down the hollyhock-bordered lane and splashed through a puddle. Bumblebees flitted from flower to flower. A mockingbird sang. Sabra heard and saw it along with the white picket fence marching across the front of the yard . . . and Mama hurrying to stand by the gate for one last look and waving.

Sabra tried to memorize the familiar scenes—Sister Wall weeding her flowers, the Harris girls playing dolls in the shade of a walnut tree, the whitewashed church. Perhaps she'd never see it again, never sit in church with her family—wiggling on the hard bench, listening to the choir with Sister Durfee's soprano ringing above the rest. Her ruined reputation and the gossip were forgotten. This was her home. Leaving it was harder than Sabra had imagined.

Uncle Hans was the first to speak. "I hadn't planned to make this trip until fall, but when I got your mother's letter asking me to come . . ."

"Mama wrote and asked you to come?"

Uncle Hans looked flustered. "She wrote about other things, too."

"But she asked you to come?"

He nodded and shrugged his massive shoulders. "I've never been good at keeping secrets."

"Did she say why?"

Uncle Hans looked sheepish. "I'm not good at lying either. Anna is always tripping me up." He grew serious, his blue eyes no longer merry. "Lizzie said you needed to get away for a while. She asked if Anna and I would mind if you came and stayed with us . . . though why she thought she had to ask is—"

Before he could finish, Sabra jumped down from the wagon, asked Uncle Hans to wait, and ran back down the street, her heart pounding and her throat constricting. Mama had written to Uncle Hans. Mama understood. Sabra ignored the bishop's barking dog, failed to see Sister Wall's startled face. *Mama . . . oh, Mama.*

Elizabeth still stood by the gate, wisps of graying hair blowing around her face, the evidence of tears on her cheeks, her apron fluttering around her narrow waist.

Sabra's steps slowed as she struggled to catch her breath and find the words to tell her mother all she was feeling. She quickly learned there was no need to explain. What were words when eyes looked deeply into eyes, when fingers touched and clasped?

"Uncle Hans said you wrote to him."

Elizabeth's nod was almost imperceptible.

"Thank you, Mama."

Elizabeth gave another nod, her eyes locked on Sabra's face, her lower lip trembling. Sabra's arms went around her mother. For a moment they were one, tears mingling as Elizabeth struggled to form the words she'd been trying to say since morning.

"Just be happy. I want my girl to be happy."

"Oh . . . Mama, I will." Sabra kissed her mother and ran back along the street to Uncle Hans and the wagon. When she reached it she turned for one last wave, one last look at her mother, then she set her radiant, tearstained face toward Matt and the mountains.

CHAPTER 18

The way to Hans Jorgensen's farm was long and arduous, rolling in a straight line across the flatland, bouncing through an *arroyo*, then climbing steeply from the canyon as it wound into the sierras. It took three days to reach it, bumping together on the narrow seat of the wagon, laughing, sometimes getting out to walk beside the straining horses. Scenery that had been no more than a blur as Sabra rushed to warn Matt could now be savored at leisure—creamy yucca blossoms, the inquisitive brown face of a prairie dog peering out of its burrow. Love and the knowledge that she was on her way to Matt had sharpened Sabra's senses. Had the desert always smelled this sweet? When had the sky been such a delightful shade of blue? Through it all she heard Uncle Hans's deep voice as he pointed to a snake coiled on a boulder or shared an anecdote from a previous trip.

"This grass used to grow tall enough to reach a horse's belly." Uncle Hans motioned to the semiarid edge of the San Diago Ranch that sprawled in undulating swells until it reached the mountains. "See what greedy men have done to God's country? The rich landowners have ruined it with overgrazing. You can already see cactus and mesquite taking over. Another few years and this will all be desert."

Uncle Hans shook his head. Like most Mormons, he had little use for the hacendados, especially the Terrazas. "They've done even worse with the peóns who work for them. Thirty pesos a month is all they pay, and every cent must be spent at the hacendado's store. It's never enough to buy the food they need, so they must put it on an account which makes the debt grow bigger and bigger, and old Don Luis gets richer and fatter. If I had my way . . ."

Sabra knew what Uncle Hans would do if he had his way. Everyone knew, just as they knew he had a soft spot for Mexicans. The big Swede was always going out of his way to befriend them. That was another reason Uncle Hans would never be rich. He was always giving things away—a young colt, a sack of flour, and himself too—happy, generous Uncle Hans who'd taken a week away from his farm at the busiest time of year to come and get Sabra. All because Mama had written and asked him to come.

Sabra shook her head, still not quite believing what her mother had done. Mama wanted her to be happy. Quiet, unassuming Elizabeth had opened the way for her to marry Matt, never once mentioning the letter as she'd helped Sabra pack her apricot dress, saying only that she wanted her to look nice. But how was Mama ever going to explain to Papa what she'd done?

Not wanting to spoil the day with worry, Sabra turned her attention back to Uncle Hans who pointed to the first of the foothills protruding onto the flats. "There's a stream just ahead where we can rest the horses and have a bite to eat."

Sabra looked past the foothills to the steep cliffs that lay beyond—coral sandstone ridges sculpted by centuries of wind and rain and crested near the top by a sable-green periphery of pine. There they were, the mighty Sierra Madre, Matt's mountains, and she was on her way to join him. *Hurry, please hurry.*

But Hans wasn't a man to be rushed. His horses must be encouraged and rested after each climb. His movements were careful and deliberate, leaving nothing to chance.

"I wouldn't know what to do without Nat and Bawley. I bought them as yearlings right after I married your Aunt Anna . . . trained them to the harness, then the plow. See how they work together. They're a team. Like a husband and wife ought to be. Like me and Anna." Uncle Hans's voice always softened when he talked of his Anna. "Ten years I've had them and they're still going strong. Most things will last if a man will just take the time to look after them."

Sabra decided Uncle Hans must want her to last for a lot of years. She'd never known him to be so solicitous, hurrying to help her down from the wagon, cautioning her about getting overtired when she insisted on walking up the steep road below the sawmill. Just because she'd turned eighteen didn't mean Uncle Hans had to start treating her like she was an old lady. But she was too happy to scold him. The heavy pall cast by the gossip in Cortéz had been left behind. Each mile brought her closer to Matt. Things would work out. Hadn't Mama opened the door?

The third day brought them into the very heart of the mountains. Summer had scattered the grassy valleys with every kind of wild-flower—yellow anise, pink begonia, a carpet of white daisies. Sabra had never seen anything so beautiful, nor had she heard so many birds—orioles and cardinals and a myriad of tropical birds, their colorful plumage flashing in the sun. No wonder Matt loved it here.

"We're almost home," Uncle Hans grinned as he spoke, his large shoulders hunched slightly forward as if he were straining to help the horses.

The horses nickered and quickened their pace as they approached the two-story farmhouse with its collection of outbuildings sitting at the bottom of a hill. The whole valley was spread before it. "Do you see why I left Cortéz?" Not waiting for a reply, he went on. "I've told your father how nice it is, but all he can think of is the short growing season. If I could ever get him up here, he'd change his mind."

She almost told him Papa *had* been to the mountains, but thought better of it. The less said about Matt, the better it would be. At least for now.

As Hans brought the wagon to a halt, four boys ran out of the house. Uncle Hans pulled on the reins and jumped down, scooping the smallest boy up into his arms and tousling the heads of the others. Everyone talked at once, the children's voices growing shrill as they vied for their father's attention. When the greetings were over, Uncle Hans helped Sabra down from the wagon and presented the boys—young Hans, Niels, Edward, and Sammy. "Remember your cousin Sabra?"

The oldest three nodded, but Sammy only sucked his thumb and tucked his blond head under his father's chin, china-blue eyes staring. Sabra hadn't seen the children since October. They had grown so much their faded overalls revealed bony ankles and grubby bare feet. But their hands and faces looked freshly scrubbed.

Anna followed the boys out of the house, tucking wisps of blond hair back into a bun, then smoothing her apron, which Uncle Hans promptly mussed as he put his arm around her swelling waist to kiss a rosy cheek.

"Hans . . ." Anna's protest was lost in Uncle Hans's chuckle.

"Thank you for inviting me to come," Sabra said. There was an awkward moment while she searched for something to say that wouldn't allude to Anna's advanced pregnancy. "I'm looking forward to spending time with the boys . . . you and Uncle Hans too."

"Mama says maybe you'll play games with us," Niels ventured.

"Not until you finish the milking." Uncle Hans had started to unload the wagon. "And only if Sabra feels up to it. Don't forget she's been traveling since Tuesday."

"I'm not a bit tired. It'll feel good to stretch my legs." She smiled at Niels, noticing he'd lost a front tooth. "How about Run Sheep Run?"

"Could we?"

"As soon as you finish your chores."

"Are you sure you're up to it?" Aunt Anna sounded concerned.

"Of course I'm up to it." What was wrong with everyone? Didn't they know she liked to play ball and run races as much as anyone?

Anna led Sabra into the house while Uncle Hans and the boys finished unloading the wagon. She liked the cozy kitchen with its freshly scrubbed floor scattered with braided rugs and everything trimmed in blue. The sight set Sabra dreaming. She wanted her home to be like this—homey and nice so Matt would look forward to coming home, just the two of them sitting across from each other at the kitchen table, a fire crackling in the stove. *Matt.* How many days would she have to wait until he came?

That night after dinner she gathered her courage and approached Uncle Hans, carrying the bundled shirt with the note hidden inside a pocket. She hated deceit, especially with her uncle, but it seemed the only way. "I almost forgot the package Sister Cameron sent for her sons." Sabra paused, not quite meeting Uncle Hans's eyes. "I'm not sure where their ranch is . . . the Whiting place, but Sister Cameron said it wasn't far. Maybe just an hour or two."

"More like three."

"Could you see that they get it?"

Uncle Hans nodded. "Brother Tenney runs some cattle up that way. One of his boys checks on them twice a week. I imagine Jake can take it up to them."

Guilt hurried Sabra from the room, eyes averted so she didn't see a worried pucker on Hans's brow, the quick look he exchanged with Anna. It was done. Now she only had to wait until Matt read the note.

The first week at the farm passed more quickly than she expected. There were always things to do—washing and ironing followed by long hours in the room Uncle Hans had dug into the side of the hill where Aunt Anna made and stored the cheese. She kept milk and butter there too, all of it sweet-tasting and cool.

Sabra watched everything Anna did with the cheese, storing the information away for the time she'd need it herself—the use of curd mills and screw presses and how the cheeses were set to cure on tiers of swinging shelves where they were daily rubbed and turned. Tasks, which had once been dreary chores, took on new dimensions. Sabra sang as she plucked a chicken and set it to simmer on the stove. While it cooked, she mixed mounds of dough to form a rich crust that tasted almost as good as Mama's chicken dumplings. All so she could practice, the skill held in readiness to please Matt . . . always Matt. How she wished he'd come.

She looked for him a dozen times a day, pausing as she gathered in the clothes, looking again just before she climbed the stairs to the little room under the eaves that she shared with the boys. Had Matt gotten back to his ranch, or was he still looking for Rafael? Her anxiety increased as the days passed. What if Jake had forgotten the package? What if Mama failed to placate Papa? And what if Papa came instead of Matt? This last thought settled like a lump of congealed oatmeal in Sabra's stomach and made it impossible to eat breakfast or concentrate on her work.

"Aren't you feeling well?" Aunt Anna's pretty features were anxious.

"I'm fine, just a touch of summer complaint. It's probably all the berries I ate yesterday." She'd say anything to keep Anna from worrying.

After that Sabra made an effort to be more cheerful, going with Edward to gather eggs, offering to help Anna in the dairy room. It was always cool and pleasant in the hillside room, though skimming the cream then washing and sunning the heavy pans took up most of the morning. When she finished, Aunt Anna set her to work with the butter. Sabra enjoyed patting out the buttermilk and molding the yellow chunks into squares while she and Anna laughed and talked.

Today Anna was unusually quiet, though several times she raised her head and looked as if she were going to speak.

Her silence made Sabra uneasy. "Is something wrong?"

"Just a catch in my back." She straightened and rubbed the small of her back. "Having babies isn't an easy business, especially the last weeks." Anna gave a final twist to the cheese press. "I hope this one's a girl. I'd like a daughter . . . someone to talk to. It's been nice having you with us." She paused and cleared her throat. "If there's ever anything you want to ask me . . . I mean about having babies . . ." Anna's cheeks turned pink. "The squeamish feeling you had this morning will soon pass. After that you should start feeling better."

"Feeling better?" What on earth was her aunt talking about?

"Until the final weeks when your back will start to bother you." Anna gave a nervous laugh and moved to the door, her steps slow and awkward. "It's time for Hans and the boys to come in from the fields. I'd better get something on the table." With that Anna closed the heavy wooden door behind her so the flies couldn't get in.

Sabra stared at the door, one hand to her lips, the other holding the wooden butter mold. Her mind tumbled with half-formed thoughts. *Babies . . . being sick?* Surely Aunt Anna didn't think she was going to have a baby. She sank down onto the stool by the churn as she recalled whispers about a Mexican girl who'd had a baby before she was married . . . and the Pace girl. Was that what Aunt Anna believed? That she and Matt had sinned and that Mama had sent her away so no one would know she was going to have a baby?

"No." The word came in a ragged whisper. Her mother wouldn't think that. Not Mama. Sabra pushed her mind over each detail of their leave-taking, remembering the love she'd felt when she realized Mama had written a letter to Uncle Hans.

The letter. What was it Uncle Hans had told her? *"Lizzie said you needed to get away for a while."* Understanding came. Uncle Hans had mistaken Mama's intent. He hadn't known Elizabeth had written the letter out of love, that it had been her way to open the door for Sabra to marry Matt. She felt a sudden rush of sympathy for what the couple had gone through, were still going through, though their mistaken assumption was something she intended to correct.

Sabra hurried to the house, skirting the chicken pen and setting the hens cackling. *Dumb chickens. Dumb Sabra.* She should have guessed what Uncle Hans thought when he kept cautioning her about being careful. But he wouldn't think it much longer. Not after she finished her talk with Anna.

Her mouth closed in frustration when she opened the back door and saw that Uncle Hans and the boys were already in the kitchen, washing their hands and calling for something to eat. She plunked plates and spoons on the table, her frustration building as the family took their places with arms folded and heads bowed for the blessing. Afterward everyone began to talk. Had Niels seen the big snake in the corncrib? Would someone please pass the butter? Sabra wanted to scream and tell them to hurry. Would they ever leave?

Anna, who usually talked as much as the boys, said little. There was a weary look on her pretty face, and one hand kept rubbing her back.

Uncle Hans was quick to notice. He noticed everything about his Anna. "Aren't you feeling well?"

"Just a little tired."

"You must rest. Do you hear me? Sabra can look after the little ones. Hans and Niels will be with me."

Anna shook her head. "There's too much to do. I'll be all right."

Hans got up and whispered something in Anna's ear. A moment later she smiled and let him help her out of the chair and into their bedroom.

"Rest," Uncle Hans admonished.

Accepting the fact that she must wait, Sabra washed and dried the dishes, then hurried the boys outside so the house would be quiet. They found a shady place under the trees where she stripped strings from a pan of snap beans and the boys dug in the dirt. Not wanting to dwell on the upsetting events of the morning, Sabra let her mind drift to Matt, her thoughts turning dreamy, everything softening as she looked with half-closed eyes at the tree arching over her head, its leaves bordered with gold from the sun.

She let her hands lie idle, felt the breeze on her cheeks, smelled the fragrance of the new-mown hay. Her world grew still. Even the boys, their hands grubbing in the soft soil, had fallen silent. There was only the faint trill of a finch, the distant sound of hooves.

Sabra's eyes flew open, the pan of snap beans and the boys forgotten as she watched the horse with its rider canter across the meadow. She got to her feet, shading her eyes with a hand. Recognition sent her over daisy-starred grass, laughing, half crying as she called his name. "Matt!"

Seeing her, he set the horse to a gallop, reining it in just before he reached her. He slipped from the saddle and stood with arms held wide to receive her, a wide grin on his dusky face. Sabra buried her face into the soft fabric of his flannel shirt, felt his muscled arms pull her close, crushing her and letting her know it wasn't a dream but a flesh-and-blood man who'd ridden three hours just to hold and kiss her.

"Sabra . . ." Matt's husky voice throbbed unevenly like his heart. He covered her mouth with his, the soft pressure filling her with delight. Each was lost in the other as they remembered their long separation, the lonely nights, and vowed it would never happen again. Never.

"I began to think I'd never kiss you again," Matt said

"I know." Sabra's voice, like her heart, was unsteady, especially when he cupped her face and kissed each of her eyelids. The softness of his lips sent shivers up her spine and seemed to turn her knees to jelly.

It took effort for Matt to pull away. "So . . . how have you been?"

Sabra told him about her father and about Mama and the letter to Uncle Hans. She couldn't bring herself to tell Matt about her uncle's assumption, only that Mama had provided them with a way to be married. That is, if he still wanted to marry her.

"Want to?" Matt laughed, his brown eyes crinkling at the corners, all of him shouting his love. "Just try and stop me."

"What about Rafael? Were you able to find him?"

The pleasure fled from Matt's face. "I've been all over the desert and now up here. There's no sign of him, no clue . . . nothing, though I know he's been seen. The man he's riding with has a bad reputation. People are afraid to say much."

"You must go to Don de Vega."

"I already have. I just got back from Valle Grande yesterday."

"And . . . ?" Sabra could tell that the news wasn't good.

"He's gone to Mexico City. They all have, even Padre Madrid." Matt didn't tell her Benito had forced him to strip off his shirt again to prove he wasn't Rafael. "Since President Diaz has fled Mexico, I think Don de Vega decided he'd better stay near the capital and protect his interests."

"How long will he be gone?"

"It's hard to say." He paused and his face brightened, an arm tightening around Sabra. "But since your mother went to all that trouble to finagle a way for you to come up here, I don't want to disappoint her."

With that said, they started back across the meadow, Matt leading his gelding, his arm around her waist. The house was their ultimate destination, though if it took them the rest of the afternoon to get there, neither would mind. It was the closeness that mattered, the joy of touching and talking and being together.

Edward and Sammy weren't that patient. Before Sabra and Matt were halfway across the meadow, the two boys set out to meet them. Eddie led the way, scowling as he demanded to know why Sabra had left them and why she'd been kissing that man.

"That man happens to be Matthew Cameron and I was kissing him because we're going to be married."

"You're going to marry a Mexican?"

Sabra felt Matt's arm tighten. "What a thing to say."

"I . . . I was only askin'."

"Well, the answer is yes. Matt's the nicest thing that's happened to me. When you get to know him better, you'll understand why I want to marry him."

"Oh." Eddie paused to take stock of Matt, his mouth growing as wide as his eyes when he took in Matt's muscular frame. "Since you're going to get married, I guess it's all right to be kissin', though I 'spect Mama won't like it."

"Eddie told," Sammy said. He was sucking his thumb, and his blue eyes were as round and curious as his brother's.

"What did Eddie tell?"

"Told Mama you was kissin'."

Edward gave Matt a quick look and set off for home, his bare feet flying over the bumpy grass with Sammy close behind. Although Sabra and Matt followed at a more leisurely pace, they were aware of Anna's round silhouette framed in the doorway. She didn't step into the yard until they got there.

"Aunt Anna, I'd like you to meet Matthew Cameron. He and his parents have lived in Cortéz for years." Sabra couldn't think of what else to say, especially when Anna, who was usually so friendly, only stared, her lips compressed, a frown etching unfriendly lines into her forehead.

Matt extended his hand "How do you do, Sister Jorgensen. I don't know if you remember, but we met at church about a month ago."

Anna remembered. There'd been talk about Matt Cameron as soon as he arrived at the Whiting place, but before anyone had a chance to know him, Matt had left again.

"I've been away most of the summer," Matt went on, "so I haven't had a chance to get back to church. My brothers have been there though . . . Harry and George. I've been meaning to ride over to visit. Then when I got Sabra's note saying she . . ."

"Note?" Anna found her tongue. "What note?"

"The one I wrote him." Sabra could feel her temper flare. If Aunt Anna didn't hurry and take Matt's hand, she was going to lose it all together. "Matt's my fiancé. We're going to get married."

Thankfully Anna reached for his hand. "It . . . it's good to see you again. Matthew, is it?"

"Most people call me Matt."

"I know your mother. She came to Juarez when we had a diphtheria epidemic." Just about everyone in the colonies had heard of Helen Cameron. Most were aware of the Mexican baby she'd adopted, too. Anna had seen them at stake conference several times, the boy sitting with his parents and smiling. Then, as now, Anna was taken by Matt's smile and dark good looks. No wonder Sabra was attracted to him. But mercy, a Mexican!

Then Anna remembered the baby Sabra was expecting. Poor mite. Think how she must feel, loving Matthew, wanting to marry him and everyone standing in the way. Sometimes young people did things they shouldn't. Anna had noticed, though, that the ones who were treated with love usually came back to the Church. Besides, there was the baby to think about. Sabra's baby needed a father.

Thoughts of the baby made it easier to be friendly. "Would you like to come in and wash up? Hans and the boys are loading hay, but they should be finishing up soon." She tried to smile. "You're welcome to stay for supper, too."

"I'd like that, but I'll wait to wash up until after I help Brother Jorgensen with the hay." Matt's eyes rested on Sabra, their warmth filling her with a promise for later. A moment later he was gone, his long stride jaunty as he led the gelding back to the barn.

As soon as he was out of sight, Anna stepped back into the house and headed toward the pantry. "With company for supper, likely breakfast too, I'll need to fix something a little special. Maybe a fruit cobbler. There's plenty of bottled peaches."

Sabra hurried after Anna, her mind groping for the right words. An inadequate "thank you" was all that came out.

Anna looked over her shoulder at Sabra. "For what?"

"For inviting Matt to stay."

Anna straightened. "I'm sorry I was rude. It was all so unexpected . . . but if you're sure you love him?" Seeing Sabra nod, Anna went on. "I'll talk to Hans tonight and see what I can do about getting things started for a wedding. Hans served in the bishopric with Bishop Carter. I'm sure if he explains, the bishop will want to make things right. Maybe you could even be married this week." She paused and gave Sabra a questioning look. "Unless you'd like to wait for your parents to get here?"

Sabra stared at Anna, her mind tumbling with the realization that her aunt had unwittingly furnished the final means for their marriage. She hesitated, her emotions in a quandary. If she told Anna she was mistaken about a baby, that she and Matt hadn't done anything wrong, then the door to their wedding would close again. Her father would never say yes to the marriage. Neither would Uncle Hans if he knew the truth. There was only one answer. She couldn't let the opportunity slip away. Her aunt and uncle would just have to go on thinking the worst.

"This week will be fine." Sabra's voice trembled as her mind leaped toward Matt and marriage. *Fine?* It would be wonderful. Who would have thought it would be so easy. She wanted to pinch herself to make sure she wasn't dreaming—to dance, sing, anything. Instead, she put her arms around Anna and gave her a hug. "You go and lie down. I'll see to supper."

Anna complied, leaving Sabra to flit around the kitchen, her mind in such a tangle she scarcely knew what she did—taking milk from the cooler when she'd meant to get eggs, forgetting to add salt. It was a wonder supper was edible, not that she actually tasted it. Her senses were centered on Matt as he sat across from her at the table, noting how his hair had started to grow over the tops of his ears, the way he constantly looked at her and smiled. Matt was the air she breathed, the sun that brightened her day, and in another week they would be married.

* * *

It was bedtime before Sabra had a chance to talk to Matt. Part of her could hardly wait to share her news, but the other part, the part that recognized Matt's pride, dreaded the moment. He'd be hurt. Mad. Maybe so mad he'd say no to her plan.

Sabra rehearsed what she would say while she washed the dishes, shutting out the happy chatter of the boys and the deeper tones of the men's voices. Uncle Hans and Matt had taken to each other, chuckling as they swapped tales about the idiosyncrasies of cattle while Aunt Anna knitted and rocked in her chair. Surely Matt would listen to reason. He had to listen.

When Anna left to get the boys ready for bed, Uncle Hans cleared his throat and mumbled something about hearing a noise from the chicken coop. "It's probably that darn coyote again." He reached for his gun.

"Do you need me to come with you?" Matt asked.

Sabra bit back a protest. Didn't Matt realize there hadn't been a noise, that her uncle was trying to give them a few minutes alone? She'd seen Anna take Hans aside before dinner and watched them exchange a significant glance just before Anna announced the boys' bedtime.

"I think I can handle the coyote by myself," Hans answered. "There's a real nice moon out tonight . . . almost full. Maybe you and Sabra would like to sit on the front steps and watch it."

Matt didn't waste time acting on Hans's suggestion, though he made a point of leaving the door opened. He pulled Sabra into the shadows, chuckling as he bent his head to hers. "Remind me to thank your uncle. He's . . ." The rest of his words were forgotten when Sabra raised her lips to meet his. He marveled again at their softness, how her body molded to his, the way they fit together. Everything was so right, just as if God had planned for them to find each other and marry.

It took considerable effort for Sabra to pull away. "We need to talk before Uncle Hans gets back."

"Talk? You're sure you'd sooner talk?" Laughter tripped through his voice.

"Please, Matt." She led him under the shadowy arch of a thick-trunked oak and turned to face him, one hand resting on his arm. "I don't want them to hear." She paused to gather courage. "Aunt Anna and Uncle Hans think I'm going to have a baby."

The words struck like a blow and left Matt speechless. Before he could recover and ask how the Jorgensens had come to such an outrageous conclusion, Sabra hurried on, explaining about the letter and what Anna had said in the dairy room. "I planned to tell her she was wrong when she finished her nap, but then you came . . ."

She lifted her head, her features indistinct in the shadows. "Then Aunt Anna said something." There was another pause, a slight stiffening, as if Sabra were girding for an argument.

"Believing what she does, Aunt Anna thinks we should get married as soon as possible. This week. She's sure Uncle Hans can get the bishop in Garcia to hurry things along."

"No . . ." Matt couldn't believe what he was hearing—Sabra's relatives thinking the worst of them, her uncle planning a shotgun wedding. He started for the house.

"Wait, Matt!"

He stopped and looked back, the moonlight accenting the high planes of his cheekbones and the stubborn jut of his jaw.

"It's our only chance. You know Papa will never let us get married. Neither will Uncle Hans. Not without talking to Papa first. This way, Uncle Hans will feel he has no choice . . . that it's what Mama intended."

"Your mother never intended anyone to think you were having a baby."

"Mama won't know that's what Uncle Hans thought. Not at first, anyway. By then I'll tell Aunt Anna the truth."

"No."

Sabra stiffened. "You're always so worried about what people think." The words were flung at him, anger overriding love. "Aunt Anna offered to fix things so we can get married and you want to stop her."

"You bet I want to stop her. It's bad enough having people think I'm a bandit, but this . . ." Anger closed his throat.

"*This* isn't true. *This* never happened." There was a moment of startled silence before Sabra's fingers closed around his arm, her voice soft and pleading. "We know we haven't done anything wrong. God knows it too. We're the ones who count, Matt. Us and God."

"Maybe." His mind groped past the anger. Perhaps he did worry too much about what people thought and said.

It's our only chance," she repeated. "I know it's not the temple wedding we planned, but it will be a bishop who marries us, not some Mexican official. We can go to the temple next year."

"Maybe you're right." This time Matt's voice was firmer. Sabra was all he'd ever wanted in a woman—more than he'd hoped to have in a wife. Did he want to ruin his chance to marry her just so he could hold onto his pride?

CHAPTER 19

The plan had seemed so wonderful at first, like an apple unexpectedly dropped into Sabra's lap, or God sending manna to the dry Chihuahua desert. The initial elation carried Sabra through the night and tripped down the stairs with her the next morning. *Matt and I are getting married!* She wanted to shout the words to the sunshine, dance into the kitchen—until she heard voices. It was Uncle Hans and Matt.

Their solemn tones and the knowledge of what they were discussing hit like a splash of icy water. *Oh, my darling, what have I done?*

The question followed her through the days preceding her wedding, lying like lead in the pit of her stomach and pressing onto her emotions like a thick, black shroud. Instead of being happy, she was miserable. Uncle Hans kept patting her on the shoulder, his blue eyes no longer merry, and Aunt Anna acted like she was making preparations for a funeral. Sabra wanted to cry every time her uncle looked at her, confess the deceit and tell him there wasn't any baby.

The day for the wedding dawned cool and clear, the grass outside the kitchen door sparkling with dew. The four boys ran through the house, their excited voices warring with Anna's shushing as she took applesauce cake from the oven. Upstairs Sabra laid the apricot dress on the bed, knowing it was what her mother would want her to wear. Then she took a warm bath, the bar of perfumed soap her aunt saved for special occasions worked into a rich lather on her shoulders and into her hair.

After she'd dressed, Anna plaited Sabra's hair into a thick French braid and puffed the sides into a pompadour. Part of her wanted to look pretty, but another part wanted to cry. Dear heaven, what had she done?

When Anna finished, she stepped back to survey her handiwork. "You look lovely . . . beautiful. If only your mother were here."

The mention of Mama was the last straw. Without knowing how she got there, she was in Anna's arms, her pent-up tears wetting the woman's neck. Anna patted and soothed, "It's all right. Things will be all right," just as if Sabra were one of her boys.

It wasn't all right. Not when everyone thought the worst of Matt. She couldn't let the deceit go on. "It's not true, Aunt Anna. Matt and I haven't done anything wrong. I'm not going to have a baby."

Anna pulled away. "No baby?"

"I was going to tell you that morning in the dairy room, but when Matt came and you started talking about a wedding, it seemed like the perfect solution." Tears closed her throat and made it impossible to talk.

"I see." But Anna didn't see. Not really.

Struggling for composure, Sabra explained how Papa had refused to let them marry, the business with Rafael, and how Mama had opened a door by letting Sabra come to the mountains. "I know it was wrong to deceive you. Matt never would have done it if I hadn't asked him. But I love him so much."

Anna was crying too, emotion blotching her fair skin as she put a plump hand to her cheek. "You love him enough to let us think this of you?"

"He loves me too. We knew Papa wouldn't change his mind." Seeing Anna's tears made Sabra feel even worse. "I know it was a terrible thing to do."

"No more terrible than what was done to you." Anna shook her head and gave an exasperated sigh. "Men . . . sometimes they can be so pigheaded." A need to blow her nose sent Anna to the dresser for handkerchiefs for her and Sabra. "You don't know what a relief this is. I doubt I'd have felt worse if it was a hurry-up wedding for my own daughter."

"I'm sorry."

"There are others to blame. Samuel had no right."

"I know Papa loves me."

"But does he have the right to choose your husband or interfere with your happiness? If my father had treated Hans like that . . ." For a second anger blazed in Anna's usually placid eyes, then she smiled and gave Sabra a quick hug, both of them pretending not to notice when Anna's swollen stomach got in the way. "Hans will have to be told," she continued. "Thank heaven he didn't say anything to the bishop."

Sabra frowned, unsure of what Anna meant.

"Hans decided not to tell Bishop Carter the reason for the wedding . . . at least what we thought was the reason. He thought it would be kinder if you told him yourselves after the baby became more evident."

The Jorgensens' innate kindness brought fresh tears to Sabra's eyes.

"Now none of that. Remember, this is your wedding day."

"Then the wedding . . . ?"

"The wedding will go on as planned."

* * *

They were married in the parlor, a vase filled with asters sharing a place on the table with the Bible and Book of Mormon. Only the two families were present. Harry and George came for Matt; Uncle Hans, Anna, and the boys for Sabra.

Sabra stood on the bottom step of the stairs, feeling shy as everyone turned to look at her, the apricot fabric of the dress molding to her narrow waist before falling in soft gathers to just above her ankles.

"Look at Sabra," Sammy whispered.

He sat on the sofa with his mother and brothers, the boys in white shirts and suspenders, their blond heads still showing the marks of the comb.

Sunlight poured through the multipaned windows, its soft light burnishing the stained pine floor with gold. Trembling with nerves and excitement, Sabra looked for Matt. Everything else was a blur—Harry winking at her, Uncle Hans standing behind the sofa, his blue eyes merry again. Her heart gave a little leap when she saw Matt talking to a balding man on the far side of the parlor, his muscular shoulders framed by the light of the corner window, his brown eyes seeking Sabra and smiling.

Everything became a blur again; the bishop's round face and balding head blended with the whitewashed walls, his voice seeming to come from everywhere. "Do you take this man to be your wedded husband?"

"Yes." *Oh, yes.* They would make the long trip to the temple in St. George when another wedding party formed. *Soon, soon . . .*

She savored the touch of Matt's hand as he took a ring from his suit pocket, the round circle of gold with the de Vega crest wound with thread to fit her finger, his own fingers sure and steady. Matt placed a chaste kiss on her cheek while the bishop looked on with a pleased expression on his face. If he thought it strange that neither set of parents was there, he didn't mention it other than to comment about the distance.

The family quickly crowded around with kisses and hearty handshakes, and Uncle Hans invited everyone outside to a table spread with plates of applesauce cake and glasses of Anna's apricot nectar.

Sabra smiled and chatted, though what she said she couldn't remember. It all seemed a dream, the soft clouds billowing over the mountains seen as if from a window—clear, distinct, as were the lavender-blue foxgloves growing in Anna's flower bed, the coral soil in the field of tasseled corn—all of it something she would store and remember forever, this day she married the man she loved.

* * *

It was late afternoon when Matt and Sabra reached the ranch. Matt brought the wagon to a halt on a rise above the meadow. They sat without speaking, Matt's arm around Sabra's shoulder while her eyes took in the native stone house butting against a hillside with a barn and granary giving balance on either side.

When she'd come with Harry, fear had blinded her to everything except Matt's safety. Now she took time to savor each detail of her new home, noting the three upstairs windows and a porch stretching across the front. Love hid the fact that the weathered wood on the porch needed painting, muted the red dirt that substituted for grass and flower beds. So what if it needed a woman's touch and lacked piped-in running water? There'd be years to make it comfortable—years to fill it with children.

"Do you like it?"

"It's beautiful. But I'd have liked it even if there were only us and the wagon." She paused and her lips lifted in a smile. "Did you know Papa and Mama really did spend their wedding night in a wagon? It took them three days to get to the St. George Temple from Honeyvale. Their parents and grandparents went with them, and they were all invited to stay with Mama's aunt after the wedding. Mama said there were beds and people everywhere." A quick glance at Matt showed he was smiling. "By then, everyone knew Grandpa Jorgensen snored something terrible, and when Papa saw all those beds . . ." Sabra hurried on, aware that Matt's grin had widened. " . . . he told Mama they weren't sleeping at Aunt Edna's. Instead Papa harnessed up his team and they drove out into the desert . . . so they could be alone." Sabra wished she'd never begun the story, wished Matt wouldn't grin so. "I guess they didn't want to listen to all that snoring."

Matt threw back his head and laughed. "Oh, Nutmeg!" Her laughter joined his, their happiness bubbling to mingle with the sparkling sunlight, the cobalt-blue sky, and the mountains. "If you'd like, we can sleep in the wagon."

"No." She gave a quick shake of her head, her eyes on the warm coral tones of the stone house. "That's where I want to sleep. That's where we need to begin."

"Sabra."

The change in Matt's voice drew her gaze, his brown eyes dark and steady.

"We'll be married in the temple too. Next year when a wedding party goes up to the temple, we'll join them. You have my promise."

"I know . . . and I thank you." Quick tears stung her eyes. It was what she'd always wanted—to love a man and know she could have him forever. Today was just the beginning.

Sabra thought about their beginning while she waited for Matt to unharness the team. There was so much she didn't know. She knew it couldn't be anything less than wonderful though. Matt only had to kiss her and she began to shiver. The sound of Matt's footsteps intruded into her thoughts. She smiled a welcome as they walked to the house, his arm around her shoulder, the other arm carrying the box with her things.

"There's not much furniture." Matt's voice was apologetic. "When Sister Doane came over this morning, she said she'd fix things up. You're going to like her. She lives on the next ranch with her grown son. She brought in dinner, so you won't have to cook tonight." Matt paused and set Sabra's box down onto the porch. "Well, Sister Cameron, are you ready to be carried into you new home?"

Sister Cameron. It sounded so good, so right. Sabra nodded her reply. Each was intently aware of the other as he lifted her into his arms, Sabra's chestnut hair gleaming in the late afternoon sunlight as Matt pushed the door open with his shoulder and carried her inside.

Except for a table, the main room was almost devoid of furniture. There was only a braided rug on the floor, a small table by the window, Matt's gun rack above the fireplace. And flowers. How could she miss the bowl of zinnias, brilliant orange and yellow heads, sitting on the doily-covered table. There were flowers on the kitchen table too. The table was set for two with mismatched plates, and a covered pot simmered on the back of the cast-iron stove.

Evidence of Sister Doane was everywhere, her little touches of friendship singing her welcome. Matt's eyes rested on the bowl of flowers. "Sister Doane said she'd make things nice." He sounded pleased.

"It was nice of her."

"She's a good neighbor." There was an awkward silence. "Would you like to see the bedrooms?"

Sabra nodded, feeling as awkward as Matt had sounded. Neither spoke as they climbed the steep stairs with only the sound of their footsteps for conversation.

Matt led her to a sun-filled room with a braided rug on the pine floor, lace curtains at the recessed window, and a bed with pillows plumped across the top of a blue woven coverlet.

"Harry and George made the bed frame while I was looking for Rafael. Sister Doane had an extra mattress. An extra bedspread too."

It was far nicer than she'd expected. Who would have thought crocheted curtains just like Mama's would be hanging at the window? "It's lovely."

"I was hoping you'd like it." A pause. "Sabra . . ."

The tremor in Matt's voice made her forget the lace curtains, forget about everything except Matt. She turned to him, saw that he'd loosened his tie and that the top button on his starched white shirt was unfastened. The reality of the moment flowed through her. This was her wedding day. Matt was her husband. There was nothing to stop her from kissing him. Nothing.

Sabra ran her fingers along the brown planes of his cheek, her eyes deep green and shimmering like a pool in the heart of the pines. Matt's arms came around her, his lips covering her mouth—soft, all softness, one hand loosening the pins from her hair, his touch making her tremble like the feathery leaves of the cottonwood.

Sabra had thought it would be night when they came together, the moon and stars the only witness to their love, a mountain breeze blowing across them. Instead, it was sunlight that warmed them, laying filigree patterns through the lacy curtain onto their skin. Sabra had never known such tenderness until Matt caressed her. Wordless, they lay together, held, touched, and knew themselves as one.

* * *

Matt wakened Sabra with a kiss. Morning light showed through the window, outlining the blackness of his tousled hair, his chin propped on one hand as he smiled down at her. "Happy?"

Sabra nodded. How could she not be happy, waking up next to Matt?

That morning set the pattern for the days to come—days that focused on being together, each hour filled with new discovery. Just watching Matt shave was an adventure, the way the short-bristled brush worked the soap into a lather, and Matt bending to see in the tiny piece of mirror above the washstand in the kitchen. Bacon sizzled in a pan, but Sabra forgot to turn it. Instead her eyes were on Matt as a swath of bronzed skin reemerged behind the straight-edged razor. She was drawn to Matt like a bee to nectar. Her lips wanted to follow the path of the razor, just as her fingers longed to comb through his tousled hair. Breakfast had to be started again, the burned bacon given to the pigs and the overheated pan set outside to cool. They laughed about it afterward, their laughter coming without thought, just like their happiness.

Matt kept the chores to a minimum, and those that needed to be done were done together. They walked hand in hand to check on the new bull in the east pasture, packed a lunch when they went farther afield. It was their honeymoon, their time of melding and discovery. For an entire week they were left alone. No one disturbed them. Not even Sister Doane.

* * *

Harry and George were the first to come. They rode into the ranch on a Friday morning, bedrolls tied to the back of their saddles, greeting Matt as he emerged from the barn.

"Thought we'd come by and see if you needed some help with the hay before we went back down to Cortéz," Harry said by way of greeting.

"I could use the help." Matt took Harry's hand as he dismounted and clapped a friendly arm on George's shoulder.

"How's it been for you over at Sister Doane's?"

"Fine." Mischief danced in Harry's eyes. "How's it been for you over here?"

"Fine."

Harry hooted and George chuckled. "Looks like you're more than fine."

Matt knew his best defense against Harry's razzing was to ignore it. "Have you eaten breakfast yet?"

Harry nodded. "Sister Doane saw to that. She also sent a loaf of bread and some fresh-churned butter."

George and Harry stayed for three days to help Matt get in the hay and check on the fences. When they left, they carried letters to the Camerons and Lindseys, telling them about the wedding.

Writing to her parents was difficult, especially when Sabra didn't know what Uncle Hans might have written. The letter was brief and said little about the circumstances leading to the ceremony. Instead it dwelt on her happiness and her hope that past differences could be forgotten.

After that, all she could do was wait for her mother to write. She knew it would be Mama. At first, anyway. But later . . . maybe later Papa would forgive her and write.

CHAPTER 20

June 1912

Samuel Lindsey paused at the end of the field, rubbing his aching back as he leaned on his hoe and looked at the rows of greening corn. The sight of the two-foot stalks filled him with satisfaction. Watching things grow always did that to Samuel, making him feel a little like God must as he planted and waited for the seeds to burgeon with new life. Farming was hard work—plowing and planting and sending the precious river water down the furrows, the need for constant weeding. But the reward at harvest time made the hours of back-breaking labor worthwhile.

Samuel's attention shifted from the rows of corn to his six sons strung out in the field behind him—backs bent, muscular arms moving as they hoed the pesky redroots and pigweed. Today was going to be another scorcher, and young Clyde was already tiring. At ten, he was experiencing his first summer to spend a full day in the fields; his excitement at being considered big enough to be with the older boys was fast fading.

"Can we stop and rest when we get to the end of our row?" Clyde called.

"We can."

Samuel wiped the sweat from his face and started hoeing on Clyde's row. Rob and Walt were almost finished. He knew they'd start back to help Jake and Willie. They were good boys, though four were missing from the field—Carl having married and gone into partnership with his father-in-law, Del just three months from being released from his mission, and Joey and Swen still too small to be much help.

Samuel had discovered that fatherhood and farming were much alike. Feeding and nurturing his children was like watering and weeding his crops—fresh combed heads and scrubbed faces on Sunday morning were like bins of golden wheat at harvest time. Unfortunately, Sabra's marriage to Matt Cameron had soured the metaphor.

He couldn't think of his daughter without a fresh stab of pain. Where had they gone wrong? Or had they gone wrong? Maybe Sabra would have gone her own way even if he and Lizzie had been perfect parents. She'd always been a furrow that wouldn't lie straight, a stalk of wheat wanting to grow in a barley field. Such hadn't stopped him from delighting in her, his bright-haired girl a sweet morsel after a steady diet of bread-and-gravy sons. Now Sabra was about to become a mother herself.

Samuel's mouth tightened as he set his hoe to a stubborn redroot. Lizzie and Mae were excited at the prospect of the baby, and had crocheted tiny sweaters, stitched gowns, and even appliquéd a quilt with frolicking lambs. The women's reaction to the news was as hard for him to comprehend as their reaction to Sabra's marriage. How could they be happy when she'd married a Mexican? How could they be excited, knowing her child would be half Mexican?

"How can I not be happy when she's happy?" Lizzie had countered. "That's all I've wanted . . . my children's happiness. If she'd married someone who wasn't of our faith or who wasn't good to her, I'd be upset. But we know Matt's good. He'll never mistreat her. Since he's the one she chose, we need to accept him as our son."

"He's a Mexican," Samuel had argued.

"And Mae and I are dumb Swedes," Lizzie had flung back. "Your children are half-Swedes, every one of them. Try and get around that, Brother Lindsey."

He'd been so surprised by Lizzie's outburst that he hadn't known what to say. It had been years since she'd exhibited that much spunk. But last summer . . . Sam thought back to when things had changed, remembering his anger when he'd learned Elizabeth had allowed Sabra to accompany Hans to his farm. Tight-lipped, he'd stomped out to the barn, planning to retrieve his daughter. He'd been shocked when Lizzie had followed him and had planted her thin frame in front of the team. Hands on hips, she'd refused to budge until he listened to reason.

"She needs to get away, Sam. Can't you see what all this gossip has done to her? What it's done to our relationship? How long has it been since you've really spoken to Sabra . . . laughed and hugged her? Weeks. Months. Soon we won't have a daughter, at least not one who loves us. Can't you see she needs time away?"

Samuel could . . . did, but his grudging acquiescence had quickly changed to blame and anger when they learned Sabra had married Matt. He never should have listened to Lizzie . . . to Mae. He should've gone after Sabra in time to stop the wedding. As for Hans—how could he have been so easily duped?

He didn't like to think of the months that had followed. Sabra's betrayal had drained all the color from his life. Things that had once brought pleasure no longer did. Distress dogged his every step, following him into the fields; it caused him to lose his temper over trifles and distanced him from those he loved.

If Elizabeth had apologized or taken the blame, it might have been easier. But she refrained from doing either. Mae took her sister's part whenever Samuel complained, the two of them bound by the invisible tie of their Jorgensen blood. They passed an uneasy winter with little being said. With the coming of the spring, Lizzie began to do special things for him—rubbing his back with warm oil, baking his favorite custard. The touch of her fingers massaging deep into aching muscles and her gentle voice going on with talk of the day's events soothed Samuel's irritation and gradually put their relationship back into its comfortable mold. In time, they were even able to talk of Matt and Sabra without quarreling.

"When love happens, it can't be stopped," Lizzie ventured one evening. "It can grow, too, like mine has for you. If we try, I know we can come to love Matthew."

He thought about this as he straightened and looked back at his sons. Could he do it? Love Matt Cameron, forget the color of his skin, accept this man Sabra had chosen as her husband? He'd been trying for weeks—praying, knowing the matter needed to be resolved so he could get on with his life.

"We're almost there," Clyde said, a grin accenting the freckles splattered across his nose. Samuel hadn't noticed the freckles or how fast Clyde was growing, shooting up like one of the redroots, destined for bigness like his Uncle Hans.

It was then Samuel made his decision, standing in the middle of his cornfield with a mockingbird singing from the fence post, the brassy Chihuahua sun blazing down onto his straw hat. It was time to stop wallowing in self-pity and the embarrassment of having his daughter marry a Mexican. It was time to give himself more freely to his sons. He'd tell Elizabeth tonight, tell her to get things packed so they could surprise Sabra with a visit for her birthday. They'd stay for the birth of her baby, too. He'd see his daughter again, forgive her, try to make things right. After that, there'd be Matt.

Samuel straightened his shoulders. Accepting Matt would take some changing on his part. Some praying too. He knew Matt was good—that in his way he was as strong in the Church as Charlie. Even so, the task he'd set for himself wasn't going to be easy, but, by George, he was going to try. With the Lord's help he knew he would succeed.

* * *

Rafael Acosta pulled up his horse and narrowed his eyes against the glare of the sun as it glinted off the walls of the hacienda. He and the bandits had waited until afternoon when the vaqueros were usually away from Valle Grande, intending to swoop down on the ranch, terrorize and kill the family, and, after taking their pick of the de Vega riches, make off with their horses as well. Instead, they had encountered a bevy of well-armed men. Each time Ignacio and the outlaws attacked, they were driven back, their casualties and frustration mounting.

"Where is this place just waiting to be plucked like a plump chicken?" Ignacio cried as they regrouped in a stand of pine trees. "This is what I get for listening to a half-grown pup."

Ignacio's insult seared like fire and added fuel to Rafael's frustration. Where was Don de Vega and that black scorpion he called his wife? Five minutes with them was all he needed. He visualized his whip lifting the flesh from the hacendado's back, the butt of his rifle smashing into the sharp-nosed woman's face—ten lashes for the insults and rejection, twenty more for the years spent in that hole of a jail.

Rafael scowled and his fingers tightened around the trigger of his rifle. He must find something to salvage from the disaster. Something or someone.

The something came like one of the miracles retold in hushed voices by old women on holy days. It rolled toward them from the opposite end of Valle Grande with the afternoon sun glinting off the top of the black carriage. The sight of the de Vega crest filled Rafael with renewed hope.

"Look!" The excitement in Rafael's voice stemmed Ignacio's anger. His pointing finger told the rest. In the space of a heartbeat, the bandits aimed and fired, the driver and outriders picked off from the safety of the trees, the matched team and carriage quickly surrounded.

Before the coach stopped, Rafael jumped from his horse and yanked open the door. Now was his chance. Now . . . He staggered as the pointed toe of a small boot struck his chest. Ignoring the pain, Rafael flung a struggling boy from the carriage. He wanted to slam Felipe's face into the ground and pull the boy's arms from their sockets, but enough reason remained to stem his emotions. If he could not have Don de Vega, perhaps his son would provide him with a means of revenge.

"Don't shoot!" Rafael cried when Ignacio pressed his smoking pistol to the boy's dark head.

"Such a puny one isn't worth the bullet," the burly leader agreed.

"Don de Vega will pay a fortune . . . perhaps all he has to get his son back."

"This scrawny rat is Don de Vega's son?"

"Sí, though why he chooses to acknowledge such a sickly one is . . ."

Felipe's boot slammed into Rafael's shin. "Traitor! Pig! My padre should have killed you when he had the chance."

"Our padre," Rafael corrected, enjoying himself.

"You're no de Vega." Felipe glared at him. "You will pay for this."

"It is you who will pay . . . or rather your padre when he learns we have taken you for ransom," Ignacio countered. The disaster at the hacienda was receding. They had found their prize, although the prize still had to be safely hidden. "Rápido! We must ride."

They rode for the rest of the day, moving at a headlong pace through tall stands of fir, past fallen logs and windfalls, their captive riding double with Ignacio. Toward evening, Ignacio called a halt by a little stream to refill their water bags and rest the horses.

"The boy is in my way," the bandit told Rafael. "From now on, he rides with you."

Rafael said nothing when Ignacio lifted Felipe onto the back of his horse and lashed their waists together with a rope. Only pride and determination had kept the boy in the saddle. Now Felipe seemed to be past caring, his slender frame slumping in exhaustion against Rafael's back. Rafael stiffened at the contact, and his lips twisted with contempt. *The weakling.*

Ignacio urged them on again. Even though there was no sign of pursuit, the outlaws continued to cover their trail by riding their horses down the middle of a shallow stream whose rocky banks were dotted with enormous oaks and sycamore. Dried leaves carpeted the ground, and crystal water tumbled over moss-green rocks. They picked their way down the stream for several miles. Caution was second nature, the predominant thread by which they clung to life.

It was dark before Ignacio finally called another halt. Since there was still no sign of pursuit, he allowed them the luxury of a small fire. But the fire failed to cheer the men. Their bellies were empty and they had lost five of their compañeros.

Rafael sat on the gnarled stump of an oak and stared morosely into the flickering campfire. His thoughts followed the disastrous twists and turns of the afternoon that had brought yet another disappointment, another night of uncertainty and hunger. Who would have thought Valle Grande would be so heavily defended? Instead of riding away with the rightful share of his birthright, Rafael had barely escaped with his life.

"I never should have listened to you," Ignacio spat.

The snarl of the bandit's voice severed the train of Rafael's thoughts. For a moment he pretended not to hear, tried to ignore the sudden chill along his spine. Ignacio Mendoza's reputation for ruthlessness was as well-known as his prowess in the saddle. Few men in

Chihuahua could outride the wily bandito. Even fewer survived his sudden rages. "How could I know Don de Vega had hired his own army?" Rafael finally asked. "When I was at Valle Grande there were only the vaqueros."

"You should have made it your business to know," Ignacio growled. "Because of your stupidity, five of my men are dead and the rest . . ."

Rafael's gaze traveled over the remains of the once-strong band. Twelve pairs of angry eyes stared back at him. Death was part of a bandito's life, but to lose five in a single afternoon bordered on disaster. Firelight glinted off the surface of the men's hard, chiseled features, the features of men who stole and killed with little thought of the consequences. Rafael could read the accusation in the silent faces—accusation mingled with bitter disappointment. They had expected to ride away from Valle Grande as rich vaqueros.

"What good is this puny boy?" one of the bandits complained. "Can we eat him? Has he made us rich?"

"He will," Rafael promised, although he was as hungry as the others. Tired too—an exhaustion so deep it made him feel as if he were already an old man. Rafael had thought the life of an outlaw would make him rich. Its only payment had been two years inside a filthy jail, and after his escape, the constant need to look over his shoulder. It was all his father's fault. If Don de Vega had acknowledged him, his life would have been much different. Instead, the hacendado had stubbornly clung to that stick of a boy who would never grow into a man.

Rafael's eyes fastened on his half brother. Felipe's bony arms were still tied, his dark head drooped, and the sound of his harsh breathing filled the night. At fourteen, Felipe should have shown signs of approaching manhood. Instead he looked more like a twelve-year-old, and a spindly one at that. But scrawny as he was, Felipe was Rafael's only chance for wealth, his last opportunity for revenge.

"We need food," the surly bandit continued. "Rafael said there was no need to worry, that we would dine like kings at Valle Grande. Instead . . ."

"*Cállate!*" The savagery in Ignacio's voice silenced the outlaw as much as the command itself. "I'm tired of complaining. Are you boys who only whine, or do I ride with men?"

For a second no one spoke, then everyone spoke at once: "A hundred pardons . . . of course we are men . . . we will follow you wherever you lead."

"Then shut up and listen."

Silence descended on the little group, and all eyes fastened on their leader. It was rumored that Ignacio Mendoza and Pancho Villa were related. Both were stocky and broad-shouldered with handsome features and bushy mustaches. They even had a similar ruthlessness. Until now, Rafael had never been the recipient of Ignacio's anger. The older bandit had treated him like a son, schooling him in the ways of an outlaw, giving him special privileges. Tonight, he sensed a change.

"I don't want to hear any more talk about Valle Grande. I made the mistake of trusting someone else's judgment. It won't happen again." Ignacio's dark eyes locked on Rafael. "Tomorrow we will make a small detour on our way to the hideout. We need food. We should find plenty at the ranch in the next valley. The gringos there have plenty and their cattle are fat. We won't go away empty-handed."

The bandits nodded in approval.

"What about the niño?" Pepe asked. "He's slowing us down."

"When Don de Vega finds the ransom note, he'll make any inconvenience we suffer worth our time."

Felipe's small head came up. "My padre will cut you into a hundred pieces before he pays the ransom."

Ignacio laughed. "I don't see him coming to do this terrible deed."

"They've gone to Chihuahua City, but when he gets back—"

"We'll be safe at our hideout," Ignacio finished for him. "From there we can negotiate. We'll see how much value your padre places on your scrawny hide."

Felipe lowered his head and stared into the fire, his narrow shoulders drooping with fatigue. The boy's lethargy didn't escape Ignacio's notice.

"I don't want the niño to slow us down. One of you will stay behind with him."

"Rafael," Pepe suggested.

"You," Ignacio said as he angrily kicked dirt into the fire. "Rafael rides with me." He was tired of listening to others' suggestions. Wasn't he the leader? Aware that every eye was focused on him, he raised to his full height. "We raid for food. If we meet resistance, don't take prisoners." Ignacio paused and picked up his poncho. "Be ready to ride by sunup."

* * *

June spread a cloak of color and sunshine over the broad mountain valley. Birds trilled from the oak tree growing next to the house, and bright yellow daisies dotted the meadow. Sabra paused on her way to the chicken pen to savor the morning. The mountains stretched before her, their slopes swathed in shadings of vibrant green etched against an azure sky. Matt had told her she would love the mountains, and she did, reveling in their beauty—summer's wild dancing colors, the softness of autumn, winter's crispness.

It seemed only yesterday that Matt had carried her into the ranch house, yet nearly a year had passed, each day awakening to fresh joy and bright expectancy. All she had dreamed and longed for was hers, gilded by Matt's gentle touch, mirrored in his expressive brown eyes. Next month they would have the baby.

Sabra touched her distended stomach, marveling at the pulse and movement inside—tiny hands and feet pummeling her ribs and interfering with her sleep at night. Her life was at cross-purposes, the girl in her wanting to run free and unencumbered over dew-damp grass, while the woman quietly accepted her growing awkwardness and reveled in the new role of approaching motherhood with the creation of life and the need to protect.

Matt was as happy about the baby as Sabra. During the long evenings of winter, he'd fashioned a cradle—cutting, pounding, sanding until the rich texture of the oak shone like autumn gold. "Ours," he'd whispered, pulling her close and resting a calloused palm on her stomach. "Ours," Sabra repeated in the bright June sunshine. She wondered if other women felt as she did—the wonder mingled with fear. Sabra had never spent much time with babies. Would she know what to do?

Sister Doane and Aunt Anna said she'd do fine. Mama had written the same assurance in her last letter, and had promised to come for the birth and stay to help during the convalescence. There'd been no mention of Papa, who hadn't penned so much as a note at the end of one of Mama's letters. His silence was the only thorn that pricked her happiness. She wondered if it would ever come—the longed-for words of forgiveness and the return of his love. In two days it would be Sabra's twentieth birthday. Maybe there'd be a letter from Papa then.

The sight of a horseman riding over the crest of the hill pulled Sabra out of her reverie. Wondering who it might be, she raised a hand to her eyes and felt a stab of fear when she saw a second rider quickly followed by several more.

"Mexicans!" Her eyes darted toward the house where Matt kept his extra gun. The house was too far away, the yard too open and exposed for her to reach it without being seen. *Dear God, help me,* she prayed while stories of roving bandits and revolutionists flew through her mind. Women had been raped and killed, children terrorized.

Heart pounding, Sabra dropped to her knees and awkwardly crawled toward the granary, hoping the tall grass would screen her from view. Her only chance was to hide inside before the Mexicans saw her. *Oh, hurry. Hurry!*

It seemed an eternity before she reached it, knees tangling in the long skirt of her Mother Hubbard, breath coming in little gasps. Sabra's shaking fingers found the door's wooden hasp. Slipping inside, she pulled it shut behind her.

Chinks of sunlight pierced the cracks and pricked the scattered corncobs and empty sacks on the dirt floor. The full sacks were stacked against the corn bin, their tied burlap corners twisted like little ears pointing into the dust motes. Instinct urged Sabra onto the sacks where she awkwardly pulled herself over the side of the corn bin and dropped down onto the loose corn. Fear pounded with her heart as she curled her arms protectively around her swollen stomach, waiting and listening.

Familiar summer sounds were all that came to her—the soft bellowing of calves from the pasture, the melodious chirping of song-birds, the contented clucking of her chickens. An ear-splitting yell and the drumming of hooves shattered the façade of tranquility.

Sabra scrambled to peer out a crack in the side of the granary. The area between the house and barn was rapidly filling with men who brandished guns and called in Spanish to one another. She watched them dismount. Some hurried toward the barn and milk room while others cautiously approached the house. What if she'd still been inside, washing dishes or sweeping the floor?

She watched as the men swarmed onto the porch, their guns ready as they savagely kicked in the door. When the dark interior swallowed the Mexicans, Sabra's eyes remained fixed on her home, caught glimpses of the men as they walked past the sun-flooded window, her nerves on edge, waiting as she sensed their ruthlessness. Every story, every scrap of whispered conversation overheard after church jangled through Sabra's mind. Were the men some of Orozco's Red Flaggers, or were they simply banditos? Neither was good news.

Everyone knew the Red Flaggers were desperate for guns and ammunition. The Mormon colonists were a ready source, one General Orozco felt no qualms in using, ordering his men to take whatever the soldiers needed. Homes were searched for guns and often looted. The owner of a store in Colonia Diaz had been held at gunpoint while his shelves were emptied. Since most revolutionists owned no uniforms, it was difficult to tell soldier from bandit.

Sabra glanced at the horses, then toward the barn, where a Mexican, dressed in coarse woven pants and a white shirt crisscrossed with a bullet-filled bandolier, hurried out of the milk room with a large round of cheese. *Not my cheese!* she wanted to shout. Having taken it out of the press that morning, Sabra had planned to share it with her mother. A loud crash followed by a burst of laughter jerked her attention back to the house.

"Rápido! Take only what you can carry," a bandit on the porch called.

Several hurried out of the house with flour and beans from Sabra's pantry. One carried a quilt, another the extra gun and ammunition.

Those in the barn were just as busy. Bridles, ropes, and Sabra's saddle joined the cheese and a ham from the smokehouse. The voices of elated bandits filled the morning air with raucous jokes and laughter. A sharp whistle pierced their laughter as the man on the porch pointed to the chicken pen and granary.

Sabra's palms went clammy when two bandits started toward her. She huddled back into the darkest corner and hoped their haste would make them forget to look inside the high-sided bin. She strained for the sound of their approach, heard footsteps and rapid Spanish. Something in the timbre of the second voice caught Sabra's attention. *Dear heaven.* It sounded like Matt.

The scrape of the granary door thrust all other thought from her mind. Would the bandits be content with the sacks of corn, or had the pot of beans she'd left simmering on the back of the stove told them that someone was hiding? Scarcely daring to breathe, Sabra listened to the soft sound of footsteps, then silence, as if the bandits were looking around, tensed and waiting, as she was. *Please God, let them be content with the sacks of corn. Don't let them see me. Please . . .*

The silence in the tiny granary spun in taut, brittle threads. Sabra waited, one hand to her mouth, the other still cradling her stomach. The sound of dry, shifting corn broke through the stillness. She closed her eyes, certain the bandit had climbed onto the sacks and was looking down at her.

The frantic squawk of a chicken jerked her eyes opened. She heard shouts of laughter and more commotion. Someone was chasing the chickens. While her brain registered the theft of her chickens, her eyes fastened on the top of the bin. *Nothing! No one!* Then her tightly strung senses picked up a small sound as someone lifted a heavy sack of corn and carried it out of the granary.

The bandit returned for the other sacks of corn, the sound of his retreating footsteps mingling with shouts and frantic chicken squawks. Anger tightened Sabra's throat when she peered out the crack and saw men stuffing her lifeless chickens into burlap sacks. They were her pride and joy, a gift from Sister Doane, providing them with eggs and sometimes a Sunday dinner. If only she had a gun. If only Matt were here.

Suddenly he was—Matt, in the form of a bandit, strode toward the granary. It was Matt's walk, his stance, and when the young man lifted his head it was even Matt's face, complete with mustache.

Sabra gasped. It was Matt, yet it wasn't—Matt in a grimy white shirt and battered sombrero. "Rafael," she whispered. She stared, both fascinated and repulsed by a face so like Matt's she wanted to reach out and touch it . . . until she saw his eyes. They were hard and cruel, and looking at the corn bin with such intensity she was certain he could see through the cracks into her hiding place.

Then Rafael disappeared out of Sabra's narrow line of vision. Experience told her he'd bent so he could take corn from the bin. She'd done it dozens of times herself, sliding up the tiny door so loose corn could spill out into a bucket for the chickens.

When he opened the door she heard the hiss of the corn as it rushed into the sack, then she felt herself sliding. She frantically grabbed for the top of the bin, but it was too late. The rush of corn continued to suck her downward while her hands clawed the corn-slick sides of the bin. *Stop! Please, stop!*

It did, but only long enough for Rafael to set the sack aside and start with the second. Sabra was caught in another downward rush, her hand scrabbling at the sides, her legs sucked down under the corn while the rest of her rode the crest. Could he see her feet? Heart pounding and clammy with perspiration, Sabra heard the door close again.

"Ven ayúdame!"

Sabra jerked at the sound of his voice, too frightened to grapple with the Spanish words. Understanding and relief came simultaneously. Rafael was only calling for help—he hadn't seen her.

Before help could come, another voice ordered them to forget about getting more corn and to hurry. Voices and footsteps receded, and by the time Sabra could free her legs and look out the crack, the bandits were on their horses with sacks of corn and food tied to the backs of their saddles. Sabra's heart plunged at the sound of breaking glass, hammered harder when she saw the butt of a rifle wielded by a bandit smash through her bedroom window.

His compañeros laughed and applauded. Encouraged, the bandit ran to the next window, then the third, smashing through the panes with his gun. When he finished, he ducked past shards of glass and stepped onto the roof of the porch where he bowed and removed his sombrero. A white patch in his hair glinted in the sun.

Tears clouded Sabra's vision as she watched Matt's twin brother jump from the roof and mount his horse. How could he be like Matt and yet so different, delighting in destruction instead of building, stealing from those who worked instead of providing for himself?

When the bandits finally rode away, Sabra's relief changed to anger as they veered toward the pasture. Whistling and twirling their ropes, they herded away Matt's prize bull, the milk cows, and all the calves. She wanted to scream out her rage and frustration. Instead she futilely banged her hands on the wall of the corn bin and wept.

Time seemed to stand still after that. Leaning back against the side of the bin, Sabra wiped her tears with the corner of her apron. Her emotions were spent, and her body felt bloated and lethargic. Shafts of sunlight streamed through the cracks and burnished the yellow kernels that radiated through tiny dust motes to gild a gossamer spiderweb. She sat as if in a stupor, having no inclination to leave the safety and warmth of the corn bin—feeling, yet not feeling, wanting only Matt.

But Matt was miles away. He'd left early that morning to check on cattle at the north end of the ranch. It might be hours before he came back and saw what had happened. Perhaps the entire day.

It was the smell of smoke that finally roused her, wafting through the granary door. Sabra struggled to her knees, lethargy replaced by foreboding when she saw smoke billowing from the ranch house.

"No!"

She was on her feet, the unsteady surface of the corn making it difficult to stand while she gripped the top of the bin and scrambled with her feet for leverage on the slick sides. She had to get out and save her home.

If it had been the year before, she might have succeeded. Now, cumbered by pregnancy, the task was impossible. She tried—twice, three times, the sides impossibly slick, her feet scrambling and slip-ping. In the end Sabra could only watch in agony while the flames leaped and caught hold of the roof.

She mentally counted the loss of her treasures: the wooden clock Matt's parents had sent them for Christmas, the rocking chair Uncle Hans had made, the cradle filled with the tiny baby clothes she'd care-fully cut and stitched.

Unable to watch any longer, Sabra slumped into a corner and closed her eyes, trying not to think of what would happen if the wind shifted and blew sparks from the roof over to the granary.

Sometime during her agony she became aware of pounding hooves. Her first thought was of Matt, but he'd told her he wouldn't be back until afternoon . . . though maybe it was afternoon. She no

longer knew time or much of anything, only that if it were the
bandits returning, she'd probably lose control.

She crawled to the crack, hope and fear warring as she searched
the yard. "Please . . . God." She pounded on the wall, her voice
turning shrill as she recognized the rider. "Matt!"

Matt yanked on the gelding's reins, its sides heaving as he took in
the scene. "Sabra . . . !" Matt's voice was hoarse.

She pounded hard with her hand. "I'm in the granary . . . in the
corn bin!"

He dug his heels into the gelding's sides and galloped toward her.
It was Matt, not Rafael, dear Matt in the faded blue-flannel shirt she'd
washed for him on Monday.

She clung to her husband after he'd helped her out of the bin,
savoring the familiar smell and feel of him, crying as she recounted
what had happened. "Rafael smashed the windows and started the
fire," she concluded. "When they left, they took your bull . . . the
cows and calves too."

Matt held her while she talked, his warm, strong fingers caressing
her shoulders, his lips moving over her hair. "I thought I'd lost you,"
he said. After he'd kissed her and wiped the last traces of tears from
her cheeks, he looked at the smoldering house. "I'll take you down to
your uncle's. You'll be safe there. After that . . ." Matt paused and his
features hardened. "After that, I'm going after Rafael and the cattle."

CHAPTER 21

Matt and Sabra left the ranch as soon as Matt rounded up the team and hitched them to the wagon, urgency sending them over the winding track down to Hans Jorgensen's and safety. Sabra hoped they'd be safe there. Even with Matt and his rifle beside her, she still felt uneasy.

Anger rushed through Sabra's unease when she looked over her shoulder at the empty wagon. Everything was gone—their clothes, the furniture and bedding, the baby's cradle—all of it left to smolder in the burned-out shell of their home.

Sabra slipped her arm through Matt's, giving him a weak smile when he looked down at her. His mouth was tense and there were little lines of worry around his dark eyes. She wondered if beneath his outward calm, Matt was afraid too. Were men ever afraid? She thought of Papa and Uncle Hans, who, like Matt, exuded an aura of strength and purpose. Thank God for their strength. Thank heaven for Matt. Without him she didn't know what she would do.

Wrapped in unhappy thoughts, Matt and Sabra substituted the quick cadence of the horses' hooves and the clatter of the wagon for conversation. They both kept an anxious watch for bandits. Sabra was the first to notice a spiral of dust at the bottom of the hill.

"Look!" Her voice was tight with apprehension.

Matt narrowed his eyes against the glare of the afternoon sun, relaxing a little when he realized the swirling dust came from a wagon and several riders.

"It looks like Papa," Sabra exclaimed when they drew closer. "It can't be."

But it was. Papa, Uncle Hans, and Rob rode horseback while Mama, Aunt Anna, and baby Sarah bounced in the wagon with Willie and the rest of the children. Sabra asked Matt to stop the wagon so she could walk to meet them, her steps awkward, laughing and crying as she held out her arms.

"We wanted to surprise you for your birthday," Samuel ventured.

His kindness undid her, and tears and words spilled out. "Bandits raided our ranch. Oh, Papa . . ."

Samuel dismounted and enfolded his daughter into his arms—soothing, patting, the swell of Sabra's stomach telling him she could never be his little girl again. "When did it happen? Are you all right?"

"Yes."

Samuel brushed a lock of hair away from Sabra's face, noting her torn dress and the smudges of dirt on her tearstained cheeks.

"They burned our . . . house." The depth of her loss quivered through her voice. "Oh . . . Mama." Sabra turned into her mother's waiting arms.

"They rode in this morning while I was out checking on the cattle," Matt said. "Took everything they could lay their hands on, then burned us out. Thank heaven Sabra was able to hide in the corn bin."

Samuel slowly extended his hand. "How many were there?"

The constraint between them eased when Matt grasped it. He'd often pictured their first meeting, the awkwardness, Samuel's scowling face and accusing words, his own anger mounting into rage. Instead they were talking calmly, their eyes meeting and holding, joined by a common concern. "About a dozen."

"Ten," Sabra said. "Rafael . . . Matt's twin brother was with them. He . . ." She swallowed and stopped. "He was the one who broke the windows and started the fire."

At the mention of Rafael, shutters seemed to slide over Samuel's eyes. Matt felt a flicker of constraint before his father-in-law's gray eyes cleared and he gave Matt his full attention.

"They rode off with my bull . . . took some of my cattle too." Matt paused and looked at Hans. "We were on our way down to your place. Could you look after Sabra while I ride after the bandits?"

"You'll need help," Hans stated.

Matt nodded. "I plan to ask Lee Doane and his hired hands to go with me."

"I'll go," Rob said.

"Me too," Willie added.

"You'll stay with your mother." Samuel's voice was firm as he turned to Hans. "Can you get the women and children back to your place?"

Hans nodded.

In a short time, everything was arranged. Samuel and Rob would ride with Matt, stopping at the Doane and Tenney ranches for additional help.

"I'll alert the ranches between here and my farm," Hans promised. "People need to be warned. You never know who'll be next." He shot a quick glance at Anna and the children. "The men will want to help. I'll let them know where you're riding."

Matt nodded, grateful for all the help he could get, yet hating to leave Sabra. His heart constricted when he looked at her, knowing the terror she'd been through, wanting to kiss away the faint shadows under her eyes, stay with her and see her to safety instead of riding after Rafael. Anger seared when he thought of his twin.

As if their minds and hearts had been running along the same path, Sabra came into his arms, her head nestled against his shoulder, her face and lips upraised. For a moment Matt's worries and the watchful eyes of his in-laws receded and he was conscious only of his wife, the familiar feel of her, his love—and when he lifted her face—her smile, glowing like a radiant moonbeam on the darkest night.

"I love you." "Take care . . ." "I'll come for you as soon as I can." Their voices merged as they kissed one last time and parted.

* * *

For as long as Felipe could remember, he'd wanted to be a vaquero, galloping his horse after one of the bulls, branding his father's cattle. The desire had always been there, as deeply embedded as cells and sinew, as visible as his dark hair and hazel eyes. It was his dream, a bright talisman hanging just behind his grasp, one the fourteen-year-old boy had been determined to obtain.

After two days of riding with the banditos, Felipe's greatest desire was to get off the horse and rest. He'd never been so exhausted, the constant jarring seeming to turn his bones to butter and make his legs flop against the sides of the horse like those of a rag doll.

"Madre de Dios, please give me strength," the boy prayed.

Although Felipe's faulty heart had robbed him of strength, it hadn't diminished his determination. It and the de Vega pride were as much a part of him as his desire to be a vaquero. *Plucky,* Matthew had called him. *Stubborn* was the word used by his madre. Felipe used his determination like a goad, ignoring his mother's injunction to stay in bed, pitting himself against the constant tiredness, setting small goals. He was a de Vega. Someday he would make his father proud. Someday. One day. The words became a litany, one he chanted in his mind whenever he felt himself flagging. He wouldn't die. He would fool the doctors in Mexico City, his madre too. One day he would ride as effortlessly as the vaqueros. One day . . .

But not today, and not at the breakneck speed demanded by Ignacio. Felipe swayed and grabbed the saddle horn. If only they could stop and rest again. He'd rested most of the morning, he and a bad-tempered bandito left behind while the others raided a ranch. Felipe had hoped the raid would take all day. Maybe by then his padre would be back from Chihuahua City. Maybe Don de Vega and the vaqueros were already looking for him. Each hour the bandits stayed away increased his chance of rescue. His hopes plummeted when the bandits returned before noon to boast of their cleverness.

"Everything was left unguarded," Rafael chortled.

"We're still not rich," José said.

Rafael scowled and waited impatiently for Felipe to mount his horse. "The boy will make us rich," he insisted. A scornful expression crossed his face when he saw how awkwardly the boy mounted his horse. *What a waste.* He'd probably fall off before they reached their hideout. Then Rafael turned practical. "Eat . . . eat," he urged, offering Felipe a slice of ham on the tip of his dirty knife.

The others had done the same, passing the ham around as they rode. They pushed on for the rest of the afternoon, thick stands of pine and oak impeding their progress, pounding hooves and the crack of an occasional whip drowning out the peaceful sounds of the wooded upland.

Felipe wasn't the only one to feel the effects of their headlong flight. Despite heavy use of whips, the stolen cattle were flagging too, their lumbering gait slowing as they were driven up another rocky slope.

"Forget about the cattle. They're slowing us down," Ignacio ordered when Matt's bull obstinately circled around a boulder and started back down the incline.

"If we don't stop and water our horses, they'll give out too," José muttered. He looked away when he encountered Ignacio's fierce gaze, but it didn't quell his rebellion. He'd pinned his hopes on the riches at Valle Grande. All they'd found was a scrawny boy who could hardly stay on a horse.

A cry from Pepe added to the frustration. "My caballo's gone lame."

Ignacio cursed and rode back to Pepe. The others slowed, casting anxious glances over their shoulders for any gringo ranchers in hot pursuit.

"Take the boy's horse," Ignacio ordered when Pepe's horse couldn't keep up.

"What about the niño?"

"He can ride with Rafael."

Felipe managed to dismount without falling, though his legs almost buckled when his feet touched the ground. He watched through a haze of fatigue while Pepe removed a sack of corn from Rafael's horse and lifted him up to take its place.

"We should leave you instead of the corn," Pepe grumbled.

Felipe pretended not to hear, concentrating on holding himself stiffly erect to avoid touching Rafael. An hour later, Felipe was so tired he didn't care if his head lolled against Rafael's muscular back, though the smell of the filthy shirt and unwashed body was hard to bear.

Immersed in misery, Felipe failed to notice when their horse began to lag. He didn't see the other bandits' impatient glances or sense Rafael's growing concern, either.

Ignacio's harsh voice jarred him out of his lethargy. "There's a stream up ahead where we can water the caballos."

Before Felipe could fathom what was happening, Rafael lifted him off the horse and set him on a fallen log. The boy slumped into a doughy heap, his labored breathing masking the sound of the stream that gurgled between mossy rocks. Felipe hadn't realized how thirsty he was until he saw the water; thirst warred with fatigue as Rafael handed him a canteen.

"Here . . . drink." Although his voice was gruff, Felipe caught a glimmer of pity in Rafael's brown eyes.

Felipe gulped thirstily, avoiding his half brother's eyes as he drank. Some of the water ran down his chin, and his thoughts were so jumbled they made no sense. If only they could rest. He was vaguely aware that Ignacio scowled and gestured toward him, that he said something to Pepe, who scrambled up a steep incline.

A moment later Pepe's stocky frame dodged back through scrub oak and boulders as he made a hasty descent. "Gringos! Gringos are coming!"

Ignacio cursed and grabbed his horse's reins. Mounting, he rode it close to Rafael. "Leave the boy," he ordered. "He's slowing us down."

"But the ransom," Rafael protested.

"The ransom won't do us any good if we're dead. The gringos are too many."

"We can hold them off."

"No!" Ignacio's face contorted into an ugly grimace.

Rafael took a cautious step toward Felipe. "The boy's Don de Vega's life. He'll pay anything we ask . . . a fortune."

"I said leave the boy." Ignacio's hand touched his gun.

Terror clawed Felipe's middle, making his heart jerk in painful spasms. He was going to die. He'd feared it from the moment Rafael dragged him from the carriage and he'd looked into Ignacio's smoking gun.

Everything grew still. Even the birds ceased singing. Rafael edged closer to Felipe. "He's mine," Rafael said. "He's my hermano . . ."

Ignacio drew his gun from its leather holster and aimed it at Felipe's head. "I'm sorry, amigo." Ignacio didn't sound sorry. He sounded angry, his senses tuned to the sound of approaching gringos. "Get on your caballo!"

Instead, Rafael sprang toward Felipe. As he did, Ignacio fired his gun, the noise reverberating along the canyon walls, filling the chasm with the sound and smell of death. To Felipe, the explosion seemed to come from a great distance, the noise meshing with fear as he felt himself falling backward into silence and tumbling blackness that had no end.

* * *

It was late afternoon when Matt and Samuel drew rein at the crest of a rock-strewn canyon. Their horses' sides were heaving and both men felt ready to drop. They'd traveled at a breakneck pace, gathering help at the neighboring ranches, their ranks swelling to over a dozen men. All were seasoned riders and fair shots, but unfortunately none had ever lifted their guns against anything more than a deer or occasional cougar. This worried Matt, especially when he knew of the bandits' ruthlessness and that only John Tenney had ventured this far into the sierras before.

Anger marched hand in hand with worry. The memory of Sabra's frightened face, the burning ranch house, and his stolen cattle seared like the white-hot edge of a branding iron. He urged the gelding to a faster pace. He wanted to smash Rafael's face—beat him, yell. The years of mistaken identity and his ruined reputation had repaid any debt he owed Rafael. The raid on his ranch was the final straw.

"What do you think?" Samuel asked Matt.

Before Matt could answer, the crack of a gun vibrated through the trees. Fearing an attack, both men bent low over their horses.

"You all right?" Rob called. He and Les Doane were just a few paces behind. Rob was off his horse by the time he finished speaking. "I'll crawl over behind that big rock and see what's going on."

The ranchers watched for signs of ambush as Rob grew still, his long frame tensing, his sandy head cautiously peering around the boulder. After a couple of minutes, he lifted a hand and motioned to Matt and Samuel.

"Come take a look."

Matt and Samuel joined Rob behind the boulder. From their vantage point they could see a stream winding through a shallow canyon. A dozen mounted men milled among the trees. As they watched, a stocky bandit lifted his hand and set his horse in a southerly direction. The others quickly followed.

Rob raised his rifle and sighted in on the retreating bandits. Samuel put a restraining hand on his arm. "We don't want a gunfight if we can help it. Since I don't see any of Matt's cattle . . ." His voice trailed away as he continued to study the canyon.

"We saw some of Matt's cattle a ways back," John Tenney put in. "We thought of rounding them up, but changed our mind when the rest of you went on."

"What's that?" Matt asked, pointing at a figure sprawled by the stream.

"Looks like one of the bandits," Rob said.

Matt left the protection of the boulder and started down into the canyon. "Keep me covered," he called.

Matt made a wary descent, using the trees and brush for cover, only dimly aware that someone followed him. His anger toward Rafael was replaced by dread and a fatalistic premonition of what he would find—not the light-hearted brother who'd saved him from the cougar, but a hardened bandit who'd raided his ranch, smashing and burning Matt's dream before he left.

Matt's steps slowed when he neared the floor of the canyon. By the time he reached the stream, Samuel had caught up with him, matching him step for step, his presence lending comfort and support.

"That's one way to end an argument," Samuel quipped.

Samuel's words went unheeded as Matt took in the glazed, staring eyes, the slack mouth and handsome features of his brother. Deep inside something lurched, staggered, and cried out in pain. "Rafael . . ."

"He looks just like you!" Hearing a moan, Samuel's attention jerked to a skinny arm partially concealed by Rafael's body. "What in heaven . . . ?"

They dropped to their knees and rolled Rafael's lifeless body aside, scarcely noting the bandit's blood-soaked shirt and pants as they stared at the chalk-white face of a boy who looked vaguely familiar to Matt.

"Felipe?"

The youth stirred at the sound of his name, but his eyes remained closed, his energy centered in getting air into his starved lungs.

Matt loosened the collar of Felipe's torn shirt, cradling the limp head onto his knees while he searched for any sign of wound or injury.

"Has he been hit too?" Samuel asked.

"I don't think so." Felipe's labored breathing concerned Matt. He remembered the diseased heart as he watched blue-tinged lips gasping for breath. "It's all right, Felipe," he reassured in Spanish. He took the bandanna Samuel had dipped into the stream and laid it on Felipe's pallid forehead. "It's Matt Cameron. Do you remember when I came to see you at Valle Grande?"

Felipe's eyes flickered open in disbelief. "Matt . . . ?" he whispered.

Matt nodded and grasped Felipe's slender hand. "Everything's going to be all right. We're here to help you."

"Matt . . ." A weak smile lifted the corners of Felipe's gray lips. His eyes closed, then quickly opened as if he didn't believe what he'd seen. "Hermano."

"Sí," Matt replied. He tried to make Felipe comfortable while questions raced through his head. What was Felipe doing with the bandits? Had he been with them when they'd raided the ranch?

"Is . . . is Rafael . . . dead?" Felipe's words were spun between rasps of harsh breathing.

Matt nodded, not trusting himself to speak.

"Rafael . . . saved my life," Felipe said.

"He what?"

"Saved . . . my life. Ignacio was going to shoot me . . . but Rafael . . ."

Matt eased Felipe into a sitting position while the boy poured out the story of his kidnapping and Rafael's grandiose plans for wealth. Felipe's voice faltered from time to time as Matt prompted and asked questions.

Since the conversation was in Spanish, Samuel had little to say, though his gaze frequently went from Matt to Rafael. He called to Rob to bring a blanket. By the time Felipe finished his story, Rob and the ranchers had joined them by the stream.

The sight of Rafael prompted more questions, which Matt answered, giving an abbreviated version of Felipe's story.

"The poor kid looks like he could use a week in bed." Rob draped his vest around Felipe's thin shoulders and offered him a drink from his water bag before he walked over to Rafael. "What are we gonna do with him?"

Matt hadn't given any thought to that. He looked at Rafael's still form. Samuel had covered it with a blanket. Instead of satisfaction, he felt sorrow as he noted the filthy shirt, the worn-out boots, and the sweat-matted black hair. It seemed impossible that he and Rafael had shared the warmth and security of a velvety dark womb—two innocents thrust into the harsh world of illegitimacy and poverty. Fate, or perhaps Helen Cameron's prayers, had rescued Matt and given him life and advantage with the Mormons. Poor Rafael had known only bitterness and rejection. The thought brought unbidden tears to Matt's eyes.

"I guess we'd better take him with us and bury him on my ranch." As soon as he spoke, Matt knew his decision was right. Rafael, who'd never had a home, would have one now. Up by that big tree about a mile from the ranch house would be perfect, he decided. It was a pretty place, one he knew their Mexican mother would have liked. "We'll bury him on my ranch," Matt repeated quietly.

CHAPTER 22

After building a fire to make Felipe as warm and comfortable as possible, they spent the night in the canyon. Although the boy needed rest, urgency sent them on their way shortly after daybreak the next morning. It was afternoon before they reached the northern end of Matt's ranch. For Felipe's sake, they'd kept to a moderate pace, Matt and his skinny half brother riding double on the black gelding while Samuel and the rest of the men rounded up the stolen cattle.

They'd almost reached the solitary tree when Rob rode back to Matt, an anxious expression on his face. "I think someone's up in those trees." He pointed to a stand of pines on a nearby rise. "Got any idea who might be comin'?"

Matt shook his head and shot a quick look at Samuel, who bore Rafael's blanket-covered body across the rump of his mare. "Not unless it's Hans and some of his neighbors coming to help."

Matt studied the pines for any sign of movement. As he did, a solitary horseman rode out of the trees with a rifle. He paused to study Matt and the ranchers, then with a lift of his hand, he and an army of vaqueros thundered down the hill toward them, firing their guns and shouting a challenge.

Matt stared at the horsemen, the speed with which they came making them blur and meld with the rolling green meadow and the cloudless sky. Knowing his horse couldn't outrun them, Matt slid from the saddle with Felipe and his rifle, half supporting his brother as they raced for the tree. Rob and Samuel sprinted to join them, their horses milling with Matt's gelding while Les Doane and the ranchers galloped after the cattle with some of the vaqueros in hot pursuit. The rest of the vaqueros veered toward the tree. Matt pushed Felipe to the ground while he peered around the broad tree trunk, rifle cocked, feeling as if a horde of black-clad devils was descending upon them.

As Matt sighted his rifle on one of the advancing horsemen, Felipe scrambled to his feet and stumbled toward the vaqueros. Matt shouted a warning and started after him. The words died on his lips when he recognized the arrogant leader.

"Padre!" Felipe held up a hand to his father who slowed his horse and swooped the skinny adolescent into the saddle while his cold eyes glared at Matt.

"Don't . . . hurt him," Felipe rasped. "He was bringing me . . . home."

Don de Vega's stony face remained fixed as his eyes moved from Matt to the body slung over the rump of Samuel's mare.

"It's Rafael," Matt said, his voice quavering despite his efforts to control it. "Felipe's had a pretty bad time of it."

Don de Vega's arm tightened around Felipe's narrow shoulders, but his angry eyes did not soften. "How do you happen to be here?" he growled.

Matt bit down on his anger. "This happens to be my ranch. Rafael and some bandits burned me out yesterday and ran off with part of my cattle. When we went after them, we found Felipe."

Don de Vega continued to regard Matt as he absorbed this information, his stoic expression giving no clue to his thoughts. The five years since Matt had seen his father had taken their toll. Deep lines were etched around his mouth, and his once-dark hair was now entirely gray.

Felipe's raspy voice broke the uncomfortable silence. "Ignacio tried to shoot me . . . but Rafael jumped in front . . . ." In halting words, he recounted the incident. "Rafael saved my life," he concluded.

"Rafael only tried to save you so he could collect the ransom," his father said.

"At first," Felipe agreed. "But later . . ." He paused and sat up straighter. "He saved my life," the boy insisted.

Benito edged his horse close, his swarthy features contorted with anger. "Rafael's a dirty pig," he spat. "If I'd been at the hacienda when he came, I would have cut him to pieces with my whip."

"Instead Ignacio shot him, and by some miracle Felipe is alive," Don de Vega interjected. As he looked at Matt, his features softened slightly. "Once again I am in your debt. If you hadn't arrived when you did, Felipe might have died before we found him."

"You underestimate your son," Matt said. "He's stronger than you think." He kept a wary eye on Don de Vega, not trusting the arrogant hacendado's sudden change of mood, especially when the vaqueros still glowered at him, and Les Doane and the ranchers were trussed up with ropes like sacks of corn.

"These men helped save Felipe too." Matt pointed to the ranchers. "If your vaqueros will put away their guns and untie my friends, I think we'll all be more comfortable."

Don de Vega ordered the vaqueros to do Matt's bidding. Although they quickly complied, Matt saw dislike in their sullen faces as they worked at knots binding the men's arms and legs. The jangle of a horse's bridle followed by a Spanish oath jarred Matt's frayed nerves. The tension didn't ease until he introduced Samuel to Don de Vega. Samuel extended his hand. There was a guarded expression in his gray eyes, but his smile was friendly. Other hands quickly followed as Matt completed the introductions.

"I'm happy to meet you," Don de Vega said in English. He chuckled when he noted Matt's surprise. "Since I deal in cattle, I must frequently do business across the border with gringos. Felipe speaks some English too. Perhaps the next time you come to Valle Grande we can converse in English."

"Please . . . come to visit," Felipe said in halting English.

"I'll try," Matt promised.

Before he could say more, Don de Vega spoke. "All of this is your ranch?"

Matt nodded, looking across the rich grazing land, seeing it with fresh eyes; lush grass ruffled in the afternoon breeze, the rocky, tree-lined stream bisected one end of the valley. Though small when compared with Valle Grande, it was Matt's, bought and paid for with his own hard-earned cash.

"You will need money to rebuild," Don de Vega observed, turning his gaze to the shell of the burned-out ranch house.

A terrible sense of loss engulfed Matt. "It will have to wait. Right now I need to get my wife down where it's safer. She . . . we're going to have a baby."

Felipe grinned when he heard this. "And I will be an uncle . . . no?"

"You will." His glance dared Don de Vega to say otherwise. The hacendado didn't appear to be listening, or if he was, it was only with half a mind.

"When you're ready to rebuild, I would like to help," he said.

For a moment Matt didn't know what to say. Part of him wanted to refuse. He'd bought the ranch without help from anyone. He wanted to rebuild it the same way. But the revolution and resulting turmoil in Mexico had altered the situation. Matt looked at Samuel, then back to Don de Vega. "Gracias." A little help from the man might not be such a bad idea.

"Now that I know where you live, I will stay in touch," Don de Vega promised. "But like you, I have someone else I must think about." He gave a quick glance at Felipe. "My son needs to get home where he can rest."

"I wish I could offer you my home."

"Since you can't, we must do the best we can. Manuel and Reyes have gone for the carriage. When we meet up with them, Felipe can rest in it as we travel."

"I don't need the carriage," Felipe protested. Although he still looked tired, the arrival of his father seemed to have infused him with energy. "When Padre and I come to visit you . . . we will bring a gift for your niño." He held out his hand.

Felipe's firm grip surprised Matt. Although the hand was small and cool, his half-brother's hazel eyes glinted with tenacity that had been honed to a fine edge by generations of arrogant Spanish dons. The will to survive was there. With Don de Vega to encourage it, Felipe would reach manhood.

Clinging to this thought, Matt watched in silence as Don de Vega and the vaqueros waved and cantered their horses away from the ranch, the outriders forming a phalanx around their leader.

"Wow," Rob said, removing his battered felt hat to wipe sweat from his forehead. "For a few minutes I wondered if we'd get out of that alive. First the bandits, then that rich don what's his name and all those vaqueros. Is that guy truly your real father?"

When Matt nodded, Rob grinned. "I wish Fred Murdock could've seen him. If he had, he'd be keeping his trap shut about you for a long time." Rob glanced at his father, expecting him to agree, but Samuel appeared lost in thought, his thumb absently rubbing the grizzled stubble on his chin.

"If you don't need us any longer, I think we'll ride on home now," Les Doane said, his voice filling the awkward silence.

"You mean you're running out on us?" Matt joked. He walked over to Les and offered him his hand. "Hope you weren't hurt. Those vaqueros were pretty rough."

"I've had gentler handling," Les admitted. He gave Matt's hand a squeeze. "What a day!" In a quieter voice, "I'm sorry about your bad luck . . . the house." A quick look at Samuel's mare. "Your brother."

"I'll be all right."

"You're sure?"

Matt nodded. "Thanks for your help. I couldn't have done it alone."

"De nada." Les laughed when Matt's dark brows shot up. "Your rich padre ain't the only one who speaks another language. That was a right nice offer he made you . . . though I'd say you've earned it."

Matt turned to Rob and Samuel. "You can ride along with Les if you want. I'll catch up with you after I finish digging the grave."

Samuel shook his head. "We're family. We'll stay and help."

The three of them worked throughout the afternoon, the rhythmic thud and grate of pick and shovel breaking the stillness as backs arched and bent, burying the tine deep into the rocky soil, shirts darkening with sweat, the restless wind never quieting. Through it all, Matt was aware of Samuel's solid presence, his deference to Matt when they made decisions, the words "We're family."

No one made much attempt at conversation until it was time to lower Rafael's body into the hole.

"Since Rafael's Catholic, what do you think we should say?" Matt asked.

Samuel frowned and leaned on the shovel. "I've never buried a Catholic before, but I don't think it will hurt to say a prayer and ask the Lord to keep the grave safe from marauding animals. It won't hurt to ask God to forgive him for all the wrong he's done, either."

Matt had already said a silent prayer for his brother when he and Samuel wrapped him in the blanket. He said another prayer now, opening the blanket to touch the patch of white hair on Rafael's head. It was their bond, their birthright—a common thread binding their lives together even though they'd chosen different paths. Not having had a mother to nurture him, Rafael hadn't learned the difference between right and wrong, good and evil. God would know what Rafael would have chosen if the circumstances had been different.

"Forgive him, Heavenly Father," Matt prayed, while another voice whispered, "You must forgive him too."

* * *

It was evening when they finally left Matt's ranch. The horses had been fed and rested, and a full moon lit the way. They rode for over an hour, their horses cantering down the same trail Matt and Sabra had taken two days before. Instead of sunshine, there was pearly grayness, the twilight stillness broken by the scurry of startled night creatures and the rustle of a mountain breeze.

Samuel was strangely quiet. So was Matt. After an hour of attempted conversation, Rob rode on ahead.

An uncomfortable silence settled over the two men, the minutes stretching on with only the soft plod of the horses' hooves and the rustling of the breeze through the pines to pass for conversation.

Samuel knew he should speak. Hadn't he rehearsed what he intended to say the week before in the cornfield? He wiped a sweaty palm on the leg of his pants. "I . . . I owe you an apology," he finally said, his voice more high-pitched than usual. "I should've believed you when you said you had a twin brother. But . . ." Samuel swallowed, saying what popped into his mind instead of what he'd planned. "You have to admit that suddenly having a twin brother sounded a bit far-fetched and convenient. Still . . ." Samuel turned in the saddle so he could meet Matt's eyes. "Me and Rob will spread the word around Cortéz. I'm sure Les Doane and the Tenneys will do the same up here. It won't be long before everyone hears about Rafael . . . how you really did have a twin brother."

"I'd appreciate it," Matt said.

Samuel knew he should say more, but the apology and words of acceptance seemed lodged in his throat. What was wrong with him?

Hadn't he seen the tender way Matt looked at Sabra, their love for each other? While Samuel willed himself to speak, the words he'd hurled at Matt when he'd asked to marry Sabra seemed to shout through the silence. *"No daughter of mine is going to marry a Mexican."*

Samuel straightened and cleared his throat. "I . . . I'm sorry for a lot of other things, too . . . some of the things I said," he finally managed. "I . . ."

"I understand." It was Matt speaking instead of Samuel, Matt wanting to make things right between them.

When Samuel turned and looked into the dusky features of his son-in-law, he saw both concern and understanding. They were two men with a common purpose, a common love. It was a beginning. For now, that was enough.

CHAPTER 23

A week later Matt and Sabra returned to Colonia Cortéz. They'd made the decision together, weighing the pros and cons, talking late into the night and praying.

"I want you safe and comfortable when the baby comes," Matt had told her. "After all that's happened here . . ." His voice trailed away as Sabra's eyes filled with tears. They'd talked often about the baby, how they wanted it born in the room where love and hope had first conceived it, Mama and Aunt Anna helping, Matt waiting outside the door. "This way my mother will be able to help too," he concluded.

Sabra saw the wisdom in it. The raid had made everyone in the mountain settlements jittery. The ranches were too isolated, the men too few, the women and children too many. Since the baby couldn't be born where they'd planned, Sabra couldn't think of a better place than her old home with both mothers helping.

Elizabeth nodded approval when they told her of their decision. Even Samuel and Rob looked pleased.

"John Tenney and Les Doane said they'd keep an eye on the place and see to the cattle," Matt explained.

"Let us know when you're ready to come back," Uncle Hans said. "The men in the ward want to help. We'll have your house done in no time."

They made the trip back to Cortéz in easy stages. It was a hot afternoon in early July when they reached the outskirts of town. A thick plume of powdery dust marked their progress, the air so still the dust settled almost as quickly as it rose, sifting into the creases on

Sabra's neck and face, its drab color speaking of home, the desert, and all that had once been dear to her.

Sabra sat up straighter and rubbed her aching back, a straw hat shading her face as she looked ahead. That big walnut tree was where Sabra had always waited for Rob and Del to come from the farm. And there was the Moffit place with the wooden gate still not hanging straight. She saw the church and on ahead her home with its white picket fence and Mama's tall border of pink hollyhocks. Everything was just as she remembered. Nothing had changed. Except herself.

Sabra was reminded of this change as Matt helped her down from the seat of the wagon. Her ankles were so swollen she could hardly stand, her body distended too, and so awkward she would have fallen if Matt hadn't supported her.

"Are you all right?" His voice and expression were concerned.

She nodded and smiled up at him. That was another thing that had changed—she and Matt allowed to openly show their love for each other without the whole town and Mama and Papa frowning in disapproval.

"I've just been sitting too long. Give me a few minutes and I'll be fine."

She went from room to room with her mother, running her fingers over the surface of the pine mantel, touching the doily on the parlor table.

"You and Matt can have your old room," Mama said. "I haven't changed a thing. I think you left a blue dress in the wardrobe. By next month you should be able to fit into it again."

Sabra looked down at the brown Mother Hubbard she'd been obliged to borrow from Aunt Anna since her own had been badly torn when she'd climbed into the corn bin. Anna had also insisted she take a crocheted shawl and two tiny dresses left over from baby Sarah. "I know they're not the ones you made for your baby, but you'll need something to cover the sweet thing."

She and Matt were grateful for what they'd been given, though being dependent upon others wasn't something they enjoyed. Someday they'd repay everyone. Someday soon, she hoped, just as she hoped they wouldn't have to stay very long in Cortéz. Good as it was to be back, she was already homesick for the mountains. The sharp sierras jutting with red crags and fleshed with spreading vistas of evergreen, stark, solitary, magnificent—they had become her true home.

* * *

Matt and Sabra soon became aware of a change in Cortéz, one so subtle Sam and Elizabeth had hardly been aware of it when they left for the mountains. Tension and a malignant suspicion and distrust between Mormons and Mexicans were sprouting up at an alarming rate. There'd been minor incidents before, but they'd quickly been settled, the involved parties shaking hands and parting somewhat amicably. Since the revolution, fear of marauding soldiers and bandits had increased, but now the fear had taken on new dimension. Mexicans, who'd been their neighbors for twenty years, were turning sullen and belligerent. Some openly stole from them and made angry threats when confronted with the evidence.

"They've turned ugly," Helen told Matt and Sabra when they gathered around her table on their second evening in Cortéz. "I never expected to see it here . . . especially not from people I've nursed and fed for more than fifteen years."

Joseph nodded as he cut his meat, a frown wrinkling his ruddy forehead. "I've told yer mother not to go to the Mexicans again."

"Mothers called their children inside and closed their doors when they saw me on Wednesday," Helen went on. "Mind, these are children I brought into the world. Some are even named after me. When I got down from the buggy, Juan Velarde told me to go away." Helen's voice quavered. "When I tried to reason with him, he raised his fist and called me a crazy old woman. As I was leaving, someone threw a rock at Dolly. Hit her on the flank and broke the skin."

"'Tisn't safe out there anymore," Joseph said.

"What's happened?" Sabra asked, remembering when she'd gone with Helen to visit the Mexicans. They'd greeted Helen like a dear friend, smiling and patting her arm, inviting her into their humble homes, their warmth expanding to include Sabra.

"'Tis the revolution," Joseph said. "Some of the men have joined it . . . the Ponce brothers from Juarez, Inéz Rodriguez from Casas

Grandes. They say we're part of the enemy, that we're as bad as the hacendados. They've spread some nasty stories about us." Joseph paused and shook his head. "Guess this isn't the best talk for dinner," he ended lamely. "Especially with Sabra aboot to have the bairn."

Talk turned to more pleasant subjects—an amusing story about one of the Johns boys who'd tipped over a can of molasses, plans for Harry's marriage to Myrtle Hamblin.

"I'm so glad," Sabra said.

Then the talk turned to Rafael and Don de Vega.

"'Twas good of him to offer to help ye rebuild yer home," Joseph said.

"It was," Matt agreed.

No one spoke for a moment, the silence stretching until it became a little awkward. Sabra studied Matt's parents—Helen, thin and spare and no longer pretty, Joseph, not as broad-shouldered and robust as she remembered—and wondered how the news of Matt's real father and brothers set with them. Did they feel threatened by fear of lost affection or were they secure enough in his love to feel only gladness that Matt had discovered a broader base for his identity?

"Don de Vega didn't even bother to look at Rafael's body," Matt went on. "It was almost as if he'd never existed, or if he had, it was for the sole purpose of embarrassing Don de Vega and making him angry." Matt stared at the clock that hung on the opposite wall. "After all Rafael did to Felipe, I can't blame Don de Vega for being angry."

"Ye've every right to be angry too," Joseph told him.

"I was at first, but when I found him dead . . ."

Sabra squeezed Matt's hand, knowing how difficult the past days had been.

"I'm glad I was able to bury Rafael on the ranch. But most of all I'm grateful I've finally been able to forgive him. For a while I didn't think I could." He smiled at his mother. "I've realized Rafael never knowingly did anything to harm me. He never knew he'd been mistaken for me or that it was my ranch they raided."

"Rafael was still an evil man," Joseph argued.

"He was," Matt agreed. "At least by our standards. But I think in his eyes, he wasn't so bad . . . just taking what was rightfully his. At least at first." Matt's grip on Sabra's hand tightened. "That's the part that concerns me a little and makes me grateful for what the two of you have done for me."

"What's that, son?" Helen prompted.

"Since we were identical twins, doesn't that mean I'm capable of doing the same things Rafael did?"

"No."

"Never."

Sabra's and Helen's protests came simultaneously, the women shaking their heads while love for Matt shone in their eyes.

"There's not a mean bone in you," Helen declared. She laughed and shook her head. "You can be stubborn, though. Between you and your father, I've had my share of stubborn men."

"That's part of what I mean. Is my stubbornness something I inherited from the de Vegas, or is it something I learned from father? How much is heredity and how much comes from example?"

Joseph held up his hand. "Yer getting in too deep for my frail brain. But one thing I do ken, Matty. Yer as good as they come, and I'm sorry I ever dooted ye."

Matt swallowed hard and met his father's gaze. It was the first time he'd heard Joseph apologize. From the look on Helen's face, she hadn't heard it often, either. Joseph's features were ruddy as he got to his feet and started for the kitchen. "Smells like the rice pudding Mother's makin' is ready."

That night, as they prepared for bed, Sabra took Matt's hand, the flickering lamplight casting light and shadows over his handsome features, her heart overflowing with love. "You're father's right. Yer as good as they come, and I've never dooted ye." Emotion closed her throat, making it impossible to say more. She lifted her lips to his, twining her hands around Matt's neck, running fingers through his dark, close-cropped hair, letting her touch tell him what she couldn't say— that she did not fear the specter of Rafael's evil. She'd trusted Matt from the day he'd first called her Nutmeg. She'd always trust him. Always.

* * *

On Friday, Sabra started into labor, the first pain no more than a tightening of her abdomen and a simultaneous ache in her back. It came just as Charlie Teasdale's mother was leaving. She'd come by a few minutes before, carrying a length of green flowered calico and several yards of white flannel.

"Brother Teasdale and I heard about your home . . . how you'd lost everything. You'll need flannel for diapers, and after the baby comes, a new dress will be nice." Sister Teasdale's slightly bulging eyes took in the plainness of Sabra's borrowed Mother Hubbard and the loose strand of chestnut hair falling into her face.

Matt said pregnancy became her, but at the moment, Sabra had never felt so drab. "How . . . nice," she stammered, her voice sounding as awkward as she felt. It *was* nice—nicer than Sabra had expected from the Teasdales. Sister Teasdale hadn't included Charlie's name with the gift. Charlie was said to be seriously courting one of the Whiting girls from Dublan.

"Since I'm needed at the store, I can't stay and hem diapers, but Sister Moffit and Sister Durfee both said they'd come by and help. As quick as Lizzie and Mae are with their needles, it shouldn't take them long to make up the dress."

Elizabeth came to Sabra's rescue, taking the flannel and exclaiming over the pattern in the calico. "Bless you," Elizabeth said. "Everyone has been so kind."

Since their arrival in Cortéz, a day hadn't passed without members of the ward bringing something for Matt and Sabra. "Now that the children are married, we have this extra bed." Or, "Here's a chair for your kitchen. Ezra fixed the leg so it's as good as new." It was as if everyone were trying to make up for their doubt and the whispered rumors, their generosity coming in a shower of household goods and offers of help—a belated wedding party without refreshments or a dance.

"Brother Teasdale and I want to do our part." Charlie's mother's voice was prim, and for a second Sabra caught a glimpse of satisfaction as if part of her were secretly glad that Matt and Sabra were having their troubles. As quickly as it came, it was gone, followed by the woman's thin smile as she made her farewell.

"Well!" Elizabeth said in surprise. "I certainly didn't expect to see this from the Teasdales."

Sabra put a hand to her stomach, feeling it swell and tighten as a dull ache built across her lower back.

"Are you having a pain?" Elizabeth asked.

"I don't know . . . maybe."

Two hours later, Sabra knew without a doubt, the cramps and pains coming with increasing intensity, each lasting a little longer, some hurting so badly Sabra wanted to pace the floor.

"I think it's time to get you settled in bed," Helen said. Mama had sent for her earlier, and the image of the slight woman with her black bag filled the house with reassurance.

"I want Matt," Sabra said, holding the edge of the table to stifle a cry. "Please, send someone to the farm for Matt."

"Willie's on his way," Elizabeth told her. "He and your father should be here in a few minutes. Brother Cameron too."

The next hour passed in a blur of pains, one building on another, sometimes coming so close Sabra hardly had time to catch her breath. Aunt Mae said giving birth was the most terrible, most wonderful thing a woman could do. Sabra thought this was probably true. A sense of joy and excitement coursed through the awful pain. *Make it stop, oh, please make it stop,* she prayed, while another part of her wanted to burst with happiness. Her time had finally come. It was about to happen.

Through it all she was aware of Helen's gentle touch, her calm voice as she told Sabra what to do while Mama and Aunt Mae hovered by the side of the bed, clinging to her hands, soothing and comforting.

As the pains got worse, Sabra was certain she was going to split right up the middle as Helen instructed her to push, then push harder.

"I can see its head," Helen said. Excitement pulsed through her voice. "There's lots of black hair . . . but you've got to push, Sabra. Push hard."

Sabra screamed, unable to stop herself while sweat trickled into her eyes, making them sting even though Mama wiped her forehead with a damp cloth. How had Mama done this for nine babies? *Oh, help! Help!*

"Push one more time."

For a moment Sabra lost control and began to cry. She couldn't stop herself any more than she could stop the terrible, wrenching pain. She'd planned to be brave. If only Matt were holding her hand. She found strength in just thinking his name and bore down with all her might until, in a wonderful release of pressure, the baby slid out into Helen's waiting hands.

"It's a girl," Helen said, the baby's cries filling the void left by Sabra's scream. "No need to give this one a swat. She's got spunk, just like her mother."

Sabra lifted her head to see the baby lying warm and slick across her stomach while Helen cut the cord and cleaned her. "Is she all right?" Before Helen could answer, Sabra added, "I always wanted a baby girl."

"Well, you've got one with all her fingers and toes and proper parts."

"She's beautiful. Just beautiful," Mama whispered, taking the baby from Helen to wipe her with a towel while Aunt Mae looked on, beaming.

Helen turned her attention back to Sabra, kneading her tortured stomach to rid it of the afterbirth, washing her so she felt clean again and snug and cared for.

"Can Matt come in now?" Sabra asked.

Aunt Mae rolled the last of the soiled linen into a bundle and set it in the corner. "I imagine he and the new grandpas are waiting by the door."

They were, Matt coming in first, followed by her father and Brother Cameron, each freshly washed and cleaned from the fields.

Matt's approach was a little apprehensive. Sabra's shrill cries had made him want to burst into the birth room, certain she was dying, wanting to stop the horrible noise. Why did babies have to come into the world in such an awful, barbaric way? Samuel and Joseph had tried to reassure him, but Matt knew he wouldn't stop worrying until he saw Sabra for himself.

She lay in Samuel and Elizabeth's big bed, her chestnut hair splayed out in sweaty tangles on the white pillow, but with such a look of joy on her pale face that Matt forgot about being worried. She was as happy as he, her green eyes bright with happiness as she looked at him, then at the baby nestled next to her.

"What do you think of her?" Sabra asked, her voice a little shaky.

It was obvious Sabra thought their daughter was the most beautiful baby in the world and that she longed for confirmation from him. It was easy to give as he looked at the tiny, dusky face, saw the perfect miniature ears and soft black hair. He felt his throat constrict with love and emotion. "She's beautiful . . . perfect."

"Would you like to hold her?"

Matt's heart seemed to falter. Although he had plenty of adoptive brothers and sisters, he'd never held any of them when they were this new.

"Go ahead. You'll be surprised how soft and sturdy she is." This from Samuel who beamed at Matt with amused affection.

Helen didn't wait for Matt's consent. She picked up the little bundle and laid her in the crook of Matt's arm. He was surprised at how light she felt . . . how good, her dark eyes opening briefly to look up at him as if she could see.

"What a little beauty," Samuel said. His voice was a croon as he reached to caress the baby's hand. At his touch, her tiny fingers opened and curled around one of his, clinging as if she already belonged to him, just as Sabra had.

The fact that his granddaughter's skin was darker than Sabra's, her hair black instead of chestnut, hardly registered with Samuel. She was his . . . theirs . . . a gift from God. A man couldn't ask for anything better than that.

* * *

It was night before Matt and Sabra were alone, their baby daughter tucked into a borrowed cradle, the two of them lying together with Sabra's head resting on Matt's shoulder. Elizabeth had looked askance when Sabra insisted that Matt join her in the big bed. Sabra needed her rest. Such things just weren't done. At least not by most women. The stubborn set of her jaw told Elizabeth that Sabra wasn't most women.

"Happy?" Matt asked as he carefully pulled her close.

"Completely."

"Even though we don't have a home?"

"My home is with you, Matt. Wherever you are makes it home. And now that we have Teresa . . ."

Matt smiled and kissed the top of her head. Although Sabra had napped, he knew she was exhausted and needed to sleep. But it was so good to finally be alone with her, to be able to talk. "You're really set on naming her Teresa? Last week you were leaning toward Amelia."

"That was before I saw her . . . before I knew how she looked."

"You don't have to name her after my . . . mother, you know."

"I want to. No one needs to know who she's named after. That way neither Mama nor your mother will be hurt. Besides, it fits her."

"It does," Matt agreed, the knowledge bringing him pleasure. The name of his beautiful Mexican mother would be carried into the next generation—the woman who'd given him life remembered permanently. She'd live again in the tiny scrap of life sleeping next to their bed, look at him through dark eyes, smile at him just like the other Teresa had done in his dreams.

"Any regrets?" Matt asked after a moment.

"Regrets for what?"

"For marrying me instead of Charlie."

"Matt!" Though exhaustion edged her voice, there was indignation, too.

"Your life would sure be a lot easier right now if you had."

"Emptier, you mean."

Matt turned her face so he could search her eyes, moonlight spilling soft light across the lace edging of the pillowcase, the faint fragrance of crushed rose petals wafting from fresh sheets. After a moment, he smiled. "I told you things wouldn't be easy, Nutmeg. But something tells me you don't care."

Matt was right. Sabra would have chosen him over a million others, followed him into the desert or all the way up to Canada, always wanting and needing him, her love running deep and true. Always. Just like Matt's love did for her.

Historical Note

By July 27, 1912, conditions in the Mormon colonies had deteriorated to the point that the United States government sent a train to bring the women and children living in Colonia Juarez and Colonia Dublan out of Mexico. A short time later, the men and older boys followed on horseback. The refugees were given shelter in El Paso, Texas. A few stayed in the homes of Mormon families while the rest lived in sheds and warehouses provided by the U.S. government. The colonists from Colonia Diaz had left a day earlier to make their way across the blistering desert in buggies and wagons, arriving at Hatchita, New Mexico, on July 29, 1912. Most thought they would be away just a few weeks, but when conditions in Mexico worsened instead of improving, they were forced to wait.

In 1913 some of the colonists returned to Juarez and Dublan, where they found their homes and farms, which had been entrusted to friendly Mexicans, in remarkably good condition. They stayed there without major incident for the remainder of the revolution. Those living in Colonia Diaz weren't as fortunate. Revolutionists had burned and looted the town, leaving little of value to be salvaged. Rather than try to rebuild, the town was abandoned. The mountain colonies of Pacheco and Garcia fared a little better.

Those of the colonists who didn't return to Mexico bought land and built communities in New Mexico, Arizona, and Texas.

Today, descendants of some of the original colonists still live in Juarez and Dublan. They speak both Spanish and English, their farms, businesses, and orchards prospering, true to the faith and heritage willed to them by their forebearers.

Colonia Cortéz exists only in my imagination, as do the people who walked its streets. In my heart, I know that after Matt and Sabra traveled to the St. George Temple, they returned to their ranch where little Teresa was joined by brothers and sisters—the invisible threads that first pulled Matt back to the Sierra Madre woven into the fabric of a rich, satisfying life.

About the Author

Carol Warburton has always loved writing and reading. Her love of books led her to work for the Salt Lake County Library for thirteen years, while her love of writing led to the publication of several books. This is her fifth novel and another book is currently in progress.

Carol's other interests are gardening and genealogy. She has served in many ward and stake callings, both as a teacher and leader. She and her husband, Roy, recently returned from serving eighteen months in the Australia Adelaide Mission. They are now serving a local mission in the Salt Lake Valley. Her love of both the Australian people and the beauties of that country are the setting for her next novel.

Carol and her husband live in West Jordan, Utah. They are the parents of six living children and twelve grandchildren, who are the joy of their lives.